TASTE the LOVE

Also by Karelia Stetz-Waters
and Fay Stetz-Waters

Second Night Stand

Also by Karelia Stetz-Waters

Something True

For Good

Worth the Wait

Satisfaction Guaranteed

Behind the Scenes

TASTE the LOVE

KARELIA STETZ-WATERS
— & —
FAY STETZ-WATERS

FOREVER

New York Boston

This book is a work of fiction. Names, characters, places, and incidents are the product of the author's imagination or are used fictitiously. Any resemblance to actual events, locales, or persons, living or dead, is coincidental.

Copyright © 2025 by Karelia Stetz-Waters and Fay Stetz-Waters

Cover illustration by Venessa Kelley. Cover design by Daniela Medina. Cover copyright © 2025 by Hachette Book Group, Inc.

Hachette Book Group supports the right to free expression and the value of copyright. The purpose of copyright is to encourage writers and artists to produce the creative works that enrich our culture.

The scanning, uploading, and distribution of this book without permission is a theft of the author's intellectual property. If you would like permission to use material from the book (other than for review purposes), please contact permissions@hbgusa.com. Thank you for your support of the author's rights.

Forever
Hachette Book Group
1290 Avenue of the Americas, New York, NY 10104
read-forever.com
@readforeverpub

First Edition: July 2025

Forever is an imprint of Grand Central Publishing. The Forever name and logo are registered trademarks of Hachette Book Group, Inc.

The publisher is not responsible for websites (or their content) that are not owned by the publisher.

Forever books may be purchased in bulk for business, educational, or promotional use. For information, please contact your local bookseller or the Hachette Book Group Special Markets Department at special.markets@hbgusa.com.

Library of Congress Cataloging-in-Publication Data

Names: Stetz-Waters, Karelia, author. | Stetz-Waters, Fay, author.
Title: Taste the love / Karelia Stetz-Waters and Fay Stetz-Waters.
Description: First edition. | New York : Forever, 2025.
Identifiers: LCCN 2025001296 | ISBN 9781538771204 (trade paperback) | ISBN 9781538771211 (ebook)
Subjects: LCGFT: Romance fiction. | Lesbian fiction. | Novels.
Classification: LCC PS3619.T47875 T37 2025 | DDC 813/.6—dc23/eng/20250113
LC record available at https://lccn.loc.gov/2025001296

ISBNs: 9781538771204 (trade paperback), 9781538771211 (ebook)

Printed in the United States of America

LSC-C

Printing 1, 2025

To lovers and foodies everywhere

chapter 1

Kia Jackson sat on the stage of the Jean Paul Molineux School of Culinary Arts in a white, double-breasted chef's coat. She was waiting to receive her diploma and, much more importantly, to find out whether she'd beaten her culinary arts school rival, Alice Sullivan, to the designation of highest ranked student in the class and the winner of the Prix du Patrimoine Culinaire award. The seed money from the award would help her start her career as a food truck influencer, something she'd been working toward for years. She knew you didn't just fall into being an influencer because you looked sexy in an apron. It was a career, and she was ready for it. She'd be even more ready if she won the money, but that benefit was a stale mini marshmallow compared to the luscious, gooey, gourmet Rice Krispies treat that would be beating Sullivan.

The president of the school stood at a podium in the center of the stage, flanked by ostentatious arrangements of peonies. He raised his hand to the ceiling.

"As graduates of the Jean Paul Molineux School of Culinary Arts, you stand as a bastion of high culture in a world degraded by the banality of modern society…"

Beside Kia, Sullivan, the only other woman in the graduating class, whispered, "Starting a food truck? Really, Jackson?"

"I'm not going to spend the rest of my life dusting fern fronds with organic bee pollen."

Kia didn't move her lips as she spoke. Four years in school with Alice Sullivan, and they could smack talk in their sleep. Kia did talk to Sullivan, in her mind, before snatching a few hours of sleep between finishing in the practice kitchen and morning classes, never quite remembering the conversations.

The president went on. "…upholding the integrity of…"

"Tursnicken," Sullivan whispered.

The tursnicken was Kia's one culinary fail (well…one of a very small number of fails). Really she just had to perfect it. The tursnicken wasn't even for class, just a genius inspiration. A chicken stuffed with Snickers bars, stuffed inside a turkey, and deep-fried in a fryer outside in the parking lot on a freezing January day. Sullivan had strolled out in her men's wool peacoat, turned off the propane, wrapped her Burberry scarf around Kia's neck, and said, *Go home, kid, before that thing blows up.*

"And now it is my pleasure to introduce the student speaker for tonight. He will be announcing the students with the three highest scores in the class and giving the award."

Kia glanced at Sullivan and tapped one finger on her breastbone to say, *Highest.*

Sullivan mouthed, *Second place.*

That mouth. Those sculpted lips, coral pink although Sullivan never wore makeup. And those chestnut curls falling over her eyes. The way Sullivan rolled up the cuffs of her sport coats. The way she tucked her tan button-downs into her tan slacks, looking like a naturalist from the 1920s. The way Sullivan flirted with the men in the program and occasionally their sisters when families visited for banquets. How many times had Kia watched Brad or John or Chad stammer, confused by their sudden attraction to this masc woman who charmed them with a smile and a strut? Probably every time, because Kia had been watching Sullivan since the first day of class.

"In competition for the prestigious Prix du Patrimoine Culinaire and the accompanying twenty thousand start-up…Would our three top candidates stand." The student speaker read Kia's name. Stage lights eclipsed the audience, but Kia thought she heard her father whistle and her aunt shush him. The student speaker followed with Sullivan's name and the name of a quiet Midwestern man she'd never talked to.

"In third place…"

The shy Midwesterner.

"In second place…"

Kia held her breath.

"Chef Alice Sullivan."

Kia had done it! All those late nights, exhausted mornings, parties she didn't go to, friends she didn't make…It was absolutely, unequivocally worth it. She'd beat Alice Sullivan.

"Coming in point six percent higher, making her the seventy-eighth winner of the Prix du Patrimoine Culinaire, Kia Jackson."

She was also the second Black woman to win, the fifth youngest student, and the student with the highest overall score. None of that mattered. She'd beaten Sullivan!

"You little brat," Sullivan said with so much affection Kia felt a lump in her throat.

I love you. Kia didn't really, but her body could not hold a higher volume of adrenaline than at that moment. She loved everyone and everything. She beamed into the spotlight shining from the theater's light booth, but inside she was beaming at Sullivan.

While the speaker adjusted his microphone, the president walked over and shook hands with Kia, Sullivan, and the Midwesterner. Then he sat back down.

At the podium, the speaker cleared his throat. "If Jean Paul Molineux was here, I think he'd agree, we've never seen a fiercer competition."

The crowd laughed. The graduating class knew all about Kia and Sullivan's rivalry.

"Losing to your most hated rival, Chef Sullivan? Is Kia going to make it out alive?"

Sullivan looked shocked.

"I don't hate Kia."

The microphone didn't catch her voice, and the speaker continued.

"For those of you who don't know these two," the speaker went on, "Chef Jackson and Chef Sullivan have been trying to destroy each other since day one. Don't worry. There are enough kitchens for the two of you. I understand Chef Sullivan got a job in Japan at Nishi Rashu."

The other graduates oohed. You didn't get more prestigious than Nishi Rashu.

"It's probably a good thing one of you leaves the country though. We don't want you fighting at the alumni dinners."

More laughter.

Was that the only way this bastion of borderline-toxic masculinity could understand what she and Sullivan were to each other? Sullivan was her muse. She'd learned more trying to best Sullivan than in half her classes. The speaker went on. The graduates kept laughing. Kia tried to cut in. Sullivan looked at her, confusion turning down the corners of her perfect lips. Kia couldn't walk off the stage with everyone thinking she hated Sullivan.

"But, in fact, we've all been competing," the student speaker went on, "with ourselves, and I would say that we are the best competition."

At the end of the student speaker's speech, the president returned to the podium. Along with two professors, he began handing out diplomas. The students were organized alphabetically except for Kia, Sullivan, and the Midwesterner.

"First in class." The president handed Kia her diploma. "Chef Kiana Jackson.

"Coming in point six percent behind Chef Jackson, Chef Alice Sullivan. You two stay out of each other's hair, okay?" The president spoke affectionately enough, but this couldn't be how it went down. Kia couldn't walk off the stage with don't-you-hate-Sullivan? seared onto the moment by a roomful of men who didn't understand the difference between fierce dislike and fierce admiration, so she turned to Sullivan, her diploma slipping from her fingers, rose up on her toes, and kissed her, tangling her fingers in Sullivan's curls the way she'd longed to every time Sullivan pulled off her hairnet.

She realized how massively inappropriate it was a split second after her lips touched Sullivan's. But before she could pull away, she felt Sullivan's hand on her waist. Their lips melted together. In that moment, every car and pedestrian and pigeon and gritty breeze in New York froze, because this was too important. Nothing else could happen in this moment except this kiss.

When Sullivan pulled away, she was obviously trying to suppress a smile. She brushed her thumb across Kia's cheek, half caress, half like she were brushing away a crumb.

"Point six percent." Sullivan shook her head. "Well played, Jackson."

Their classmates cheered. Deep in their hearts, they didn't

want the story to be about hate. This was graduation. They wanted a happy ending. Applause rang in her ears, and the lights dazzled her eyes as Kia picked up her diploma and made her way off the stage. The other graduates received their diplomas in the alphabetical order of the bottom ninety-seven percent of the class.

After the ceremony, friends and family pressed into the banquet hall. Kia introduced Sullivan to her father, aunt, uncle, and cousin. Sullivan introduced Kia's family to hers, including her grandfather, who wore the same dapper vest and tie that Sullivan wore when she wasn't in her chef's whites, and a woman introduced only as Miss Brenda. The woman glanced knowingly between Kia and Sullivan and smiled. Music played. Hors d'oeuvres circulated. She lost track of Sullivan for several hours, but when the graduation party was over and Kia was just about to admit that she'd seen the last of Sullivan, Sullivan appeared beside her where Kia leaned against the wall by the door.

"You blew their minds," Sullivan said.

"Did I blow *your* mind?"

Flirting was not Kia's forte. Cooking was. Charming people into letting her use their fancy restaurants' kitchens. She also had a few impressive, if less-than-useful, superpowers. She could sail a yacht and train a dog to use a composting toilet thanks to a father who thought a yacht full of spaniels was a good place to raise a child. (He was right.) But her flirting always landed at the extreme ends of the spectrum that started with so-subtle-no-one-would-notice and ended with cheugy-enough-to-be-creepy. But Sullivan's appreciative grin told her tonight's flirtation hadn't failed.

"You want to go back to the practice kitchen and finally show me how you make those pear Rice Krispies treats?"

Kia was also the only person to ever make Rice Krispies treats at the Jean Paul Molineux School of Culinary Arts. Some of the professors had refused to taste them. Everyone else agreed they'd beaten all the other desserts combined.

"If you tell me the secret ingredient in your gazpacho."

Sullivan nodded. "You're on."

Sullivan met her in the kitchen twenty minutes later. They hadn't turned their keys in yet. The kitchen rested in after-school silence, lit by the security lights. All the stations immaculately clean. Everything put away. Kia reached for the lights, but Sullivan stopped her, gently placing her hand over Kia's. Kia's whole essence—mind, body, and soul—sparkled like the bubbles in a fine Veuve Clicquot. And Sullivan kissed her again. Sullivan pressed her up against the wall with a quick, "Is this okay?" It was more than okay. It was everything Kia had wanted since she'd walked into class on the first day.

Sullivan didn't take their kiss further. Maybe she knew that Kia would be so overwhelmed with fangirl delight, she'd pass out. Still, Kia was breathless when Sullivan drew back and said, "Well? Your secret technique, Chef?"

They'd cooked all night. First Kia showed Sullivan the secret to her Rice Krispies treats (brown butter) and a pear reduction sauce. Sullivan had produced a packet of heirloom tomato seeds and explained that growing the tomatoes from seed was her secret technique. Kia swatted her gently and Sullivan pulled her into a casual kiss, then released her and said, "Do you ever notice, you never get to eat anything at these social gatherings. You have to shake people's hands and hold your wine. Where do you hold the yellowfin hand rolls? You don't have any hands. I'm starving."

So they whipped up a plate of soup dumplings and goong hom pha. The dumplings led to debate about vol-au-vent. Could you really make a good vol-au-vent with ham and cheese? Kia said yes. Sullivan said no. Or foie gras? Kia said no, Sullivan said yes. So they had to make both types and taste test. They agreed the foie gras was superior.

"No one can make foie gras like you," Kia said.

"Thank you, Jackson," Sullivan said. "You're not bad in the kitchen yourself."

Eventually, they'd ended up sitting on the floor with a bottle of wine, legs stretched out. And Kia thought it was the beginning of something. They'd kiss again. Maybe they'd sleep together. And they'd figure out a way to be together. True, Sullivan was moving to Japan. True, Kia planned to park her food truck in all forty-eight contiguous states in two years. But there had to be a way…But when they'd finished the wine and the vol-au-vents, Sullivan had said, "I'm going to miss you, Jackson. Stay in touch," and that was it.

six years later

chapter 2

"You will submit," Chef Alice Sullivan said mildly, pushing her knuckles into the recalcitrant ciabatta dough, "to my superior strength and intelligence."

Across from her, her childhood friends—Nina Hashim and Opal Griffith—had just sat down to mugs of fair trade Assam tea at Sullivan's kitchen island.

Though rain was on the horizon, the early evening sunlight filtered through the Douglas firs in her backyard, illuminating the trays of microgreens in the windowsills. (She grew all her restaurant's microgreens in her house.)

"You know there's this thing called a…" Nina flourished acrylic nails that had never touched bread dough.

"You don't even know what it's called." Opal was the sous-chef in Sullivan's restaurant, Mirepoix du Bois. "Nina's right though. You'll give yourself carpal tunnel. Use the mixer."

Sullivan's hands ached from kneading, but it was good to feel the stick and pull of the notoriously hard-to-work-with dough.

"The more we do by hand, the smaller our carbon footprint." Bands of gluten stuck to her fingers. "I know you think you can control this relationship."

"Is she talking to us?" Nina asked.

"She's talking to the dough." Opal pushed her bright red glasses up her nose with her index finger. "They have a complicated relationship."

"Drink your tea." Sullivan tried to flick a bit of dough at Nina's designer tracksuit, but the dough held her like quicksand.

"The goddess always protects me from uncooked evil," Nina quipped as she whipped her curly hair back and forth. Each ringlet seemed to have a life of its own.

It was the perfect Sunday evening in May. Sullivan's high-end eco-restaurant, where she worked alongside Opal, was closed Sunday through Tuesday, so her weekend had barely begun. Two more full days of hiking and testing low-waste recipes in her own kitchen lay ahead of her. Her best friends gathered at the kitchen island for tea before they moved on to drinks at Opal's favorite bar and Sullivan wandered through the urban forest to the Oakwood Heights Neighborhood Association meeting. Not exactly a wild party, but a nice chance to reconnect with some neighbors she hadn't seen in a while. Evening sunlight dappled the ciabatta dough. Often she forgot that May was close to the solstice. It was usually so rainy it felt like an extension of winter, but not tonight. Tonight felt like the beginning of summer.

"Check this out." Opal reached into her Portland She-Pack women's rugby satchel. "A Black woman won the American Fare Award. Youngest woman and the first food truck owner."

"Ooh, shit," Nina said. "Sullivan's conniption fit in three, two, one." She counted down on her fingers.

Food trucks were nomadic salt bombs, crawling across the country leaving plastic forks and environmental apocalypse in their wake. Sullivan pointed it out every time she saw one.

"She's gotta be a rock star to get past that wall of

prime-rib-loving white guys on the award committee." Opal flashed the magazine cover in Sullivan's direction.

Sullivan glanced at it for the second the magazine deserved. The cover photo featured a woman with a loose Afro standing in front of a food truck. (It was the hair Opal wanted but never had the patience to grow.) Turquoise sunglasses shaded the woman's eyes, picking up the specks of turquoise on her splash-patterned overalls. She beamed, raising both hands to form a heart. Why did this talented Black woman have to destroy the earth with microplastics? And of all the talented Black chefs, why did *American Fare* pick a food truck owner?

"It's offensive," Sullivan said.

"Because you didn't win?" Nina asked.

"Because they didn't pick Chef Gregory Bruselle of Maple Savor or any of the Renaud sisters or Tyron Hisaki."

Opal opened the magazine and pushed it across the island toward Sullivan.

"They're all old school. Look at her," Opal said, her pointer finger stabbing the page. "She's drippin' style. Look at those glasses."

Sullivan looked for real this time.

Behind the glasses.

Beneath the Afro.

Sullivan stopped kneading. And for a moment her friends and the dough and the sunlit microgreens disappeared. Sullivan was standing in the practice kitchen at the Jean Paul Molineux School of Culinary Arts. A fire she'd almost forgotten surged in her lungs.

"Kia. Fucking. Jackson. You little brat."

The American Fare Award. Kia had gotten there first. Sullivan shook her head.

"You know her?" Nina asked. The definitely gold, not gold-plated, rings on her fingers gleamed brighter with surprise.

"We went to school together."

Opal picked up the magazine again. "She's the one you kissed!" She pumped her fist as though she'd just scored a winning try on the rugby pitch.

"I want to see." Nina snatched the magazine out of Opal's hands. Her voluminous mane of wavy hair swirled around her as she turned to look at Sullivan.

"The woman you kissed in front of the whole auditorium." Nina nodded. "The one who beat you by point six percent."

"Didn't you say she was the best chef you'd worked with? I'm offended, by the way," Opal said, not looking at all offended. "Kia was the one who got away." She gave Nina a knowing look. "Sullivan had feelings for her."

"Not like that." Sullivan missed the look in Kia's eyes when Kia realized Sullivan's coq au vin beat hers hands down. She missed Kia's gloating grin when Kia's mille-feuille had a million more feuilles than Sullivan's. Their competition had made Sullivan want to be better than Kia at everything Kia was great at. But she hadn't had those kind of *feelings* for her. "And it was one kiss."

A lie.

She'd never told Nina and Opal about kissing in the practice kitchen after graduation or why, no matter how much she changed her dessert menu, she always featured the Golden Crisp Experience. It was such a Mirepoix staple now, she'd almost forgotten that she first prepared it to tease Kia for her inexplicable love of the Rice Krispies treat.

Those kisses didn't fit the story Sullivan told herself—and then told her friends—about that night. The way she'd told the story, they'd competed, came in first and second, kissed once, and went their separate ways. They'd had thousands of hours in the kitchen to figure out if they had romantic feelings for each other, and they didn't. They'd just been riding high on the night's excitement. It was a special night, but Sullivan was heading to Japan. Kia was about to set off in a food truck. (What a shame.) So Sullivan left the story at *we kissed once*. She'd dropped the night of kissing and cooking out of the story when she told it to Opal and Nina. Adding it later made it feel too momentous.

God, if Opal knew Sullivan and Kia had kissed more than once, she'd drag Sullivan to the American Fare Awards and ask Kia out for her. If she had to, Opal would send Kia a postcard reading *Will you go out with my friend. Check this box.* ☐ *Yes* ☐ *No*

"I respected her cooking, so I kissed her."

Opal raised a naturally arched eyebrow. "As one does."

Kia would be close to thirty now. Funny to think that twenty-year-old prodigy was a grown woman. If the magazine was any indicator, she still dressed like a *Fresh Prince of Bel-Air* rerun. And it was still cute.

Opal pushed her bright red glasses up again and read from the article. *"Kia Jackson, who goes by Kia Gourmazing—"*

"Gourmazing?" Sullivan rolled her eyes.

"—made her mark on the street food scene with the tursnicken, a take on the classic turducken. Instead of the usual turkey-duck-chicken combination, Jackson stuffs Snickers bars inside a whole chicken, inserts that into a turkey, and deep-fries. 'It can be hard to find turkeys large enough,' Jackson says, 'but if I can't find one through my regular vendors, there's always a local farmer who can hook me up. That's a beautiful thing about America. We go big.' Jackson made her mark on the social media scene, jumping onto the newest social media platform U-Spin, and making it her own. 'I love Insta and the classics,' Jackson says, 'but U-Spin is my new love.'"

"You should reach out," Opal said, closing the magazine.

"Sullivan won't eat at a food truck. She's not going to date a food truck owner," Nina said.

"I said reach out! Not date! Why do you think I'm always trying to set her up?" Opal's freckles rearranged themselves to spell the word *innocence*.

"You've tried to set Sullivan up with every woman on your rugby team. And you said she has feelings for Kia."

"*Had* feelings," Opal said.

"I did not have 'feelings.'" Sullivan put *feelings* in air quotes.

"I didn't try to hook her up with Megan," Opal said to Nina, ignoring Sullivan. "Megan has a girlfriend."

"Okay, you tried to set her up with the other four hundred women on your team," Nina countered.

"Fifteen plus alternates," Opal said firmly. "But you could rekindle your old flame if you wanted to." Opal adjusted her glasses. "You own Mirepoix. You could get a ticket to the award ceremony."

"They'd probably let you give a speech," Nina added.

"You were friends," Opal said. "It'd be nice."

"It'd be weird." Sullivan sank her knuckles into the dough.

"Or DM her and say, *Congrats on American Fare*," Opal suggested.

"You know I'm not on social media."

Opal's face softened. "You've got to get out there, buddy."

"Just because Aubrey ate up your life with her stupid Instagram feed," Nina added, "doesn't mean you need to get off social media forever. Insta will always take you back."

Aubrey's dreams of being an influencer had replaced Sullivan's life with a fake, glittering facade. Everything staged. Everything filmed a dozen times until Sullivan's smile was sexy enough, her shoulders were straight enough, and any finger cots she'd incurred in the process of chopping through the hard skins of butternut squash were hidden.

"I hated social media, even before Aubrey."

"Just because you fumbled at the line-out doesn't mean you can't get back on the pitch," Opal said gently.

Nina fluttered her fingers in Opal's direction in affectionate dismissal. "No one knows what that means."

"I mean go out. Have fun. Maybe meet someone at a bar," Opal said. "Skip that HOA meeting and come to the Tennis Skort tonight."

"The Oakwood Heights Neighborhood Association meeting is a nice way to connect with people." Sullivan regretted the statement the moment it left her mouth.

Opal wanted her to meet someone, but Sullivan didn't need that. She just needed to get out, see a few people, make small talk. That was as close to dating as she needed to get, even if sometimes her body ached for a person's touch and the house echoed with emptiness. She was lonely at night, but that meant there was no one filming a carefully constructed version of her life, a life where Sullivan and Aubrey had always been happier than other couples. And if Sullivan did tear up, it was carefully edited for maximum pathos. After all, one of Aubrey's biggest influencer rivals got ten thousand comments when their parakeet died. You could sell sadness but only in small doses in the right lighting.

"Connect with people," Nina groaned. "The Oakwood Heights Neighborhood Association meeting is where your sexuality goes to die. Remember you took me once? Said we just had to *stop by*. It was two hours before they got to your agenda item. What was it? Moss abatement?"

"Do you know how many species of beneficial insects die if they use Moss Out!?"

"If you think the neighborhood meeting is where you meet people," Nina said, "your vagina will suck back into your body, close its doors, and die."

"I have to go tonight. They're reconfirming the Bois as green space for another two years."

The Bois (French for forest) was the undeveloped land at the center of the Oakwood Heights Neighborhood and directly between Sullivan's house and her restaurant. Every morning and every evening she followed a narrow path through the woods. As a child, she'd explored the Bois under her grandfather's loving eye. *Did you know that a newborn opossum is the size of a jellybean? Doesn't the stairstep moss look like a tree in a Japanese painting? An epiphyte is a plant that grows on another plant without hurting it. That's how we should all be, Alice.* (Only her grandfather called her by her first name.)

"Is something going on?" Nina got that gleam in her eye that said, *Can we sue someone?*

"It's just a formality. They'll confirm its status for two years. By then the Oakwood Greenbelt Land Trust will have enough money to buy it and make it green space permanently." That was Sullivan's promise to her grandfather. He had protected the land for fifty years. She would protect it forever. "It's slow, but we're getting there."

"Your grandpa would be so proud of you," Opal said.

"But you're not thinking of this *formality* as your social life." Nina wasn't asking. She was commanding.

"You two are my social life."

"Dating life," Opal amended for Nina. "Hey, I know! My cousin's coming in from Savanah. She's queer. Why don't you take her out." Seeing Sullivan's look, Opal added, "Just as friends. Or that nice guy who comes into the restaurant and eats alone. He likes you."

"No cousins. Definitely no customers." Sullivan laughed. "If you keep it up, I'm going to make *you* go to the neighborhood association meeting. After they approve the green space, we're talking about on-street parking and storm drains."

Nina put her arm out in front of Opal as though protecting her from an attack.

"Opal's our girl. You can't do that to her."

And the three of them were off, bantering back and forth about Sullivan's bread dough and the trays of microgreens in her windowsills, Opal's rugby team, and Nina's latest divorce case in her life as attorney to the rich and dysfunctional.

An hour into their banter, Sullivan's phone rang with a Miriam Makeba song, "Pata Pata."

"Miss Brenda," Opal said, recognizing the familiar ringtone.

Miss Brenda was Sullivan's grandfather's friend. The two of them swore they'd never been anything other than friends and fellow activists fighting for the earth and running their respective restaurants. They were still so perfect for each other, everyone put "friendship" in quotation marks when they talked about them. Or they had. When her grandfather was still alive.

Sullivan took the call on the porch. A moment later she returned.

"Speaking of storm drains, Miss Brenda's green roof is leaking again."

"It's a roof made out of lawn. Of course it's going to leak every time it rains," Nina said.

"Green roofs are rarely planted with grass." Sullivan noted the first drops of rain on her window. You couldn't hope for too much sunlight in Oregon in the spring. Sullivan's mind jumped from broken pipes to clogged gutters to errant nieces and nephews climbing the fire escape to water the roof (which did not need watering). "But yes. The thing leaks every time it rains.

"I'm going to go scope it out for her. Otherwise she'll get up there herself. Can you wait until the bread comes out before you head to the Tennis Skort?" Sullivan nodded toward the oven. "It's got another ten minutes on four hundred and then drop it down to about—"

"Would I be your sous-chef if I couldn't smell when the bread is done?" Opal asked.

"How long will you be?" Nina asked. "Do you need us to go to the association meeting for you? I know we could sue someone."

"I will be back in an hour, and no one is suing anyone. There's more tea and a decent Rapaura Springs sauvignon blanc in the fridge. Stay as long as you like."

"We're going to the Tennis Skort after this," Opal said. "Go to your meeting, get them to sign whatever they're signing, and come out with us."

"I'll think about it."

Sullivan would think about it. She'd go to the meeting and then sit on her porch, listening to the night creatures emerge from burrows, sniffing the air with little twinkling noses. Hopefully it'd have stopped raining by then. She'd think about how lucky she was to have friends who loved her even if she didn't want to drink Pickle Balls and 30 Loves surrounded by screens showing every sport known to womankind. She was lucky to live in a city that valued green space. She was lucky to have her restaurant and her home a mossy stroll from each other so she never had to drive to work. And she was lucky to have once known Kia Jackson, who was now basking in the glory of deep-frying candy inside raw chicken. If someone was going to win an award for that culinary abomination, it might as well be Kia.

chapter 3

Kia Jackson stood at the back of the Oakwood Heights Grange Hall watching her assistant, Deja, set up an induction hob, a portable burner to hold the crepe pan and spreader where Kia could exhibit her craft. Meanwhile she'd be making a persuasive argument for why the Oakwood Heights Neighborhood Association should sell her the green space called the Bois.

Several men and women of the indeterminable age of fit, rich, white people hovered next to her, each holding a water bottle stickered with their favorite causes. SAVE THE DOLPHINS. SAVE THE RAINFOREST. LOVE WINS. Outside, it had started raining, but it didn't feel like a bad sign. The grange hall turned event space hummed with welcoming, rustic charm. Its high ceilings were adorned with exposed wooden beams, and the walls were lined with vintage barn wood. Soft string lights hung along the walls. In the center of the room, rows of metal folding chairs had been set up for the neighborhood association meeting, and people were milling around them shaking hands and hugging friends.

"You have absolutely nothing to worry about," Save the Dolphins said.

The white people with liberal water bottles all belonged to the Oakwood Heights Neighborhood Association board. Save the Dolphins was the board chair.

A woman whose water bottle wanted to stop the I-5 bypass extension said, "We've already floated your plan, and the Oakwood Heights community is excited about bringing in food trucks."

Kia was excited, too, although everything was moving so fast. Her heart rate hadn't dropped below 110. She'd been living on jalapeño cotton candy.

"In some ways, this is just a formality," the board chair added. "You'll present your plan for Taste the Love Land."

That was Kia's long-held dream of owning land where food trucks could set up for weeks or years depending on their needs. It could be a place for Kia to put down roots. Growing up on a yacht with her father, she'd had love and security, scenery and adventure, everything she needed and more…except a permanent address. For a long time, she'd thought she didn't need an address, but more and more the open road had felt like the empty road.

"There will be time for community discussion and time for another buyer to put in a bid but—" The board chair raised a finger like Tony the Tiger preparing to declare, *They're grrreat!* "There's nothing in the charter that says we have to advertise that we're putting the land up for sale, so it's just you."

A trio of women moved around them on their way to their seats. They inclined their heads in polite greeting, and the board introduced Kia as the *developer we're all excited about.*

"Of course, if there's a legacy landowner…" Love Wins said after the trio moved on.

The board had explained the situation before. If someone's family had owned land in the neighborhood since its incorporation in the 1800s, they got an opportunity to buy any land jointly held by the association if the association decided to sell, and they got to buy it at fair market value.

"But don't worry. The only legacy landowner left hasn't been at a meeting for ages."

"And couldn't afford the land if they wanted it," another board member added.

Kia pictured a wealthy, old man with a young blond wife and self-serving politics. She didn't feel too bad about buying the land out from under him, not that he—whoever he was—had expressed any interest.

"So unless the community wants to keep paying HOA dues on a plot of land no one uses"—the board chair smiled sympathetically—"it's yours. Like your marketing manager said, this will give restaurateurs who've been pushed out by gentrification a second chance."

Kia surveyed the grange hall filling up with people greeting each other and shaking rain off their coats. The smell of urn-brewed coffee scented the air. This could be her community, a brick-and-mortar home.

Kia's ex-girlfriend turned marketing manager, Gretchen, had pitched Taste the Love Land to the board while Kia had been mounting the stage at the American Fare Awards. With the help of investors who were excited to put their money into American Fare's most charismatic winner, Kia would clear the land and build a food truck pod. Food truck owners could rent, or they could be co-owners in the venture. She'd have a covered pavilion, children's play area, maybe a space for live music. Most importantly, she'd make a place for people who needed it. Young entrepreneurs without enough money for a startup. Old restaurateurs pushed out by rising taxes or natural disasters.

She'd make a place for herself too because living on the road—one city after another, one fair after another—felt lonely. It had all meant something when she was meeting real people and sampling local cuisine, promoting small businesses and hearing stories about life and love and struggle. Now she'd achieved an influencer's dream and got so many sponsors she barely had time to spend the money she made. But it felt like all she did was hawk products without a chance to make real connections.

The grange hall was filling up. Deja had finished setting up for Kia's cooking demonstration.

"Excuse us," the board chair said. "I guess it's time for us to sit." The board made their way to their seats at a table at the front of the room.

The meeting started with minutes from the previous meeting and a brief announcement from the Social Committee. Kia hung back by the door, waiting to be called up.

"Now, we'd like to introduce our guest of honor," the board chair said. "As you know from our past few meetings, there's been interest in selling the Bois. I know we all recognize that the taxes and liability insurance on a property like that are expensive. With the funds from the sale, we could pay off the association's debts incurred by the unfortunate landslide two years ago. As you know, we owe the city for subsidence abatement work they did for us. And a sale could also prevent our dues from going up for several years. But—" The board chair held up his hand as though someone had protested, which they hadn't. "Previously, we've foregrounded preserving the Bois as a green space, but interest in that cause has dwindled, and Ms. Kia Jackson…why don't you tell us why you think we should sell the Bois to you and your investors."

The crowd gave a polite round of applause. Time for Kia to

do what she did best: charm. She had enough charm to get into the White House without a hall pass. Kia took a deep breath and took her place in front of the board's table and behind the cooking station.

A month ago she was changing a flat tire on Old Girl—the name of her restored Gulf Stream RV—in Niobrara County, Wyoming, on her way to the Denver Fresh 'n' Foodie Festival. Then Gretchen was on the phone. *You know that idea you had for a food truck pod? I've found land you can buy, and you'll have the money you need soon. Food trucks are hot. Wait six months and everyone will be onto boba and Brazilian steak.* She'd thought they were making conversation. *You won the American Fare Award,* Gretchen had said, like an afterthought. *American Fare will call you today.* Before Kia could take that in, Gretchen had told her to make her move now or regret it for the rest of her life. *Here are the numbers for six investors. Charm them the way you do, and get them to give you the money.* Gretchen had been a passionless girlfriend; she was a passionate business partner.

Kia took out her phone and projected a slideshow onto the screen to the side of the table.

"This is Me'shell. She's actually on her way to Portland right now. She sent this picture yesterday."

The image showed a food truck parked in front of a motel, the words THE TROPICANA glowing incongruously against a backdrop of craggy mountains. A few lumps of snow still lined the parking lot. A dark-skinned Black woman stood with her arms crossed, cold and determined. Next to her stood a teenage girl in a green sweater.

"Me'Shell cooks the best fish fry I've ever tasted. Her daughter there, Crystal, she's trans, and the places they've lived before this haven't been friendly. They needed to get out, but they didn't have money, and they didn't have a place to set up Me'Shell's food truck. Me'Shell and Crystal encouraged me to really visualize Taste the Love Land. What if I created a place where talented food truck owners from around the country could set up? Bring new cuisine. Build community. Belong. I told Me'Shell about it one night while we were sitting by the water just watching the moon on the Everglades."

They'd actually met at a Waffle House because the Everglades was full of snakes large enough to eat Kia, and she was not going to die by being swallowed whole by a creature with ten thousand vertebrae. Sitting in the moonlit Everglades made a better story to present to the neighborhood association.

"Me'Shell said if I started Taste the Love Land—that's what I want to call the food truck pod—she'd pack up her truck and her car and start driving that night. Well, I didn't make a move that night, but when I won the American Fare Award—"

Another round of applause.

"—and investors got interested..." Kia gave the audience her best smile and moved to the next slide.

The next slide showed three white men in crew cuts and Army T-shirts, the youngest man in a wheelchair.

"This is Chet the Third, Chet Junior, and Chet Senior. I know, cute right? They go by Chet, Chaz, and Gramps. They're a cooking family. Always ran a food truck. They're a military family too. Three generations of service. When Chet Junior got injured, they wanted to find ways to make culinary work more accessible. It's almost impossible to find work as a chef if you're paraplegic, but it doesn't have to be like that. The way Chaz explains it, if everyone had four arms and you only had two, folks would say, *How could he possibly do the job?* Well, heck yeah, Chet Junior can do the job! Best barbecue. No cap."

Next, she had a chef who'd lost his restaurant in Houston when his neighborhood gentrified. Then a pair of sisters who'd started a food truck while they were unhoused, sleeping on the floor of the truck and dreaming of a city that would appreciate their eccentric fusions.

Kia's heart rate slowed as she advanced through the slides. These people were the reason why she'd drunk nothing but black coffee with coriander and mint syrup for days and was nearing dehydration.

"I'm fortunate." Kia started winding down her speech. "I've accomplished a lot, and that's because of talent and hard work. But the thing is…there are a lot of people who are talented and hardworking and don't get where they want to be, not because they're not worthy, not because they don't deserve it. They don't have what I have in buckets—"

The end of that sentence was supposed to be *luck*. She was going to follow that with, *I've been blessed to have a great family with enough resources to support my dreams etc., etc. But not everyone has that, and so I want to build a place for people who are talented and hardworking but who haven't had my privileges, etc.*

She didn't get to finish her sentence. The word *luck* died on her lips as someone crashed through the door at the back of the grange hall, muddy and out of breath as though she'd just run from a bear. (Or python. It could happen. They were everywhere.)

"Stop!" the woman gasped. "You can't sell the Bois!"

chapter 4

Everyone in the grange turned and stared at Sullivan. Rows and rows of Oakwood Heights residents, many of them customers who'd eaten at Mirepoix, looked at her with mild horror. Understandable since mud soaked her jeans up to the knees and the rain had turned her hair into slippery ringlets all falling in her eyes.

Sullivan had been on the roof when Miss Brenda had called up, her voice hoarse, *Agnes's nephew Patrick just sent her a text saying that Barb Preeters is at the association meeting, and she says they're selling the Bois.*

Sheer luck had saved Sullivan from breaking a leg in her haste to get down the fire escape.

Only then had Sullivan checked her watch. She'd lost track of time, the threat of a roof collapsing on beloved Miss Brenda's restaurant had distracted her. It shouldn't have mattered. The association vote was a formality. The Bois had always been green space. The Oakwood Greenbelt Land Trust would be buying it in a few years. No one had talked about selling.

She'd been half an hour late when she started running toward the meeting. For once she wished she'd driven.

She'd tried to find her phone, hoping a glance at the agenda would show her that Agnus's nephew Patrick was wrong about Barb Preeters. There was no way things could get lost in that game of telephone, right? But in fact, nothing had gotten lost.

Sullivan had searched frantically for the email with the meeting agenda on her phone. The phone had kept slipping out of her muddy fingers, like a dream where you tried to run and you couldn't. But she finally got a hold of it and opened the attachment. There was the usual approval of last month's minutes and presentation of committee reports. Following that was *Taste the Love Land, discussion and questions* followed by *Vote to sell the Bois to Taste the Love Land Food Truck Paradise Inc.* She clicked the link to last month's minutes. Her hand shook and not just from the rain that had started falling but because the association was talking about selling the Bois, and no one had told her.

Not one of the customers who'd eaten at her restaurant had thought to mention it when they came in to celebrate their birthdays or anniversaries. She'd stayed open on Christmas, Thanksgiving, and New Year's to give people a place to celebrate, and no one had said, *Isn't Alice Sullivan raising money to make the Bois a permanent green space? Shouldn't we let her know the association is talking about selling?* She felt betrayed. Her grandfather's dream, her peaceful backyard, the namesake land of her restaurant, and all the lobster mushrooms, yellow violets, baby racoons, and the rare tree snake. She'd seen it only a few times, and every time had been magic. Now all of that would be tilled under for a bunch of food trucks.

Sullivan was fit, but she hadn't run like this since…She'd never run like this. She'd run all the way from Miss Brenda's biscuit restaurant in downtown Oakwood Heights to the grange. She felt like someone had stabbed her in the side. Now she was standing between flanks of folding chairs, the mild-mannered neighborhood members gaping at her. Sullivan doubled over, gasping.

"You can't—" Her vision blurred from lack of oxygen or shock. "Sell the Bois."

A long table had been set up in front of the board members' seats. An extension cord trailed to one of the outlets. A portable induction burner sat on the table. In her oxygen-deprived state, it looked like an approximation of an altar with the board seated behind it like disciples.

"Ms. Sullivan." The board chair's voice cut through the haze. "We were surprised you weren't at the last few meetings. We've discussed this extensively. The neighborhood is in favor." Sullivan's mind reeled. She clenched her jaw, berating her own shortsightedness in choosing to attend the two Sunday evening She-Pack games instead of the association meetings.

She gripped her side and struggled to an upright position. The hall's high ceilings looked vacuous. Night darkened the high windows. Suddenly the folding chairs and the board's table stripped the grange of everything that had made it elegant and cozy. This was just another industrial space where lots of people made bad decisions without thinking through the consequences. She just had to speak up and—

And then her mind cracked and she froze. She had to be hallucinating, because Kia Jackson stood at the front of the room wearing flipped-up turquoise sunglasses and holding a pink spatula with a crepe draping off it like a Salvador Dalí clock. She wasn't the skinny kid she'd been in school, although she still wore the same ridiculous amount of color. Bright green jeans. Yellow sneakers. A tight pink T-shirt. She'd replaced her Afro puffs with a glorious Afro. She still had the same luminous light brown skin, although she wore more makeup.

Kia dropped her spatula on the pan. Then Kia was running toward Sullivan. The gathering turned their heads as one.

"Whaaaat?" Kia reached Sullivan and almost threw her arms around her but stopped. "Oh my god, I didn't know you'd be here." Kia held her arms open waiting for her hug. "Chef Sullivan! Still trying to make up your point six percent? You look amazing."

"What are you doing here, Kia?" Sullivan kept her arms crossed and body guarded.

"I'm…buying…the Bois." Kia went from confident to hopeful to hurt. "To put in food trucks?" It came out as a question. "Who's ready to be gourmazed!"

"No." *This isn't real.* Sullivan was in a dream. Kia Jackson was buying the Bois? Had Sullivan conjured her out of the pages of *American Fare*? Sullivan could hear the room around her. She needed to text Nina. *You're a lawyer. You have to stop this.*

Sullivan shook the imaginary cobwebs out of her head. She noticed a screen standing to one side of the board members, lit up with a splashy photo gallery of gaudy food trucks. She glanced from the board members' faces, back to Kia's stunned expression. But then another feeling washed through the mix of confusion and anger that had taken over her mind and body: nostalgia. Sullivan breathed in the familiar scent of coconut and chocolate floating like a spring breeze around Kia's hair. How could someone who had once been her comrade be capable of such betrayal? How could Kia Jackson be the person behind Taste the Love Land. What a cheesy name! Sullivan took in the whole scene of conspirators. The board. The audience sitting silent and unmoving, uncomfortable with the tension in the air.

"Please sit down, Ms. Sullivan," one of the board members said.

"You are not paving over the Bois so you can sell elephant

ears and fried grease and…and…and kratom!" Sullivan said to Kia, her voice trembling with a mix of shock and defiance.

Kia had the audacity to look genuinely wounded. *No hug?* her face seemed to say.

"The Bois is not for sale," Sullivan barked.

"Ms. Sullivan, you are disrupting our meeting and being disrespectful to Ms. Jackson. Those are not Oakwood Heights values."

Sullivan half sat, half fell into an aisle chair.

Kia looked like she might tear up. Her brows were raised in surprise, and she stifled a shuddered breath from fully escaping.

"Land held by the Oakwood Heights Neighborhood Association can be sold at auction to the most competitive bid—barring a claim by a legacy landowner—after discussion at an association meeting and a vote," the board chair said.

"I'm a legacy land owner!" Sullivan's voice soared in panic. Aubrey, her ex, always made her redo the video if Sullivan squealed. *You are sexy, stylish, masc-of-center,* Aubrey had complained. *Please stay on brand.* Sullivan tried to lower her voice, but it came out in a squeak. "My great-great-grandfather signed the original charter. Our family has owned land here since the beginning."

On a normal day, that fact made Sullivan profoundly uncomfortable. Her family had not owned land since the *beginning*. Nations of people had lived on this land for thousands of years before Jedidiah Marius Sullivan planted his first survey stake. That was all the more reason to protect the Bois. It wasn't theirs to sell.

"I claim it. I'm a legacy holder. I claim it!" Sullivan said.

Kia stood in the aisle a few feet from where Sullivan had fallen into a folding chair. Kia bowed her head, as if to hide reddened cheeks. Her shoulders slumped and her arms dangled. For a second, Sullivan felt sorry for her. Was Kia really a developer now? Was this one of a dozen properties, or was this purchase a first? And how awkward to run up to someone to hug them in front of an audience only to be rebuffed, especially when you were giving a business pitch. That was up there with the classic naked-in-public dream, except no one was mad at you in the naked-in-public dream. No one was shooting daggers at you with their eyes, which Sullivan was doing. It was the only weapon she had right now.

"Ms. Sullivan, are you able to pay for the land in full by the end of the month following clause 12a in the charter?" The board chair's question hung heavily in the air.

"I…no…"

Sullivan felt everyone's eyes on her, their faces a sea of curiosity. How could they go along with this?

"You had ample time to raise objections to the sale."

"We know the Bois was important to your grandfather. We contacted you, Sullivan," one of the board members said. "We sent you several letters asking if you'd like to attend a meeting?"

She vaguely remembered letters with the Oakwood Heights Neighborhood Association logo and return address. She'd assumed they were just the usual flyer they sent around advertising holiday gatherings or alerting people to new parking regulations. She'd recycled them without opening them. Besides the bank and the IRS, who sent important documents through the mail?

"You knew I was setting up the Greenbelt Trust. I thought I had more time. You could have called me." Tears roughened Sullivan's voice. "You ate at my restaurant, and you didn't mention… no one warned me."

"Please continue," the board chair said to Kia. "We apologize for this interruption."

"We'll talk...wait for me afterward?" Kia whispered to Sullivan.

Sullivan was not going to wait for her, but she sensed that Kia would stand there looking down on her until she said yes. She gave a noncommittal nod.

Kia walked back to the front of the room and continued her speech.

Sullivan half listened as Kia cleared her throat and resumed cooking and returned to her speech. Kia verbally stumbled.

"I was staying. Uh, saying. Um, at Taste the, um, Love Land," she began, her voice strained, "we believe in the power of food to bring people together. Our f-food truck pod will feature food. Of course it would. Obvs." She laughed nervously. "Um, um. It will be a culinary destitution. Destination." The color drained from Kia's face as a crepe slid off her spatula, landing with a wet slap on the pan.

But Sullivan couldn't feel sorry for Kia. Kia was buying the Bois. Sullivan's front porch looked out on the Bois. Mirepoix's outdoor seating bordered the Bois. But more importantly, pileated woodpeckers tapped the old trees for bugs, and racoons gazed down from the branches at night. She had to do something. What? Beg Kia? *We were friends.* But they weren't exactly. She should have looked Kia up. Stayed in touch. *Don't do this.*

"Wait. Hold everything." A man's calm, reassuring voice spoke from the back of the room. "Kia Jackson is not buying the Bois."

Sullivan whirled around.

Three white men in boxy, black suits had entered the room.

"I'm afraid you've left out one provision of the land trust charter." One of the men walked to the front of the room, positioning himself in front of Kia.

He represented the Nature Conservancy. Greenpeace. The Sierra Club. He was there to save them. Sullivan hoped.

"We're here on behalf of Mega Eats Corporation." The man spread his hands in a welcoming gesture. "This meeting is to establish the highest bidder, right? Provided no legacy landowner claims their right to purchase land. Any legacy landowners here?"

"I am." Sullivan dropped her head in her hands.

Sullivan felt sick. Blood was leaving her extremities to protect her vital organs.

"You can buy it at fair market rate. No bidding war," the man said, as though he was delivering good news. "You have a week to put the funds in escrow. Are you going to buy?"

Sullivan's fundraising hadn't raised half the cost of the Bois. If she sold Mirepoix and her house, she still couldn't make it.

"I can't." Sullivan choked out.

"The charter requires that after you vote to sell, you must sell to a legacy landowner first. If there is no legacy landowner, you must sell to the highest bidder," the man continued, speaking to the crowd. "Clause 14b. *To maximize the benefit to the neighborhood, and to eliminate the risk of cronyism.* We've been looking at the Oakwood Heights neighborhood for a while. Did you know there isn't an insta-dining option within a quarter of a mile of Oakwood Heights?"

"We don't want a Mega Eats. We want Kia," someone yelled.

"We want the food trucks."

"We get to decide who buys."

"And," the Mega Eats rep said as though no one had spoken, "we can probably get Portland to put in a dedicated off-ramp. You'll just pull off the freeway, pick up a Family Mega Pack, and be home."

Kia had the audacity to turn to Sullivan as though Sullivan

should save her. For a second, the bit of Sullivan's heart that wasn't raging broke a little. She'd always wanted to beat Kia; she'd never wanted Kia to lose.

"I can up my bid," Kia called out.

"Whatever you bid, Mega Eats will add twenty percent."

"We didn't advertise this sale publicly," someone said. "How did you find out?"

"*You* didn't, but she did." The man stepped aside so everyone could get a good look at Kia. "Mega Eats would never have heard about it except that Ms. Jackson is an influencer. Isn't that right, Ms. Jackson? We wouldn't have heard about the sale except you've been live streaming about it for a week."

chapter 5

Kia's candy corn and rice paper crepes sizzled. She smelled sugar burning. The Mega Eats representative made a shooing gesture at her. This was supposed to be a done deal. She should be taking selfies with the board. She should be live streaming the birth of Taste the Love Land. She stared at Sullivan. A whirlwind of emotions swept through Kia. Her breath quickened. Her heart raced. She was wide-eyed with disbelief. Sullivan was here! But Sullivan's face was like a landscape in an ice storm, breaking apart in slow motion.

Kia had dreamed of meeting Sullivan again a thousand times. Sitting on the front steps of Old Girl—named for her vintage charm. And no matter how many years passed, something connected Kia and Sullivan. They understood the tension that had filled the room that last night at school. Sullivan would embrace Kia. *I've always wanted you*. Kia would clutch her and whisper, *I missed you*.

And it was because she missed Sullivan that she hadn't looked her up for years. What if real Sullivan ruined the fantasy? What if real Sullivan posted dumb memes and was a personal chef for some bad politician? But now Kia didn't need to see Sullivan's vita to see the same person she'd known in school, but reality was still ruining the fantasy, because Sullivan was doubled over in her chair, her face in her hands.

Around them, the crowd protested.

"We don't want Mega Eats!"

The Mega Eats reps strutted through the crowd handing out flyers with a Mega Eats complex pictured on the front. The board chair conferred with one of the board members. The audience whispered *live stream* and *her fault*. The moment lasted. Kia was supposed to be cooking. Deja was supposed to be passing out crepes. Kia had never felt so exposed. She couldn't just slink away without a word. She didn't know how to fight with the Mega Eats representative. She wanted to run down the aisle and throw herself at Sullivan's feet. *I didn't mean for this to happen.* Instead she just stood in front of her cooking station, like a kid getting booed at a school talent show.

"Are you okay?" Deja appeared at her side.

Of course she wasn't okay.

"Sullivan, I'm sorry," Kia whispered.

"You know her?" Deja asked under her breath.

"I did."

"Excuse me," the board chair said to the crowd. "Listen up. I'm very sorry. Clause 14b does say legally we are required to take the highest bid."

"The board will have to vote. I'm sorry. We're here to make sure the association follows the charter rules. In this case, we don't get to decide based on what we want."

Sullivan rose.

"I can't believe you'd let this happen." Her voice landed just below a yell. Then she stalked out of the room with the stride of a powerful warrior who had just lost the war.

Kia didn't see the vote. She was already racing down the aisle toward the door Sullivan had slammed behind her.

"Wait!" Kia's steps pounded hard enough to rattle the glass cases of grange ephemera on the walls.

Sullivan had pulled up short at the EMERGENCY EXIT ALARM WILL SOUND sign on the door at the end of the hall.

"Sullivan." Kia put one hand on Sullivan's back.

Sullivan pulled away as though Kia had touched her with a hot pan.

Tears streamed down Sullivan's face. She was the same woman Kia remembered, but horror and grief replaced her cocky grin. This was wrong. Sullivan never lost her cool. Yes, she barked orders in the kitchen when the students cooked together, with Sullivan playing the role of expeditor, but that was to be heard over the kitchen noise, not because she was distressed. The closest Sullivan got to upset was muttering comically hyperbolic threats to stop her Mornay sauce from splitting.

Kia felt a wave of something she'd never felt for Sullivan: protectiveness. Sullivan had never needed protection or comfort. Had she? She did now. She needed someone to scoop her whole body into their arms and rock her and say, *It's going to be okay.*

"Say something. Look at me," Kia begged. "Are you okay?"

The question was as dumb now as when Deja asked her.

"How can you ask?" Sullivan stumbled backward, paused at the ALARM WILL SOUND sign on the door, and then pushed it open.

A dull siren throbbed around them.

Sullivan broke into a run, heading straight for a black wall of trees, her feet splashing through puddles. It looked dangerous. In her distress Sullivan was running toward…whatever horrors lurked in that haunted wilderness. If she got hurt, it'd be all Kia's fault.

"Wait!"

Kia followed Sullivan. The rain had intensified. The clouds blotted out the moon and absorbed the ambient city light. Entering the forest felt like racing into a cave. Sullivan had almost disappeared into the darkness when Kia entered the forest, her vision going black as she stepped from the parking lot lights into the damp forest.

"Sullivan, please." Kia fumbled for her cell phone flashlight.

Sullivan stopped and turned, shielding her eyes.

"Put that thing down. We're not in a mine."

Kia pocketed the light.

"Did you know I was here?" Sullivan asked.

"Of course not."

"So you're doing all this and you didn't even do your research, did you?" Raindrops and tears streaked Sullivan's face. "You didn't google the Bois?"

Gretchen had handled everything. She'd told Kia she would never get a deal like this again, and the investors would only be interested for a minute. The sponsors were clamoring for new content. And Kia had been excited to tell Me'shell she could pack up her life and start the drive to Portland because Kia's dream of a beautiful food pod where small businesses fed love to the community was coming true.

Except it wasn't. And she had done something terrible to Alice Sullivan. Sullivan, who had inspired her. Made her laugh. Filled her with lust. Sullivan, who had been the focus of her life the whole time they were in school, some of the happiest days of her life. Kia had made Sullivan cry. She'd never made anyone cry, and now Sullivan looked so broken.

"It happened so fast. I didn't know you were here."

"That's my house." Sullivan pointed into the darkness. "And that's my restaurant. And this is the forest I grew up in. And Mega Eats is going to strip every inch. They'll destroy this place. Birds can migrate because they land in urban green spaces. Rain fills up the water table because it can get into the ground here.

Beautiful little creatures live in every part of this forest. And now all that'll be left will be a burial ground of plastic fucking forks."

In another context the hyperbole would have been funny. It wasn't funny now. Sullivan was trying to pull herself together. The streaks of tears on her cheeks and her sudden, brittle arrogance wrenched Kia's heart.

"Mega Eats should never be allowed to do that," Kia whispered.

"And before Mega Eats was going to strip this place, *you* were."

"Taste the Love was different." Suddenly it mattered that Sullivan understood that. "It was going to be a place for people to belong. I'm sorry Mega Eats came in. I'm sorry I live streamed." She'd ruined everything. "I am *so* sorry." Kia remembered all those nights teasing each other in the kitchen, pushing each other to do better, teaching each other. And those kisses. She'd fucked up everything. She couldn't walk away with Sullivan thinking she was as bad as Mega Eats. She needed Sullivan to see the beautiful thing she'd tried to build.

"I've been to thirty-eight states." *I missed you.* Kia wanted to grab Sullivan's hands or throw her arms around her. "Every single place I've been, there's been mom-and-pop restaurants getting run out of business because some developer decides to change everything. I want—"

Sullivan cut her off.

"Fuck, Kia." Sullivan scrubbed her hands over her face. "What do you think *you* were going to do to *me*?" She gave a little snort as though this confirmed some ugly truth she'd accepted with disgust. "Food trucks."

"It wasn't supposed to be like this. I…I didn't mean…I didn't know. Please, Sullivan, don't hate me." Kia heard how pathetic the words sounded as soon as they left her mouth.

"I don't hate you." The way she said *hate* suggested a technicality. *Based on the fine print, I don't exactly hate you.* Hate adjacent.

"You're an entrepreneur whose business deal failed." Sullivan raked her hand through her curls, the bitter version of a gesture Kia had admired so many times. "My life is collateral damage."

With that, Sullivan stepped off the path, walking without a light, the underbrush parting for her. She kept her head up, although the rain was still coming through the trees. Eventually, Kia saw the spark of a porch light, then a glimmer of a barely visible window. And then the light went out.

Kia stumbled out of the forest. The lights in the parking lot felt like spotlights. Clumps of mud clung to her sparkly boots. Her phone vibrated with texts. It had probably been vibrating the whole time she had talked to Sullivan. She just hadn't noticed. They'd all be texts from potential sponsors funneled her way by Gretchen. More sponsors. More branded posts. More product placement. Gretchen had already signed her up with Mayonaisia margarine mayonnaise, Solo cups, and American Spirit breakfast sausages. Gretchen would be on her if she didn't text them back immediately, but how could she think about American Spirit breakfast sausages when she had just ruined Alice Sullivan's life. She shivered as the cold edged out the adrenaline in her bloodstream. Across the parking lot, Deja stood in front of Kia's F-150, waving with her whole arm.

"Kia! Over here. That was terrible. Do you want to talk? I'm here for you. I'll drive you to Old Girl, and then we can go out."

Deja had been working with Kia for over a year. She wasn't the first superfan who'd wanted to work with Kia, but she was the first one insistent enough and talented enough—serving as everything from fill-in cook to videographer to crowd control—to get on the payroll. What Kia hadn't been prepared for was the fact that Deja's fangirling hadn't diminished. Kia Gourmazing hadn't lost her luster in Deja's eyes. And sometimes, like now, Kia wished

Deja would silently do her job like any other bored employee in America instead of taking passionate interest in Kia's every move.

"I'll drive. It's *my* truck." Kia didn't want to be the kind of influencer who snapped at her assistant, but today was a fail all the way around.

"You can't drive," Deja said seriously. "You're upset."

"I'm upset. I'm not drunk." Kia felt around for her keys.

"You left your bag inside." Deja held up Kia's sparkling turquoise purse. "The meeting's gonna let out soon. Let's go." She pulled out Kia's keys and hopped in the driver's seat.

Kia got in the passenger side. She sighed and touched the truck's screen, tapped home, which would locate Old Girl in the Riverview RV Park north of Portland. When they stopped in the middle of nowhere, Deja sometimes slept on the pullout couch in the RV. But they weren't in the middle of nowhere, and Kia couldn't take too much more Deja cheer.

"You got an Airbnb, right?" Kia asked. "Don't forget to charge it to my account."

"Yes, but I can stay with you if you want."

"No. No. Thank you."

"I can't believe what happened in there. And that woman Alice Sullivan…what did you talk about? On a scale of one to a hundred, how pissed was she?" Deja continued talking a thousand words a minute. "It's kinda like Amazon reviews though. If someone gives it one star—"

"Gives what one star?"

"Anything. A blanket that looks like a tortilla. Taxidermized bat. And someone gives it one star and they're like, this is the worst thing ever. You know they're probably just mad at their life, but if they give it a three, then maybe you believe them. So do you think she was one star angry or three stars angry?"

"Probably one star."

"Not your fault then. She's just angry at her life."

Because I ruined it.

Kia pulled out her phone. Interspersed with sponsors were texts from her people, starting with her cousin Lillian.

Lillian: *Congrats on the sale, right?*

She'd sent that several hours earlier, before Kia had gone into the grange hall.

From her aunt Eleanor she'd gotten a perfectly punctuated text telling her that Eleanor was proud of her and Kia's father would be too as soon as he sailed close enough to land to get cell phone reception again and heard about the sale.

Eleanor: *Also, don't hesitate to call your father on the emergency radio; I know it's for emergencies. However, I think this counts as a happy emergency; he would be delighted to hear you won the American Fare Award and are entering the landowning class.*

So much punctuation.

Me'Shell wasn't as optimistic.

Me'Shell: *How'd it go? I'm looking for your post????*

Me'Shell: *You haven't posted. Did the sale go through. We're in Wyoming right now. We should still come right? I don't think we can afford the gas to get back. Ha ha ha HA*

Me'Shell: *But for real what's goin on*

Gretchen texted, *I heard. Call me now.* Kia couldn't debrief with Gretchen. Sullivan's tears had robbed Kia of words.

Portland blurred by outside the truck's window, rainy and dark. The traffic lurched. The highway backed up like rush hour even though it was after eight p.m. Everyone said Portland had gotten too big for its infrastructure. Too many people wanted to call this rainy, green city home.

"So what do you think?" Deja asked. "What are you going to do?"

It took Kia a moment to realize that Deja had stopped talking long enough to wait for an answer.

"Leave town I guess." Sometimes her life felt like driving on an empty freeway with no landmarks and no GPS to tell her if she'd ever reach home.

"I mean about Alice Sullivan," Deja prompted.

"Fuck. Nothing, I guess." Kia leaned the side of her head against the window. Rain and city lights hit the window.

"But she's totally into you."

Please don't let Deja be writing fan fiction about her love life. (Deja's fanfic would be Kia's only love life.)

"And you've got tons in common. There's not much about her online. Nothing recent. She used to be all over the foodie scene, then she kind of disappeared a year or two ago. No social media. My friend Trey isn't a hacker but—"

Nothing legit started with "isn't a hacker but."

"They found out Alice Sullivan owns this fancy eco-restaurant called Mirepoix du Bois. Mirepoix of the woods. She lives on the other side of the Bois."

"I know." *I wish I didn't.*

"And Trey found a video of your kiss at graduation."

Kia lifted her head from the cold window and looked at Deja.

"Where? How?"

"Someone filmed your graduation. And they didn't exactly put it online, but Trey is good at research. The way that guy was talking shit about how much you hate each other, and then you just grabbed her and kissed her, and she kissed you back like… fire. There was so much there. I can't believe you didn't get together after that. It was obvious you've been in love with her since that kiss. And I could tell she saw you looking all snatched and realized she feels the same way."

Deja's words hurt like grabbing the handle of a pot that had been in the oven. For a split second, the body didn't register pain. Then pain washed in on a wave of how-could-I-have-been-so-dumb because Kia had played this fantasy in her mind a thousand times. Sullivan saw her again and suddenly realized what their time together had meant and how irresistible she found Kia. They kissed and skipped into the sunrise of happily ever after. (The exact details of HEA were hazy. Did Sullivan move into Old Girl? Would Sullivan like living in a vintage RV? Did they buy a farm and raise chickens? There was definitely a lot of sex and cuddling on comfortable sofas and planning birthday adventures.) Hearing how ridiculous the fantasy sounded coming from Deja made Kia feel like a fool a thousand times over.

"I don't want to talk about Alice Sullivan." *Please take a hint.*

"Yes. But," Deja said with enough pep to make the sun rise early. "This is your chance to connect with your long-lost love. God, I wish I had someone like that. It's so romantic. What tore you apart? Was it another woman?"

"What? No."

"A man? Anyway. Doesn't matter. Maybe you'll even get married. Hell, maybe it'd make you a legacy owner. But that's not the point. The point is you get a second chance at love. You could live with her. Portland's hella expensive. Seattle too. When I lived in Seattle, I had four roommates." Deja relayed something about a roommate who ate everyone's condiments. "But like way more mayo than normal. It's like, *What did you do with it?* You don't think it was something sexual, do you?"

Deja paused, apparently genuinely waiting for an answer.

"I so can't answer that."

This morning Kia "Gourmazing" was living the elusive American dream. Now she'd betrayed Me'shell, ruined Sullivan's life, opened the door for Mega Eats to barge into a neighborhood that didn't want them, and Deja was asking her about sex and mayo. And she wanted to cry, but there was no one to cry to. Her father was yachting out of cell phone range. No one had ever cried on her aunt Eleanor's shoulder. And ever since her cousin and best friend Lillian had moved to Paris with her girlfriend, Izzy, Lillian had started scheduling their calls. The gaps between Lillian's texts had gotten longer. Kia had been Lillian's person. Now it was Izzy. And even though Lillian loved her and would listen to her all night long if Kia wanted to talk, it didn't feel the same knowing that some part of Lillian wanted to get off the phone and get back to Izzy.

When Kia got back to her RV, she threw herself on her bed. She'd always been an optimist. She found solutions. She tried new things and they worked. She expected people to like her and they did. She gave a bitter laugh, thinking about Deja's romantic fantasy. Sullivan hadn't missed her. There was no lost love to rekindle. They weren't moving in together. Kia wasn't going to become a legacy owner by marrying Sullivan. Marry Sullivan. Ha! Right.

Deja was sweet but she was ridiculous sometimes. So ridiculous it wasn't even worth googling the Oakwood Heights charter to see if marrying a legacy owner made you a legacy owner. Deja needed a lesson on identifying realistic plans. The last thing Kia was going to do was show up on Sullivan's doorstep and beg Sullivan to marry her so Kia could build Taste the Love Land and torture herself by imagining a world in which Sullivan loved her.

chapter 6

Sullivan stood in her living room. Nothing had moved since that afternoon. Chenille throws still draped the sofa. Her grandfather's books still lined the built-in bookshelves over the fireplace. Her stereo was still queued up to the audiobook she'd been listening to. But now the vaulted A-frame ceiling swallowed up the light from the table lamps, casting the room in gloom, like a mix between the Midnight filter and the Gritty filter on Insta. (She couldn't believe she remembered the names.)

She'd shooed Opal and Nina out after three hours of Nina trying to ply her with expensive tequila and Opal hugging Sullivan like a Little League coach comforting a losing player. Spring rain like nothing she had seen before slashed her deck as though the world raged at Kia, Mega Eats, the board, the neighborhood, and, most of all, Sullivan. She used to go to the neighborhood association meetings. Before Aubrey's unrelenting pursuit of social media content had eaten up every minute of Sullivan's free time, Sullivan had been involved in the association. She probably would have run for board president except Aubrey said it didn't play well on Insta. Food festivals slapped. Going to rugby games and doing charity cooking classes together served up sexy, sapphic couple. There was no way to make board membership exciting. And Sullivan let some of Aubrey's hunger for likes pull her away from the causes she believed in and the community she wanted to serve. For a while it had felt worth it. After all, she had Aubrey, the love of her life, what more did she need? It turned out other things she needed included room to be herself, privacy, and a chance to live her values.

Sullivan would have heard about the sale if she'd been more involved. She could have read the handwritten letter her grandfather wrote to the board the last time the board discussed selling, the letter that persuaded them to protect the land for fifty years. That was her grandfather's legacy. And Sullivan could have led guided tours of the forest, pointing out trillium and clues that pointed to bobcats gliding through the Bois. She jumped as the wind knocked a pot of cilantro off her porch railing.

Who was she kidding? The world wasn't mad at Kia or even at her. Climate change had turned the patter of spring rain into a hurricane. What did dear Miss Brenda used to say? *Unleash the fury of a changing sky and then duck and hide!* Climate change brought about by a thousand causes, but tonight all she could see was a pile of single-use plastic mounting in front of her house.

A spark reflected in her living room window. Sullivan turned to see what appliance had flashed in her kitchen, but the kitchen and living room rested in darkness. Her living room looked out on a deck set a story above the garden, a lovely vantage point to observe deer and raccoons without disturbing their habitats. There were no walking paths behind her house, as she had been painfully reminded when she'd stalked away from Kia, refusing to flinch even when a blackberry vine snagged her cheek like a fishhook.

The light grew closer. Maybe it was someone's lost dog with

an LED collar, but no, the way the shadows flailed around the flashlight said *person*. Who would walk in this weather, let alone tangle with the armed and vindictive blackberries? A tremor of fear interrupted her fork-ridden despair. She checked the lock on the slider and then the front door. The light got closer. She should call the police, but there'd be flooding all over the city. The police would have to leave someone stranded in their second-story apartment so they could rush to Sullivan's rescue, and *then* she would find out it was someone's golden retriever. Her backpack lived in a front closet. She was always ready for an impromptu hike in the Cascades or overnight backpacking trip near Camp Sherman. When she was stressed, she'd go camping solo. It was safer than people thought if you were prepared. She pulled it out and grabbed a Nitecore spotlight that could light up a mountainside. She'd never used it, but you had to be prepared when you were alone. God, she felt alone tonight.

She hurried to the window and turned on the spotlight. A person was lying on Sullivan's low-water moss "lawn," where they had obviously slipped. It was a girl. Probably a teenager who'd snuck out to smoke pot and gotten lost. Sullivan pulled open the slider, letting in a tidal wave of rain.

"Are you okay?" Her words got lost in the storm.

She dialed back the lumens on the Nitecore and shone her light on the girl. No, not a girl, a woman, with a glittery handbag lying in the mud beside her and dark hair streaming over her eyes. Sullivan hurried to the porch railing.

"Are you hurt?" She projected her voice.

"No, I'm just frickin' wet! Fuck, it's raining!"

The woman sat up. And the tableau all came together…or didn't, because it was impossible that *Kia* was sitting in the mud in Sullivan's backyard.

"What the hell are you doing here?" Sullivan called. "Wait. I'll come down." Sullivan must be dreaming. "Hold on." She headed for the front door.

Had Kia sat around the grange for hours waiting to stalk Sullivan in the rain?

"*What* are you doing?" Sullivan said.

Kia looked so disheveled, Sullivan couldn't be quite as mad at her as she wanted to be. She gave Kia a hand up.

"I wore Converse," Kia said, as though the Converse—which might have had heels, Sullivan couldn't quite tell in the mud—were at fault. "That magic path only opens up for you." The cold had gotten into Kia's brain. She wasn't making sense. It didn't have to be sub-zero to get hypothermia when you were this wet.

"There is no magic path. Come on."

How could this soggy, unexplainable apparition be the woman who'd inspired Sullivan to push her craft to perfection? Be *her* Kia Jackson? Sullivan stopped for a second. Where had that thought come from? Not *her* Kia. Just Kia fucking Jackson who never should have come back into her life. Kia shook with the cold. Sullivan put an arm around Kia, willing her body heat into Kia's side. Kia leaned against Sullivan as Sullivan guided Kia around the house and up the front stairs, and sat her down on the bench in the foyer.

"You should get out of those wet clothes. I'll get you something to wear. And then you'll leave."

"I have to talk to you."

"You can talk while you wait for an Uber."

Uber would take forever in this weather. Kia must have a car somewhere. Maybe Sullivan could drive her back to it.

"You made it look so easy." Kia's chattering teeth bit the words into barely discernible syllables. "You just walked away into the woods, like a...an elf, an elk, a wood elf." Coats, hanging on pegs behind the foyer bench, brushed Kia's shoulder, and she jumped. "There are probably a million snakes out there."

"Did you hit your head when you slipped?"

"Fear of snakes is not a sign of hitting my head. I have a plan."

Sullivan looked down at Kia fumbling with the buttons of her ridiculously shiny silver lamé jacket, her hands shaking too much to get purchase.

"I do not want your plan."

"You—" Kia gave up on the buttons and tried to pull the jacket over her head. "Haven't heard"—the stiff plastic caught on her elbows—"my plan." She yanked the jacket down in defeat.

Kia looked up at Sullivan with wide, pleading eyes, ringed with smeared mascara. Sullivan had forgotten the gold color of Kia's eyes, like polished tigereye. Sullivan knelt before her, undid the jeweled buttons of Kia's jacket, and eased it off her shoulders. She hung it up on one of the pegs. The back of the jacket read LET'S GET GOURMAZING! in glittery letters.

Sullivan shook her head.

"Kia *Gourmazing*. Really, Jackson?"

"It's—" Kia's teeth chattered. "A brand name."

"Can I?" Sullivan gestured to Kia's soaking blouse, an artsy number with tiny buttons Kia would never get undone if she couldn't even get her jacket off.

Kia nodded. Sullivan undid the first button, careful not to look at Kia or let her fingers touch Kia's skin, even through the fabric.

"I didn't know you felt that way about me, Chef," Kia said, teeth still chattering.

"I do *not* feel that way." Sullivan stood up. "I have first aid training. If you have hypothermia, you need to get dry fast."

Kia wriggled out of the blouse without undoing the remaining buttons. How could Kia think Sullivan was looking at her like that? Sullivan glanced at Kia, but only because Kia had planted the idea in her mind. Kia had filled out since school, full breasts cupped by a translucent bra. Little rolls softened her hourglass waist, although her belly was flat and muscular.

Suddenly Sullivan lost the ability to form words. Kia was gorgeous, and her bra was so sheer spiders made webs more substantial. Sullivan could see Kia's nipples. Sullivan was thinking about Kia's nipples while Kia was probably suffering hypothermia and hallucinating that Sullivan was an elk (or elf). And for some unexplainable reason, Sullivan suddenly imagined warming Kia's chilled lips with her own. Sullivan's body woke up in a way she hadn't felt since before she and Aubrey broke up.

Opal was right. She did need to get out more, and not to the Oakwood Heights Neighborhood Association meeting.

"I was not." She spun around so she couldn't be accused of ogling Kia.

"Not what?" Kia asked, still breathless from the cold.

"Anything. Nothing. I was minding my own business. And who wears *that* bra in *this* weather?" That wasn't appropriate; she realized that as soon as the words left her mouth. She tried to fix her mistake, still not looking at Kia. "A bra can be a significant source of warmth when layering for inclement weather. You missed a significant opportunity for forest preparedness."

Sullivan turned around, keeping her eyes fixed on Kia's golden gem eyes. Kia bowed her head. Was that a hint of a smirk visible behind the coils of Kia's hair?

"Go clean yourself up." Sullivan pointed to the hallway. "Shower's down there. Don't get mud on the carpets. They're Turkish."

"Thanks. By the way, I don't *want* to be prepared for the forest." Kia wrapped her arms around herself, hiding the translucent bra. "Ever. Again. I don't do forest. I made an exception for you because I need a small favor. Really, it's more like a favor to both of us."

"You *do* remember that you ruined my life, like, six hours ago, right?"

Kia looked up at her innocently.

"What do you want, Kia?"

"Alice Sullivan, will you marry me?"

chapter 7

Sullivan had a beautiful stone shower stall and a variety of expensive-looking bottles: organic bergamot bodywash, cedar shampoo and conditioner, cinnamon facial toner, Himalayan salt scrub, and several large bars of soap resting on teak soap trays. She wouldn't have guessed Sullivan was a fancy-soaps person, but now that she saw the buffet of body products, it fit. You didn't smell as good as Sullivan without product. And Kia was standing in Sullivan's shower. She was touching a bar of soap that Sullivan might have rubbed against her skin, could have rubbed over her...

What was Kia doing?! What was happening? Had she been flirting with Sullivan and then blurted out her proposal? She was supposed to be logically, professionally laying out the argument for getting married. Had she ruined that possibility with the kind of line tipsy men at the Oklahoma State Fair tossed her way when she sprayed whipped cream on their cinnamon fried ice cream bread pudding balls?

I didn't know you felt that way. Sullivan definitely did *not* feel that way. Although she had noticed Kia's bra, but only because she was trained in first aid, and you couldn't help a person without at least glancing at them. Kia leaned back, letting the water hit her face. This would never work, but what was she supposed to do? She let the water cascade over her, blissfully warming her to the core. She stayed for as long as she could without Sullivan thinking she'd passed out in the shower. Then she turned off the water and stepped out.

As if on cue, Sullivan spoke through the door.

"I've left some clothes for you." Sullivan's footsteps jogged away.

On a decorative table next to the bathroom door, Sullivan had left sweatpants and a sweatshirt, tan with gray racing stripes down the arms and legs. Kia put them on and stepped into fleece clouds and the faint hint of cloves and sandalwood. Kia toweled off her hair—no salvaging her Afro, named Georgie because something so fabulous deserved a name—and stepped out of the bathroom.

Sullivan sat at her kitchen island, wearing flannel slacks and a gray button-down shirt with the sleeves rolled up to her elbows, looking dignified, annoyed, and so, so, so hot. She'd gotten tattoos. Those contrasted with the whole I-quote-Yeats-and-draw-ferns-in-the-conservatory look, but it worked. Black-and-white geometric patterns extended beyond her rolled-up sleeves. They hid the scars and burns on her forearms. Chefs got hurt no matter how careful they were. The whole effect was tough and stylish, and it made Kia's heart flutter.

"When did you get all tatted up?" Kia blurted.

"I went through a phase."

"A phase?"

"Of having too much money and not enough hobbies."

"Did you get them in Japan?"

Her eyebrows lifted in an expression that said, *Are you here to make small talk, kid?* Except in school, amused admiration would have tempered the look. Now the look was tempered with, *I hate my life.*

Kia had brought a peace offering. She hurried to her bag slumped in the hallway. Thank god the bottle hadn't broken and the to-go container hadn't leaked. She set the muddy present on the table and opened it.

"Cayenne-pear Rice Krispies treat."

"Of course it is," Sullivan grumbled.

"With calvados. Your fave, right? They go together perfectly."

"I'm not going to drink away my problems."

"What problems?"

"*You.* And the shitstorm you brought with you. And why are you really here?"

It'd take a minute to get Sullivan on board. An untouched shot stood at attention on the table. Kia smelled it. Tequila. She took the shot and refilled the glass with calvados.

"Try it." She set the shot and the Rice Krispies treat in front of Sullivan.

"No."

"I have a solution to our problems, but first you have to try it."

"My problem is you coming out of the Bois in the middle of the night like a serial killer."

Sullivan folded her arms, looking aggrieved but still looking like a dapper 1920s naturalist. Kia had always imagined Sullivan would sit around her house in men's silk pajamas or a smoking jacket. The button-down and tattoos weren't quite what she'd pictured, but they still fit. The sight filled Kia with delight, like a fangirl getting a behind-the-scenes glimpse of her on-screen crush.

"Your address isn't online," Kia said. "Not even on Been Verified."

"Oh *that* doesn't make me think I'm going to end up in an oil drum in a storage unit somewhere."

"I had to talk to you. I only knew where you lived because you walked away through the woods. It was like the forest opened up for you. Mean trick. It did *not* open up for me."

"I own a restaurant. The hours—when I am there, coincidentally, because I am the executive chef—are posted online."

"But you're closed tomorrow, and Tuesday. We only have a week. Try it." Kia pushed the Rice Krispies treat closer to Sullivan.

"A week to do what?" Sullivan sat back.

The plan had almost made sense when Kia saw the provision in the charter. Now it made about as much sense as suggesting they conjure up a genie.

"To get married."

"I think you hit your head. Let me check your pupils." Sullivan began to rise.

"Wait. Listen. I don't want Mega Eats to buy the Bois. You don't either. If you marry me, I become legacy, and I can buy the Bois."

"I don't want you to buy the Bois."

"But I'm better than Mega Eats."

That hurt. The only thing she had to win over the woman who'd driven her to be the best, whose blue eyes she'd dreamed about, whose strong hands she'd watched, longing for Sullivan to touch her the way she massaged her lacinato kale, whose teasing friendship had made the practice kitchen feel like home, was the fact that Kia wasn't a union-busting monster corporation who might be deliberately mixing plastics with their meats but no one knew for sure because they settled their lawsuits with gag orders. But just because Kia's plan was crazy didn't mean she hadn't thought through her argument.

"I looked at your website," Kia said. "You're smuggling pepper into the country so it won't go on a container ship."

The Pepper Trail was a program where tourists—who were going to travel anyway—returned with spices, thus eliminating the need to ship them by sea.

"You know it's not making a *big* difference for the environment, but it's making *some* difference," Kia went on.

"It's not going to make *any* difference," Sullivan said bitterly. "It offsets about as much carbon as not running my air conditioner for a day."

"But every little bit counts, right?"

"Says the woman with the plastic forks."

"Yes, we're going to use plastic forks. And yeah, biodegradable would be better. Metal would be better. But the restaurateurs I'm bringing in can't afford that kind of stuff. Do you know how much more expensive biodegradable plastic is? I know you don't want me here. And I'm still cutting down the trees, and I'm still putting in a food pod, but Mega Eats will cut down the trees and dump piles of trash in your front yard to get you to go. I'll leave you alone." Kia closed her eyes, her exuberance fading back into shivering. "A lot of people are counting on me."

"No."

"I know you hate Taste the Love Land, but your other option is Mega Eats." Kia set each word down with the finality of a checkmate. "You and me...we don't like to lose. We never did. I want this land. And if Taste the Love Land moves in, it's a quirky Portland thing next to your restaurant. If Mega Eats moves in, they become an anchor store for everything you hate, and you will be in their way. And they will *crush* you."

Kia had been so focused on her pitch, she hadn't noticed Sullivan's shoulders hunching in and her arms tightening around herself.

"But I'll leave a green space around your house. You can have a say in the plans. But we have to do something tomorrow. There's a three-day waiting period to get married. If we sign the paper on Monday, that gives us the three days, plus a day to register my bid on the land."

"There are animals that live here and nowhere else." Sullivan looked very tired and very sad.

Kia wanted to put her arms around her. But according to Sullivan, she was ruining her life, so that wouldn't be comforting.

"At least one," Sullivan said. "The miniature Oregon tree snake. It's so beautiful. It's like this thin green ribbon that's come to life. It's magic."

"Snakes! Save anything but snakes." They were the definition of toxic with their beady eyes glinting, their scales glistening. "Uh. Gross. The way they move. Totally unnatural," Kia said, shivers intensifying. "Wait, does that mean there's a regular Oregon tree snake?"

Or worse. Maybe there was a *jumbo* Oregon tree snake.

"Not anymore," Sullivan said mournfully.

Kia regretted her outburst of snake hate. There was no understanding Sullivan's apparent grief at this fact, but she was grieving nonetheless. It was written on her face, in her posture. Even her chestnut curls looked sad.

"Eat your Rice Krispies treat," Kia said gently.

No one had ever looked so deflated by taking a bite of a Rice Krispies treat.

"With the calvados," Kia urged.

Sullivan took a small sip. There was that hint of grudging admiration behind her sadness, irritation, and defeat. Something in the way Sullivan rolled her eyes said she knew it was the best. They'd never needed a judge to tell them who'd won.

"I'm not going to marry you. That's not how things work."

Sullivan swallowed a few times. Her jaw tightened. The world didn't make sense when a brilliant, invincible woman like Sullivan looked so vulnerable.

"Please think about it. I told a lot of people to risk everything because I promised I could give them a better life."

"But you couldn't." Sullivan sounded as sad as she looked. "I'll drive you back to wherever you parked."

After all the times Kia had tried to crush Sullivan in the kitchen, seeing her crushed in real life made Kia want to lie down on the floor and cry.

"There's nothing I can say?" Kia asked.

"Absolutely nothing."

chapter 8

Early the next morning, Sullivan arrived at Margino's Coffee. The barista sat at the baby grand piano at the front of the coffee shop, plucking out a melody that might have been Taylor Swift's "Shake It Off." There was no shake, shake, shaking it off for Sullivan. The barista jumped up with a wave. Sullivan ordered for herself and her friends, then dropped her messenger bag on a bay window seat. Margino's usually cheered her up. The white walls and delicate potted ferns felt cozy in the winter and breezy in the summer. Now it felt like she was watching herself in a dream where everything looked normal, but a dream where you knew that something terrible was about to happen. She stared out the window. Outside, the denizens of Portland's Pearl District were emerging to walk their purebred dogs, oblivious to the bizarre and depressing turns Sullivan's life had taken.

Nina arrived a minute later dressed in a butternut squash–colored velour tracksuit.

"Damn, girl. You look some kinda way." She rested her fists on her ample hips. "It's not the end of the world." She squeezed herself onto Sullivan's window seat, pulled a lipstick out of her purse, and lunged for Sullivan's face. Sullivan pulled away.

"You can't face the world without some color on you." Nina tipped Sullivan's chin up. "It'll make you feel better."

"We don't exactly wear the same colors."

"You can make it work. Blot." Nina handed her a cloth napkin.

Sullivan didn't have the energy to tell Nina that a lipstick-stained napkin would probably be thrown away, adding to the massive waste produced by the restaurant industry.

Opal banged through the door with a rugby ball under one arm. She dropped the ball as she wrapped her thick arms around Sullivan.

"Were you up all night?" Opal sounded a little teary too. "It's going to be okay."

If Mirepoix closed, it'd hurt Opal too. Sullivan felt like an ass for forgetting.

"I'll make it right, Opal. Maybe this is your chance to open your own place."

"Oh, honey. I don't want to open my own place. I want you to have Mirepoix. I want *us* to have Mirepoix."

Opal pulled up a chair in front of the window seat table, nodding her thanks for the triple Americano Sullivan had ordered for her. There was no cause for thanks. The coffee was under-roasted. The foam on Sullivan's cappuccino clogged her throat.

"Who're we going to sue?" Nina dropped the lipstick back in her bag.

"There's no one to sue." Sullivan stared into her unsatisfying cup.

"There's always someone to sue." Nina cradled her London Fog, careful to keep the steam away from her mane of curly hair.

"Kia showed up last night."

"At your house?" Opal asked. "Why didn't you call us?"

It hadn't seemed fair to call her friends in the middle of the night after they'd already spent hours comforting her.

"We *do* have someone to sue." Nina set her drink down and pulled out a tablet.

"We're not suing Kia," Sullivan said.

"What did she want?" Opal asked.

"She brought me a bottle of calvados and a Rice Krispies treat and asked me to marry her."

Despite everything, it was fun to watch the sentence land. Nina and Opal looked at her, then at each other, then back at her.

"What?" her friends said in unison.

"Why did she propose marriage?" Nina asked, starting to look hungry. In Nina's mind marriage meant divorce, and divorce was the expensive, Dior-scented water she swam in.

"Not that you aren't a beautiful, talented woman who deserves love," Opal added. "By the way, there's a new guy working at my brother's office. When this is all over—"

"No. No. No brother's office."

"But you can't sue her," Opal added. "You know how hard it is to get into *American Fare*, just to make it as a high-end chef. And as a Black woman! You can't sue a young Black entrepreneur, even if you did kiss her—"

"I'm not suing Kia." Sullivan slumped in her seat.

"So why did she want to marry you?" Nina asked.

"She came by to tell me how Mega Eats is going to run me out of business. I think she said they'll crush me."

"Romance is not dead," Nina said.

"When did she come over?" Opal asked.

"After midnight."

"In the storm?"

"She walked through the Bois."

Sullivan could see the gold sparkling in Kia's eyes. Kia wasn't the culinary arts school ingenue anymore. She wasn't a wunderkind anymore. She was grown. She was a businesswoman. And even covered in mud, she was a force to be reckoned with. It wasn't fair. They might have been friends if they'd reconnected in another way. Maybe there was an alternate reality where Sullivan messaged Kia. *Congratulations on American Fare.* Kia wrote back and somehow that tripped a fuse in the universe, the butterfly effect, and because of that, none of what happened had happened.

"Did you have hate sex?" Nina asked.

"No!"

"So Mega Eats is going to destroy you, and you should marry Kia because…?" Nina looked like her mind was racing through every possible scenario with the speed of a high-end laptop. She slapped her palm on the table. She'd arrived at the end of the calculation. "You're a legacy landowner. If she marries you, she can buy the Bois."

Nina's enthusiasm was unnerving. The barista came by with complimentary tuiles because Nina lived in the high-rise above the coffee shop and probably spent more at Margino's Coffee than any other customer.

"I like her." Nina drew out the words, then punctuated the sentence by crunching a cookie in half. "That is smart. That's even serving ruthless. She'll do anything, with anyone to get what she wants. I'm feeling *I do.*"

"You think I should marry her because she's *ruthless*?"

Nina nodded as though *ruthless* was high praise.

"And savvy. Decisive."

"I don't believe she asked you that," Opal said. "People don't marry for property rights." She picked at the stitched seam of her rugby ball. "Marriage is about love and commitment."

Nina looked at Opal as though Opal had said Beyoncé was a mediocre talent, then pulled out her phone and started typing.

"Marriage is about money. Always," she said with a hint of sadness. "I like her. She's smart." Nina kept typing. "There's no way she can just give you the money. If she's got investors, they're not going to go for that, and even if they did, that kind of contract takes time we don't have."

"What are you talking about?" Sullivan asked.

"I'm contacting my associate. He'll draw up a boss-ass prenup." Nina shrugged without looking up. "Anything goes south, we take her down. I'll need access to her info. Net worth. Income streams. Any pending actions. What's her lawyer's name? You have to register the marriage as fast as possible." Nina's fingers flew across the screen. "Get me her number and all the deets. I was going to blow out my hair this morning, but for you, I'll wait."

"I am absolutely not marrying Kia."

"Yes. You are." Finally, Nina looked up. "You don't have options, girl. It's marry Kia Jackson or die under a pile of Mega Eats wrappers."

It was still pouring rain Monday morning, the day after the Oakwood Heights Neighborhood Association meeting. The RV park had planted orange cones around the lanes to indicate high water. The cone nearest Kia had tipped over and floated in a lake-sized puddle. The weather fit Kia's mood, and the pounding rain was the right backdrop for what she had to do. She had to call Me'Shell.

"There was a problem with the sale." That felt small compared to everything that had happened last night. "It didn't go through, and it probably won't." No point in giving Me'Shell false hope. "It won't. And I'm so sorry." Kia propped her elbows on the foldout table in Old Girl. "I am looking for other options. I will find you a place to set up your truck. I'll help you pay the lot fee until you're up and running."

"But Taste the Love Land was a sanctuary. You said so. It'd be different than just renting space. We'd be in it together."

Behind Me'Shell's voice, Kia heard Crystal say, "What's wrong, Mom?" and then: "Watch the road, Mom!"

Kia was going to make Me'Shell wreck. That was the kind of person Kia was. She should put on some Miley Cyrus because she was coming in like a wrecking ball.

"It's just for a little while until I find a different place to buy."

Gretchen had told her she had to move fast because investors wouldn't stay interested for long. She was exciting. She was new. But she wasn't a sure thing. As the American Fare hype died down, that'd feel more important to them than her surge of fame. Plus the Bois had seemed like the perfect location for the perfect price. She shouldn't promise Me'Shell another Taste the Love Land. She'd already broken that promise once.

"I am so, so sorry," she said.

Her throat clenched with unspent sobs, but she didn't get to cry now. She was the bad guy, not the victim right now. She didn't have a right to make Me'Shell feel sorry for her. Or Sullivan. But, damn, she felt sorry for herself.

"Please pull over so you can process this. Call me back, okay?" Kia said.

Then she called the Chets.

Then she burst into tears.

Since the day couldn't suck more, Kia had driven down to the Chicken Feet and Chow Festival, where she'd installed her food truck—named the Diva, because obviously. It had her face on it. Deja would have stayed all day to help sear oxtails, but the festival was dead, and Kia sent her away with grudging thanks. Even the amazing Kia Gourmazing couldn't attract customers. She'd had about ten since she opened, despite a dozen upbeat live streams. She was supposed to be hawking a name-brand barbecue sauce, but they would want livelier videos. She'd have to apologize and make something better tomorrow.

Kia flipped the sign on her food truck to CLOSED and walked out into the festival to stretch her legs. Liver More Food Truck was packing up and leaving. The turnout was poor because of the unrelenting rain, or maybe Portland wasn't ready for trucks like the Chitlin Shack. Sullivan would like Chicken Feet and Chow, Kia thought. The festival was all about using the parts people didn't eat. Waste not, want not. Now that Kia thought about it, she really should use more of the spare parts. Maybe if she brought Sullivan a serving of her sweet soy and adobo patas de pollo she could convince Sullivan she wasn't a wasteful capitalist? Probably not. Kia sighed.

Her turquoise glasses did little to protect her eyes against the slicing rain as she trudged through puddles big enough to swallow small cars.

"This weather!" she said into the wind. The weather wasn't the real problem.

The men operating the Krispy Kraken were huddled around a smoker, their backs turned against the blowing wind. Instinctively, Kia headed their way, ready to cheer them on, but she stopped. She didn't have the right to raise anyone's spirits. She'd disappointed so many people already. The wind kicked up and blew her rain jacket hood off. Cold rain splashed her neck, and she flinched from the shock.

At least the Diva was warm. She let herself back in and sat down with her back against one of the stainless steel cupboards, checking her phone. Lillian hadn't responded to her last text: a picture of the rain pouring down around the fair.

She had just reached the depth of self-pity and was taking the next emotional staircase down to full-blown angst, when someone knocked on the frosted glass service window. The figure stood silhouetted in the dull light. Kia wiped her eyes and put on her Kia Gourmazing smile. Then she pulled herself off the floor. Maybe she could make someone a sandwich and make their day a little brighter. Maybe it was a fan hoping for a signed napkin. She'd give them a free LET'S GET GOURMAZING! T-shirt.

She opened the window. Sullivan stood in front of her holding two travel mugs, hunching against the rain. Her face said she did not want a sandwich or a napkin or a T-shirt.

"I'm going to regret this." Sullivan handed Kia a mug.

"Come in." Kia bounded to the door, then hesitated with her hand on the latch. Nothing fun or pleasant was going to come of Sullivan trudging through the rain. She let out a long breath to calm her nerves, opened the door, and beckoned Sullivan into the small space.

Sullivan looked around the inside of the Diva.

"Nice layout."

Sullivan liked the layout. That was something. Kia pushed a button and a bench unfolded from the ceiling. That always impressed people. Kia gestured for Sullivan to sit. Sullivan wore a camel-colored overcoat and a scarf of some sophisticated tartan.

Kia clutched her mug. Where should she sit? Sitting next to Sullivan was too close. Standing over her was weird. The floor was too greasy. She chose leaning against the counter in a pose she knew said, *I'm trying to look casual*, while not being casual at all. She tried to think of something to say.

Sullivan broke the silence.

"You're the lesser of two evils."

Was the correct response *fuck off* or *thanks*?

"You're better than an off-ramp." Was there just a touch of humor in her long-suffering look? Like Sullivan couldn't believe she was speaking the sentence out loud? "I talked to my friend, who's a divorce attorney for the rich and dysfunctional, and she says she'll work with your lawyers on a prenup."

It took Kia a moment to register the words.

"You're going to marry me? Oh my god. Thank you. Thank you!" Kia stood up straight. Sullivan had said yes! "Can I hug you?"

"This is not a hugging situation." Sullivan sat back, reminding Kia of an affronted cat. "And the second you sign the papers for the sale, we're getting divorced."

Hysterical laughter threatened to well up in Kia. Her spirits lifted. She could call Me'Shell back. *Don't panic. We might still do this.* Then tears welled up behind her laughter. She'd spent all that time in a passionless relationship with Gretchen, and now she was going to marry a woman whose highest praise was, *You're better than an off-ramp.* And it was Sullivan whom she'd adored. She hadn't looked Sullivan up because she didn't want anything to ruin her fantasy that one day they'd meet again and Sullivan would adore her. And now they'd met again. And Kia was tired, sad, and scared, and Sullivan wanted Kia out of her life as fast as possible.

Kia held her breath to hold in her feelings.

"Okay. Well. Now that we've settled that." Sullivan touched her eyebrow as if to smooth it out, although the only thing in need of smoothing was the chestnut curls dripping rainwater. "So we'll get married."

Kia nodded, not trusting her voice.

"Try the coffee." Sullivan motioned to the mug in Kia's hand.

Kia took a sip. For a second, the taste washed away the damp, sad festival and Sullivan's weary expression, the panicked relief at saving Taste the Love Land, and the sudden reminder that she would probably be alone forever. Suddenly, Kia was standing in a field impossibly poised between spring and late summer as the taste washed over her tongue.

"Sumatra with mint and coriander simple syrup," Sullivan said. "And one Jet-Puffed marshmallow."

Kia's favorite. Kia had made herself this special coffee every morning. She'd always offered one to Sullivan, and Sullivan had always refused. *Not with the marshmallow, Jackson. I have standards.* It had become a joke, and Kia had snuck marshmallows into Sullivan's coffees, for the delight of watching the taste dawn on Sullivan's face. *Jackson! You are in so much trouble.*

"You remembered," Kia whispered.

"I couldn't forget that insult to the culinary arts."

Kia swirled a sip around her mouth.

"You made the simple syrup. It's fresh."

"I have standards, Jackson."

"And you bought the marshmallows for me, didn't you?"

Sullivan would never have store-bought marshmallows on hand.

"And I will keep them in the car because those pillows of horror are not coming into my house. Get your lawyer to call mine before I change my mind." Sullivan set a business card on the counter, picked up her own coffee, and walked out.

Kia's thoughts bubbled like a pot boiling over. Adding to panic and relief and sadness and exhaustion, she felt a touch of excitement that had nothing to do with Taste the Love Land. And it wasn't the excitement of boiling water hitting a hot stovetop but the fizz of freshly made soda. Little sweet bubbles appearing out of nowhere. For all that you're-not-as-bad-as-an-off-ramp stuff,

Sullivan had brought her favorite coffee. What if they spent time together, and Kia was so charming and delightful, Sullivan fell madly in love with her? And because Kia was hopeless and determined to throw herself headlong into disappointment, when she got to her RV, she opened the neatly organized box of accessories stored in a built-in cupboard above her bed. She took out a rhinestone ring she'd bought in Albuquerque. She put it on her ring finger and held out her hand to admire it.

"I do."

chapter 9

Kia paced inside her RV, her laptop counting down to the minute Lillian clicked into their scheduled Zoom call. Scheduling calls made sense with the nine-hour time difference, but it made Lillian feel farther away. There was a time when they'd texted and called each other for no particular reason at any hour of the day. Now Lillian was waking up next to Izzy. It wasn't Lillian's fault, but it made Kia feel lonely.

For years, Kia had wanted her life on the road more than an address and a committed relationship (unless Sullivan decided she was desperately in love with her, in which case Kia had been ready to settle down…at least she could pretend that was true so she could enjoy her seeing-Sullivan-again fantasies). She met so many wonderful people on the road. It made up for not having a lot of close friends or a girlfriend. But now she was spending most of her time promoting sponsored products at name-brand restaurants and corporate-sponsored fairs. She wasn't meeting lobster fishers in Maine or building community gardens in Detroit or watching grandmothers teaching their grandchildren how to make fry bread. She was making a ton of money promoting American

Spirit breakfast sausages. She was the person every aspiring influencer wanted to be.

Then she went back to Old Girl alone. She could charm her way into any after-party. No backstage bouncer was immune to the confident friendliness that said, *Of course I belong here.* But when it came to flirting—as she'd painfully illustrated with Sullivan—she was hopeless. (Probably hopeless in bed too, although she hadn't had enough experience to know for sure.) And while thirty was *very young*, Aunt Eleanor had told her once when she was fretting about the approaching big three oh, she was almost thirty with one passionless relationship behind her. And now she had to tell Lillian that she was marrying her culinary arts school rival and crush to secure a land deal. She wasn't ready for the lecture. Lillian might be all calm and happy in Paris with her lover, but she was still her mother's daughter. *This is an unorthodox way to conduct business. Have you considered other options, Kia?*

Kia climbed the steep steps to her bed loft. Usually she loved being in Old Girl, which she had parked in an RV park outside the city. She crawled into her loft, where she could sit up, although not stand. (On a good day her Afro, Georgie, brushed the ceiling, but today it had deflated in the humid air.) Out of the back of Old Girl she could see snowcapped Mount Hood and airplanes crisscrossing the sky. It was a pretty park compared to some of the places she'd stopped.

Old Girl was her sanctuary, filled with plants, mirrors, jewelry, and books. Her kitchen and her bed loft vied for favorite space. Old Girl was where she collected herself at the end of a busy day, the place where she could channel the peacefulness of clear skies and open highways. But today, it felt like a vehicle, not a home.

Kia looked at Georgie in a little mirror that hung beside her bed. Her hair was lopsided in an unflattering way. She tried to pick it into shape, a pit growing in her stomach. *Breathe.* She took out the old digital camera she kept in a cubby in the headboard. Her favorite camera. With an actual memory card and no Bluetooth. A safe space. She pressed the stiff on button and scrolled through the pictures. They were all of her. Not selfies—she set the camera on a stand. But not self-portraits either. *Portrait* implied art and planning. They were just *her*. Often naked. Never posed. No filter. Not trying to look sexy. She didn't smile in the pictures unless it was a true smile. She hadn't been smiling that much recently.

"I am me," she recited.

No matter what happened or how many Kia Gourmazing selfies she edited, deep inside, Kia Jackson was Kia Jackson. She was a girl reading Sappho on the deck of her father's yacht the *Serendipity*. She was sixteen talking to Lillian on the phone in the middle of the night. She was alone on a Montana highway towing Old Girl and blasting Beyoncé. The pictures calmed her. Everything was happening so fast, and it felt like it was happening *to* her. But deep inside there was part of her that none of this could touch.

"I am real."

The Zoom chime sounded to tell her Lillian had logged on.

She opened her laptop on top of a pile of velvet pillows. She willed her facial muscles into her signature Duchenne smile and turned on the camera. Kia and her lopsided Afro had a job to do, a confession to make, a scolding to take. Lillian appeared in her tiny apartment, sitting on the fire escape. She held up her phone to show Kia the Eiffel Tower lit up behind her, visible between two buildings. Did it get any more romantic than that?

"Cuuuz! What's up?" Feigning casualness was Kia's bread and butter, but it felt impossible to slow the adrenaline coursing through her. She kept talking. "You look amazing. How's the ballet school? Did you buy those Parisian tea towels you wanted?"

"Forget the towels. How was the meeting? Are you a land baron now?"

Kia nervously brushed her left hand through her Afro. Lillian froze. For a second, Kia thought the internet had stalled.

Then Lillian said, "Kiana Jackson, that's not an engagement ring?"

"What?"

Kia was still wearing the ring.

"Did you get *engaged*?"

"I…" Kia opened her mouth, but a desert's worth of sand swallowed her voice. This was like lowering a tursnicken into hot oil. You had to move carefully and with confidence. "I am getting married."

"You didn't even tell me you were dating someone." Lillian sounded hurt.

Kia could hit her with, *When would I tell you? It takes a week to schedule a call with you.* But that wasn't fair.

"It's not what you think."

"How can marrying someone not be what I think?" Lillian asked.

"I would have told you if I was dating."

"Oh my god, Kia!" The reproach softened to amusement. "Did you meet her three days ago? Aren't you supposed to be in the middle of a land deal?"

Right. Hadn't her aunt Eleanor always called Kia and her father *colorful parrots*? They were fanciful. They didn't make sense, and they didn't have to, because it wasn't in their nature. Lillian had to be perfect, but Kia just had to show up in her turquoise sunglasses and make everyone laugh. She wasn't going to get a lecture, because Lillian expected her to do crazy things like getting married to a woman she'd just met while in the middle of the biggest business transaction of her life. But being a colorful parrot wouldn't save her from letting Me'shell down. Being fanciful and funny wouldn't make Sullivan like her.

Kia felt Georgie droop.

"It's all fucked up, Lillian."

Even from across the world and through the screen, Kia saw concern fill Lillian's face.

"I didn't get the land deal, and now I might, but it's not…it's not how I wanted it."

"And you got married."

"Not for love."

Lillian waited. Kia started with the meeting at the grange hall.

"Do you remember Alice Sullivan?" Kia asked. "The other woman at Jean Paul Molineux."

"The kiss!" Lillian said. "Yeah, I remember her. That was rich. You're not the grab-a-woman-and-kiss-her type. Wait. You're marrying Alice Sullivan?"

Kia dropped her head into her hands, then remembered Georgie would cover up the camera. She sat back up again.

"Is that good?" Lillian asked. "You liked her, but have you talked to her since school?"

If only they were having this conversation because Kia and Sullivan had really fallen in love. If only Sullivan had swept Kia up in her arms. *I always wanted you, Kia.*

"I haven't, and I had no idea she was going to be there. You know how my dad is always going on about serendipity. Serendipity is like karma. It's not always good. I must have bad karma too. Or maybe I just fucked up. Obvs I put a bunch of stuff about the sale on my channels. And Sullivan wasn't the only one who showed up."

Lillian had never eaten at a Mega Eats, so Kia gave her some context for the next part.

"You remember that story about schoolchildren in Pennsylvania being fed pink slime passing for ground sirloin? That's Mega Eats slime." Kia described the men from Mega Eats sweeping into the grange hall. "They outbid me. And they knew about the sale because I live streamed it." The thought made Kia want to empty the contents of her stomach into the RV's incinerating toilet and never eat again. "I'm such an idiot."

"You're an influencer. It's your job to live stream things."

It didn't make Kia feel better.

"Sullivan lives right next to the land, and she owns a restaurant, and she's all into the environment and hates food trucks and hates Mega Eats even more."

"Kia, I'm so sorry. Was she pissed?"

"Really pissed. But there's a clause in the land's trust. It says if someone's family has owned property in the neighborhood since it was incorporated, they get to buy the land at fair market value. No one can bid against them. So the only way I can compete with the highest bidder is to be a legacy owner, and the only way to become a legacy owner is to—"

"—marry a legacy holder," she and Lillian said at the same time.

They could still finish each other's sentences, even if Lillian had a new life with Izzy.

Lillian frowned. "Sounds kind of like redlining."

Kia hadn't even thought of that uncomfortable part of the scenario. In the past, people wrote laws like that to keep Black people out of white neighborhoods.

"I guess this is revenge?" She winced. "Now we're using the clause so a Black woman can buy the land and rent it to minority-owned businesses."

"It's bold." Lillian bobbed her head side to side as if considering which way she wanted to go on the topic. "So you talked Sullivan into marrying you so that you could buy the land instead of Mega Eats."

"Yep. And now Sullivan low-key hates me…more than low-key. But she hates Mega Eats more."

"So you got married?"

"Tomorrow. In court."

"How did you talk her into it? I mean, anyone should be happy to marry you. You're a rock star, but did you just catch her outside the meeting and say, *Want to get married?*"

"She ran off during the meeting. She was really upset. All through school I thought she was invincible. Nothing fazed her. She just floated through school dressing like some gorgeous nineteen twenties drag king. But she was crying outside the meeting. I made Alice Sullivan cry."

This time Kia didn't care that Georgie covered the screen as she rested her forehead on the keyboard, probably reprogramming the computer to do nothing but search the web for the life cycle of starfish. She didn't care. All she could think about was Sullivan's face contorted with the effort not to sob, then the cold resignation that had filled her face in the forest. *What do you think you were going to do to me?*

"So then I didn't know what to do. I came up with this ridiculous marriage idea. I don't have any contact info for Sullivan, and I couldn't wait until her restaurant opens on Wednesday, so I walked to her house. I'd seen where she went when we were in the woods. It was raining. I showed up looking like someone had thrown me in a lake. I did bring her my signature Rice Krispies treats."

"How could someone not marry you after having those?"

That was a huge compliment from a woman who'd spent most of her life declaring that carbs were the devil.

Kia described her conversation with Sullivan. She left out the part where Sullivan unbuttoned Kia's jacket and she awkwardly flirted with Sullivan.

When she'd finished, Lillian said, "It's weird, but I'm kind of happy for you. Maybe you and Sullivan can reconnect. You adored her in school."

Kia nodded slowly.

It wasn't fair. If she'd met Sullivan in any other way, Sullivan might have wanted to be her friend. And just maybe Kia had seen a spark of interest as Sullivan glanced at her body. The chance that that passing attraction was enough to light a fire were slim. The chance that that passing attraction was enough to light a fire *now* was nonexistent.

"She did make me a coffee," Kia said. "With a marshmallow, mint, and coriander syrup."

"See?" Lillian said. "She can't hate you if she made you that... creative drink."

Kia said goodbye to Lillian and flopped down on her bed, staring up at the skylight. It was close enough that she could almost touch it while she was lying down. The stars, on the other hand, were a bazillion light-years away. Kia rolled Lillian's words around in her mind. Was there any way Sullivan could forgive her? Was it possible that remembering Kia's favorite coffee and tasting the Rice Krispies treats could equal something like affection? Tolerance? Nostalgia for the practice kitchen? Something that wasn't a strong dislike mixed with several cups of desperation and probably a tablespoonful of *I can't believe I kissed this woman back in the day?* Her father would say yes. Happiness could be right around the corner. Newly in love Lillian would say yes. Kia's heart and mind said no. The whole reason she wanted to build Taste the Love Land was that she'd seen too many people struggle and suffer. On-screen, she was bubbly Kia Gourmazing. On her old digital camera, she was Kia Jackson, who had seen the world, knew how beautiful it could be, and knew how often sad things happened to good people.

chapter 10

Sullivan couldn't believe she was getting married. A huge abstract of swirling oranges and blues graced the expansive lobby of the Multnomah County Courthouse. Men in suits and women in power sweater sets hurried across the marble floor. Beside her, Opal stood in an ironed rugby jersey and Nina in a red suit that said, *I'm going to annihilate you in court before mimosa brunch at the Ritz*.

Sullivan had always wanted to get married. For a while, she'd thought she would marry Aubrey. To have someone who loved you forever. Loved your foibles. Adored the eccentric habits you hid on the first date. And of course, every marriage saw difficult times, but love made those hardships sacred. This was not that marriage. And, logically, she knew her arrangement with Kia had nothing to do with whether or not another person would love her. But somehow being married for money made her feel like no one would ever want her. She stuffed the feeling deep in her pocket and tried to forget it. She had a enough reason to feel sorry for herself without inventing things.

Sullivan spotted Kia as soon as she entered the huge, open space. The girl who'd helped serve crepes bounded beside Kia.

"I can't believe I'm going to witness Kia Gourmazing's

marriage," the girl said by way of greeting. Her eyes got wide like an anime character looking at a cake. "I know you've been in love this whole time. You have total chemistry. Are you eloping?" She expounded on how signing their wedding license was almost as amazing as having Jesus as a houseguest. "I mean, I've never had Jesus as a houseguest. Like, spiritually, I have. But not, like, IRL."

"I'm Nina," Nina cut in. She extended her hand to Kia. "We talked on the phone. This is Opal. She'll witness too."

Kia shook Opal's hand, then introduced the girl.

"This is my assistant, Deja."

"I am in love with your love story. You two." She made her hands into a heart and held it over her chest. "Hashtag 'relationship goals.'"

Please don't let this marriage be anyone's #RelationshipGoals.

"Hi," Kia said to Sullivan, fidgeting with her phone, which she clasped in one hand. "Thanks for this."

Kia wore a formfitting dress. Bands of fuchsia crisscrossed her body. A stripe of pink held the weight of her breasts. The dress stretched over her hips. Dark orange glitter sparkled in her hair. She wore white boots that could have stepped off a runway or out of a military operation in the snow. She also looked tough, a little terrified, and...*pretty*. How had Sullivan been so immersed in the competition for flavor and technique, in the intensity of the rivalry, that she failed to see Kia fully? If someone had asked, Sullivan would have said, *Yeah, sure, of course she's pretty*. But she'd never *felt* Kia's beauty, not the way she felt it now. Kia's beauty was classic like an African queen. Kia's golden-brown eyes danced. Her lips looked soft and sumptuous. The sweep of her curves was so tempting...

"Hey," Nina prompted.

Shit. Had she been staring at Kia in a way that suggested... the kind of interest a person should have (and Sullivan absolutely should not have) in their future wife? A hint of *gotcha* pulled at Kia's lips, just like when she bested Sullivan at lyophilization, managing to freeze-dry quail eggs and broccolini into a stunning and delectable dish.

"Let's get this over with then," Sullivan said, gesturing toward a wide flight of stairs.

Kia fell in step beside Sullivan as they mounted immaculately polished stairs to the second floor.

"You look nice," Kia said.

Sullivan had worn a suit.

"You also"—Sullivan looked as far away from Kia as she could without turning her head around like an owl—"look like you dressed for the occasion."

"I thought I could make it a little special at least." Kia dipped her chin and blinked a few times, as if Sullivan was so wonderful she couldn't believe her eyes. Her fake charm was not working.

"I already said I'd marry you."

"My marketing manager said I should take some pics of the wedding in case we want to put it on the channel," Kia said with less charm. "Maybe. When we get divorced that'll be off-brand, but we might just cut you out slowly and hope people forget about you. Like when Bowling Ball the bulldog died. They didn't do a big death announcement, just got a new puppy and let it ride. You knew Bowling Ball, right?"

Sullivan stopped midway up the marble stairs.

"No."

"He was almost as popular as Noodle the pug."

Sullivan grabbed the railing like she might fall.

"I don't mean cut you out as a person," Kia added quickly. "Just on the channel. I mean, if you wanted, we could pretend to be married forever. You'd look great on my U-Spin account."

Opal, Nina, and Deja had stopped at the top of the stairs and were watching them.

"Do *not* put me on your socials," Sullivan spat.

"Is being seen with me that bad?" Kia's face radiated hurt.

"I don't want to be seen online. Period. You're infinitely better than an off-ramp. But this"—Sullivan's gesture took in the courthouse and everything else that was wrong with her life right now—"is too much. And being splashed all over social media… that'd be the last straw."

"Everyone splashes everything all over social media."

"Just, please, Kia, don't put me out there like that."

"Okay. I won't. I promise."

To Sullivan's surprise, Kia sounded absolutely sincere, like she took the request as seriously as Sullivan did because she could tell it mattered to Sullivan.

Nina was waiting for them at the top of the stairs. She fixed Sullivan with a look, the same look she'd given Sullivan when they were kids and Sullivan had broken some rule of play or as teenagers when Sullivan crushed on an obnoxious boy.

"Are you two fighting?" Nina took Sullivan's arm while glaring at Kia. "I like to see a marriage dissolve as much as the next divorce attorney." She flicked her other wrist, exhibiting a bracelet full of diamonds. "Make it rain. But I asked Judge Lavigne to waive the three-day waiting period. Marriages are the only fun part of her job. Act like you love Kia so much you cry when she smiles at you."

"We're not fighting," Kia said.

"Sullivan." Nina drew out her name. "Kia is a strong Black businesswoman breaking into a male-dominated field. If she wasn't buying the Bois, you'd love her. Play nice."

"We're not fighting," Sullivan repeated.

"Fine, let's go," Nina said, in the same tone mothers used with children in grocery stores at five o'clock.

The group followed Nina down the hall. Nina sat them on a bench while she went for paperwork.

In front of them, a young Latine couple adjusted each other's corsages. One person wore a jewel-blue suit and the other person wore a simple yellow dress. An entourage of friends and grandmas and little children surrounded them. The person in the dress put their arms around the person in the suit and kissed them on the cheek. Blue Suit lifted Yellow Dress an inch off the ground and spun them around.

Kia jumped up. "Y'all are too cute!"

The couple beamed.

"Could I take your pictures? I run a little social media thing. Kia Gourmazing. I just love to meet new people."

Kia held out her phone, presumably showcasing the fabulous new people she'd already immortalized on her feed.

"I know Kia Gourmazing!" Yellow Dress exclaimed. "My uncle runs a food truck."

"Great! I'll tag your uncle's truck."

The couple was already posing for Kia's camera. Kia beamed, took some pictures, typed a caption at light speed, and sat back down.

"Don't worry," Kia said to Sullivan. "I won't put you on my channel."

"Do you do that constantly?" Sullivan should leave it alone, get married, walk away. But Aubrey's photo shoots had interrupted every date Sullivan had planned. She should at least get through this miserable experience without watching people cheesing for Kia's camera.

"It's my job," Kia said. "If I lose followers, I lose money."

"Real money?"

"About three hundred." Kia started typing again.

"A month?"

"Ha. I'm not *that* big. A year." Kia didn't look up. "How do you think I'm buying your ancestral forest? I've got investors putting up the down payment. I'm financing everything else. I can't do that selling hot dogs."

Three hundred a year. Did Kia mean…

"Three hundred thousand?"

Over a quarter of a million for posting hot dogs?

Kia flipped her phone over on her knee and looked up.

"Yeah."

Nina always said men married for money or looks. Women married for money, but they were attracted to power. *Money represents power. That's the real draw.* Sullivan hadn't gotten it. Until now. The casual way Kia dropped the sum…was impressive.

It was hot.

Objectively.

Not to Sullivan personally.

"I'm sorry. I shouldn't have said *your ancestral forest*," Kia said. "I didn't mean to make fun of it."

Sullivan didn't say anything. Kia had been a worthy rival in the kitchen. She was apparently a worthy rival in life too.

Kia looked at the young couple. "They're going snorkeling in Hawaii for their honeymoon."

"Think they'll make it?"

"Snorkeling?"

"Marriage."

"I hope so." Kia rested her elbows on her knees, chin on her steepled fingertips. "They look happy." She turned toward Sullivan without lifting her chin, her eyes wistful. "I'd love to be them. To find someone to love forever." She exhaled a soft snort. "That's not in the cards, is it? Have you been married?"

That's how little they knew about each other.

"No. You?"

"I'll have time for that when I'm dead." A faraway look clouded Kia's eyes. "But when I do…if I do…I want it to be someone I have fun with, someone who's always got my back. Shotgun rider."

"Someone who loves me exactly the way I am." Sullivan heard Aubrey complaining. *Pull your shoulders back. You look like a cat in the rain.*

"How could they not?" Kia covered her lips with her fingertips. "Sorry." She shrugged. "You're kind of a snack."

Sullivan gazed past Kia's shoulders. "I always thought I'd get married just once. I guess I'm old-fashioned. I don't think people should stay in bad marriages, but I thought I'd choose someone who'd want to be with me forever."

"The one thing in your life you wouldn't have to question," Kia added.

"Yeah." Sullivan gave a rueful shrug.

"That's what I wanted too. I don't know how I thought I'd find her living in a different city every week though. I think my dad never married because he's always moved around too much to find true love, and he wouldn't settle for less."

"And look at us now."

For a second, Kia looked like she'd stepped off a bus at an empty station only to find the person she'd expected wasn't waiting for her return.

A woman in a floral jumper stepped out of the courtroom. "Sullivan? Jackson? Judge Lavigne is ready for you."

"They'll use vow seven point five in the contemporary vow set," Nina said when Sullivan, Kia, Opal, and Deja were standing in front of the judge's dais. Deja vibrated with enthusiasm.

The ceremony took about five minutes.

chapter 11

Outside the courtroom, their party stood in awkward silence, like actors waiting for someone to call action on the set of *Law & Order*. Only Deja radiated happiness. She radiated so much, Kia wished she'd found a different witness. It felt wrong to let Deja believe Kia and Sullivan were really in love, she'd have to take her aside and tell her the truth sometime. Kia and Deja weren't exactly close. It was hard to get close to someone who imitated every detail of your style and frequently declared you the *frickin' hella dopest* person on the internet. Deja only saw Kia Gourmazing. Still, Deja deserved a modicum of honesty from Kia Jackson. Later.

"I guess we'll leave y'all alone to enjoy your wedding night!" Deja said. "But let me know if you want me to film the after-party or a honeymoon. Are we going to do a real wedding ceremony with cake and a dress? I know. I know. Too much to think about right now." Deja hugged Kia. "I got you whenever you're ready. You two can bake the cake together. It'll be fire!" Deja bounded off in fireworks of delight.

Nina and Opal exchanged a look.

"I've got a cheating husband to take for everything he's worth," Nina said.

Opal said, "I'll come with you."

They walked fifty feet down the hall and paused, watching Kia and Sullivan with the subtlety of a stop sign.

People doing courthouse business flowed around them like a river. But Sullivan was the only person Kia saw.

"Do you want to get a drink?" Kia tried to keep the pleading out of her voice.

Please, let this be okay.

Sullivan shook her head slowly.

"Later? We could catch up? Did you hear Professor Howard got fired for having sex in the practice kitchen? You dressed up for me." That had to mean something. You didn't dress up if you hated someone. Kia shot Sullivan her enchanting smile.

"Nina says her clients don't wear REI. It'd ruin her image."

That killed the last shred of romance in their wedding.

"Oh. We could still go out."

"Nina's right," Sullivan said. "If you'd bought a vacant lot on Eighty-Second Avenue, we'd be cool. But you didn't. Thanks for blocking Mega Eats though."

"That's goodbye?"

Sullivan looked expressionless, but she was upset. They'd spent so many nights in the practice kitchen and so many days in class. You couldn't watch someone do the thing they loved most and not learn their tells. Kia could see the tension in Sullivan's shoulders.

"I'm sure we'll run into each other while you're getting Taste the Love Land up and running, but yeah. Goodbye, Kia."

With that, Sullivan strode toward her friends, who were obviously *not* in the process of suing a cheating husband. Nina took Sullivan's arm and led her down the hallway like she was rushing her away from the paparazzi. Opal headed in Kia's direction with equal speed.

"We need to talk," Opal said when she reached Kia.

Sullivan's friend had one of those faces that nature crafted to be happy: light-skinned with freckles dancing across her cheeks and a gap between her front teeth, big eyes hidden behind bright red glasses. The face of a loving first-grade teacher or a pastor at one of those queer-friendly churches that played "YMCA" at the end of the service. All that made her scowl look fiercer. *I love all God's little children* except *you; you I'll push into traffic.*

"It's good to see a young woman of color get the recognition she deserves. I really mean that. I just want you to know, outside of all this, I appreciate what you're doing for the industry." Opal put her hands on her hips. "But I'm going to be really clear about something. Sullivan hates social media, and you're not going to take one picture of her."

A lot of people hated social media until they found their thing: French bulldogs, DIY videos on caulking. But Sullivan probably wouldn't find a thing.

"She told me, and I checked. She doesn't have social media." Kia offered the *trust me* smile that charmed everyone from security guards to CEOs. "I can't believe she doesn't have her own hot chef channel."

"And don't tag Mirepoix. It's important to her."

"Is she okay?" Kia asked.

Social media was a lottery. The more people saw you, the bigger your chances of success and the higher the chances there'd be a fan you didn't want. Sullivan had been careful. Of course, Kia had looked for her. She didn't even have a forgotten Tumblr account, not a trace of fanfic on Wattpad. The thought struck Kia like a cold wave.

"Is there someone…looking for her?"

"She just doesn't like it. That's all you need to know."

Opal turned to go. Kia caught her arm. "You have to tell me."

Opal pulled her arm away.

"Her life is none of your business. Do what you're going to do. Knocking out Mega Eats is a boss move. Respect. Like I said. If it weren't Sullivan, I'd be breaking ground with you if you'd let me. But it is Sullivan, and she doesn't deserve any of this, and she doesn't need her face all over Kia Gourmazing."

"If someone is stalking her, I need to know. I do this for a living. I can protect her."

"I doubt that."

"This marriage just put her name in the public record. If she's hiding…" Sullivan's information was now part of the Bureau of Vital Records. "We can go back to the court and see if they can hide her name. I can find someone to monitor who's looking for her."

Had something in Opal's face softened just a little bit?

"It's not that," Opal said. "She's just had some shitty experiences. Don't make it worse."

Relief left Kia momentarily speechless. Thank god Sullivan didn't have to worry about a bad person catching up with her.

"Thanks for looking out for her," Kia said.

Sullivan must be having the worst day. She'd always seemed invincible. But no one was invincible. Maybe if she'd asked Sullivan about her childhood. Maybe when Chef Guillaume called Sullivan's Toulouse-style cassoulet *a misunderstanding of flavor* Kia should have offered Sullivan a hug, not a grin.

She'd wanted to ease the tension in Sullivan's shoulders. She'd wanted to rub Sullivan's temples when she obviously had a headache. She'd wanted to break Sullivan's unflappable confidence—not by cooking a better white bean, pork, and duck dish, but with tenderness. Maybe if she'd done that, she'd be playing the role of supportive friend. Or something more. Instead, she'd put Sullivan on a pedestal and then thrown her whole soul into building a taller pedestal. And she'd succeeded by point six percent as though maybe that would make Sullivan see her as more than a talented kid. Sullivan probably didn't think she was a talented kid anymore, but she definitely didn't think Kia was a sexy, talented businesswoman either.

Opal hurried back to where Nina and Sullivan waited around the corner in front of another courtroom. The doors opened, issuing a never-ending stream of anxious and dejected-looking people, fidgeting with crumpled papers. Opal put her arms around Sullivan in a big mom-coach hug, like Sullivan had lost the game and gotten kicked in the process…which was basically the case.

"Let's get a hot chocolate," Opal said, giving Sullivan one more squeeze.

"Oh my god, Opal. This is not a time for hot chocolate," Nina said. "We'll go down to Makers Bar and get you a martini the size of your head."

Sullivan didn't have the energy to complain that she didn't drink martinis, *and* it was before noon.

Nina's driver was waiting in the fire lane by the time they got downstairs, ready to drive them the (only) four blocks to Makers Bar.

"I'm wearing Louboutins," Nina said as she settled into the third row of seats in her black SUV.

A Shanghai tunnel under the city would've fit Sullivan's mood. Unfortunately, the owner had transformed the massive drainpipe into a cozy hideaway, the walls covered in hammered bronze plates, sconces flickering with artificial candlelight. Nina pointed to a circular booth at the back and headed to the bar to order. She returned a moment later with coffees for herself and Opal and a glass of cold gin and olives for Sullivan. The martini had never made sense to Sullivan.

"Don't worry," Nina said. "Your prenup is so tight the NSA can't get in."

"I don't think that's what the NSA does." Sullivan took a sip of slightly salty gin. Nina was correct; it was the right drink for the day. "Not exactly how I thought I'd celebrate my first marriage. I always thought I'd be a one-and-done. Mate for life. Be old women sitting on the porch spying on the neighbors. Die within minutes of each other and get composted for soil."

"Oh, honey," Opal said.

"You are not dying." Nina put her hands on her hips, which had the same scolding effect sitting down as it did when she was standing up in her Louboutins. "And Opal and I are glad it's Kia and not Aubrey."

"Nina," Opal protested.

"Tell me you'd pick Sullivan marrying Aubrey over a simple business deal with Kia Jackson?" Nina said.

Opal's freckles scrunched together apologetically as she winced.

"Yeah…sorry. I'd pick Kia. She's pretty impressive."

Great. Her friends liked Kia because Kia was ruthless and impressive.

"I told her you didn't want any social media," Opal added.

Nina leaned in. "How'd it go? Do I need to add another clause to the contract?"

"She said she'd keep you out of her socials." Opal folded her arms on the table. "She was pretty cool about it. She was worried that someone was stalking you. Like *genuinely* worried, like she cared about you. You kissed her in front of your whole graduating class. That must have meant something."

"It was like when two straight women kiss onstage at the Oscars to support gay rights."

The night came back like an old reel, still as clear as when it was posted. Kia gazing into her eyes, frozen for a second before the kiss, more focused than Sullivan had ever seen her. Most of the guys in the program had flirted with Sullivan. Back then, Sullivan walked into bars and picked her next date like selecting a mango from a vendor at the Manhattan Fruit Market. But she and Kia were just friends...friendly rivals. Colleagues bonded by mutual respect and competitiveness. Then Kia kissed her with a fire that felt like the end of the world or the beginning of everything. That hadn't been about Sullivan. That had been about graduation, about winning, about the first step into their new careers.

Right?

The first days of being married to Kia Jackson were just like not being married to Kia Jackson. Except for the impending food truck invasion. Sullivan went to work. Strawberries were in season. Her customers loved the mushroom risotto. Blake, her intern from the Portland Night High School apprenticeship program, was on his phone in the kitchen again. Opal shot her the usual you-know-you-have-to-let-him-go look. As usual, Sullivan couldn't bring herself to do it. It was all weirdly normal.

Sullivan resisted the urge to look at Kia's social media for a few days. Then she gave in and downloaded one of Kia's social media apps. The app and her phone remembered her account even though she had supposedly deleted it. She didn't sign in. She just wanted to look.

Sullivan couldn't help herself; she smiled as she scrolled to a video of Kia making hot-and-sour empanadas in New Orleans. The video started with Kia's face close to the camera, her eyes wide and playful. *All right, folks, today we're cooking empanadas with my helpers, Grady and Tyler.* Two boys, one white and one Black, stood at her side grinning. *Or as I like to call empanadas, little pockets of joy.* Kia held up an empanada. *Let's see how many I can drop on the floor before we get one perfect!* The video showed a series of bloopers, Kia laughing as she fumbled with the dough. The bloopers were almost certainly on purpose. The final shot was of a perfect empanada, golden and steaming. *Couldn't have done this without my little pockets of joy.* She set down the empanada and ruffled the boys' hair.

The early posts were a delightful mix of humor, culinary tips, and snippets of Kia's travels. There was a post about the food experimentation Kia did to keep her menu fresh. This reel was about a disastrous one, a lobster ragout in Boston, complete with a picture of Kia covered in lobster guts. *Note to self: Secure the lid on the blender. Oops. #LobsterRagoutNah!* The only things Sullivan thought might be fake about the videos were the mishaps. She guessed they were usually to cover up something one of her guest chefs had done. There were so many moments of genuine connection. A photo of Kia sitting with a group of older women in a park, all of them laughing and sharing stories. *Met these lovely ladies in Milwaukee today. They taught me more about life and love over a cup of sweet tea than I've learned in years. #MidwestHospitality #LifeLessons.*

Sullivan found herself charmed and drawn in. Kia's posts were not just about food; they were about people, places, and the small moments that made Kia's life rich and meaningful. There was an authenticity that Sullivan hadn't expected. No wonder Kia had a staggering number of followers. She made them happy. Her posts made Sullivan happy. Maybe there was hope for humankind. Maybe, despite their differences, people across the country, across race and political divides, could come together and eat tursnicken.

And yeah, as the posts got more recent, Kia was obviously getting more sponsors. She spent a lot of time working American Spirit breakfast sausages into her recipes, and the number of Fizz Bang soda cans strategically placed in the shot defied coincidence. But she still seemed sincere. In the most recent post, she was split-screen chatting with a handsome man in an Army T-shirt sitting in a wheelchair. *Taste the Love Land is a game changer for us*, he said. Kia beamed through tears that seemed real. And Kia didn't mention Sullivan anywhere. In Kia's online life, everything was going as planned, all filtered and sparkling. As promised, she'd left Sullivan out of it.

Then it was Sunday morning. Mirepoix was closed Sunday, Monday, and Tuesday. Sullivan drew a deep breath as she stepped out of her house. The Bois smelled of clean, damp soil and conifers. The vegetable garden in front of her house looked like a little Eden. There were the green peas. There was a marigold planted to lure bugs away from her lettuce. A few birds trilled in the underbrush. You could hear I-405 in the background, but you could pretend it was wind. You couldn't pretend away an off-ramp cutting through your front yard. She looked up at a glimpse of white clouds beyond the fir trees. The storm had cleared, like the sky had cried itself out.

Did I do the right thing?

Her grandfather wasn't sitting on a cloud looking down, but if he was, he'd say something about trusting her heart.

What if my heart doesn't like any of it? She pictured Kia in her blue sunglasses and beautiful hair. She saw Kia in her chef's coat whirling fire in a pan as their professors looked on with curiosity that said they'd forgotten they were supposed to be grading her. How could Kia run a food truck? How could she throw away her talent to be an influencer? Kia's career was none of Sullivan's business, but it wasn't Sullivan's morning coffee that made her stomach roil. Influencer-Kia was also saving her from the off-ramp. She didn't want Kia here, and she had to admit she'd missed Kia too. Sullivan's heart was a failed fusion, poke spaghetti or peanut butter stuffed inside le religieuse pastries. Probably something Kia would cook.

Sullivan knelt down in the muddy soil and gently extricated a vetch plant from her kohlrabi.

"How did you get here?" she asked. She moved down the row, slowly getting muddier as she pulled the weeds by hand.

Near the end of the row, she stopped to examine an owl pellet tucked between kohlrabi and a clump of oregano that had jumped from a nearby pot. A white skull was perfectly preserved in the clot of gray fur.

"Look at you. The cycle of life." Owl pellets weren't creepy. This was the owl turning its head three hundred degrees. Seeing in the dark. Swooping down.

A soft voice startled her from behind.

"What is it?"

Sullivan turned. She'd been so focused, she hadn't seen that a woman with a golden retriever had strolled down her driveway. As she drew close, the woman gave a little wave. The dog sniffed at the owl pellet.

"Stop it, Hazel," the woman said.

"The owls spit them up. It's the parts they can't digest," Sullivan said. "They're not gross."

"Just the cycle of life." The woman knelt down beside her. Her chocolate-brown hair was pulled back in a ponytail. Her smile was friendly, and she was pretty.

"Yeah," Sullivan said, a little surprised. "They're kind of beautiful. That's probably a mouse." Sullivan pointed to the skull.

"I thought about being a biology major in college," the woman mused.

Opal would say the woman was flirting with her. Through all the noise of Kia and Mega Eats and food trucks and loggers and her bizarre marriage of convenience, Sullivan felt a little thrill of pleasure. Maybe after this whole thing with Kia was over, Sullivan would get back out there and find an outdoorsy woman who hated social media.

The woman stood up.

"You live around here?" she asked.

Sullivan nodded back toward her house.

"What's your name?"

The woman *was* flirting. And unlike Aubrey, this woman didn't think owl pellets were, sin of sins, *off-brand*. No one was filming this. She didn't have to arrange her face into perfect Instagrammability.

"I...um...Sullivan."

She never used to feel shy flirting with someone. Kia used to tease that Sullivan could make any guy in their program fall in love with her, just by giving him shit about his filleting technique. Once Kia had said Sullivan had a great smile. She'd followed it up with, *Do you have more teeth than other people or are they just whiter?* because Kia couldn't give Sullivan a compliment without throwing some friendly shade.

"Sullivan." The woman rolled Sullivan's name over her lips with satisfaction, like Sullivan was exactly who she'd been looking for.

Sullivan could get back to the woman she'd been, the woman with the white teeth.

"First or last name?" The woman looked like she was ticking something off on a mental list.

"Last, but no one calls me by my first name."

"Which is?"

"Alice."

"Alice." The woman nodded. "Alice Gwenyth Sullivan." She whipped an envelope out of her windbreaker and shoved it at Sullivan. "You've been served."

chapter 12

Kia stared at the caramelized kale chips as they scorched in grape-jelly barbecue sauce. She kept stirring as the smell of burnt sugar and cruciferous vegetable filled her RV. Classical music blasted through her earbuds: Jean Sibelius's Symphony no. 2. Her father always played classical music on the *Serendipity*. The music usually calmed her. Symphony no. 2 reminded her of Sullivan: strong and certain. But Sullivan wasn't impenetrable, and thinking about Sullivan wasn't calming, because on the table lay a manila envelope full of incomprehensible papers.

It had happened so fast, like everything had the last few weeks. Kia had been cooking at Portland's Cruciferous Carnival. Then a fan was asking if she was Kiana Renee Jackson. The man actually took a selfie with her before handing her the papers. *You've been served.* Mega Eats was suing to stop the land deal and questioning the validity of their marriage.

Now she was stress cooking. She'd tried taking some pictures with her old digital camera, but putting her naked, unfiltered self on a memory card had done nothing to stop her panicking.

"I am me." Right now, she'd rather not be. "I am real." Ditto. Today, it'd be better to be an avatar.

If only she could turn back the clock, to not press start on the live feed that brought Mega Eats' ravenous boars snarling at her front door. Hers and Sullivan's. Kia tried to focus on the candied kale and not on how much of Sullivan's life she was destroying. She poured more sauce on the kale. Maybe she could stuff it in yeast dough. Add cheese. A cruciferous Hot Pocket. She stuffed the cabbage into her food processor and reduced it to shreds.

She couldn't call Gretchen. Gretchen was at an important site visit and off her phone. Kia could call Aunt Eleanor and ask for help, but she couldn't face Eleanor. She couldn't even face Lillian. She thought she'd fucked up before. She'd almost lost the deal. She'd messed up Sullivan's life. But this was so much worse.

Kia leaned on her elbows on the counter. She'd felt a blaze of excitement when Sullivan handed her the marshmallow coffee. That was gone now. Sullivan hadn't wanted anything to do with her before this. What happened when you got sued? She couldn't go to jail, could she? The papers said something about fraud. She returned to the stove and stirred frantically as though stirring could salvage the kale…or her life.

Reaching for salt in the built-in spice rack, she noticed a person walking toward Old Girl, head down in the rain. Kia peered out the window to get a better look. The strides, even and deliberate, were familiar. They neared. She'd seen that posture too many times not to know it was Sullivan. But what had happened to her? Gone was her 1920s retro style. She looked like a bushwhacker, dressed in dirty overalls, complete with knee pads and a sheath around her waist. She looked ambush-ready. When she looked up, she had fire in her eyes, a scowl anchoring her face, and a manila envelope in her hand.

Of course, Mega Eats had served Sullivan too. Kia wanted to hide, but it was too late. Sullivan locked eyes with her, standing in front of the large kitchen window. Kia wanted to close her eyes and make it all go away, but she could feel Sullivan's hot impatience through Old Girl's sheet metal.

Kia went to the front door and hesitated. She didn't have to open it. If she stayed in Old Girl for the rest of her life, she'd be safe. Wasn't there some law like that? Maybe it was churches? Or maybe that protected you against vampires.

"I know you're in there," Sullivan said.

Kia unlocked the door and quickly stepped back to her stove.

Sullivan waved the envelope in Kia's direction. "Did you know?"

"I got one too," Kia managed. "I'm sorry. I'm the one to blame. I got you into this fake marriage, and now we're both in hot water." It came out in one breath.

"Did you read the complaint?" Sullivan demanded.

"Some of it." There were so many legal terms and they all meant *you're fucked*. Kia blew on a forkful of kale and tasted it.

"Let me get this straight…you're named in a lawsuit. And now you're cooking?" Sullivan said with all the incredulity of a news anchor announcing some clickbait story. Sullivan picked up a clean spoon, touched it to the barbecue sauce, and tasted it. "What is that? Burnt high-fructose corn syrup?"

"Grape jelly and kale."

"You're burning grape jelly and kale while we get sued?" Sullivan paced around the kitchen floor.

"I had to stop reading the complaint. I got overwhelmed."

"They're accusing us of fraud." Sullivan's pacing continued. "And you're making kale grape jelly. And so much cabbage."

"It's my therapy. Don't you cook to calm down?"

Sullivan looked at the cabbage shreds bursting out of the food processor.

"I cook to make food."

"I'm not out-the-box ready to fight." Kia grabbed a handful of cabbage and clutched it hard enough that her knuckles went white. "I'm processing."

"Your feelings or the cabbage? And this isn't food," Sullivan added. "This is a cruciferous massacre."

"I know I fucked up."

"You're a tornado. You're an earthquake. You're climate change. You're ruining everything. And you're taking the healthiest vegetable and turning it into a blackened Jolly Rancher."

It was too much. Kia felt her whole face tremble.

"I'm trying to pull it together. I know it's bad. I'm sorry. I came crashing into your life, snatching your Bois and your hand in marriage all so I could chase my crazy dream. I've promised too much to too many people." Kia focused her eyes on the floor, because looking at the anger in Sullivan's eyes would make her cry for sure. "I know I'm going to hurt everyone. And I should call Gretchen, my publicity manager, but I know she's busy, and I haven't, and my cousin's in love, and my dad's on a yacht with a million spaniels and no cell phone, and you hate me." She wiped her eyes with the back of her hand, still clutching the wad of cabbage. "And I didn't need the American Fare Award. It should have gone to someone else, but I'm still a great cook." She stifled a sob. "You can't judge my panic kale. You can't make fun of someone's kale when they're…they're…" *Crying.*

Sullivan laughed, low and deep in her throat. Kia looked up, ready to tell her that it was mean to laugh, even if it was all Kia's fault. But when she met Sullivan's eyes, Sullivan's expression was soft and rueful.

"Come on, Jackson." Sullivan walked over, gently took Kia's hand, and eased her fingers off the cabbage. It fell to the floor like sad, damp confetti. "Obviously someone likes candied kale. You won the American Fare. That's huge."

"It doesn't feel like a win."

"It is."

And Sullivan hugged her. Sullivan, who was still wet from the rain. She smelled of soil. It was a tender hug. Sullivan pressed her hand to Kia's back, not patting her, just holding her close. Kia's body warmed in ways it shouldn't. Her heart warmed too. She needed this hug, and she needed it from Sullivan.

Sullivan whispered, "I'm proud of you."

Then Sullivan stepped away quickly, her scowl reasserting itself, but it felt like Sullivan directed it at the two ominous manila envelopes, not at Kia.

"I don't understand the whole thing either," Sullivan said. "But I know we're both fucked if we don't address it. My last relationship was a train wreck, and I got screwed. I won't stand for it again. We're fighting this crap together."

Sullivan might have meant *together* as in *don't think I'm going to handle this mess alone*, but it almost sounded like *we're a team*.

"This lawsuit is offensive on so many levels," Sullivan added.

"They don't know who they're messing with," Kia ventured.

They'd been a team in school. That's what their classmates didn't get until their kiss. They only wanted to beat each other after they'd beaten everyone else.

"What are we going to do?" Kia asked.

"Call Nina," Sullivan replied. "She lives for this stuff."

That afternoon, showered and out of her gardening clothes, Sullivan arrived at Nina's condo on the twenty-fourth floor. Inside, floor-to-ceiling windows owned the room. The view of Portland commanded attention. A Vietnamese silk orchid graced the dining table. Sunlight gleamed off deceptively low-end kitchen appliances. Nina did not cook. Nina was already seated at the end of her oyster-gray sofa.

"Espresso?" Nina gestured to her Nespresso machine. "Don't panic," Nina said before Sullivan could speak but definitely *after* she'd started to panic.

Kia arrived a moment later. She looked so overwhelmed. Sullivan wanted to put her arm around her again. The way Kia had sunk into her when she'd hugged her in her RV had made Sullivan feel protective and appreciated. There was a thank-god-you're-here quality in the way Kia melted against her. How could Sullivan not be a tiny bit happy that this beautiful woman wanted her there?

"Don't worry. This is what Nina does," Sullivan said.

"So I've got good news and slightly…inconvenient news," Nina said before Kia had settled onto the sofa.

Nina could be dramatic, but she never overreacted, which meant her idea of *inconvenient* might be Sullivan's idea of end-of-my-life-as-I-know-it. Wait. That had already happened. Something worse. Something inconvenient like falling off a cliff was inconvenient.

"Good news. I read the complaint, and it's bullshit. They're saying you entered into a fake marriage to secure a land deal, which you did." Nina paused to sip her espresso. "But that's okay. Everyone's marriage is fake, and it is always about the money."

"That's—" Kia sat down at the far end of the sofa on which Sullivan was quietly panicking.

"Not true?" Nina said. "You understand food. I understand love and law. The beautiful thing is that it's okay. Nothing says you can't marry for money."

"What do we do?" Kia looked at Sullivan. "I am so sorry."

Part of Sullivan wanted to point out that *sorry* barely began to touch on how bad Kia should feel, but that felt like kicking a puppy, because Kia looked devastated. The way she looked at Sullivan, it almost seemed like she felt worse about Sullivan's predicament than her own. Despite the impending inconvenience (e.g., earthquake, prison sentence, murder hornets), Sullivan felt comforted by the thought that Kia cared.

"I thought I was doing the right thing." Kia's lip quivered.

"Move over, Nespresso; is it time for gin?" Nina asked. "I can make you a martini."

That was the extent of Nina's culinary abilities.

Kia shook her head.

"Here's how it's going to go. First, Kia, you'll have to stop any work you've got planned for the Bois. The judge has granted an injunction. That basically means no one can do anything until we've got this settled. Then we'll have some depos, collect some evidence for what's called a hearing for summary judgment. That means we'll all show up in court. Mega Eats will say what they say. I'll point out that there's no law against a self-serving marriage, and—Sullivan, don't look that way. You're getting something out of this too even if it's not exactly what you want."

"It's not at all what I want."

Out of the corner of her eye, Sullivan saw Kia hang her head. Why couldn't Kia have bought a defunct car dealership lot on Eighty-Second Avenue? They could be celebrating together. It really would have been nice to have Kia back in her life, but not like this.

Nina waved away Sullivan's comment.

"The summary judgment is when we tell the judge that Mega Eats' lawsuit is bullshit, and the judge ends it because the law is on your side one hundred percent."

"You mean they just say Mega Eats can't sue us?" Kia looked up.

"Exactly. There's no judge on the Oregon bench who's going to say marriage has to be for love. And there's no judge who's going to say Kia can't take advantage of the legacy clause in the Oakwood charter. It's crystal clear. You can marry whomever you want—with a few obvious exceptions—for whatever reason you want and do whatever you want with your money provided you're not embezzling or hiring assassins."

"As one does," Sullivan said.

Kia gave a wan laugh. Sullivan had always liked Kia's laugh. It was best when Sullivan had beat Kia at some cooking challenge and gloated about it so extravagantly that Kia had to laugh.

"I know it's stressful, but this is paperwork." Nina's matter-of-factness was comforting. "Businesses fight with each other. Rich people go after rich people. You're Rich People now, Kia. Give this a month and it'll all be over, but in the meantime..." The way Nina trailed off was not comforting. She got up and made herself another Nespresso. "I think you two should live together."

Oh, hell no.

"Why?" Kia asked.

"This is not the big deal you two will think it is, but I got these."

Sullivan hadn't noticed the manila envelope on the end table. Sullivan was starting to hate manila envelopes. Nina took out a stack of photos.

Nina handed half the stack to Kia and half to Sullivan.

Sullivan looked at the picture on top. It was a nighttime photo, taken at a distance, of someone sitting in an RV, the window a bright square of light against the darkness. A person with an Afro bent over a table.

"Is this the inconvenience?" Sullivan's voice squeaked. "Wait, is someone stalking you?" She looked at Kia.

Kia was an influencer. Someone's parasocial relationship with the online Kia could have gotten out of hand. It happened. Kia might be in the process of ruining Sullivan's life, but Sullivan didn't want anyone to hurt her!

"Trade," Nina said mildly.

The next stack of photos showed Sullivan silhouetted in her bedroom alone.

"Mega Eats hired an investigator to prove you're not living together, hence it's a fake marriage, and they should get everything they want."

"You said it didn't matter if we loved each other," Sullivan said.

"Yes. And if living together equaled love, I'd be out of a job. The judge will take one look at the claim and throw it out. Don't worry. But why give them any ammunition? Plus"—Nina turned to Kia—"Sullivan is lonely, and she could use the company."

"I am not." She often felt lonely sitting in her living room listening to an audiobook in the evening or crawling between cold sheets at night, but that wasn't the kind of lonely living with Kia Jackson was going to fix.

"She doesn't get out." Nina continued as though Sullivan hadn't spoken. "Maybe you can get her to go to a bar, chat someone up. Discreetly. Because you are married. And you're in a bit of a situationship."

"I do not—"

"Maybe just get her tipsy. Opal and I try, but she's all *I go out. I go to the Oakwood Neighborhood Association Meetings.*"

"I am right *here*. And I do not need to get tipsy."

She thought about Kia and her Rice Krispies treat. Kia was

nothing if not optimistic. How could she possibly have thought that ridiculous marriage proposal would work? And yet, here Sullivan was, getting sued for marrying Point Six Percent Kia Jackson. Oddly, a tiny part of her wished they could have fun the way they used to. At the time, Sullivan had always focused on Kia as competition, but Kia had been fun too. Sullivan had missed Kia's energy when Sullivan moved to Osaka, with its serious-minded, hierarchical kitchens.

"Kia, Sullivan's house is gorgeous. Plus living together could look good if we sue Mega Eats for emotional distress." Nina eyed Kia and Sullivan. "How distressed are you feeling?"

"Sullivan?" Kia said, ignoring Nina the way Nina had ignored Sullivan (which was satisfying). "Can I move in with you?"

chapter 13

The next day, tired from a sleepless night, Sullivan stood on her porch watching a massive pickup tow an orange and brown RV down her driveway. Sullivan had lived alone since Aubrey left. The house was her safe space. Now she'd be living with an influencer again. Sullivan would be innocently gardening or talking to a melon she was carving into a swan because…what else did she have to do when she wasn't working? And there'd be Kia live streaming herself. At least Kia wouldn't be filming Sullivan. It'd be like living on a movie set. There'd be cameras, lighting, lamenting about angles, but she wouldn't be in the shot. And she knew that if Kia did want to get her in the picture and Sullivan said no, Kia would respect that.

For all that Kia was destroying her life like a kitchen fire, Kia hadn't *knowingly* done anything to hurt her. She'd been honest and—from her pleading expression, Sullivan guessed—extremely sorry about all of it. Aubrey had been sorry that Sullivan broke up with her. She'd never really been sorry that she put their life on display.

The truck stopped. Kia leaned out the window and pointed to a strip of grass near the house.

"I'll pull in there." Kia still looked shell-shocked.

Sullivan felt sorry for her. Kia had gone from the top of the world, to losing everything, to getting it back, to getting sued, and now she was moving in with a woman who wished Kia hadn't come back into her life. (Although it was getting harder not to appreciate Kia's sincerity...and her golden-brown eyes.) Sullivan saw the wistful expression on Kia's face when she'd said, *I'd love to be them.* Maybe Kia had her own sadnesses she'd rather not put on display for Sullivan. It made Sullivan want to call out, *I really don't hate you.*

The thought died as Kia began backing her RV toward the vegetable garden.

"The garden!"

Kia was going to drive over the vegetable garden and back into a tree. It'd fall on the house. Maybe the tree would hit Sullivan. How poetic. Kia swiveled her whole body around and put the truck in reverse, pointing the RV in the general direction of the house.

"I'm really good at this." Kia hung out the window, one hand on the steering wheel.

"Could you at least measure?" Sullivan called out.

Kia stopped the truck. She flipped up the lenses of her turquoise sunglasses.

"Yes, of course. Sure. Anything you want." She sounded desperately eager to please and like it had never occurred to her to measure a parking spot before wedging her RV into it.

Before Sullivan realized what Kia was doing, Kia projected herself out of the truck window *Dukes of Hazzard*–style. She grabbed hold of something above her head and boosted herself onto the roof of the truck. Kia had changed into a puffy white vest—too wintry for May and too sleeveless for the rain. It showed off well-defined muscles in her arms. It was distracting, as was the way she'd let her short Afro puffs grow into a glorious 1970s Black Power Afro. Even wearing a T-shirt reading I ♥ TURSNICKEN she looked like a powerhouse. The fact that she was driving a truck so big it'd give Texas an insecurity complex didn't hurt the image, even though trucks like that destroyed the environment. At least Kia was towing something with it. Sullivan couldn't stand seeing people driving trucks to pick up their dry cleaning.

"Why not use the door?" Sullivan called out.

"I'm showing off." Kia looked down at Sullivan with a hopeful smile that said, *Play along. Please?*

"Trying to hold on to your point six percent?"

"I *own* my point six percent." Kia held up her phone and pointed it at the tree she was about to displace.

"Are you live streaming already?" Sullivan asked.

"I have a measurement app," Kia said, as though explaining that her truck had windshield wipers.

Kia grew still, her eyes flicking from her phone to the too-narrow space beside Sullivan's house.

"I got it," she said after a moment.

With that she clambered off the truck, hopped back into the driver's seat, and as fast as if she were pulling a sedan into a parking spot, backed the RV between a tree and the vegetable garden.

"Mic drop," she said when she got out.

Sullivan was not impressed. Not at all.

"I don't even use the backup camera." Kia smirked, but her smile faded as she approached Sullivan. "I've been backing Old Girl up for years."

"Old Girl?"

"The RV. Because she's vintage. I wouldn't back her in if I

wasn't absolutely sure I knew what I was doing. Want an official tour of Old Girl?"

Sullivan would have said no except that Kia looked shy and proud, like a kid holding a drawing to her chest, eager to turn it around and share it.

Sullivan had been too fixated on the lawsuit to appreciate the RV before. The space was much tidier than Sullivan expected. The walls were eggshell blue with accents of a light brown around discreet crown moldings. The door led into a sitting area with a couch and small dining table, folded out from the wall. Across from that, a kitchenette featured white cabinets and glossy, white enamel appliances. There were succulents in the windows, their pots anchored to the sill, and framed postcards that must have been souvenirs from Kia's travels.

"Like it?" The way Kia asked said the answer meant a lot to her and she kept talking like she was afraid to hear what Sullivan had to say. "I bought Old Girl on eBay. She needed work. The electrical wiring was a mess."

"Please tell me you hired an electrician to fix it?"

"Don't worry. It's not going to catch fire." Kia put her hands on her hips. "Unless you come in here to flambé something in the middle of the night."

"Because I do that all the time."

"I don't know. You lit my crème brûlée on fire."

It sounded dirty, although Sullivan had *literally* lit her crème brûlée on fire. They'd been standing in front of the professors, ready to exhibit, and Kia's torch had run out of butane. Sullivan had whisked past her, setting the rum on fire before anyone noticed. Kia now turned and then looked back over her shoulder flirtatiously. She looked adorable, and she looked like she was trying on an unfamiliar persona, like she didn't know how to flirt but she'd seen people do it on TV. Sullivan raised an eyebrow. Kia's face morphed into embarrassment.

"Sorry." Kia pushed her hands into her pockets. "I made that awkward."

The space felt too small. Kia looked too pretty and too earnest. Her vest was too tight, her arms too muscular, and the desire to look at her—just to compare Kia now with Kia then—was too strong. She gave Kia an obviously appraising look.

"What do you mean? What's awkward?" She hoped her look conveyed *that's your dirty mind, not mine.*

"I collect art from all over," Kia said, obviously changing the subject...the subject they hadn't actually been talking about. Kia pointed to a postcard of a painting of cacti. "This is from New Mexico. They're barrel cacti in bloom."

The pink flowers on top of the round cacti made them look like breasts.

"Are they now?" Sullivan said.

A pretty rose glow flushed Kia's cheeks.

"What about this one?" An accompanying photograph looked like a Georgia O'Keeffe–esque orchid which, of course, meant that it looked like a vulva. "What's this one of?"

Kia started fussing with a loose drawer pull.

"It's just a flower with petals that...It doesn't look like...That's not why I bought it. I like the purple." She looked like she'd die from blushing.

Sullivan wasn't sure what game they were playing, but Kia wasn't good at it.

"You can dish it, but you can't take it."

"Dish what?"

"Light my crème brûlée on fire," Sullivan said, as if to herself. "Tsk. Tsk."

Sullivan had definitely won this round.

"The thing I really want for Old Girl is the 1968 Wind Searcher Pop-Up Pavilion," Kia said too loudly. "They only made them for one year. They're these pop-up pergola-type things that you mount on top of the RV. Then you can sleep up there or just sit and watch the sunset, and there's no way anything can get you."

"Like people?"

"Like snakes. And you can hang netting to keep out bugs. I've been looking for one for years."

"If you don't want the snakes and the bugs, why do you go camping?" Sullivan had to ask.

"I don't camp."

"So this RV is for…?"

"My home."

Kia hadn't had a chance to study Sullivan's house when she'd stumbled in covered in mud and determined to secure an engagement, like some odd version of a Jane Austen heroine. Now she followed Sullivan in. The house definitely said old money, but in a cozy way. Miele appliances gleamed in the kitchen. The marble counters were spotless. White ceramic trays in the windowsills held a variety of greens that blended into the greenery outside the windows, giving the space a springlike feel.

"That's the kitchen," Sullivan said, although it was obvious. "Don't cut directly on the marble. Knives are hand-wash."

"Chef Sullivan, you dragging me? That's low." Kia stepped in front of Sullivan, smiling to let her know she was trying to play. "As if I would cut on your marble and then throw the knives in the dishwasher. I was not raised in a barn."

A smile twitched at the corner of Sullivan's mouth.

"I don't know. Someone who'd forget to calibrate the dough sheeter before running their puff pastry dough…"

"That was one time," Kia complained.

"And who saved your ass before you ruined the whole batch?"

"You did." Kia pretended to huff. "But who saved your ass every time you forgot the aromatics in your beef bourguignon? How could you forget *every* time?"

"I was just testing you to see if you cared," Sullivan said.

"I cared."

"I know." They froze for a second. Had they just had a moment?

Sullivan whirled away as if to deny what she had just said. "I try to do as much by hand as I can, but there's a stand mixer up there." She pointed to a cupboard. "And in the pantry I've got a sous vide, blender, immersion blender, food processor, mandoline. Wine fridge is over there. Help yourself." She paused as if a wearisome thought had crossed her mind. "Opal and Nina think I should be drinking at the Tennis Skort."

"Because you drink…" Kia opened the wine fridge and pulled out a bottle. "Two thousand fourteen Gevrey-Chambertin alone?"

"No, because they think I should meet someone." Sullivan looked like she hadn't meant to say it. She pressed her lips together, searching the ceiling. "I guess I have." Sullivan turned away. "There's the living room."

The living room was comfortably cluttered. A chenille blanket pooled at one end of the sofa. Built-in bookshelves housed photographs and ephemera: driftwood, stones, pottery vases of dried herbs. A record player sat on an ornate cabinet by the window, records in sleeves spilling out on the floor in front of it. A surprisingly lacy bra draped over the back of the staircase banister. And two life-sized abstract nudes framed a large fireplace.

"Chef, I would never have guessed," Kia said.

"They're by Janice Domingo." Sullivan looked put upon. "She's one of the best painters in Costa Rica."

"I mean this." Kia picked up the bra as Sullivan led her to the staircase. "You just throw your clothes off as you go upstairs."

"I didn't expect to have a roommate."

Sullivan blushed, and Kia remembered how much she'd loved to make Sullivan blush or roll her eyes in exasperation. Then she remembered that she'd just touched Sullivan's bra. She'd been dreaming about touching Sullivan's body for years. Kia felt heat spread across her own face as she tried to quash the thoughts.

"Give it back." Sullivan snatched the bra. "Are you going to stand here all day and critique my undergarments or can I show you to your room?"

She was reading Kia's lustful thoughts. And while Kia might have made Sullivan blush a tiny bit, her own face was flaming with…it wasn't quite embarrassment. Sullivan was teasing her. If she didn't know better, she'd say Sullivan was flirting with her, but her ability to read women was abysmal, so probably not.

"It's hand-wash, and it was drying," Sullivan added. "Air-drying is an excellent way to conserve electricity."

Sullivan led Kia upstairs and showed her to a guest room furnished in somber burgundy curtains and a four-poster bed with dark gray bedding. A rolltop desk filled one corner.

"Very lord of the manor," Kia said.

"It was my grandfather's study." Sullivan's voice was flat. "He spent a lot of time trying to protect the Bois. Those are his drawings." She pointed to botanical drawings displayed in gold frames.

"I'm sorry," Kia said as she stepped closer to the artwork.

"If it hadn't been you, it would have been someone else."

Kia leaned in for a closer look at a photo of an old white man. She stood with her hands clasped behind her, careful not to bump into a vase resting on the desk. "What was your grandfather like?"

Sullivan walked over to the window, pushing up her sleeves as if she were getting ready to till the land with her grandfather. Kia stared at Sullivan's tattoos. What did they mean? Who designed them? Kia wanted to trace the lines with her fingertips and then kiss her way up Sullivan's inner arm until Sullivan shivered.

"He was an environmentalist," Sullivan said without turning around. Then, as though the matter was closed, she said, "The bathroom is down the hall. Extra linens are in that closet. Make yourself comfortable. This evening let's set some house rules."

"I don't think *comfortable* and *house rules* go together," Kia said.

"I don't think *marriage* and *lawsuit* do either, but here we are."

Kia hoped they'd go straight to the kitchen to talk, but Sullivan had scheduled a visit to an organic pickle distributor in Washington. Kia spent the day driving around Portland with Deja getting footage for her socials. It just felt exhausting. That night, Kia set up her laptop at the kitchen island and waited for Sullivan to finish admiring Washingtonian pickles. Kia replied to fans' messages as she waited. Messaging with people online used to be one of the best parts of her online life. Now Deja and AI did most of it. She felt disconnected from the people she had once thought of as her flock. After she'd sent as many messages as she could muster the energy for, she opened Google and continued her ongoing search for the 1968 Wind Searcher Pop-Up Pavilion. There was one for sale in Iowa, but that was too far to go right now, and she shouldn't buy something frivolous.

She was relieved when Sullivan finally came home.

"How were the pickles?"

"The farmer has found some brilliant ways to use nematodes to target soilborne larvae of cucumber beetles."

"That is so not appetizing."

"Neither are pesticides."

Sullivan looked so serious, Kia wanted to snatch the beanie cap off her head and ruffle her hair, but that would go over about as well as showing up on Sullivan's lawn with a marriage proposal.

"Ready to go over the house rules?" Kia asked. "I've just been chopping raw meat on the marble counters."

Sullivan rolled her eyes.

"Set anything on fire?"

"Your heart." It flew out of her mouth before she could stop herself. She made that kind of too-obviously flirtatious comment to lots of people. She was joking. It didn't mean anything.

Sullivan let out an equally too-obvious sigh.

"Oh, Jackson. What have I gotten myself into?"

Sullivan took out a French press and ran some beans through the grinder. When she opened it and some grounds fell out, she muttered, "I did not fill you that much. You're just doing it for attention." She swept the grounds into her hand and tossed them into the sink.

Despite everything, Kia felt a real laugh bubbling up. She held it back, but that didn't change the fact that Sullivan was adorable.

Kia took a sip. "Kenyan? From Muranga?"

"Southern Nyeri."

"So right above Muranga."

"I'm not giving you that one, Jackson. Muranga is not Nyeri."

"Fine."

"What are you working on?" Sullivan asked.

"My dream."

Kia turned her laptop around so Sullivan could see the idyllic photograph of a couple watching the sunset from beneath a 1968 Wind Searcher Pop-Up Pavilion.

"That's your dream? To have a little tent on top of your RV?"

"It's not just a little tent. It's got features and it matches the RV."

Sullivan snorted.

"If you slept on the ground, you wouldn't need all that."

"If I had to sleep on the ground, I'd get a different job. Now stop hassling my dream. You wanted to talk about house rules. I already deep-fried a tursnicken on your stove, so that's covered."

Sullivan gave her a melodramatic sigh. "Before we discuss that culinary affront, how about a few vital statistics. Just in case someone asks me what sign you are or how many siblings you have."

Kia listed her vitals. No siblings. Gay single father. Allergic to Goldschläger.

"That's just weird," Sullivan said.

"It's my allergy. It's not weird. Are you writing this down?"

"I'll remember everything."

"You will not."

Sullivan rattled off everything Kia had said.

"You always memorized your recipes at school. Why not just keep them on your phone?"

"What if your battery dies and you have to make a dacquoise cake?"

"You charge your phone."

"What if there's no electricity?"

"You wait for the power to come back on."

"If it doesn't?" Sullivan asked as though she'd just made a winning argument.

"Like, ever? I'm not going to be making a dacquoise in the zombie apocalypse."

"Quitter."

Sullivan sounded so disapproving, Kia almost missed the affectionate way her lips quirked upward.

Kia woke her phone up so she could type Sullivan's answers, because she could not memorize how to make a dacquoise cake in the apocalypse.

"Age and birthday?"

Sullivan's birthday was coming up soon.

"You're only six years older than me," Kia blurted. "That's nothing. When we were in school, I thought you were so…grown up."

"You were a child when you started the program."

"I was *twenty*."

The difference between twenty and twenty-six had meant something. But now? They were both grown-up business owners. Kia had caught up. If Sullivan had thought of her as a kid before, maybe now she could think of Kia as a woman. Kia closed her eyes to press the thought out of her brain.

"So what's your dream birthday?" Kia asked. "I might have to plan something for you. I mean, you are my wife and all."

"I'd have a partner." She didn't add *real*, but the way her shoulders dropped implied it. "They'd take me camping."

"Don't you go camping all the time?"

The real issue was why someone would want to sleep outside with bears, snakes, and serial killers, but Kia didn't bring that up.

"For my birthday, they'd plan the whole thing. I'd just wake up and they'd say, *We're going camping*, and they'd have everything ready."

This was obviously more personal to Sullivan than just getting eaten by bears on a trip someone else planned. This was about being cherished. Kia guessed no one had cherished Sullivan like this. It clearly made Sullivan sad. Despite Kia's adamant aversions to getting eaten by bears and poisoned by tent-dwelling snakes, Kia knew there was no world in which she didn't take Sullivan camping for her birthday.

chapter 14

It was the end of another night at Mirepoix, and Sullivan was in and out of the refrigerator rotating inventory, first in, first out. From across the line stations, Opal gave her a look.

"I know. I know," Sullivan mumbled. "Blake?"

Blake dropped his phone on the stainless steel counter, then pushed it behind a stockpot, which did nothing to hide his guilt.

"Outside. We need to talk." Tonight was the night Sullivan fired him. She really would do it this time.

Behind the restaurant, the Bois rested in darkness, the quiet interrupted by lugubrious howling. Kia would probably think it was wolves…or werewolves. Sullivan shook her head remembering the horror with which Kia had pronounced the word *snakes*, shivering as though one were crawling on her at that very moment. Sullivan hadn't laughed. It was a real fear. It had still been comically endearing.

Blake began apologizing before they'd had a chance to sit down on one of the outside dining tables.

"I know I shouldn't have been on my phone." Apologies

poured out of him. "But people were talking shit about Mickey on Insta," the boy pleaded.

Mickey was his pit bull mastiff mix, which was currently howling his loneliness from the back of Blake's pickup.

"People were saying pit bulls are vicious and Mickey should be put down."

Mickey was as vicious as a bag of cotton balls and about as smart.

Social media did this. Some jerk online took twenty seconds to bash pit bulls, and this kid would risk his job to defend the dumb bag of cotton balls. He was lucky. Some jerk trolled his dog; Sullivan's girlfriend had turned their life into a stage play. Blake must have seen the look on her face, because his words came like a dam breaking.

"Are you firing me? Please don't. I'll be better."

She had to fire him, but she didn't have the energy tonight. She'd been thinking about losing the Bois. Living with Kia was fine right now. She'd expected Kia to be a presence, to leave glittery clothes on the bathroom floor and pools of corn syrup on the stove, but Kia was immaculately tidy, quiet, and often gone. But eventually Kia would hire loggers, and the Bois would be decimated. Trees turned into scrap lumber. Every time she thought about it, she wanted to cry.

"This is your last chance. Now take Mickey home before he pisses off the whole neighborhood."

"Didn't do it, did you?" Opal said when Sullivan returned to the kitchen for a final check.

Sullivan shook her head.

"Let me know if you want me to." Opal was everyone's loving coach, but like a good coach, she could do what had to be done.

"I have to do it. It's my job."

The walk home through the Bois would have made her feel better, except that walk was a funeral procession. There was the fir tree shaped like a tuning fork. There was the stand of holly planted by some past gardener. All gone in a year.

She sighed when she saw the lights on in the kitchen at home. She didn't feel like making polite conversation. She considered sneaking in the back door, but she'd scare the shit out of Kia when Kia realized someone was in the house.

"I'm home," Sullivan called out as she entered.

Kia stood at the stove in one of Sullivan's aprons, her hair swooped up in a purple scarf, defying gravity with its height. Two eggs sizzled on the stovetop griddle, their yolks shimmering wet like she'd cracked them the moment Sullivan put her key in the lock. Kia turned to face her, arms at her sides, centered perfectly in front of the stove like a Wes Anderson film.

"I made you a breakfast sandwich." Kia nervously twirled the spatula she was holding.

The smell of frying onions reminded Sullivan that she hadn't eaten since breakfast.

Kia flipped the eggs, buttered some English muffins that had been grilling alongside them, delivered the eggs to the muffins, closed the sandwiches, and produced two nests of caramel-colored hash browns. All with one movement like fast culinary tai chi.

"You never ate when we were in school. You'd make all this great food and leave it for everyone else. And then you'd get a breakfast sandwich at Ravi's Deli." Kia must have sensed Sullivan's dour mood. Kia's words came out in a rush as fast as Blake's apologies.

Kia pushed a plate across the kitchen island. The over easy eggs looked hopeful gazing up at Sullivan.

"That's sweet, but I've had a long day. I'm just going to grab a protein bar."

Sullivan got a box of cricket-flour protein bars out of the cupboard. Kia snatched the box away.

"I can't let you eat these."

"Insects are sustainable."

"Crickets are fine." Kia waved the box. "Deep-fry them, and they're Cheetos of the land. But I tasted these, Sullivan, I can't let you eat them. They taste like sad dirt."

"I had a sad dirt kind of day."

"Want to talk about it?" Kia pushed the plate an inch closer to Sullivan.

Sullivan gave in. The cricket bars did taste like sad dirt.

"I have to fire someone." Sullivan sat down and took a bite of the sandwich.

The yolk broke against the buttered muffin. The crunch of hash browns nodded to the russet in one direction and the potato chip in the other. The pendant light over the kitchen island cast a warm circle around them.

"What happened?"

"My intern prep cook. He's on his phone all the time, posting on his *dog's* social media. He's had a tough life—he needs that job—but it's a small staff. We have to be able to count on each other."

This was the part where Kia told her about the importance of mentoring young chefs or not following a corporate model or how Kia would give a kid like that a food truck to run.

"Sometimes you have to fire people, and when you do, you're going to be kind. You always are." Kia looked sincere. "You didn't leave me lying in the mud. You saved my ass so many times in school."

Sullivan took another bite. The sandwich tasted exactly like the ones she'd bought at Ravi's Deli back in New York. For a moment, she was walking out of the practice kitchen into the darkness of February or bright threads of daylight in June. Sunlight filtering through the flyers on the window of the deli. Still grinning about some comment she and Kia had riffed on all night.

"What would you do?" Sullivan asked.

"I never work with anyone long enough to have to fire them, but I think I'd take his phone, tell him to delete the dog's profile, and, if that didn't work, fire his ass."

Sullivan's own laugh surprised her.

"What about supporting young professionals?"

"Young professionals stay the fuck off their phone when they have the opportunity to work with one of the best chefs in the country."

Sullivan hid her smile behind another bite of her sandwich.

"Jackson, you're slipping. What about your point six percent?"

Kia arched her back, the tower of her hair in its purple scarf lifting regally.

"I said *one* of the best chefs."

And Sullivan remembered one of the things she had always appreciated about Kia: Kia could tease her, gloat, and talk shit, and it never made Sullivan feel small. Smack talk was something they did together, not something Kia did to her.

Days passed quietly and then it was Sunday morning, the day before their court date. Tomorrow, Nina would clear everything up. The case would be dismissed. Kia and Sullivan wouldn't be a team anymore. It'd be back to Kia the developer and Sullivan the small-business owner. Even though they'd been friendly to each other, Sullivan would expect Kia to move out. The thought swirled around Kia's mind as she sat at the kitchen island trying to focus on her fans' messages.

Deja and her AI social media program responded to

comments, driving up engagement. But Kia wanted to write back to as many personal messages as possible. People shared their stories, their memories, their family recipes, and sometimes their grief. *I watch your reels when I'm in the hospital with my kiddo. We cooked your Snickers potato pie at my gran's funeral.* She couldn't let AI reply with a generic *Hope you're doing well.* So she sat at the island in Sullivan's microgreen-filled kitchen, her laptop and her special coffee in front of her, typing and typing.

Her neck ached and it was barely ten a.m. (Sullivan was still asleep, which was a charming surprise. Kia expected her to be an up-at-six kind of person.) Kia sat back and stretched. A confetti of early sunlight sparkled through the trees and the greens, casting dancing points of light on the blond wood cabinets. Two colorful Turkish-cotton dish towels adorned the oven door. After tomorrow, she might never sit here again.

Kia was wearing tight jeans and a Kia Gourmazing T-shirt, but the kitchen invited fluffy robes and slippers. It felt like a home, like Old Girl and her father's yacht except immovable and old. Sullivan's family had owned this house for generations. Nicks in the hardwood could have been made by kids who'd grown up, lived their lives, and passed before Kia's father had been born. It'd be nice to live in a place like this with friends she saw every day.

"Morning." A sleepy voice broke Kia out of her reverie. "What are you doing up?"

"It's after ten."

"How did that happen?" Sullivan sat down on an island stool across from Kia. She tugged at the cuffs of her pajama top (a subtle tan plaid, like Burberry without the red stripes).

Kia hopped up and turned the water boiler on for another pour-over. Without thinking, she put her hand on Sullivan's shoulder.

"Don't wake up too fast. You'll hurt yourself."

Sullivan rolled her eyes.

"How long have you been up?"

"Since five."

"That's obscene." Sullivan laid her head on her crossed arms as though preparing to go back to sleep.

Kia placed a cup of coffee beside her. She resisted the urge to ruffle Sullivan's hair. Sullivan sat up and took a sip.

"So I had an idea," Sullivan said, sleep clearing from her eyes. "You're buying the Bois. I guess that'll all start soon after Nina puts Mega Eats in their place. And you haven't seen the whole Bois. What do you think about a picnic? There's a beautiful spot I want to show you."

The coffee soured in Kia's stomach. She read the subtext. *Tomorrow you'll get the go-ahead to destroy the Bois. Want to see it before you wreck it?* But Kia couldn't say, *Nah, I'd rather not see your ancestral forest before I pave it over.* And a stupid part of her ached for this to be real, for Sullivan to invite her on a real date. Sullivan wasn't, but it'd be exquisite if, after all those years of pining for Sullivan, Sullivan took her hand—*I've always wanted you, Kia, I was just too scared to tell you*—and kissed her.

"No?" Sullivan asked.

Kia felt her face flush. Please don't let Sullivan read the fangirl lust in her heart.

"No. I mean yes. Of course."

An hour and a half later, they headed out, Sullivan wearing a backpack. An actual *backpack*. The Bois wasn't backpack big. Why not carry their sandwiches in a sling bag? Or just hand one to Kia to carry on her own? The Bois felt bigger as they walked through the woods. Eventually, they arrived at a flooded field. Short, gnarled trees jutted out of brown water. In the distance, a line of trees looked like they swallowed up children in fairy tales. Kia flipped up her turquoise sunglasses and peered around.

"It's a wetland," Sullivan said.

Kia assessed the location for its appeal on U-Spin and its Instagrammability. Instagrammability about eight percent. U-Spin, zero.

"I can see it's wet."

"Isn't it gorgeous?"

It was hard to imagine how anyone could mourn this M. Night Shyamalan landscape, but Kia thought she saw love and grief flash behind Sullivan's eyes, more intense than anything Kia had felt for the villages and bayous she'd visited on her travels.

"There's a footpath through the wetland," Sullivan said. "Follow me."

They were going to walk on a *footpath* across water? This really wasn't something to love.

"Are there snakes?"

"They're not poisonous out here."

"That was not the question. They aren't going to fall out of the trees and land on me, are they?"

"No." A shadow passed over Sullivan's face. "I haven't seen a miniature Oregon tree snake in at least a year."

Sullivan headed toward a wooden sign that read DENNY E. ELWOOD MEMORIAL WETLAND TRAIL. He'd probably fallen in and gotten eaten by the snakes. That happened in Florida. With climate change, those ropes of Satan had probably made their way to Oregon.

Kia pinned her location for Deja to look for her body. She took a picture and WhatsApp-ed it to Lillian.

Kia: *She's taking me on a picnic in a WETLAND* 📷

For once, Lillian texted back immediately like she had before she gave up ballet and fell madly in love with Izzy.

Lillian: *Iz says they're beautiful*
Kia: *Iz is OREGONIAN*
Lillian: *Facts* 😂

Kia texted a picture of her De Luxe Heel Platform Converse.

Kia: *She hates me*
Lillian: *Everyone loves you*

"You could have warned me about this," Kia called after Sullivan, but Sullivan was practically dancing down the narrow muddy path between decaying clumps of reeds. "Georgie does not like it out here," Kia grumbled.

Sullivan set the pace, moving with the grace of a TikTok dancer, floating and gliding just above the path, whistling.

"That's a blue heron." She quoted some poetry because *that* was appropriate in the minutes before being eaten by pythons. *"I have looked upon those brilliant creatures, and now my heart is sore. All's changed since I, hearing at twilight, the first time on this shore.* That poem's about swans though."

Kia's heel sank in the mud. Every step felt like a struggle, amplifying her frustration. Sullivan glanced over her shoulder.

"Keep up, Jackson." Was the lightness in Sullivan's voice teasing or mocking?

Sullivan widened her lead, still pointing at bushes, although Kia could no longer hear the botany lesson. Kia tried to hurry but her heels stuck. The path dipped. Water flowed slowly across it. Sullivan had jumped it. Kia would fall in the mud like she had outside Sullivan's house and break her neck.

"Alice Sullivan!"

Sullivan turned and waved. Didn't their days at Jean Paul Molineux mean enough to Sullivan that she wouldn't strand Kia in a swamp? Was Sullivan going to hike out of the forest behind the wetland, call an Uber, and leave her? A drop of rain hit her face.

A nearby clump of reeds trembled. So did Kia's Afro. Her anxiety spiked. Something rippled in that water. Inside her chest, Kia's heartbeat sounded like a boxer landing blows on a punching bag, forceful and a little erratic. Snakes. She yelled the only thing she could think of. The truth.

"I'm scared of snakes, Sullivan, and I'm stuck."

With the grace and speed of a steeplechaser, Sullivan closed the distance between them.

"There are fucking snakes out here." A drop of water hit her cheek. "Ugh!"

"Oh shit, I'm sorry, Kia." Sullivan sounded earnest. "This is my special place, and I was excited for you to see it. I wasn't thinking."

Kia's frustration softened. If this mud bowl really was Sullivan's special place, Sullivan had terrible taste in special places, but it was kind of sweet that she'd taken Kia here.

"I can't jump over that." Kia pointed to the water.

"Do you trust me?" Sullivan asked.

"After this? No."

"Sorry." Sullivan shrugged, looking suddenly shy. "I took search and rescue training. I can carry you over it."

"And drop me."

"No. I promise." Sullivan held open her arms as though preparing to receive a large basket. "Okay?"

Kia would regret this.

Sullivan stooped a little. Then Kia felt one of Sullivan's arms under her knees and the other around her back. Instinctively Kia draped an arm around Sullivan's neck. Then Sullivan lifted Kia in her arms, leaning back a little so Kia's weight rested against her chest. It was epically sexy. Sullivan walked through the water and set Kia down gently on the other side, like relocating a lost baby bird to its nest. She kept a hand on Kia's lower back until Kia got her balance. And it was the hottest, most romantic gesture Kia had witnessed in real life. As soon as Sullivan put her down, she missed the warmth and safety of Sullivan's arms.

"I won't race ahead." Concern flickered in Sullivan's eyes.

"Maybe we can work on our communication and coordinate better next time?"

"Of course."

The path seemed drier with Sullivan beside her, and soon they were stepping into the forest behind the wetland. The path widened, so they could walk side by side. Kia glanced at Sullivan, who managed to look glamorous stepping over roots and rocks with her laid-back confidence.

"Do you really love this place?"

"Just wait."

"What am I waiting for?"

Sullivan looked a little chagrined.

"You really will like it. At least your followers will."

Sullivan smiled up at the canopy of trees. Kia's eyes darted to Sullivan's mouth—a mouth that she had watched for countless hours. Expressive lips parting to show beautifully white teeth, curving into an electric smile that Kia had found so mesmerizing. Sullivan looked like a hot REI commercial with all her gear. Had she ever made love to a woman in a tent? Or under the stars? That could almost make Kia want to go camping.

The path turned.

Sullivan announced, "We're here."

Kia had been too busy trying to turn the heat down on her thoughts. But her brain wasn't a gas range where you could turn it off in a second. It was an old coil stove where the coils stayed hot for an inconveniently long time after you'd decided you were done with it. She hadn't noticed the sound of water growing louder as they approached, but here was a small waterfall. Maybe ten or twelve feet. Ferns surrounded the small pool at its base. It made Kia think of a scene in a snow globe. A perfect, peaceful place set apart from the rest of the world. A place that should be protected in a glass globe so no one could touch it without loving it the way Sullivan obviously did.

"I used to come here when I was a kid," Sullivan said. "They hadn't put in the path, so I had it all to myself."

"How'd you find it?"

"My grandpa showed me. He knew every inch of the Bois."

Kia tried not to think about what she'd need to do to this mud pit to run in electricity and plumbing, pour concrete pads for the trucks, put in an accessible playground, ADA bathrooms…at one point she'd thought about a small stage. Fuck. She'd have to pave the whole thing. Sullivan would kill her. If Mega Eats didn't get them first. Nina had sounded so confident, but what if…? Before Kia became the kind of influencer who spent her time doing promotional videos for her sponsors, she'd been the kind of person who spent afternoons fishing on the banks of dirty creeks listening to people talk about the unexpected disasters that had shaped their lives.

There was so much to think about, and none of it went together. She was excited about Taste the Love. She was worried about Mega Eats. She was lusting after Sullivan. She felt terrible about what she would have to do to Sullivan's precious Bois, but she was definitely going to do it, because Taste the Love was her dream. But wasn't part of the dream about Lillian and Izzy coming back to Portland, and all of them going out to brunch together and throwing prom parties in the winter when everyone needed an excuse to dress up? But Lillian hadn't said they were coming back, not anytime soon. Was Kia putting her life savings and her investors' money (not to mention risking Mega Eats' wrath and Sullivan's) for a dream of home that you couldn't buy? She stared at the waterfall.

"You okay?" Sullivan set down her backpack.

Kia sat down on a rock. "I shouldn't complain to you."

Sullivan shrugged. "We didn't make any house rules about complaining."

"We're going to court tomorrow, and it's just...a lot." The waterfall hid the tremor in Kia's voice.

Sullivan waited. Kia wanted to sink against Sullivan's strong, REI-clad chest and pour out her worries, but you couldn't ask to be comforted by the person whose life you were ruining.

"I'm fine," Kia said.

Sullivan took her jacket off and handed it to Kia. "You look cold."

The warmth of the jacket felt impossibly intimate.

"Sandwich?" Sullivan opened her pack.

Suddenly, Kia was starving.

"Roasted vegetables with Gruyère, or pulled pork with caramelized onions?" Sullivan asked.

"Which are you more proud of?"

Sullivan considered and handed her the roasted vegetables. "Notice how the miso glaze melds with the sear on the rocotillo peppers."

"Yeah, yeah." Kia took a bite. She had visited restaurants in thirty-eight states and she hadn't had a sandwich this good. "Fuck you, Sullivan," she said through a mouthful.

Sullivan's smile said she knew it was a compliment.

Above them, the clouds were parting.

"Here it comes," Sullivan said, gesturing to the sky.

And like magic or something out of a religious painting, a ray of light shone into the pool, illuminating every droplet of water in the air. Kia's mouth opened in an O of wonder.

She was just about to say how much she appreciated Sullivan taking her out even though she'd almost drowned in the wetland, when a giant, poisonous viper slithered out of the underbrush. It moved in for the attack. Kia screamed.

Sullivan stood up and moved toward the monster.

"Shoo," she said. "Kia doesn't want to know you."

Kia considered wading into the water to escape. Could this kind of snake swim? Her skin crawled at the thought.

"It's just a garter snake. They're harmless," Sullivan said.

The snake disappeared back into the bushes. Now that it was gone, Kia could admit that maybe it wasn't *that* big. Maybe it was more like shoelace big. Short shoelace. It was still hideous.

"Why are you so afraid of snakes?" When Sullivan sat back down, she was closer to Kia, their hips touching. She hadn't moved closer on purpose, had she?

"It's the way they move." Kia waved her arm to imitate the unnatural slither. "The way they just appear. And everyone says, *Oh, there're no snakes at the fairgrounds. There're no snakes in Cincinnati.* And then, bam, there's one under my RV. That's why I want the Wind Searcher Pop-Up Pavilion. And don't make fun of me. Everyone's scared of something." Kia trembled in Sullivan's coat.

Sullivan looked at her, confused but sympathetic.

"I wouldn't make fun of you." She touched Kia's knee, just a fleeting gesture but Kia felt it vibrate through her body. "Even though you put marshmallows in your coffee."

"You already made fun of me for the marshmallows." Kia pretended to scowl.

"Shit. I forgot. Sorry. I won't make fun of your snake thing."

Sullivan's calm dispelled Kia's nerves.

"You know I grew up on a yacht, right?"

"I did *not* know you grew up on a yacht."

"I did, and my dad and I sailed all over the world. He's got money. Smart tech investments. He always said nature wants you to look at it, not touch it. No snorkeling off the boat. No swimming with the dolphins. We went to gorgeous places, but sometimes we were far off the grid. He knew it'd be fun to swim off the yacht in the middle of the ocean, but if your eight-year-old kid gets stung by a jellyfish or hits her head as she's jumping off the boat, nobody can get there in time."

Sullivan looked like she was impressed by Kia's adventuresome childhood. It made Kia want to tell Sullivan more stories.

"Nature was like a fairy-tale house that's made of candy. You want to eat it, but it'll kill you. And sea snakes." She gave a dramatic shudder to illustrate the horror. "The Dubois' snake. The spiny snake. The yellow-bellied sea snake just drifts around in the ocean its whole life waiting to eat human children."

"How big is it?"

"Like two feet!"

"How big are the children?" Sullivan's smile said, *I really am sorry this scares you, and also you're funny, and I'm trying not to tease you.*

"This is *my* phobia." Kia gave Sullivan's arm a little slap. The gesture felt natural. Exactly what you do when your friend teases you in a way that doesn't hurt. "Small enough to eat."

"I'm sorry," Sullivan said more seriously. "Stuff like that can be terrifying when you're a kid."

"It was worth it to get that life. Sometimes the ocean was so blue. Sometimes we'd see dolphins. Fish of every color. If we were married for real, I'd take you sailing." That sounded way too romantic. She pivoted. "We always had spaniels. My dad got them life vests in their own tartans, and he taught them to poop in a composting sandbox." She counted on her fingers as she listed off the names of her favorite dogs.

"What did you do on a yacht for all that time?"

"Read. Talked. FaceTimed my cousin when she wasn't dancing. Wherever we landed, my dad got someone to teach me something. His friends are expat drag queens mostly. They taught me chess, Spanish architecture. And sometimes he'd get an old abuela to show me how to make tortillas."

Kia could almost see the setting sun stretching shadows over a chess board.

"It was an anchorless life. I don't know if I have a high school diploma. I took some tests for homeschooled kids. I might have failed."

Sullivan shrugged and bumped her shoulder against Kia's.

"My grades in high school sure wouldn't have gotten me into Harvard, but look at us now. Total rock stars."

Kia loved the way Sullivan lumped them together, like they were real friends. She was probably being kind because Kia was just a few minutes past a snake-induced panic attack, but still… it was nice.

"My dad said I knew everything I needed for a good life," Kia went on. "My aunt got me some sort of international student's high school equivalency paperwork so I could get into culinary arts school."

"I wasn't great at school, not the books and computers part," Sullivan mused. "I love audiobooks, but reading on paper…" Sullivan winced as she crumbled the parchment sandwich wrapper into a ball. "Dyslexic."

"I didn't know."

"Why did you think I memorized all my recipes instead of reading them on my phone?"

"Because you were brilliant?"

"Thanks. And my folks and brother are all professors. They didn't put me down, but it was my grandpa who showed me there are a lot of different ways to be good at things."

"Is it weird that we went to school together and we don't know this stuff about each other?" Kia asked.

"It kind of is. I like knowing that you grew up on a yacht. Do you live in an RV because you're used to living on a yacht?"

"Yeah."

"Do you like it?"

"Moving around? Absolutely. I read Sappho off the island of Lesbos. Who doesn't want that?"

Feeling her ass going numb from sitting on a rock, Kia shifted. The movement settled her hip firmly against Sullivan's. She felt Sullivan's warmth. She didn't imagine it this time. Sullivan leaned into her.

"My cousin Lillian was my only friend, but that worked because I was always moving around and she was a ballerina. She didn't have time for a social life, and I didn't have a place for a social life. We understood each other. It wasn't weird that we were always in different time zones. She's in Paris now though. With her girlfriend. I'm not jealous." She was jealous. "I thought maybe they'd move back to Portland, and we'd all…I don't know. Live together. That's dumb. They're so in love. They don't want a third wheel, and I love living in a fifth wheel." Kia made the thumbs-up gesture she'd offer her fans, but she didn't feel it in her heart. "So I guess when this is all done…"

"Will you move out of the house?"

Kia felt Sullivan's hip shift uneasily.

"Of course," Kia said quickly. "I'm going to move as soon as we get rid of this Mega Eats thing."

"Oh." Sullivan almost looked hurt. "So, like, you'll leave tomorrow?" Did Sullivan want Kia to stay? Was she offended that Kia had spoken so quickly?

"I mean your house is beautiful. I'd love to stay forever." She gestured to the waterfall. "But I'm used to being on the road."

"It'd make sense to live closer to your food truck." Sullivan sounded like a business adviser, helpful and disinterested. Sullivan tucked her balled-up sandwich wrapper into a pocket in her backpack. With that, the clouds above them closed. Sullivan handed Kia a napkin from her pack. Kia couldn't shake the feeling that she'd said the wrong thing, but she wasn't sure if it was *I'm going to move as soon as we get rid of this Mega Eats thing* or *I'd love to stay forever.*

chapter 15

"Go! You have to pick up Kia and get to court." Opal made a shooing gesture, indicating Sullivan needed to leave the Mirepoix kitchen. They'd been making mini quiches for a Portland Night High School fundraiser. "Do you not understand that I could do this blindfolded without you?" Opal added.

Sullivan understood. And she was nowhere near being late to court. It would just be nicer to whip eggs with Opal than to put on a suit and drive Kia down to the courthouse. The judge would dismiss the Mega Eats case, which would be great, but then Kia would start work on Taste the Love. There was no way it wouldn't devastate the land and Sullivan's heart. She had promised her grandfather she would preserve this land in aeternum. Forever. Now bulldozers would plow under the wood sorrel and the trillium. Loggers would take down tree after tree. They'd drag the logs to the edge of the Bois, leaving meter-deep gashes in the land. Kia would be smart to recoup some of her costs by selling the lumber. Sullivan had a flight to Palm Springs saved in Expedia for when they started logging, and the site kept asking her if she wanted to book it, but she couldn't escape the development forever.

"I'm going." She took off her chef's coat and hung it by the back door. She kept her eyes on the ground as she walked through the Bois back to her house.

In the house, Kia was sitting in the kitchen, her purse in one hand, a sparkling green coat laid over her lap, as though she'd been waiting all morning and they were late. Which they weren't. Kia just couldn't wait to move out. That added a layer of sadness on top of everything else, like a bitter coffee glaze on a burnt cake. Sullivan didn't know what she wanted. She couldn't possibly want Kia to stay and plan her destruction of the Bois on Sullivan's kitchen island, but when Sullivan turned off the part of her brain that remembered what was happening outside her house, it was nice to have Kia around. She felt like they picked up right where they left off, gently giving each other shit and smack talking without hurting each other's feelings. They knew when to throw shade and when to tread carefully. Usually. She felt bad about dragging Kia into the wetland. Part of her had hoped Kia would see its beauty and feel crushed by guilt for what she was about to do. Realistically, she'd suspected Kia would hate it, and had taken Kia out there for that reason. Neither inclination had been noble, but once she got outside with Kia, she really did want her to see nature's beauty. She didn't want Kia to be frightened. She could still feel Kia's body in her arms, warm and solid and smelling of honey-spice perfume. And just like you couldn't imagine someone throwing a softball and not imagine its trajectory, she couldn't think about that moment without feeling like it should have ended in a kiss. Had Kia felt it too? Did Kia have to be so forceful about her desire to move out? Couldn't she have been a little wistful?

Sullivan shook her head. What the fuck was she thinking?

"Let's get out of here," she said.

Kia nodded and stood up.

"You're not going to change?"

Sullivan shrugged. She'd meant to change, but why bother?

"Mega Eats can hate me in jeans."

Nina was seated on a wooden bench outside of courtroom 3A when Kia and Sullivan arrived. She looked like the act of sitting on a bench offended her. Her iridescent navy suit found it too public. But when Nina looked up, she smiled, upbeat as though they were meeting for drinks.

"How's it going?" Kia asked.

Nina motioned to the bench, almost patting it, but lifting her hand away as though reluctant to touch it.

"Splendid as a ray of sunshine. Ready to get this over with?" Nina said a little too loudly.

Kia and Sullivan had barely sat down when the courtroom door opened and they were ushered into a spacious, wood-paneled room. They sat in the first row of seats.

"Do not worry," Nina said quietly. "Their case is a ridiculous bluff to intimidate you, and the judge will see that immediately. Put your order in at the Makers Bar. We'll be out of here before it's ready."

In a commotion of noise and bluster, the Mega Eats contingent burst through the courtroom door, causing it to bang against a rail. The lead attorney—guessing by the fact that he burst in first—wore a boxy, 1990s suit and a wide tie that screamed *Miami Vice*. He was accompanied by a phalanx of corporate lawyer types similarly attired like cartoon versions of the Mafia. Their presence still made Sullivan feel like a rock had sunk to the bottom of her stomach. These weren't cartoon lawyers. Even if Nina said they'd be out in five minutes, these were men hired by one of the biggest corporations in the world to crush her.

"That guy—" Nina nodded to the first attorney, who was making a show of talking on his phone even though a sign on all four walls read SILENCE YOUR PHONES. "That's Armand Mulroney and his first-year associates. He'll mistreat them so badly they'll be gone by the end of the year."

Mega Eats' lead attorney and Nina exchanged a quick nod of recognition before turning their attention to the bench, where Judge Edward Harper's chamber door squeaked open.

"All rise," the bailiff said. "The Honorable Edward Harper presiding."

The older man had a calm, fatherly presence until he spoke.

"Mega Eats versus Jackson-Sullivan on the respondent's motion for summary judgment. Let's get this over with," he said curtly.

Nina's posture straightened. She buttoned her blazer. The iridescent navy seemed to sober to black. They'd been friends for years, but Sullivan was still impressed. Nina would be almost as frightening as the Mega Eats attorneys if she weren't on their side, but she was on their side. They were fine.

Sullivan placed her hand on Kia's shoulder, an awkward gesture since they were sitting next to each other, but Kia gave a wan smile.

It's okay, Sullivan mouthed.

"As the court is aware," Nina said, "we are asking for a motion for summary judgment. Mega Eats contends that my clients' marriage is orchestrated to steal a land deal. This is not only untrue, but, legally speaking, it is a moot point. They are arguing that the marriage is invalid because Ms. Jackson and Ms. Sullivan haven't known each other long enough to fall in love." Nina exuded confidence, her voice smooth, persuasive, and slightly amused. "The thing I find peculiar about this situation is how a billion-dollar corporation known for harassing landowners and businesspeople who stand in their way would have such a romantic outlook on marriage. It doesn't matter if my clients are in love. As you know, Your Honor—but perhaps Mr. Mulroney does not—I am a divorce attorney. If lack of love—and Mr. Mulroney has offered no proof that Ms. Sullivan and Ms. Jackson do not love each other—but if a lack of love annulled relationships..." Nina shrugged and held up her hands in a helpless gesture. "What would I do all day?"

When Nina finished, Kia swore she saw the judge nod with a hint of approval in his eyes, which was comforting and somehow a little depressing. No need for love? Not even affection?

"Mr. Mulroney, your response?" the judge asked, his tone cool and skeptical.

Mega Eats' lawyer stood up; his cartoon-Mafia bluster had morphed into calm composure. He walked to the podium with a quiet confidence, his eyes meeting Judge Harper's.

"Thank you, Your Honor. Nina's argument is well crafted."

Nina's face tightened at the use of her first name.

"But her argument overlooks several key pieces of evidence that create genuine issues, which must be evaluated thoroughly by a fact finder." He went on. "The evidence we have submitted shows that Ms. Sullivan and Ms. Jackson have only just moved in together. Photographs taken just a little while ago show them living completely separate lives and, as I mentioned in my brief, they've only known each other for a few days."

Nina stood. "Objection," she said. "My clients met over ten years ago and spent four years in culinary arts school together. It's quite possible they have known each other longer than Mr. Mulroney has been practicing law. Not that that matters. And while we are talking about cohabitation, Your Honor, I've met your wonderful wife at various legal conferences. In Seattle.

Where she lives and practices law for most of the year. I assume you would not consider yours a fraudulent marriage."

"You will not bring my personal life into this courtroom."

"My apologies, Your Honor."

"We'd also like to point out that Ms. Sullivan does not appear anywhere on Ms. Jackson's social media, even though Ms. Jackson makes a point of being a member of the LGBTQ community."

Nina was on her feet again. "Objection. Being out does not require that she broadcast her private life."

"It simply seems odd that a woman who has featured her egg timer on her feed would fail to mention her 'real' marriage to Alice Sullivan," Mulroney said.

"A very good point, Mr. Mulroney," the judge said.

"We'd like to call on case *Saville* and *Saville*," Mulroney added.

"Those are powerful precedents," the judge said. "Have you overlooked those cases, Ms. Hashim?"

"Those cases aren't on point. In both cases, the marriage was an attempt to defraud. If, hypothetically, my clients did marry to secure the land in question—and I am not proposing that they did—that is the opposite of an attempt to defraud through marriage. That is working in the open for mutual benefit."

"It is an attempt to defraud Mega Eats."

"Your Honor, this feigned innocence is wearing thin. Mega Eats believes in the power of true love, and now they think it's fraud if two businesswomen outsmart them? Would Mr. Mulroney like me to hold his hand too?"

Mulroney's face reddened. His associates leaned back as though waiting for an explosion. It didn't come. Sullivan thought she saw the judge and Mulroney exchange a look, a look that was more frightening than an outburst. They knew something. She caught Nina's eye.

"I know," Nina whispered.

The pit in Sullivan's stomach morphed into a canyon-sized hole. Judge Harper seemed to turn on Nina.

Mulroney said, "Your Honor, it is imperative that this case be heard on its merits."

The judge stood.

"Your Honor, I haven't finished," Nina said.

"You can finish at the trial. I find in Mega Eats' favor. I can't dismiss this out of hand. We will proceed to trial to see if Ms. Hashim's musing on love and business hold water." He hit the striking block with his gavel. "Next."

This was what shock felt like. Kia felt like she was watching herself, Nina, and Sullivan from above. There they were standing on the sidewalk in front of the courthouse. It was a dream. It wasn't happening. Nina would explain that Kia had misunderstood the judge's decision. They were fine. Nina had been right.

"What the fuck was that unfounded bullshit?" Nina said, pulling out her phone and typing furiously. "I'm texting my associates, and my driver is on his way. We're going to the Makers Bar."

A few minutes later, they were ensconced in a circular booth. A waiter in black jeans and a black button-down glided over to their table.

"Champagne or martinis?" he asked Nina.

"Martinis."

"I'm sorry, Ms. Hashim."

"One of those days," Nina said. Behind her breezy tone, Kia heard something ominous.

"Are we fucked?" Sullivan asked.

"Well."

No one wanted to hear *well* in response to *are we fucked*.

Over drinks and a charcuterie board no one ate, Nina talked, and Sullivan asked questions. Nina was going to ask for a new judge. There was no way the judge should have let the case go to trial.

"Totally sus!" Nina commented. "That's a legal term. One other thing," Nina said as she closed the vintage cigar box that held the bill and pushed it to the edge of the table. "I'm sorry about this, Sullivan. You two should get on Kia's social media. Be cute." Nina rolled her eyes like she couldn't imagine what that might look like. "I am so sorry this didn't go our way, and I'm going to prove that this should never have gone to trial. The case Mulroney cited is so distinguishable. But in the meantime, just in case, let's get you all over the internet serving serious love vibes."

Poor Sullivan. She hated social media enough that Opal, her jolly rugby coach friend, was ready to throw down over it.

"It's off-brand," Kia blurted. "I mean Sullivan is. We are. I can't cook tursnicken with Chef Mirepoix."

Sullivan looked like a soufflé that had deflated down to its base ingredients: an omelet. A sad omelet.

"It's not that you wouldn't look great on Kia Gourmazing," Kia added quickly. "You were the hottest woman in our class."

"I was the only other woman in our class." Sullivan's sigh carried every word in the sentence.

Kia couldn't let Sullivan think she didn't want her on Kia Gourmazing because she wasn't good enough, cool enough, hot enough.

"I still had a massive crush on you when we were in school." Kia let out a manic laugh. "I mean, not for real, but I could have. Look at you. Who wouldn't?"

Nina looked back and forth between them, eyes narrowed.

"I don't care if marrying Sullivan is off-brand," she said. "Put some glitter on her and make it work."

Kia held it together until the second call and fourth text to Lillian. Now she sat cross-legged on her bed—Sullivan's guest bed—her phone clutched in her hands. It was late afternoon in Oregon, which meant the middle of the night in Paris, so it wasn't fair to expect Lillian to answer, but before Izzy, Lillian would have. Before Izzy, Lillian had had a sixth sense for when Kia needed her. Before Izzy, Lillian just danced and talked on the phone with her best friend/cousin wherever Kia was and however mismatched their time zones.Kia tried one more time.

Kia: *You awake?*

Nothing. Kia counted to twenty, then fifty. It was too much. She was supposed to be filming a promo for August Harvest granola, spontaneously working in the phrase *crunches like summer.* Gretchen would have her ass if she was late. She had to call Gretchen and tell her what had happened. Gretchen would show her love by immediately outlining a damage-control publicity plan, with a dose of cautionary tales about clients who ruined their brands and went broke. And Me'Shell was getting to Portland tomorrow, ready to help Kia plan Taste the Love Land, and there was no love and no land, and Sullivan wanted her out of the house, and now she couldn't leave because it'd look like they weren't in love, and she had been secretly crushing on Sullivan since she was twenty, and Sullivan had every reason to *exactly* hate her. Kia was about to lose everything. No woman would ever love her. She'd die alone and she wouldn't even have her father's good sense to buy a dozen spaniels. She rounded herself into a ball, her phone clutched in her lap, her arms wrapped around her knees, and burst into tears.

She didn't hear the door open. She only realized Sullivan was there when Sullivan put her arms around her.

"It sucks," Sullivan said, rocking her gently. "All of this."

Her words and her embrace made Kia cry harder.

"This is all my fault." Kia tried to catch her breath.

"Technically yes," Sullivan said without any anger in her voice. "But also no."

Kia could feel Sullivan shake her head.

"You were trying to start a business. I own a business. I can't come at you like you were trying to burn down my house."

"You don't have to be nice to me." Her whole body shuddered with the effort to suck back her tears.

"Is it more than the lawsuit? Is there something else?" Sullivan asked, still holding Kia.

"Isn't that enough?"

"It's absolutely enough. It's too much." Sullivan released Kia but kept one arm around her shoulder. "But *is* there anything else?"

"My cousin used to be my best friend, and she still is, but she's in a relationship, and I feel like she doesn't have time for me, which is selfish. And my dad's out of cell range. And Gretchen's a great businessperson, but she never loved me when we were dating." A litany of woes poured out of Kia. "And that's the only relationship I've had. And I shouldn't be upset. People love me, and not everyone has that, but I'm always traveling. I used to think it was an adventure, but I started to think of Taste the Love as a home base. I'd travel but I'd have a home here. But it's just a business. You can buy a business. You can't buy home. And now I've ruined your home too. And you have to live with me, and you hate it. And you have to be on social media, and you hate it. Oh god, and now I've laid all this on you and got snot on your shirt."

Please, let her not actually have snotted on Sullivan.

Kia scooted to the end of the bed and stood up. She took a deep breath. Oddly, she felt a little better. She walked over to the mirror and assessed how much concealer she'd need to do a live stream. More than LYS Beauty made last year.

"Fuck me," she said to her reflection. "I didn't accidentally tell you you were the hottest woman in our class, did I?"

She heard Sullivan chuckle behind her. "And that you had a massive crush on me. I was very flattered."

Thank god; the way Sullivan said it told Kia she hadn't taken Kia seriously.

"I just didn't want you to think I said you were off-brand because you weren't…"

"Massively hot?"

"Right. That. And Opal said you hated social media."

"So you were going to fight Nina on the social media bit?"

"Yeah."

A pause.

"Thanks."

"We could plan a whole bunch of social media things and do them all in one day. Then you wouldn't have to think about it," Kia offered. "I could make a list, and you could see what you hated least."

"And you could bring some stuff in from your RV. Make this place yours. Hang up some of your sexy flower art."

"You've got life-sized nudes!"

"Then it'll all match," Sullivan said. "Hell, you've already shook up everything. Get us a rescue dog. Isn't that what queer women do?"

"I don't think I should get us a rescue dog." Kia laughed. It felt like sunshine after a storm.

Sullivan was smiling.

"Not even if it has emotional issues? I was hoping for something that would eat the sofa." Sullivan shook her head, but her smile widened, revealing a cute dimple that hadn't made an appearance when they were in school, perhaps because Sullivan's smile had always been a little guarded. Kia hadn't noticed that until she saw this unguarded smile. As though she'd felt Kia's admiring gaze, Sullivan touched her index finger to her lips for a second. "But, seriously, Kia, I don't hate living with you. Make this feel like your home. You don't have to live here like a ghost."

chapter 16

Sullivan felt both relieved and nervous that Kia was taking the initiative with the social media campaign. They sat down at a table by the window of Mirepoix, like a couple on a date at a quiet café. Sullivan rarely experienced her restaurant from this angle. It was peaceful. A white gravel path lined with low boxwood hedges led from the parking lot to the front door. In a few weeks, she'd set up the outdoor seating area and turn on the string lights that lit the forest like fairies. And next year…it was hard to transpose Kia, perfectly coiffed with dark purple glitter sparkling in a halo around her Afro, onto the image of Kia in a hard hat bulldozing the Bois. It felt like Sullivan should be able to say, *Let me help you find another property.* Kia would say, *Thank god. I hoped you'd say that.* Then they'd drive around the industrial neighborhoods looking for attractive vacant lots. In the evening, they'd cuddle on the sofa, with Zillow open on Sullivan's laptop, and Kia reading off the specs because the concentration it took Sullivan to read the screen made her eyes tired.

Sullivan must have been lonely like Opal said. Images of Kia floated in and out of her mind all day. If she'd just been noticing

Kia's attractive body or gorgeous hair, that'd be one thing. Having dirty thoughts about Kia would be inappropriate, but it was natural to notice a woman as striking as Kia. But Sullivan hadn't been ogling Kia's ass. Well, okay, she had once or twice. But mostly she thought about Kia reading on the sofa, Kia cooking in her pajamas, Kia standing in the bathroom doing whatever it was she did to style her hair in a perfect sphere. Sullivan pictured sitting beside Kia in Kia's truck watching the ocean on a rainy day at the coast (which really meant there was something wrong with Sullivan, because using a truck that size for all-purpose transportation—over the Coast Range at that—was unconscionable). Sullivan pictured falling asleep next to Kia, and her own bed felt emptier than it had before.

"Are you ready?"

Sullivan jumped.

"I'm sorry. Yes. What?" She'd been staring at Kia's purple nail polish and the collection of glittery bracelets on Kia's wrists. There was something very personal and very crush-like about pondering a woman's wrists.

"Do you want to talk about things we could do for social media?" Kia asked, although that was the express purpose of their meeting. Of course, we'll have to do wedding-y stuff. Then after that, I asked the manager at the Tennis Skort if we could stage a spontaneous cooking challenge at the bar. You know. You. Me. Throw down on the cocktail napkins."

"They'd let us use their kitchen?"

"Sure. I asked nicely. We need to go on dates. The socials love cute couples on dates. There's a new exhibit at Hopscotch. We could do a mani-pedi."

"Do you know how much formaldehyde is in nail polish?"

"No. And I don't want to," Kia said. "What about zip-lining?"

"Terrifying."

"Thank god."

"You don't want to zip-line?"

"I'm just trying to be helpful here and think of dates for us, something that might go viral. You definitely have to come to the state fair and watch me cook. And we can play Ping-Pong at Pips and Bounce."

"You grew up on a yacht. Do you know how to play Ping-Pong?"

"Of course not. And going back a few, I think we should make our own wedding cake. That'd give great reels. I've had this idea for a piñata cake with....wait for it...Pop Rocks! I haven't quite figured the engineering, but when you cut open the cake, the Pop Rocks spill out, and somehow they get activated. With water. Or liquor." Kia scrunched her lips to the side, looking adorable. "And maybe you could set it on fire. But anyway, flaming Pop Rocks would look great against a traditional three-tiered cake. You could do the cake. I can do the Rocks."

"Sweetheart, I am never making anything with Pop Rocks." Sullivan only said *sweetheart* to take the sting out of her teasing since Kia was obviously (and unexplainably) delighted with her Pop Rocks wedding cake. And calling Kia *sweetheart* was funny, because they weren't sweethearts. That was the whole reason they were discussing Pop Rocks wedding cakes. And yet the endearment felt natural, and Kia smiled shyly.

"Fine," Kia said, looking up at Sullivan coquettishly. "What do you want to do to look sexy and in love on social media?"

"Mushroom hunting?"

"Oh, babe, there is nothing sexy about mushroom hunting."

Kia calling her *babe* didn't mean any more than Sullivan calling her *sweetheart*, but the word still felt friendly.

"You don't know how sexy mushroom hunting can be."

To Sullivan's surprise, Kia said, "You'll have to show me."

Sullivan was thinking about mushroom hunting when her mind flashed to her parents and her brother, Paul, with their wood-paneled offices at the University of Chicago and Northwestern University.

"Who do we tell about the wedding? I don't want to lie to my family."

"You're not going to tell them what's really going on?" Kia asked. "I told my cousin Lillian, and she'll tell her folks. I'll tell my dad as soon as he's back in cell range." Kia sighed. "Don't worry. They won't give up our secret. I absolutely trust them."

"I trust my family," Sullivan said slowly. She tried to picture their reaction. *I'm in a marriage of convenience with a developer who wants to buy the Bois. Yeah, the land Grandpa spent his whole life trying to preserve.* They wouldn't know what to think. She wasn't an unruly child who made bad choices. But she didn't fit in their PhD-ed trio. They didn't keep her confidences because she never shared any. They talked but they never *talked*. "I mean, if I told them that I'd be in trouble if they talked about it, they wouldn't."

Kia sat quietly. Her back straight, her elbows resting on the table as she leaned forward ever so slightly.

"Tell me about your family."

Kia's wide eyes were fixed on Sullivan, and Sullivan felt like Kia was soaking in every word.

"We like each other. They want good things to happen to me, and I want good things to happen to them. But they're a set. They make puns. They've read the same German philosophers, and they have in-jokes about them. And it's been that way since I was a kid. They tried to include me, but it was like trying to include Nina in a rugby match. So we see each other on holidays. They live in Chicago, so they always get together. I'm always invited, and I go when I can."

"Did you grow up in Chicago?"

"Suburbs. But I feel like I grew up in the Bois." That sounded pointed, but Sullivan couldn't tell her story without talking about the Bois. "I came alive when I visited my grandpa. I loved being in the woods with him. Climbing. Jumping off things. Catching bugs. Getting dirty, except it never felt dirty. I never thought, *Eww gross.* I knew what was dangerous. My grandfather taught me what to do if I saw a cougar or a paper wasp nest. I was part of nature, so stuff like touching slugs or getting mud in my mouth when I went swimming in a creek didn't make me uncomfortable. It made me feel…whole. I was home. The Bois was home. Chicago and school felt like a nice prison. When I was home in Chicago and I couldn't go outside because it was twenty below, I'd cook. When I was cooking, I had the same feeling of being *in* my body. Using all my senses. Being a part of something that wasn't my own body.

"My parents suggested I go to culinary arts school and paid for it. They believe in education even though no one in our family had ever done physical work. But they wanted me to have the best, so they paid for the Jean Paul Molineux School of Culinary Arts. That's them. That's us. They love me, even if they'll never care about filleting techniques and I'll never spontaneously say, *Putting Descartes before the horse.*"

"That's a good pun," Kia said grudgingly.

"I feel weird telling them I'm getting fake married. We're not close enough to tell things like that, but it would be wrong to lie and tell them it's for real. What would I do when we get divorced? Tell them we fell out of love a month later? But I don't want them to find out online and think I got married and didn't invite them. And what about the She-Pack and my regulars and the other chefs

I know? What about the kids I've worked with from the Night High School? I hire interns from there. If they all found out I'd been lying? Or if they all think you dumped me after a month, they'd all try to comfort me."

Like they had when she'd left Aubrey. She should have taken advantage of all those invitations to dinner and coffee and double dates and meditation classes instead of just hiding away.

"They'll send me links to empowerment webinars." Sullivan put her head on the table in mock despair.

To her surprise, she felt Kia's hand ruffle her hair and then Kia's fingers glide closer to her scalp, massaging the back of her head. Her touch was luxurious. Sullivan never wanted her to stop. Could she just stay like this forever?

"I'm sorry," Kia said. "That's a lot to think about. It's easy for me, I've got five people in my life."

"You've got followers," Sullivan mumbled into the bliss of Kia's touch.

"They used to count. I used to have real conversations online with some of them. Now Deja does most of my replies. Now Fizz Bang pays me five thousand dollars for every recipe I write that features their soda."

Kia sounded so sad, Sullivan tore herself away from the best feeling she'd had in ages and sat up so that she could look at her.

"That sounds really hard."

"I just want to be me, to be real," Kia said.

"And this is even less real than usual."

"Yeah."

Sullivan wanted to take Kia's hand, but she didn't. Kia had touched her and if she touched her back…that would change something, and Sullivan didn't know what, and she wasn't sure if she wanted it to happen.

"If we pour a can of Fizz Bang soda over the wedding cake, will they give us ten thousand dollars? Because I need a new walk-in freezer."

"After everything I've put you through, wife," Kia said, her smile returning, "I will buy you a whole new kitchen."

"You could afford it, couldn't you?"

"If I wasn't sinking my money into Taste the Love Land, I totally could. But even so, I'll find a way." Kia sounded both deflated and defiant. Before Sullivan could find something sympathetic to say, Kia said, "I got it. We'll do an engagement scene. I'll surprise you by asking you to marry me. Then we'll kind of skip over the whole getting married part. And find a different occasion to make a Pop Rocks piñata cake."

She winked at Sullivan, a gesture so cheeky and cute, Sullivan could have kissed her.

"Then if your family sees it or your customers, you can tell them we were never serious." Did a shadow flit across Kia's smiling face? "Tell them we went out for a hot second, and it wasn't for real, but you got tons of free press for Mirepoix. And I—" Kia shrugged.

"Just did it for the engagement?"

"Ha!" Kia slapped the table.

"What?"

"Your family's got nothing on you."

It took Sullivan a second to catch on. Then she laughed and pretended to polish her nails on the shoulder of her jacket.

"I'm pretty good, aren't I?"

"Alice Sullivan, you are very good. That's why I married you."

"I suppose," Sullivan said slowly. "We should have some rules about…you know. Consent-type stuff. I'm okay with holding hands, arm around your shoulders, kiss on the hand."

"You really are old-fashioned." Kia gestured toward the tweed sports coat Sullivan had put on when they left for the restaurant.

Sullivan closed in on herself, like she wanted to hide the jacket or defend it.

"Come on, Chef. Your fashion is dope as fuck. It always has been."

Sullivan relaxed and went on. "I guess we probably want…no lips unless the whole room is shouting, *Kiss, kiss.*"

"Where are we going to be with a bunch of people shouting, *Kiss*?" Kia asked.

Sullivan could have sworn she sounded more curious than disbelieving, like she would be on the lookout for a room full of people chanting, *Kiss.* Sullivan kind of liked that.

"At a rugby drink-up?" Sullivan ran her hand through her hair, messing up her curls, then stopped, suddenly hyperaware of the nervous gesture.

"And what if we do get bullied by the rugby team that wants us to kiss?" Kia asked, a grin hiding behind her faux-serious expression.

"If a whole rugby team tells us to kiss, I guess we should probably kiss."

chapter 17

Kia and Sullivan decided on a mélange of activities for their first social media shoot. They'd invite friends to the Tennis Skort, where they'd challenge each other to a cooking competition. That would be social media gold. At the end, Kia would whip out one more dish—her signature dessert—and on top would be a ring. The ensuing engagement speech and congratulations would fuel her socials for a week.

Actually, Kia was looking forward to creating some unsponsored content. She was *not* going to propose to the woman she'd had a crush on since she was twenty (even if it was a fake proposal) with a can of Fizz Bang in one hand and the ring stuck in a Pronto Pup.

Sullivan had asked Opal to *just happen* to bring the She-Pack to the Tennis Skort, and, all the way from Paris, Kia's cousin's girlfriend had rallied her burlesque troupe. They would also coincidentally be there. Mixing with the rugby team and the burlesque troupe would look fantastic on Kia's diverse, colorful, fun-loving socials.

Now they were sitting in a booth at the Tennis Skort, which gave a serious I-met-my-wife-playing-softball vibe, and waiting for

Sullivan's friends to show up. Naturally, Opal and Nina would be there. Sullivan and her besties didn't do *everything* together, but they were tight. It was sweet. Kia hadn't see that side of Sullivan in school. She socialized with everyone in the program and dated several of the guys, but she didn't seem like the kind of person who'd have bestie ride-or-dies from childhood. It was nice getting to know her better. She liked the real Sullivan even more than the version of Sullivan she'd idolized in school.

The server checked on their drinks—Megan Rapinoes with Bombay Sapphire gin—and they ordered a second round. Sullivan looked like she needed it. She kept looking around and wincing when anyone pulled out their phone for a picture. Next to their table, a trio of women took a dozen selfies and laughed at the outtakes.

"We should probably…?" Kia asked tentatively.

"I guess that's what we're here for." Sullivan's whole body sighed.

Kia leaned toward Sullivan, trying not to sniff Sullivan's freshly washed hair. She had no right to think about how good Sullivan smelled or how wonderful it would be to snuggle under Sullivan's arm, to lean against her, to feel the curves hidden beneath her masculine clothing.

She took a quick selfie and started typing the caption.

"Aren't you going to take a thousand more to make sure I'm smiling right?"

"You always smile right."

Kia kept typing. Sullivan looked over her shoulder.

"You don't care that my mouth is open and I'm not wearing lipstick?"

"You never wear makeup."

"But I look washed out in the picture."

"Do you want to borrow a lipstick? We can redo the photo."

Sullivan's sudden insecurity made Kia want to hug her. Where had that come from? Why did gloating, boastful, irresistibly charming Alice Sullivan disappear when the camera came out?

"No," Sullivan said cautiously. "I don't care, but I'm not photogenic. I thought you'd want to get a better picture."

Sullivan was so photogenic Kia's phone was swooning.

"You look like one of those hot, queer influencers who make a million dollars wearing jeans."

Kia felt herself blush. She'd just called Sullivan hot. Again. She might as well run with it. She captioned the photo, *Kickin' it with my boo. Damn, you're fire, girl! And you make me so happy. Here's to the best chef I've ever met*. She added some emojis and showed it to Sullivan.

"The best chef." A smile spread across Sullivan's face. "You finally admitted it."

"The best chef I've *met*." Kia elbowed her. "I didn't *meet* myself."

"Little brat," Sullivan said under her breath.

The way Sullivan said it—with grudging admiration and a hint of affection—made Kia feel more special than a million likes from her fans.

A cheer went up as someone scored something on a TV mounted above the bar. Kia spotted Nina striding through the door, looking out of place in her suit. Opal followed wearing a rugby jersey and looking like she'd been born in a sports bar. A pack of women in similar striped shirts followed her, splitting off in fours and fives to move tables together and get beers.

"That's Opal's rugby team. They just finished a match," Sullivan said.

The smell of sweat and mud confirmed that.

A moment later, Nina and Opal took the seats Sullivan had saved for them.

"This is lovely." Nina's tone said it was not.

"She doesn't understand sports," Opal said. "I have tried to explain them to her."

"*All* of them." Nina cast Opal a baleful look.

"Hello, Kia," Opal said, her ready-to-smile face held in a neutral expression.

If she could just get Opal and Nina to like her. Hadn't Sullivan grumbled something about Opal trying to set her up? If Opal liked Kia, she might decide Sullivan should date Kia. Why not? Didn't every chill, über-cool masc woman need a peppy femme on her arm? What if they had fun tonight and went home tipsy enough to relax but not tipsy enough to blur any lines of consent? What if Sullivan said, *It's been too long, and I need you, Kia*? The what-ifs were going to her head faster than the gin Megan Rapinoes.

"I read the article you wrote for *Portland* magazine about health trends in soul food," Kia said. "You were so on point."

Opal really had been.

"You said there's been this resurgence in chitlins," Kia said. "Do you think we can sell white people on intestines?"

Opal didn't get to answer, because a cohort of top hats, boas, and rainbow-striped suspenders had come in like confetti blown in on a breeze.

"My cousin's girlfriend's burlesque troupe. Okay, it's showtime," Kia whispered to Sullivan.

"Listen up, everyone!" Deja, dressed in a purple LET'S GET GOURMAZING T-shirt and orange bustle skirt, had hopped onto a chair. "I want to make a toast to two of my dearest friends. The amazing Kia Gourmazing and the James Beard Award–winning Chef Alice Sullivan from Mirepoix."

"You won a Beard award?" That was huge. How had Kia not seen that online?

Sullivan shrugged as if it were nothing, and Kia swatted her arm gently.

"There they are!" Deja pointed to Kia and Sullivan.

A dozen cell phones pointed toward their booth. Kia felt Sullivan stiffen again. They were pretending to be in love. It made sense to take Sullivan's hand. *It'll be okay.* She expected Sullivan to flinch when she touched her, but Sullivan squeezed her hand back.

"These two have the best love story." Deja described an unrequited love going back to the first day they met at school. She alluded to circumstances that tore them apart which seemed like an extreme way to say they got jobs in different countries. "When I saw them together again... Deja put a hand over her heart. "The way Chef Sullivan melts when she sees Kia and how Kia looks at her like she's been dreaming about Sullivan every night for all those lonely years..."

Sullivan grinned at Kia.

"Really?" she whispered.

Yes. Really.

"Shut up." Kia swatted at Sullivan again.

Deja went on. The crowd loved it.

"Did you tell her about the real us?" Sullivan asked quietly.

"Not yet. I feel bad," Kia whispered to Sullivan. "I can't tell her the truth. She's so..."

"Talkative?" Sullivan said without taking her eyes off Deja.

"Yeah. I'm not sure she wouldn't say, *Even though they think the marriage is fake, I know they're secretly in love with each other.*"

Kia glanced at Sullivan's handsome profile.

I was in love with you, she said in her mind. It was hyperbole. She hadn't been *in love* with Sullivan, but all those years of infatuation, respect, lust, and the fiery need to beat Sullivan at everything...that added up to something love adjacent. But their story wasn't anything like Deja might imagine. Despite the raucous crowd and the pleasure of Sullivan sitting next to her, their story was sad. It was a story of unrequited...something and missed opportunities.

"Kia?" Sullivan asked as if sensing the turn of Kia's mood.

"Deja will feel like a fool when she finds out," Kia said. "We're not super close, but she's a great assistant. I'm an asshole."

"With all this lawsuit bullshit," Sullivan said quietly, "she's safer if she doesn't know. What if Mega Eats said she was an accomplice? You look out for people. That's what Taste the Love is about, right? Looking after people?"

How could Sullivan know this was just what she wanted to hear from her? This is what Kia had desperately wanted Sullivan to see when they argued in the woods. *I'm not Mega Eats.* Sullivan released Kia's hand and put her arm around her, pulling Kia a fraction of an inch closer. Their bodies touched. Kia wanted to melt into Sullivan.

"Thank you," she said quietly.

"Now," Sullivan said, "are we ready to do our thing?"

Kia stood up, pulling Sullivan with her.

"Thank you, Deja." Kia waited for the crowd to turn to her. "In honor of our time at school, I've invited Chef Sullivan to a cooking competition. Right here. Do you want to settle this OG style?" Kia put on a thousand-watt smile. "You. Me. Half an hour. Five ingredients that the audience chooses. Or are you afraid of all that ketchup and no sustainable pepper?"

Kia planted a light kiss on Sullivan's cheek to soften the question.

The noise of the bar faded. She'd kissed Sullivan. It was just a kiss on the cheek, but *her* lips had touched *Sullivan's* face. The sensation of Sullivan's soft skin lingered on her lips. Kia tried to face the crowd, but she couldn't tear her eyes off Sullivan, searching for the micro-expression that would tell her if Sullivan minded.

Sullivan looked at her, one eyebrow raised. For a moment, Kia's whole world was Sullivan's blue eyes. Then Sullivan put her arm around Kia and kissed Kia's forehead.

"You're on. *Babe*."

Sullivan had forgotten—and in another way she could never forget—the way the air in the kitchen changed when she and Kia concentrated. Sullivan barely noticed Deja dancing around taking video. The noises of prep and line cooks still making orders for the bar faded. It had been like that at school. Only Kia was real. She was the only one to beat. And how the fuck was Sullivan going to beat Kia when most of her ingredients came from a deconstructed Bloody Mary?

"Is that a sauce or a soup? I can't tell," Kia teased.

Sullivan glanced up.

"Eyes on your own plate, Jackson."

The words *I missed you* almost left Sullivan's mouth. Then she lost herself in her cooking. She didn't realize she'd been talking to the onions she was chopping until Kia called out, "Are the onions giving you shit, Chef? I'll kick their ass for you."

The onions had made Sullivan tear up, and she wiped away a tear with the sleeve of her shirt.

"I am dominating these onions." Sullivan chopped defiantly. To the onions, she said, "Don't think I can't cry through a hundred more of you."

"You tell 'em, Chef." Kia blew her a kiss.

It had always made her feel special when Kia teased her. Kia had never teased anyone else in school. Sullivan had once asked her why. Kia had answered without hesitation. *Because I like you best.*

Half an hour later, they stood at either end of the bar. Their presentations were immaculate. Sullivan's tiny cups of Bloody Mary gazpacho lined up in front of her. Kia's stuffed Bloody Mary chicken wings standing at attention.

The bartender picked judges from the audience.

A server who'd been filming them in the kitchen bit into Kia's chicken.

"It's so good!"

Five judges tasted the food. Two picked Kia. Two picked Sullivan. One claimed there was no way they could choose.

"Who's going to break the tie?" the bartender asked.

Half the audience volunteered.

"Kia can judge," Sullivan said. "Babe, come over here and taste real food."

The crowd gave a collective "Ooh."

"Kia can't be a fair judge," someone called out.

"She can when she tastes my sensuous gazpacho," Sullivan said.

They had had so much fun in school. Why had Sullivan walked away from that?

"You're going down." Kia drew out the word *down*.

A bar full of U-Haul lesbians got the double entendre. Kia shrugged. The crowd parted to let Kia stroll toward Sullivan.

"Just try my gazpacho, babe." Sullivan pushed the last cup toward her.

The crowd pressed them together. Someone knocked into Kia. Instinctively Sullivan put a hand on Kia's back to steady her. But the crowd jostled them, and her hand landed on the curve of Kia's ass. Soft and firm. Sullivan's mind stalled like it did when she read a long list of measurements, the letters and numbers knocking up against each other until *12 t* became *21 T*. A vision of Kia naked in her bed filled Sullivan's mind, the softness of Kia's body in repose, light brown skin against white sheets, legs sprawled open. She snatched her hand away.

"I'm sorry," she choked out before she remembered they were in love.

"Babe, you can grab my ass any time you like." Kia smirked at Sullivan and made a grabbing motion.

"I did not *grab*—"

"Whatever. I don't mind. You can do it again."

Sullivan blushed so hard she felt like her cheeks might catch on fire like an ill-fated bananas Foster. Kia bumped her hip against Sullivan's.

"Don't dish it if you can't take it." In a softer voice, Kia added, "This is fun. I really am happy to be here with you."

Had her full lips always been a little higher on one side, making her look mischievous?

The sounds around them had once again faded away until Kia projected over the crowd, "Now I will decide the winner." Kia made a ridiculous show of licking her lips as she tasted Sullivan's gazpacho. "I'm afraid to say, Sullivan's got it. Nice job, Chef."

"You're going to let me win?"

"No."

Just like in school. They always knew whose dish was best. And despite all the smack talk, they were too good to each other not to admit it.

The crowd cheered.

"But you only won that round," Kia said, half to Sullivan and half to the crowd.

Deja kept her camera on them.

"What? Another round?" Sullivan sounded like a kid acting in their first play, but the crowd's gasps said they believed the whole act.

"Yes," Kia said. "I have another dish I want you to taste."

Another "oooh" from the crowd. The bartender brought over a plate Kia had prepared in Sullivan's kitchen. Her signature pear Rice Krispies treat, a ring planted prominently on top.

"This is my favorite dish in the world and the very best thing I can give you. And you are my favorite person in the world."

She took the small plate in both hands and gracefully lowered herself to one knee.

Someone in the crowd squealed, "It's a ring!"

"Chef Alice Sullivan, will you marry me?"

It was surprisingly hard to extricate a ring from a Rice Krispies treat, but Sullivan managed.

"Did she say yes?" someone whispered.

"Yes!" Sullivan projected over the crowd. She helped Kia up.

Kia hadn't shown her the ring. She'd said it was a surprise. It was surprising. The ring screamed, *I bought this at gay pride in Vegas.* It was a large, emerald-green crystal set in a circle of smaller, rainbow crystals. It looked like you'd need an oven mitt to handle it.

From across the room, one of Opal's rugby mates, called out, "Kiss, kiss."

"I guess we covered this in our rules," Sullivan said quietly. "If we get bullied by a rugger…I get to kiss you?" She left it a question in case Kia wanted an out.

"I always follow the rules, Chef." Kia put her arms around Sullivan's neck, looking up at her. "I'm a very rule-following person."

Cooking a tursnicken at the Jean Paul Molineux School of

Culinary Arts. Trudging through a stormy forest to ask a woman to marry her to thwart a multibillion-dollar company.

"You so aren't, and I love that about you," Sullivan said. "But maybe this time you should follow them."

In that moment, Kia exuded an irresistible allure that captivated Sullivan completely. The subtle, enticing scent of her perfume wafted through the air, the soft shadows on Kia's face, accentuating the delicate contours, her eyes sparkling with an intoxicating blend of intelligence, humor, and passion. Her smile was like a secret invitation, and Sullivan felt her heart skip a beat as she moved closer. And it hit Sullivan like a match to sweet liquor: She wanted Kia. She wasn't just attracted to Kia. She wanted to hold her, touch her, comfort her, talk to her, laugh with her. Suddenly it felt like she'd always been…infatuated? Enchanted? Just a little bit in love with Kia Jackson? If she rolled all the passion she'd felt for her hookups, her dates, and for Aubrey, she'd been picking up crumbs at the bottom of a bowl compared to the intensity she'd felt for Kia.

Kia pulled back just enough to cup Sullivan's cheek. She met Sullivan's eyes, but she seemed to be looking beyond Sullivan at some future they might or might not have together. She stroked Sullivan's jaw with her thumb. Sullivan was vaguely aware of the crowd going wild with enthusiasm. Kia didn't seem to notice them.

"Kiss me, Chef?" Kia asked, and her expression was so earnest it brought tears to Sullivan's eyes. To hide them and because she desperately wanted to…she kissed Kia Jackson again.

Sullivan touched her lips to Kia's in a light but lingering kiss. Kia's lips were soft. Her hands curled in Sullivan's hair the way they had all those years ago on the graduation stage. Sullivan wanted to run her hands through Kia's hair too, but a little voice in the back of her mind told her not to mess up such a remarkably symmetrical hairdo. Instead she placed her hands around Kia's waist, pulling her closer. She let their hip bones touch. She rested her hands on Kia's lower back. If she'd sensed the slightest resistance on Kia's part, she would have broken the kiss instantly, but Kia let out a soft moan of pleasure that filled Sullivan's body with the colorful, bursting feeling of spring.

Still, when they pulled away, Sullivan whispered, "Was that okay?"

"Only if you say it was point six percent better than any kiss you've ever had," Kia said, turning to capture Sullivan's lips for one more second.

"Yes, Jackson," Sullivan murmured. "It was more than point six percent better."

chapter 18

The small stained glass window in the center of Sullivan's front door glowed from the foyer light within, her concession to seeing the front steps without adding another light bulb to the city's light pollution. She held the door for Kia. After living in the house like a ghost—not even a toothbrush in the bathroom—Kia had started to leave a few things around: AirPods on the kitchen island, a sweet-smelling hair cream in the bathroom. It was hard to remember that this fun wouldn't last and that a lawsuit was hanging over their heads.

Sullivan should go to bed with a quick good night.

"You want a glass of wine?" she asked instead. "Red or white?"

"Got anything pink in a can?"

Sullivan glanced over her shoulder. Kia grinned. She was cute.

"Ugh. I'll Grubhub you some."

"I'll have red."

Sullivan poured two glasses and picked up the bottle. She gestured to the living room. She opened the slider to the porch, letting in the cool night air.

"This will be wasted on you," Sullivan said as they sat at opposite sides of a love seat.

They should have sat on the sofa. But they sat down at the same time, as if they always sat a few feet apart on the comfortable furniture, Kia with her feet tucked under her, Sullivan with one arm draped over the back of the sofa.

Kia dabbed her lipstick on the back of her hand before swirling the wine and taking a sip.

"Bordeaux. Late 2010s. You should have kept it another five years. It's too young." Kia reached for the bottle Sullivan had set on the coffee table. "Château Cazauviel 2017. I'm right."

"Lucky guess."

"I know my wines, Chef. *I* can still cook pâté en croûte. Even if *you* haven't learned how to deep-fry a tursnicken."

"I will never cook tursnicken," Sullivan said. "But I do like the idea that Chef Guillaume's best student is churning out turducken knockoffs. You should drop into the alumni newsletter with that. Serve him right for all that *You will never be a true chef until you've cooked at Restaurant Mirazur.*"

Kia laughed. "I was his favorite."

"I will not admit that you were the best."

"You don't need to," Kia said in a teasing, singsong voice. "I know."

Sullivan swatted the air in Kia's direction. "Brat."

They sipped their wine. A comfortable silence gathered around them. Finally, Kia pulled a mustard-yellow scarf out of a pocket in her hoodie and wrapped her hair up as if getting down to business.

"Want to look at the pictures Deja took? See what you want me to post?"

A sip of wine burned the back of Sullivan's throat. Kia was right. It was too young.

"Can you just not tell me anything about them?"

They'd had fun at the Tennis Skort. She didn't want to see it curated for social media, her real memories filtered, emphasized, or erased for someone else.

Aubrey's posts cascaded through Sullivan's mind.

"Sullivan?" Kia placed her open hand in the space between them. "Why do you hate social media?"

"Fake news. FOMO. The servers have a huge environmental impact even if the companies say they're using sustainable energy."

"The day we got married, Opal pulled me aside and suggested that if I put you on social media, she'd kill me."

"Opal would never say that."

"She didn't *say* it. Opal didn't tell me what happened. She just said you had a bad experience."

Sullivan should brush it off. *Bad experience. No big deal.* The memory of Kia's fingertips lingered on her face, and her body was a longing, lonely creature that didn't know anything about the legacy clause and just wanted to feel Kia touch her again. She wanted to hear Kia tell her she was perfect exactly as she was.

"I was with a woman, Aubrey. She was the first woman I'd dated seriously. It was all new, and it was…great. She liked all the same things I did. She loved backpacking, and she worked for Blue Sky Clean Air, an environmental nonprofit. And she loved social media. At first, we'd go hiking out of cell service, and when we got back to the car, she'd post a hundred pictures.

"Then one day we were camping. We always brought a few of those survivalist food packs. We didn't eat them. They were just for emergencies. But I made one to see if it was any good. It was so bad, it was funny. We took videos of each other's reaction as we tasted it. She's so animated. Her smile was the best. When she smiled at me…but this time, she made the video look like I'd served it to her for real. She pretended to like it, and then when I turned around she made this *great* face. Have you ever seen someone taste Malört for the first time?"

Kia chuckled. "Yeah. It's terrible."

"It was like that, and the video was funny, and we both cracked up about it. And it went low-key viral. She loved that. So she kept making these videos. They started out sweet. Just things we did that she thought were cute and funny. Our handle was Love Sullivan n Aubs."

Sullivan stroked the velveteen surface of a throw pillow Aubrey had bought to add color to living room scenes. So many times she'd longed for real affection, only to find Aubrey holding a camera to capture their kisses.

"At first, I was flattered. She posted nice stuff about us. But then everything became about her social media. We had to redo everything because I didn't stand right or look happy enough. Or I had to change clothes because my sweatshirt wasn't on-brand. It felt like everything I did was wrong. I lost my confidence. I'd *never* lost my confidence before that."

"Not even by point six percent?"

Sullivan's hand rested on the back of the sofa, and Kia covered it gently with her own, as if to let Sullivan know that her teasing was just a way of saying she cared. She was saying, *I can tease you because you're strong, because you're still you.* Kia's skin was warm, and Sullivan felt that warmth suffuse her body, like Kia could keep her safe. Sullivan turned her hand over so she was holding Kia's. She half expected Kia to pull away, but instead Kia stroked Sullivan's wrist with her thumb, looking at her tenderly.

"No. Not even when a ridiculously talented prodigy beat me by point six percent."

"Good." Kia squeezed Sullivan's hand. "What happened then?"

"Aubrey quit her job to become an influencer. She wasn't making a lot of money, but the restaurant supported us fine. That wasn't the problem. The thing was her channels became everything to her. We stopped having sex. Why do it since we weren't putting it online? All I wanted was for her to kiss me or touch me or give me a compliment or a present that wasn't for her reels."

Tears suddenly threatened Sullivan's eyes.

"Oh, Sullivan." Kia's expression was soft with kindness.

"It ended when I had a celebration of my grandfather's life. I like to do it once a year. Some friends of his come over. Miss Brenda makes his favorite biscuits. We say a few words about him, read from his botanical journals. He wrote the most beautiful things about the forest. He was really important to me. *Is* really important to me. I was feeling sadder than usual. I don't know why. I told her I needed her present with me. No phone. No videos. No social media. I did not want to be Love Sullivan n Aubs."

"And she put it online," Kia said with an infinite gentleness.

"Yep. She said sadness was trending. Other influencer couples had posted crying videos and they'd gone viral. I didn't find out until Nina saw it. She knew I'd told Aubrey not to film. And the comments people had posted were actually really sweet. A lot of people who'd known my grandpa commented. It'd almost have been okay, except when I told Aubrey I'd seen it, she had all these bullshit excuses. She hadn't asked me to change anything about the day. I should have noticed her filming at the ceremony. Why did I care that she was filming; I never looked at our feed anyway? This was her dream, and I just treated it like some annoying hobby. We fought that night. I hate fighting. Finally, I asked her if social media disappeared, and there was no Love Sullivan n Aubs, would she want to be with me. She said it was a stupid question because social media wasn't going away."

"Did she say she loved you?"

"Not that night. She said it when she realized I was breaking up with her the next morning; she said it over and over. I almost took her back. I was just about to. Then she said, *What happens with Love Sullivan n Aubs if we break up?* She was more upset about losing her influencer status than she was about losing me."

Kia's arms were around her before Sullivan had drawn another breath.

"I will dox her until she leaves the country."

"Don't get yourself arrested. She's not worth it."

Kia leaned in and caressed the back of Sullivan's head where the barber shaped her hair into a short undercut. It was an intimate touch, the kind of touch Sullivan would never expect—or want—from Opal or Nina. Sullivan felt a wash of pleasure and release. Her shoulders loosened. Kia squeezed her closer.

"Alice Sullivan, you are so easy to love."

It felt like Kia was trying to press the words into Sullivan's heart with her embrace, like she wanted to hold Sullivan and the sentiment in her hands until they melted together and Sullivan believed her entirely.

Then Kia froze as if she'd realized she'd crossed a line. She pulled away. Sullivan wanted to pull her back. *Say it again. Hold me.*

"I get why you don't like social media," Kia said with a nervous cough.

"I'm sorry. I know it's your job."

"Exactly. I do it for a living, not to make myself feel important. My relationships are real. I don't love people for show."

"I wonder, sometimes, if Aubrey and I would have lived happily ever after if there wasn't social media. I think we really clicked before the whole influencer thing. When she's being real, she's amazing."

Did a flash of jealousy cross Kia's face? No. That must be

Sullivan's imagination because...did she want Kia to be jealous? Just a little bit?

"Now Opal is trying to set me up with every single person she knows."

"You're *my* wife."

"Are you jealous?"

"Of course I'm jealous." Kia turned away haughtily, then turned back to Sullivan and grinned. "But I already cuffed you, so I don't have to be." Kia winced dramatically. "I didn't cuff you very romantically. No one is giving me prizes for wooing women, but...I do succeed at everything I try."

She settled back into the love seat. The distance between them felt shorter. Everything Aubrey had done felt farther away. Kia's words and her touch pushed Aubrey down in the algorithm of Sullivan's memories. Kia poured some more wine in their glasses, even though they'd only taken a few sips. The gesture seemed to say, *Let's stay awhile.* They chatted about the Tennis Skort and about Opal and Nina. Kia told stories about her father's spaniels, and they compared preferences: lemon or lime, notepad or Post-its, summer solstice or first snow. Eventually it was time for bed. Kia lingered, perched on the arm of the love seat after they'd ostensibly gotten up.

"Sullivan? Tonight when we kissed, did you...I mean...you didn't...You kissed me because you had to, right?"

"I didn't have to. I'm not that afraid of ruggers. But you're lovely to kiss, and it is part of our plan."

Had Kia wanted their kiss to be real? Had she felt the same thrill of desire and recognition Sullivan had? *Has it always been you?* Sullivan stared at Kia. Sullivan had half a second to make the most emotionally fraught decision of her life. She could say, *I think I feel something for you.* That would probably lead to Sullivan's bed and a glorious, ill-advised night and then emotional upheaval on par with an earthquake. Or Sullivan could stick to what she'd said. *It's part of our plan*. Her body longed for Option One. Her heart liked it too. Her brain was an overtaxed parent trying to corral two bad children.

And the moment passed.

"I…I think we should go along with the plan."

"Absolutely," Kia said. Sullivan felt like she was watching a door closing. "We won't kiss again unless we're bullied by ruggers." Kia's laugh was the live equivalent of an emoji. The meaning was clear, but there was no heart in it. Then with a singsong "good night," Kia disappeared upstairs.

Kia was sending the message *that won't happen again.* That was as it should be, even if it didn't feel right.

"You forgot the sage?" Opal asked as Sullivan dug through drifts of rosemary and oregano on the Mirepoix counter.

Sullivan knew she was off her game. The herbs should be chopped by now. They should never be in this messy pile.

"I woke up late."

More like she hadn't slept all night.

"Do tell." Opal had been waiting for an opening.

"I had insomnia."

"Thinking about Kia?" Opal asked, checking to make sure Blake was out of the kitchen (probably texting his dog). "I've seen you kiss randos at the bar, and it wasn't like that."

"She's not a rando."

"I know," Opal said, as though she'd just caught Sullivan in a trap. "She's your wife."

"Nothing happened…besides what happened at the Tennis Skort."

"Did you want it to?" Opal started stemming rosemary, keeping her eyes on Sullivan.

"Shouldn't you be taking the bread out?"

Opal sniffed the air.

"No, and I will let it burn if it means you spill the tea. Talk to me about Kia, because I know she's the reason you had insomnia."

Sullivan leaned her butt against the counter in violation of health code. She sighed.

"I cannot—not, not, not—think about Kia that way."

"Why not?"

"She's going to tear down the Bois, and the first tree that goes down is going to make me hate her. I can't pretend that's not coming and kiss her now."

"What if you didn't hate her?"

"I will because she could stop." That was the knife's edge of truth behind everything. "She could find another property."

"But Mega Eats would buy the land."

"It's like she has to destroy everything I love to protect me, and doing that is going to get her everything she wants. It's like some fucking Greek tragedy where every option is bad."

"Oh, hon." Opal put her arms around Sullivan, carefully holding her gloved hands away from Sullivan's back. "It's going to be okay."

"In a cosmic, cycle-of-life way. Not in a real-life way."

Blake came through the back door.

"I wasn't texting. I made a real call just like you guys did in the fifties."

"He thinks we were alive in the fifties." Opal shook her head. "Chef, go home and get some sage. I'll school this young'un."

chapter 19

Kia spent the morning after kissing Sullivan trying to focus on her menu and supply order and failing to pay attention to anything except her memories of Sullivan's kiss. She had felt passion in Sullivan's kiss. She had seen desire and affection in Sullivan's eyes, but Sullivan didn't want that even if she felt it.

By ten a.m., Kia had wasted four hours pretending to calculate costs and answer DMs at Sullivan's kitchen island. She straightened. Her shoulders were stiff. Her hands were stiff. She slid off the stool. She should do a live stream. There were a dozen filters that would make her look fresh and relaxed.

"Fuck it." She shoved her phone in her back pocket.

It must be nice to be Sullivan and do everything by hand or by mind. No social media. No pictures on the Mirepoix website. She wasn't just a legacy owner; she was a slice of life before smartphones.

And Sullivan was at work. She wouldn't be back until after midnight. Kia went upstairs and retrieved her old digital camera from a duffel bag under the bed. She checked the memory card. Still room for about a hundred photos. There'd been a time before cloud storage when you had to choose which photos to keep. You had to know what mattered. Her father rhapsodized about that time almost as much as he rhapsodized about the serendipity of life.

She wandered back downstairs and took several pictures of Sullivan's kitchen, trying to capture the details that made it real. Then she wandered over to the two large nudes hung beside the fireplace. She studied them. Slightly larger than a real person. The paint strokes angular and rough and yet the whole picture was rounded, the rough edges somehow creating a smooth whole. She popped in her earbuds. Sibelius poured into her ears.

Then she set the digital camera on a bookshelf across the room from the paintings and pulled off her Kia Gourmazing T-shirt. She unbuttoned her jeans. Sullivan's hands would be steady and certain as they unbuttoned her jeans, but Kia did *not* get to think about Sullivan's hands, which she would never feel unclasping her bra, never feel smoothing over her breasts or dipping inside—she didn't get to think that way.

She stripped naked, set the timer for thirty-second bursts, and walked in front of the painting. Then she moved the camera and sat in the curve of the love seat, the velveteen fabric caressing her body. She tried not to pose, just to exist without reference to the camera.

Kullervo crescendoed in her earbuds.

Had Sullivan walked around the house naked before Kia moved in? Had she felt the soft upholstery against her bare thighs? Had a person gone down on her as she gripped the arm of the love seat?

Kia had told herself that she didn't care that she and Gretchen only ever had sex a few times a year, and it was always disappointing. Lots of things were disappointing: broken timing belts and rain at a fair. She had been busy working on her art and her brand. But what would it be like to be naked on this couch with Sullivan on top of her, their legs intertwined, the constraints of the sofa teasing them with what they couldn't quite have? What would it be like if—

"Kia!" Sullivan's voice broke through the fifth movement.

Kia's earbuds jumped out of her ears as her brain exploded with *What, why, how?*

"You're supposed to be at work." Kia leapt up, which only made her feel more naked.

"I forgot the sage for the butternut squash risotto." Sullivan wore her chef's coat and clutched a bunch of sage. "And you're supposed to be clothed in the house, although we didn't explicitly say that because…" Sullivan looked around as though she'd seen something more distressing. "Are you with someone?"

"Of course not."

Sullivan stood right next to the chair on which Kia had thrown her inside-out clothing.

"*Why* are you naked in my living room?"

"It's *our* living room, and how could you forget sage in the butternut squash risotto?"

Sullivan stared at Kia's face with the intensity of someone trying not to look down, and then she did, and she blushed a lovely pink, like rose petals on a wedding cake. She glued her eyes to the floor. She shook her head as if to say, *How did I get myself into this?*

"I was taking pictures."

"For Kia Gourmazing?" Sullivan looked up.

"No, for me. So when I'm ninety I can look at how hot I was." *And to remember I was real.*

This time when Sullivan's eyes found Kia's body, they lingered. Did Sullivan want her to feel her gaze like a touch? If they were lovers, Sullivan would touch her there and there and there. She could not be turned on in Sullivan's living room. She should tell Sullivan to look away. She should cover her breasts and pubes with her hands and make a grab at her clothing. But she was already naked, and already turned on, and Sullivan looked more amused than distraught, so Kia pulled her shoulders back to accentuate her breasts and sashayed across the room. Sullivan didn't like her like that, but that didn't mean Kia wasn't hot. She'd eaten enough tursnickens to give her curves she hadn't had when they were in school. What queer woman wouldn't want to look? She brushed past Sullivan and picked up her clothing.

"You've seen naked women before." Kia gave Sullivan an innocent look. "Pretend we're in the locker room."

"I've never changed in a locker room."

Sullivan had never changed in a locker room?

"Even I've changed in a locker room."

"I like exercising outdoors. Locker rooms smell funny, and it's weird that you can't even show your nipples through your shirt, but then you're going to get naked with a bunch of people you don't know."

"Is it better if you know them?"

They were actually having this conversation. With Kia naked and Sullivan clutching sage. Then they were both laughing.

"So you're not sending these selfies to someone?"

"No. And they're on a memory card, not in the cloud." Kia stepped into her pants and tucked her underwear in her pocket. "I love being an influencer. It's fun. I meet great people. And everything I put online is at least half-true. But it's a job, and it means all the pictures I have of myself are half-staged. Except these. I want a way to remember my life without a filter."

Sullivan looked pensive. "I think I get it." She turned around.

"And now I'm going to go, and we're going to pretend this didn't happen. I never saw you. I was never here." She headed for the door.

That was the most intimate moment she'd ever have with Sullivan, naked, talking about locker rooms.

"Hey, Sullivan," Kia called after her. "You could just sub in marjoram."

Sullivan waved a bunch of sage over her shoulder without turning around.

"I have standards, Jackson."

Sullivan was so cute and so untouchable. Kia felt a pang of sadness.

Sullivan stopped before she opened the front door.

"Just for the record," she said with her back to Kia, "your ninety-year-old self will be impressed."

"Blake, wash and chiffonade that sage from Chef Sullivan," Opal said as Sullivan burst through the back door of Mirepoix. To Sullivan she added, "Don't act like Mirepoix was going to fall apart because you left for thirty minutes."

Blake was in the corner, earbuds in, surreptitiously looking at his phone.

"Blake!" Sullivan yelled.

She never yelled in the kitchen. She raised her voice over the sound of cooking, but she didn't yell in frustration. Opal raised an eyebrow. Blake hurried over.

"Sorry, Chef. Sorry. It wasn't for me. It was for Mickey."

"Do not tell me you were updating your pit bull's social media page," Sullivan said. "We need a mountain of Parmigiano-Reggiano grated, garlic minced, and mushrooms sliced."

"Why are you rushing in like there's some kind of situation?" Opal asked.

Sullivan dropped her voice. "She was naked! In my living room taking pictures in front of my Janice Domingos."

"How did she know you'd be coming home?" Opal asked.

"She didn't."

"Oh." Opal sounded disappointed.

Sullivan knew it was good that Kia hadn't stripped in the living room to surprise her. Kia was just doing her weird thing.

"She was taking pictures."

Sullivan needed to marinade the Osceola wild turkey, or it'd be tough, and start fermenting the cabbage. All she could think about was Kia's look of shock at Sullivan's presence, Kia's embarrassment, and then the moment when Kia seemed to think, *Ah fuck it. I'm here now*, and strolled over looking like a goddess. Like the kind of woman one of Sullivan's legacy relatives—a woman maybe—would have fallen in love with and painted and hidden the paintings because the world wouldn't let her love that body. So beautiful. A port-wine stain birthmark on her hip and the requisite chef's scars on her forearms. A spattering of faded tattoos decorated her body like stickers applied by someone who thought it was fun to stick them on but didn't care about the overall effect. A fried egg on her thigh. A rose on her breast. The interlaced women's symbols above her short, dark pubic hair. Her neck and arms were tanned a beautiful, toasted coconut brown, and her belly was almost as pale as Sullivan's. Some worthless AI filter would have erased her birthmark, made her skin a uniform color, lengthened her waist and slimmed her hips. It'd be terrible to erase so much beauty. Kia walked with the grace of a river, and she glowed like sunrise. And Sullivan had wanted to take in every detail.

"Not for her social media?" Opal drew closer, a look of concern crossing her face.

"No. She had an old digital camera. She said she saves the pictures on a memory card. She wants to have something to look back on when she's ninety. Pictures that weren't staged. It was kind of sweet really."

"She gets that that social media stuff is fake," Opal said. "That's way better than Aubrey. I swear she always thought she was *making* her life, not living it."

"Kia is smart as hell. But she can be smart with clothes on."

"Was she pretty?" Opal said conspiratorially.

"No." Sullivan couldn't let the lie stand for a minute. She could see the look of hurt that would cross Kia's face if she heard Sullivan say it. Kia had been brash and young in school. She'd never shown Sullivan the human side, the side that stress cooked and slipped in the rain.

"Yes. Very."

"Was she upset that you saw her?"

"I think she liked messing with me."

"How was she messing with you? She didn't think you'd be home."

"She was…flirting."

"Mmm." Opal's eyebrows raised in interest.

"Not for real. To mess with me."

"And it messed with you?"

"I came home to find my fake wife–roommate naked and posing with my Janice Domingos!" Sullivan hissed.

"Were the Domingos the issue?" Opal said, opening her eyes wide in mock curiosity.

"Yes. No. Obviously not."

"If you saw her, and you're attracted to her, maybe that's a good thing. You get to be attracted to people again. It's good to notice a beautiful woman. It means you're over Aubrey. And if you didn't make her uncomfortable. If you worked it out, and it wasn't too weird, well…"

Sullivan's mind raced to Kia's body and imagined tracing every curve, tattoo, and tan line. Every bone. Every scar. She closed her eyes to push the thought away, but that only brought it into focus.

"I'm not in love with Kia Jackson," Sullivan said.

"Oh." Opal's eyes widened behind her glasses. "In love. I thought we were just talking about her supple, young body."

"She's only six years younger than me."

"And you're in love. Wait till I tell Nina."

"I am not. You should not. I'm just—"

Opal ambled a few steps away. That was as much ambling as the small kitchen allowed. Nonetheless, Sullivan knew her protests would be lost in the sound of searing scallops unless she projected her voice like she did during service. Blake did not need to know her business. Sullivan threw up her hands.

After that, Sullivan poured every ounce of focus into her prep work for the butternut squash risotto, trying to replace the memory of Kia's body with thoughts about seared ahi and arugula. It didn't work.

chapter 20

Saturday morning Kia and Sullivan stood on the sidelines of the She-Pack game. Kia took a selfie. In a few minutes, Georgie would start to deflate in the humidity, but for now, the mist caught in her hair, turning the tips white like a dandelion. She was going to use the selfie as an excuse to put her arm around Sullivan and take another picture, but Sullivan looked exhausted. She hadn't come home until three. Kia had been simmering with curiosity verging on jealousy at the thought that Sullivan might be with someone. Maybe Sullivan needed to blow off steam with a discreet friend with benefits. But when Sullivan came home, Kia had wandered downstairs in her thin, low-cut striped nightgown, pretending to be half asleep and surprised to see Sullivan. Sullivan had explained that she'd had to do extra prep to make time for the She-Pack game in the morning. Then she'd invited Kia, and only on her way up the stairs had Sullivan added, *It'll be good stuff for your socials.*

Now Kia held out her coffee with marshmallow.

"Want some?"

Sullivan took it gratefully. She put her lips on Kia's travel mug. She smiled over the rim. Kia felt like she was going to swoon.

"I will never admit that coffee is good," Sullivan said.

"But you know it is."

Sullivan stared at the field while the players, unexplainably, bunched together and lifted a teammate over their heads so the player could throw the ball.

"Everything you do is good."

Kia wasn't sure she'd heard Sullivan right. Could a person's desire for their crush to like them cause auditory hallucinations?

Sullivan glanced at her. "I don't mind that you're here. Minus the lawsuit and all that. It's nice to have company." Her gesture took in the damp grass and cool, gray sky. "The Tennis Skort was fun. Maybe we should cook together again. People are always asking me to do fundraisers. I don't want to always tap Opal for that stuff."

"I'd love that." Kia's heart glowed, and for a few minutes, passing the coffee back and forth with Sullivan and watching the most inexplicable game known to humankind, Kia felt perfectly happy.

After the game, which the She-Pack lost for reasons Sullivan tried to explain but Kia did not understand, they went to the Tennis Skort. The team piled into the bar, and soon the whole bar was chanting a call-and-response.

Opal started them off. "If I were the marrying kind, and thank the Lord I'm not, sir, the kind of rugger I would be would be a rugby…"

"Flanker, sir!" one player called out.

The team answered, "Flanker, sir, why is that, sir?"

"'Cause I'd get off quick," the player sang out.

The team answered, "And you'd get off quick, we'd all get off quick together. It'll be all right in the middle of the night if we all get off quick together."

Opal conducted them as if they were an orchestra.

"If I were the marrying kind, and thank the Lord I'm not, sir, the kind of rugger I would be would be a rugby…" She pointed to Sullivan, who blurted out, "Wing, sir."

The team answered, "Wing, sir, why is that, sir?"

Sullivan said, "I'd spread it wide." And immediately blushed.

The team answered, "And you'd spread it wide, we'd all spread it wide together. It'll be all right in the middle of the night if we all spread it wide together."

Kia and the rest of the bar patrons were bent over in stitches.

Sullivan finished her verse and shrugged.

"When in Rome…" she said.

"Do I get a verse?"

"Absolutely. You could be a fan from far away."

"And I'd…?"

"Come for hours or eat out. There're options."

Sullivan shot her a teasing grin, and a realization slammed Kia like a rugger. *I love her.* She'd thought those words on the graduation stage, but that had just been a metaphor for the overflowing excitement she'd felt. The words *I love you* felt solid now, a statement, not a question. But she couldn't be in love…with the way Sullivan grinned, the way she talked to her cooking, the way she had been kind to Kia every day of their marriage when she could have made Kia's life miserable. Love would make everything so, so, so much harder. *Am I really in love?* She stared at Sullivan.

Sullivan, missing Kia's existential crisis, looked over her shoulder to see what Kia might be looking at. Nina had just walked in the door, and Sullivan waved. Nina hurried over. She didn't look enthusiastic about the song.

"Slight complication." Nina's expression said she was bringing more than a slight complication.

"To our case." Sullivan didn't pose it as a question.

"This can work to our advantage," Nina said, "but I still don't like it."

They waited.

"So I was doing some research," Nina said. "Follow the money. There's a company called Perfect Foods Distribution. I found out that a majority shareholder gave a large amount of money to a PAC." Nina must have read Kia's confusion. "That's an independent-expenditure-only political committee," she added, clearing up nothing.

The part of Kia that wasn't floating away on a tide of renewed panic got stuck on why independent-expenditure-only political committee spelled PAC not IEOPC. But the point was, PACs were set up to gather money for political candidates and causes. This PAC was set up to give money to Judge Harper for his next campaign. And the majority shareholder was Harper's daughter-in-law.

"That's not so weird, is it?" Sullivan asked. "Families give politicians money."

"It's not, except Perfect Foods Distribution is Mega Eats' primary supplier. Judge Harper's daughter-in-law practically owns Mega Eats' biggest business partner, and that big business partner gave a shit-ton of money to Harper. If Harper pisses off Mega Eats, he pisses off their business partner and his daughter-in-law. I know family dysfunction, and I know money."

"Harper is in Mega Eats' pocket?" Kia didn't have to ask.

"Big facts," Nina agreed. "Perfect world: Harper would recuse himself without our even asking. He hasn't. So I'm going to use this to destroy Harper with the Judicial Fitness Committee. His career is over, it's just that I don't know if I can end him before your case. So standard procedure would be to ask for another judge."

Kia didn't like the rawness in Nina's voice. She might be all flash and sass, but she cared about Sullivan. Kia could see it in her eyes. And she was worried.

"Did we get a good judge?" Sullivan asked.

"That's the complication," Nina said. "I asked for a new judge, and the court denied the request. They say the connection between Perfect Foods and Mega Eats is too tangential."

"What do we do?" Sullivan's eyes were wide.

"Don't worry."

"Don't worry?" Sullivan's voice soared with the same panic Kia felt.

"I'm going to keep working on getting a new judge. And you and Kia are going to do more of the same. I want to see you in *love*. We might do bus ads?"

"Bus ads?" Sullivan looked perplexed.

"To advertise Kia's channel, but you just happen to be in the picture, kissing or something."

"I'm kissing Kia on a bus ad so Mega Eats doesn't win a lawsuit?"

"You're right. Not worth the cost. Just get all up in her—" Nina took a sip of Sullivan's drink. "All up in her socials."

To make the moment a little more surreal, Opal had started leading the ruggers in chanting, "What's long and firm and full of sperm? Dick da dick dick."

"Why is a women's rugby team singing about dick?" Nina asked. "Aren't half of them gay?"

"It's a rugby thing," Sullivan said.

Opal waved her arms in front of her muddy choir.

"I don't understand her," Nina said absently.

"But you love her," Sullivan said.

"Yeah." A sweet look crossed Nina's face, quickly replaced by her sharp, professional smile. "And you love Kia. Got it?"

With Nina's warning fresh in their minds, Sullivan and Kia planned their next date. Kia was working a fair, but that was a perfect opportunity to promote Kia Gourmazing and their love story. Sullivan would "surprise" Kia at work. Kia would feed her, and then they'd explore the fair. Kia always hired local chefs to help in her food truck, so it'd be easy for her to get away.

Around nine p.m. on date night, Sullivan was walking across the grass parking area toward the county fair. It was a waste to crush a grass field to make a temporary parking lot. She'd made that point when her grandfather had brought her to the fair as a teenager. In his slow, thoughtful way, he'd said, *That's true.* Then he'd pointed to the roller coaster bedazzling the dark horizon. *But that doesn't make it any less beautiful.* It could have been the same roller coaster swirling across the horizon tonight, the moon hanging high above it like a creamy dinner mint. Everything was complicated. Beautiful things hurt the world and were still beautiful. The thrill of seeing Kia in her element cooking in the Diva kept pushing panic about Judge Harper's conflict of interest to the back of Sullivan's mind. Was this what it was like to be in the right relationship? Even the hard times glittered when you were with your person? Of course, their relationship was a tangled mess of history, feelings, and impending doom.

It was just hard to remember that with carnival music twinkling from invisible speakers. Inside the gates, people meandered between stalls, their faces hidden behind clouds of cotton candy. No one's sticky child was screaming yet.

It wasn't hard to spot Kia's food truck. IRL, the Diva was even flashier than in the *American Fare* article. A life-sized LED screen on the side of the truck showed a GIF of Kia eating stars. Another LED screen flashed the menu. Destiny's Child played from a speaker at the top of the truck. Deja danced to the beats while flipping something on a grill. Sullivan got in line. There was something about watching Kia from afar. Kia took naked pictures to remember her real self, but this was Kia's real life too. She sparkled.

"Love the vibe!" Kia motioned to a customer's jumpsuit and Afro. She noted the next customer's T-shirt. "Metallica, heck yeah!" She made devil horns. She'd praise whatever the customers chose. "Y'all know what the good stuff is!" Then she'd hand out a glittery pink pager, call the customer *my friend*, and move on to the next. Impossibly, she seemed genuinely fond of everyone.

"Hey, baby!" Kia's voice bounced over the sound of music when she spotted Sullivan. "That's my wife." She pointed to Sullivan.

People in line cheered because…no one had ever gotten married before?

"Hey, gorgeous," Sullivan called back.

"Sorry, folks, I gotta see my boo. My crew will take good care of you." She motioned to the other chefs. "Babe, I'm making you a plate. Grab a seat."

Kia had set up a dining space next to her food truck. String lights hung on poles. Signs invited people to give up their seats to people with mobility challenges. Sullivan sat down. A moment later, Kia set a plate in front of her. She'd piled the plate with baked beans, greens, something that might have been beets, fried jalapeños crusted with what looked like Cheetos, a caramelized corn fritter (maybe…it could have been a caramelized anything), and a corn dog. Kia pulled the colorful scarf off her hair. Her hair exploded from its confines. Then she slid into place behind Sullivan, wrapped her arm around Sullivan's chest, and took a selfie. Then Kia sat, shifting in her seat and looking embarrassed.

"Sorry. I should have asked first."

"You have selfie privileges."

"Forever?"

If only.

"Absolutely."

Kia traced a finger along the edge of her plate in a gesture she probably didn't realize was sexy. Then she reached over, took a caramelized something off Sullivan's plate, and popped it into her mouth.

"Damn, I'm good!" Kia said. "Admit it, Sully, I'm the best."

"Sully? I get a nickname now?"

"You are my beloved wife. Of course you get a nickname. Is it okay?"

More than okay.

"I was thinking you'd go for *princess* or *goddess*, but I'll take Sully."

"Eat your corn dog, Princess Sully." Kia held out the corn dog, looking eager.

Kia cared what Sullivan thought. It'd hurt her if Sullivan said she hated it. Sullivan took the corn dog. No matter how much grease coated her mouth, she'd say she loved it. She didn't need to pretend. It was everything a corn dog should be. It was winning every carnival game. It was road trips with your best friend. It was a ride on the Ferris wheel when you were a kid, before you knew the rides were installed by underpaid day laborers.

"Do you like it?"

Sullivan savored the flavor.

"I've been to five-star restaurants that weren't this good."

Kia beamed. "Say it again."

"I will not give you the satisfaction." Sullivan grinned.

Kia held up her phone in one hand and a fork with a slice of fried jalapeño in another.

"Boomerang fork toast for the fans?" She gestured for Sullivan to pick up the other fork.

"I'm not even sure what that means," Sullivan said, but she speared a piece of jalapeño nonetheless.

"Just toast." Kia held the phone out and they tapped their jalapeños together.

Kia checked the video and posted it, speaking the words, "Nothing means as much to me as my wife saying she loves my cooking." She checked the text, touched the screen, and put her phone down.

Sullivan took a bite of greens, savoring the collards, ham hock, vinegar, and spices. She glanced at her hand.

"Shit. We should do that toast over." She held out her wrist to show Kia where a potato had splashed hot water on her and scalded her wrist that morning. "Occupational hazard."

"Baby!" Kia held out her hand for Sullivan's, gently turning it from side to side.

"It's nothing."

In the world of kitchen injuries, this didn't rate a level one. Sullivan wouldn't have thought about the welt distorting the geometric pattern of her tattoo if Kia wasn't filming. The world didn't want to know that even the best chefs' hands were a quilt of scars and burns.

"Wait here," Kia said.

She went back to the Diva and returned a moment later with a glass bottle with a dropper.

"It's THC-infused aloe. I make it. It works great, but I have to dump it every time I go to a state without legal weed. This stuff could literally get you high."

"High-wrist behavior?"

"Oh my god, Sullivan! How can you say your family makes puns and you don't."

Kia laughed, as warm and wide as the sunshine in July. She held out her hand for Sullivan's again.

Sullivan hadn't been aware of the raw heat of the burn until Kia placed a few drops of cool salve on the inside of her wrist and smoothed it in with her fingertips. Her touch was so gentle, tender…loving?

"Is that better?" Kia continued to cradle Sullivan's hand.

Her skin was better. Her heart ached. Sullivan nodded.

"We'd better take the video again without evidence that a Yukon Gold jumped out of my hand to scald me. Evil little thing."

"We don't need to redo it," Kia said. "That's what it's like to be a chef. We have to curate some of what we show the world, but curating doesn't mean hiding what's real."

Sullivan almost said, *Like our marriage?* She didn't, but Kia added, "I know the marriage isn't real, but your restaurant is. The dangers of cooking evil Yukons are real. Tonight is real." She brushed at a drift of hair that had fallen across her forehead. "It's real that I'm happy to be here with you."

Sullivan stroked her thumb across the back of Kia's hand. Kia closed her eyes and sighed.

"I'm happy to be here too."

Sullivan was in so much trouble.

chapter 21

Kia watched Sullivan transfer a slip of spicy honey-garlic aioli onto the back of her spoon and pass the spoon over her tongue. The gesture was just as sexy as it had been in school.

"Now that you've tasted my food, do you question your life choices?" Kia teased.

"Everything about you makes me question my life choices."

That could have been a diss except the way Sullivan said it, the slight roughness in her voice, the way her eyes lingered on Kia's face…

"That was a compliment," Sullivan added through a mouthful of honey-coated fried beet.

"Do I make your life gourmazing?"

Kia sat on her hands to keep from picking up her phone and taking a thousand pictures of the warm fair light caught in Sullivan's hair, like every gold wheat field Kia had driven through at sunset, only more beautiful. She wished she had her digital camera so she could take those pictures where the internet couldn't touch them.

"Yes," Sullivan said. "You make my life *gourmazing*."

The words *for now* hovered between them. Soon Judge Harper would either rule in Mega Eats' favor and ruin Kia and Sullivan or, hopefully, he'd do the right thing and rule against Mega Eats. But then Kia would start work on Taste the Love Land. Sullivan had hinted that she'd leave town while Kia had the land logged. Maybe Sullivan would stay away for the whole development. And Kia had to get back on the road. Her followers missed Kia Gourmazing's travels.

Kia pushed the thoughts away.

Sullivan finished her food. "Want to take some pictures?" she asked like someone who didn't loathe social media.

They got up. Kia took Sullivan's empty plate and plastic fork and dumped it in a trash can. She waited for Sullivan to say something so Kia could defend plastic. Biodegradable forks made out of cornstarch cost ten times as much, and growing corn took energy too. Everything humans did was bad for the environment, but they weren't going to sit on a rock and eat lichen for their whole lives. But Sullivan didn't say anything, and Kia felt a wave of sadness for the waste the fair would leave in its wake.

Her sadness ebbed away as they headed into the crowd of fair-goers. They fell into the kind of conversation that felt silly and meaningful at the same time. What was their favorite toy as a child? Did they ever dream they were naked in public? (No for Sullivan. Yes, cooking naked in the Diva for Kia.)

"Ever dream you're taking naked pictures in the living room when your innocent wife of convenience walks in?" Sullivan rested her hand on Kia's lower back as she said it, the gesture so confident and subtly seductive, Kia knew why every man at the Jean Paul Molineux School of Culinary Arts fell for Sullivan.

"Ever dream that you forget sage when you're making *sage* and butternut squash risotto?"

What were their favorite movies? If they were an animal, what animal would they be and why?

"A dragon," Kia said, skipping ahead to avoid a letter board advertising caramel corn.

"And why?"

Kia spread her arms, walking backward so Sullivan could take her in.

"Because obviously."

She waited for Sullivan to tell her *because obviously* wasn't an answer, but Sullivan just smiled and said, "Fair enough."

"And you?" Kia asked.

"A frog," Sullivan said without hesitation.

"Baby, you're so much sexier than a frog! But truth—" A memory Kia had totally forgotten popped back into her mind. "When I was a kid, I read that frog prince story, and I thought I'd rather have the frog than a boyfriend."

"Look at you all outdoorsy, kissing frogs."

"I wouldn't actually kiss them! That's how you ended up with a prince you didn't want."

"Did you always know you were lesbian?"

"Pretty much. When did you know you were bisexual…or pan?"

"Probably pan, but I grew up with the word *bi*, so that always felt comfortable. And I guess I always knew, although there've been times, like in school, when I was more interested in men. Other times, women."

"And right now?"

The crowd pushed Sullivan and Kia together. Sullivan took Kia's hand.

"Are you fishing for a compliment, Jackson?"

"What compliment am I fishing for?"

"That there's no way I could be married to you and notice anyone else."

Had she been fishing for that sentiment? It would hurt if Sullivan was surreptitiously checking out the people they passed. Kia didn't say anything.

"Because it's true." Sullivan squeezed her hand. "I'm not looking at anyone else."

All the lights at the fair brightened, as if someone had turned on an extra generator.

"Well, I've been desperately in love with you since I was twenty, which totally ruined my dating life, by the way!" Kia spoke the words with maximum drama so Sullivan would think she was kidding.

"Right," Sullivan drawled.

Kia had better cover up the truth with a quip.

"Don't flatter yourself, Chef," Kia added. "My dating life isn't hard to ruin."

They walked on, commenting on the merchandise for sale and the families enjoying the fair. Kia wished she didn't have to stop them every few minutes to take pictures, but the more she took now, the less she had to subject Sullivan to her influencer lifestyle later on.

"So you hire local cooks?" Sullivan asked as they stopped to photograph themselves in front of a donkey in a stall decorated with prize ribbons.

"It's great publicity for them," Kia said. "I highlight their restaurants, and I pay them, of course. If there's a culinary arts student dreaming of having their own food truck, it's a line for their résumé. Cooking with the amazing Kia Gourmazing."

"You help people," Sullivan said.

"You expected me to be a ruthless capitalist?"

Sullivan shrugged. "Nah."

"I want to live my father's values," Kia said as they continued. "He said you should always leave a place as good or better than you found it. The first time was in Arkansas right about the time I really started drawing crowds. It was at a fair. I was making way more money than the local people. But their fry oil was stale. They all sold the same bad elephant ears people had been eating at fairs since forever. So I closed my truck and went around to each of the other chefs and helped them think of one thing they could do to distinguish or improve their food. They didn't love me at first. Young, know-it-all kid busting in on their thing, but they made more money that night than in the last three nights. I realized, this is what I want to do."

"So you started hiring local people?"

"And featuring local restaurants. If there's a food truck that's struggling, I give them some good recipes, show them how to be more efficient. But I've lost that vibe. I only do bigger fairs now. That's what my sponsors want. I'm sick of pushing American Spirit breakfast sausage and Fizz Bang soda." She hadn't realized how adamant she felt until she spoke the words. "That's why I want to start Taste the Love Land." It mattered that Sullivan got it. *Please, see me.* "My cousin's girlfriend has been in Portland for years. She says people are getting priced out of neighborhoods their families lived in for generations. A lot of people of color. Taste the Love Land can be an incubator or a place for people to survive if they've lost their brick-and-mortar."

They'd reached the end of the exhibition hall and stepped out. Beyond a fence made of orange plastic netting, the dusty parking lot stretched into the darkness. A plane crossed the sky, looking large in its proximity. The airport was just a mile away. Sullivan watched its ascent, then closed her eyes to the sky.

"Are we going to get through this lawsuit thing?" Kia asked, although it was hard to imagine a world where things did work out. If they lost the lawsuit, they were fucked on so many levels. And they probably would lose if Judge Harper was on Mega Eats' side. But if they won and Kia built Taste the Love Land, Sullivan would hate her for the rest of their lives. If Sullivan didn't hate her, Sullivan would at least feel terrible about the Bois. That kind of terrible wasn't the foundation for a relationship. "I feel like it's wrong to have fun or relax with Mega Eats at the door."

"Where there's life, there's hope. My grandpa used to say that." Sullivan hesitated for a moment, then added, "He said happy people don't wait until they've got everything they want to be happy. The art of living well is learning that you can be happy and worried at the same time. You can be sad and joyful. You can even be angry and at peace. The best activists are like that. Life doesn't have to be perfect to be wonderful. Let's go do something fun even though we might be fucked."

Kia looked up at the spinning carts on the roller coaster. How many scenes like this had she seen? Hundreds? Tonight it felt special. It was beautiful and bright, as though someone had plucked the stars out of the sky and adorned the roller coaster with their glow.

Sullivan caught her looking, smiled, and then took her hand as easily as if they'd been holding hands forever.

"Come on," Sullivan said. "I have a wonderful ride for a photo op."

The ride, if it could be called that, looked like two mobile homes strung together and painted in shades of pink, with hearts lined with light bulbs, some burnt out, some flashing erratically. A sign above the contraption read THE LOVE TUNNEL.

"When I was a kid, if you really liked someone, you took them to the Love Tunnel," Sullivan said. "If you really, really liked each other, you'd make out."

No one else was in line. Sullivan gave the attendant two tickets.

"Did you ever make out with someone in the Love Tunnel?" Kia asked when they were settled in their seats.

"Brian Cotswell. Sixth grade. My true love." The cart rattled and began moving slowly toward an arch of pink lights.

The cart rumbled past a scene painted on plywood. Silhouettes of a man and woman stood near a lake. Hidden lights above the scene faded from bright daylight to twilight to night, and stars twinkled in the plywood.

"And then there was Daisy…I can't remember her last name," Sullivan went on. "She broke my heart as much as someone can when you're fourteen and don't know their last name."

Sullivan rested her hand on Kia's knee. The lights dimmed.

"This is the part where I kissed Brian Cotswell."

"Does that mean these exact same rides have been going around since you were in sixth grade, and we should be worried?"

"Every summer. A few nights and then they're gone. Like you," Sullivan added pensively.

"But I'll come back. Lillian and Izzy will move back to Portland eventually. Taste the Love will be my home base."

"It'll be a business that you visit. It's not the same thing as home," Sullivan said gently.

What if I stayed? The thought appeared in Kia's mind like a package at one of the FedEx stores she used as a traveling mailbox.

"Would you like to…kiss?" Sullivan touched Kia's cheek. Kia covered Sullivan's hand and held it in place. The neon lights in the tunnel turned Sullivan's curls a chestnut pink. "In honor of my thirteen-year-old self who thought this was the most romantic place to kiss?"

"Yes," Kia breathed.

Sullivan's kiss was as gentle as sunlight and cotton candy. But she had a storm chaser's confidence, tempered with a strength that didn't need a storm to feel alive. Kia melted like sugar into caramel. She closed her eyes. Sullivan was kissing her the way Sullivan did everything. Like the way she rolled up her cuffs, the way she stretched her shoulders, or tasted a sauce, like she was completely alive in her body. Kia melted and glowed and throbbed. Sullivan's lips parted. Their tongues touched. Sullivan moaned softly. It was everything, and Kia had never needed *more* so badly.

Then Sullivan pulled away and handed Kia her phone. Kia didn't realize Sullivan had been holding it. The screen was open to a picture.

"Are you proud of me?" Sullivan said, pulling away. "This is the first picture I've taken for your followers."

In the picture, Sullivan leaned in for a kiss. Kia beamed.

"I'm sorry I didn't appreciate what you do," Sullivan said. "I get it now. Being a real influencer is a job, and you're really good at it. I'll help you take photos and videos so you don't have to do it all yourself."

Kia held the phone, but she wished she could toss it off the ride and into the fake lake they were passing, and never take another photo unless it was on her digital camera.

"We *are* cute," Sullivan said proudly.

But do you really, really like me? Kia thought.

chapter 22

The next day, Kia sat at a picnic table a few yards from the Diva. At the window, Deja sang out orders and compliments. Superfans could be annoying, but right now Kia was glad to have someone who was willing to play head chef in her food truck.

"Slay, girl! Looking fly." Deja tapped an order into the Square. "Two double-bacon-wrapped fig omelets with extra gravy coming up."

The two cooks Kia had hired in addition to Deja repeated the order, interrupting their rendition of "We Are Family" but singing the orders to the melody. The line to the Kia Gourmazing Experience was as long as ever, even though Kia was sitting by herself. It was possible the line of white Portlanders thought Deja *was* Kia. If only Deja could take over her whole life, and Kia and Sullivan could just escape to a chalet in the woods. (They were not *camping* in her escape fantasy.)

Kia's phone chimed and Lillian appeared on the screen, her tiny Paris apartment visible in the background. Kia wandered in between two other food trucks. Today she was parked at the Hawthorne Asylum. The food pod reminded her of some Lewis and

Clark fort, the trucks circled to prevent intruders except those that came through the large wooden gate propped open with the word ASYLUM fashioned in wrought iron above it.

"How are things going?" Lillian asked.

"We're still gearing up for a lawsuit against a multibillion-dollar company. Sullivan's friend Nina says we shouldn't be too worried. It's just business. But I don't know."

Kia walked over to a truck selling microbrew. It was rude to order while talking on the phone, but Kia handed a twenty to a man working and motioned to the taps.

"Which one?" he asked, looking annoyed.

"Any one."

She waved away the change and tasted the beer. Portland brewers were in competition for the bitterest IPA. When she built Taste the Love Land, it would need a michelada truck. One that served the classic Mexican drink with gummy worms and Doritos. *If* she got to build Taste the Love Land.

"Does she have a strategy? Do you want me to talk to my mother about it, get her lawyer friends involved?"

"No. Nina is the best according to Gretchen, and you know how Gretchen likes to do background checks. I don't know. It'll be fine. Or it won't. No, it won't be fine."

"Are you talking about the lawsuit?"

"We kissed!" Kia blurted out. "Twice."

"Oh?" Lillian's voice filled with curiosity.

"It was…fuck. It was everything I ever wanted."

It had left Kia trembling because she wanted more. Kia gulped a mouthful of beer and sat down at a damp picnic table in between the beer truck and a Mexican food truck.

"Tell me." Lillian drew out the words.

And it all came rushing out like Kia was a talkative tween

swooning over her Love Tunnel crush. She told Lillian about the Tennis Skort and the kiss in the Love Tunnel.

"Sullivan hates social media, but she pulled out her phone while we were kissing and took a picture, and was like, *This is going to make an awesome post.* I mean…of all the times to get on board! But I don't know if any of it means anything. There was literally a crowd of ruggers waiting for us to kiss, and then it was for a post."

Lillian chuckled.

"Aren't you going to tell me to stop being an idiot?" Kia asked with a sigh.

"Aren't I going to be rigid, judgmental, preachy?" Lillian filled in the blanks without a hint of resentment.

"Maybe?"

"I went on reality TV and then quit ballet at the height of my career to be a teacher. I ran off to Paris with my lover. Love changes you, Kia. You see the world differently when you have someone who's standing next to you forever."

"You're supposed to tell me not to do this. How am I going to make good life choices if you don't tell me to act right?"

"Love blossoms in weird places."

Love blossoms in weird places?! This was the same woman who'd told the dancers in her company that emotion was an unforgivable distraction.

"I saw that picture of you in the Love Tunnel," Lillian said. "She didn't need to kiss you to get that picture. I thought you two were just looking at each other. She kissed you because she wanted to kiss you."

Kia's heart thrummed with hope. If prima ballerina Lillian Jackson could leave a life of brutal, lonely discipline, maybe Sullivan would fall desperately in love with Kia…until Mega Eats took everything she had or until Kia's loggers felled the first tree.

"Do you want to sleep with her?" Lillian asked.

Kia should be thinking about the injunction, or her deposition responses, or her testimony. If not that, she should at least be inventing a tursnicken redux. She wasn't.

"Yes!" Kia took a sip of beer and lowered her voice.

The two women gossiping at the next table looked like they'd enjoy hearing about her romantic predicament, but Kia didn't need to broadcast that part of her life.

"But I don't know what I'm doing. I mean about sex. Sullivan's good at everything, and she's slept with men and women. She's going to have standards."

Before meeting Izzy, Lillian was queen of one-night stands, and she'd had a lot of nights. When Kia was with Gretchen, Kia had never asked for advice. Lillian could have handed her the secret to mind-blowing sapphic sex and Gretchen would have said, *Did you see what* Wired *magazine said about AI-based algorithms?*

"What do I do, Lillian?"

"You be honest and you communicate."

Kia could not just pour Sullivan a cup of coffee and say, *I've been thinking about our rules, and I wondered if you'd like to break them and have sex with me.* No. Their relationship was already too much like a business deal. Sullivan deserved romance. Kia could sprinkle rose petals on Sullivan's bed. No, she'd better use an invasive flower that looked beautiful on your lover's bed but was bad for the forest ecosystem. Then even if Sullivan didn't appreciate the romantic gesture, she'd appreciate that Kia had cleared a few feet of destructive flora.

"You let her know that you like her. You could tell her you're nervous about having sex."

"That's very emotionally intelligent, but what do I *do*? Her last girlfriend was all about their image and not their real relationship. I want her to know I'm not like that. I want her to feel special." *I want her to feel loved.*

"Plan a date for her, something you know she'll like."

"But we already have to go on dates for social media and this lawsuit."

"Turn off your phone and relax," Lillian said.

"Isn't *relaxation the gateway to failure*?"

Lillian was so mellowed by love she just smiled. Kia was pretty sure aliens had abducted her cousin and reprogrammed her brain. At least alien Lillian was happy.

"If you think she's special, she'll feel that. If she likes you, she'll like whatever you do for her."

"What if she doesn't like me?"

"Does the way she's acting say she doesn't like you?"

"No."

But just because things were looking good today didn't mean that disaster wasn't around the corner.

"Just let her know how you feel. And, Kia?" Lillian hesitated. "Make sure you do really like her. If she likes you, and you leave… you'll have put her through a lot. But if it's meant to be, it'll be. Look at your dad's boat. Believe in serendipity."

———

Sullivan sat on her bed and slipped off her work shoes. It was late. It had been a long night but a good one. Mirepoix was bustling, and absolutely everyone loved their meals. Blake had forgotten half the garnishes, but at least he hadn't been on his phone.

She hadn't seen much of Kia since their kiss. It wasn't unusual. Kia was often out of the house before Sullivan woke up and in her bedroom when Sullivan got back from work. The past week, Kia had been on a late-night street food kick, eating from every food truck she could find at two in the morning and live streaming mini interviews with the food truck owners. Still, it felt deliberate. And Sullivan wasn't sure if she minded. They both knew the kiss didn't—couldn't—mean anything. The next time they passed in the kitchen, Sullivan making coffee, Kia bent over her laptop, her spine curved like a shrimp, they'd have to recognize the truth. It was a sweet kiss, and nothing more could happen, no matter how much they both wanted it.

She hadn't told Opal or Nina she and Kia had actually kissed in the Love Tunnel. She wanted to keep that detail to herself for a little while. Before Opal's reflexive attempt to set her up reminded her ironically of how impossible it would be to be with Kia. Before Nina said something sarcastic about love. She just wanted a day or two to savor the memory as though she were sixteen and Kia was her first girlfriend, and they actually thought the Love Tunnel was romantic.

Sullivan closed her bedroom door and drew the blinds. She got into bed, but she felt restless. The house was too quiet. The light coming from under the door was too bright. She rolled over. Her body longed to be touched. She loved sex, the way she could be fully in her body.

Now the only thing she could think about was Kia. The way she'd absentmindedly rest her hand on the side of her neck and tilt her head when she was thinking, appreciating something, or pondering a problem. The way she kicked her hip out when she stood at the kitchen counter, her curves unmistakable.

Now she grabbed the extra-firm body pillow she never used when she was sleeping. She lay on her side and tucked the pillow between her legs, clamping her knees together. Sullivan loved being touched. She stroked her clavicle and down her chest, savoring the sharp angles and softness of her skin and the way her body responded. If only she could touch Kia like this. If only Kia could touch her.

Sullivan pulled out her favorite vibrator, the Labianator. When she bought it, the box had promised *silent, toe-curling vibrations.* In reality, it sounded like a helicopter taking off. Quickly she rolled onto her belly, thrusting into the pillow and vibrator. The first vibrations on her mons were exhilarating.

She stopped at a sound. Had Kia come home early? Was that Kia opening her own bedroom door? Going downstairs for a snack? She wouldn't knock on Sullivan's door and ask where Sullivan kept laundry detergent or cream of tartar, would she? So far, they'd respected the sanctity of closed doors. No, it was just the house creaking.

She thrust into the pillow, clenching it between her thighs, chasing the muffled vibrations until she felt her whole insides contract. Relaxation washed over her, and it should have helped her to sleep, but several hours later, she was still tossing and turning. No deep sleep to be sure. She might as well get up and walk around for a few minutes, step out on the deck and breathe the forest air. This time next year, there wasn't going to be a forest. There'd be fried tursnicken air. Maybe that thought would quell the desire that masturbating had done nothing to dispel.

Sullivan didn't see Kia until Sullivan had taken a few steps into the kitchen. The kitchen was dark except for a single pendant light. Kia sat on one of the stools at the kitchen island, her arms folded next to her laptop, on which showed her U-Spin account and a browser open to RV accessories, her head pillowed on her arms. She leaned precariously, obviously asleep. One startling dream and she'd slip off her stool.

"Kia?" Sullivan said softly.

Kia's back rose and fell with her breath. She looked adorable with her cheek squished against her arm and her scarf unraveling from her hair. Sullivan crossed the room. She couldn't just wake

Kia with a loud *Hey, there*. But she also couldn't leave her teetering on the stool.

"Kia?" Sullivan placed a gentle hand on Kia's shoulder.

Kia woke up like she'd been caught sleeping on the job. She listed to one side as though she'd forgotten where she was and expected the back of a chair to steady her. She grabbed at the counter to stop her fall, then slipped off the stool, heading for a backward tumble. Sullivan caught her and held her.

"What...I..." Kia mumbled.

"You fell asleep."

Kia slumped against Sullivan, her head resting on Sullivan's shoulder.

"What time is it?"

"Almost three."

"Fuck. I have to be up by five."

Sullivan held her, gently stroking her back, trying not to notice Kia's paper-thin T-shirt, the clasp of her bra easy to feel through the fabric. Sullivan didn't let her hand drift over the band. She shouldn't be stroking Kia's back at all. Kia looped her arms around Sullivan's waist. It felt as natural as breathing and as miraculous as a bird landing on her hand.

"When was the last time you slept all night?"

"Before I won the American Fare." Kia rubbed her eyes without stepping out of Sullivan's embrace. "Nothing feels like a win. There's no end when you're an influencer. If you're losing followers, you need to get them back. If you're getting traction, you have to get *more* traction. I guess it's like every job. You go to work on Monday, and then you go again on Tuesday."

"And at a regular job you have days off, and you leave at the end of the night."

Kia should be in bed, rolled on her side with Sullivan's arm around her. The thought suffused Sullivan's body before she could push it away: Kia sleeping naked, her head on Sullivan's pillow. When Kia finally went to bed—if she went to bed—did she long for someone's arms around her the way Sullivan's body yearned for that comfort? Yearned for it even more than she yearned for sex, although the tension between her legs reminded her that she was holding a beautiful woman. Not just *a* woman. Kia. Sullivan tightened her thighs as though that had ever dispelled desire.

"And you should go to bed," Sullivan said.

Kia pulled away and looked at Sullivan, more alert than she'd been a minute ago.

"I will. I just really want to write back to some of my fans. The Love Tunnel is trending. The picture you took." Kia slumped with an amused sigh. "That's the gayest I've been online, and a lot of kids are coming out to me. One more hour. Then I'll go to bed."

Sullivan glanced at the clock on the fridge screen. Two fifty-nine. Kia wouldn't go to bed at all if she stuck to her five a.m. wake-up. Sullivan felt a wave of tenderness so intense it felt like a physical ache.

"Come and crash out on the sofa for a few minutes," Sullivan said. "You're not answering fans if you're sleeping in the kitchen. You might as well be comfortable." Without waiting for an answer, Sullivan put a hand on Kia's elbow to guide her to the sofa.

"I never had a sofa this big," Kia said as she lay down. "Not a sofa you could stretch out on or cuddle with someone. When I tried to cuddle with Gretchen on her sofa, she said I didn't know how."

Kia was lying on her back, looking up at Sullivan, her eyes sleepy and bright at the same time.

"She shouldn't have said that," Sullivan said. "She could have showed you."

"She wasn't a cuddler. We were perfect for each other." Kia gave a little snort. "That's what she said, not what I said. Is it that hard?"

Sullivan sat down on the edge of the sofa so she wasn't looming over Kia.

"No it's not. You just have to enjoy being in your body and tell the other person if your arm is falling asleep."

Sullivan should not offer to show Kia. She knew that.

"Do you want me to show you?"

Kia's eyelids were drooping. "Yes."

"You'll be the little spoon." Sullivan lay down beside Kia in the deep sofa and wrapped an arm around her. "Now I fold my other arm like this." She tucked her arm between them. "And you just cozy up."

"*Back that ass up?*"

"That is not how I would describe it." Sullivan chuckled. "But basically, yeah."

Kia snuggled her back to Sullivan's chest.

"I like the way your hair smells." Sullivan had not just said that out loud.

"It's a conditioner this great hairstylist in Memphis makes. I wanted to promote her, but I couldn't because of some contract with Ma Belle products. I just want to be real, Sullivan. I want everything I do to be for real."

Kia took Sullivan's hand and cupped her own hands around it. The way she cradled Sullivan's hand made Sullivan feel like Kia held her whole body.

"Am I doing this right?" Kia brushed Sullivan's knuckles with her lips. Such a soft touch, Sullivan wasn't sure she'd felt it.

"As long as you're comfortable, you're doing it right."

"Are you comfortable?"

The way Kia's ass pressed against her hips turned Sullivan on. If Kia woke up, said, *Want to get naked and scissor on the couch?* Sullivan would have pressed their bodies together until every fold of her vulva kissed every fold of Kia's, and for the ten or twelve seconds before Sullivan came, she wouldn't think about a single consequence. But she wanted this tender moment even more. It was all they could allow themselves, and it was as sweet as raw honey from a field of wildflowers.

"I'm very comfortable." Sullivan felt her own sleepless night catching up with her. "I don't think anyone has ever cuddled on a couch better than we are."

"Are we point six percent better than everyone else?"

Leaving aside the impending heartbreak?

"We're more than point six percent better."

chapter 23

The following Tuesday, the last day of Sullivan's "weekend," she woke to a dream about Kia. In Sullivan's dream she and Kia spun in the red and purple basket of a carnival ride. Kia swirled around Sullivan's body like a cloud, touching every part of her, turning her on in a way that made every cell in her body sing. And Sullivan was so close to orgasm. The ride spun faster. Kia whispered, *Come for me*. Her words lit up the sky like calligraphic fireworks.

And Sullivan woke up.

Like she always did when she had a sex dream, her body was aroused and yet…not. Like she had a dream body that was vibrating on the excruciating edge of release while her real-world body was inert. Her real body had been asleep while her dream body lifted to the height of pleasure.

Her subconscious hated her.

Sullivan sighed, got up, and pulled on sweatpants and a sports bra. She rubbed her eyes as she descended the stairs. She needed coffee, then a cold shower.

But Kia—who was supposed to be gone by six a.m., in her food truck or touring around the city looking *gorge* in her turquoise sunglasses—stood at the counter with a cutting board and ingredients before her. The kitchen smelled of fresh bread and coffee.

"I like your bra," Kia said.

"Shit. Sorry. I'll put on a shirt."

"Not fair." Kia's eyes drifted down Sullivan's body. "You've seen *me* naked."

"Not on purpose. Not that I minded."

Kia turned away, but Sullivan could see she looked pleased.

"You said you didn't have anything to do today, right?" Kia said. "I want to take you on a date."

Kia poured Sullivan a cup of coffee.

"Are we lagging in the algorithm?"

"No. I just want to show you something special. There's a new exhibit at the Portland Art Museum, and we can picnic inside."

"I don't think they let you picnic in the museum."

"They'll let me." Kia gave her a sweet, self-deprecating smile.

An hour later, raincoats dripping, Kia and Sullivan arrived at the side door to the museum. A man with a museum name tag ushered them inside.

"The exhibit isn't open yet, so you'll have it all to yourself." He led them up a concrete staircase and pushed open a door at the top. The door led into a high-ceilinged gallery with white walls and gleaming blond wood floors. And the biggest Janice Domingo nudes Sullivan had ever seen.

"I saw on the website that they were having a *Divine Nude Muse* exhibit. I thought you'd like to see it."

Sullivan was mesmerized. Her paintings were tiny by comparison; these nudes towered over them. Not all of them had been hung. Some rested against the wall. Others were still wrapped in protective cloth.

"Obviously don't touch anything," the man said and disappeared down the staircase.

"How did you...?" Sullivan looked at Kia, who'd set her picnic basket on a bench in the center of the space.

"I asked."

"You can't just ask to picnic in a museum exhibit that isn't even open yet."

"I can." Kia took off her turquoise sunglasses and tucked them in the picnic basket.

"You want to look around?" Kia asked.

Sullivan absolutely wanted to look around at the nudes. The paintings that had already been hung had been placed so that the women's vulvae were at eye level. The nearest one showed the woman's vulva peeking out beyond her pubic hair.

"I didn't know they'd be quite so...close," Kia said.

Her light brown skin did not hide her blush.

The next painting was even more explicit. Kia tried to hurry past it.

"Don't you want to admire the composition?" Sullivan teased. "You're blushing."

"Of course I'm blushing." Kia motioned to the painting's vulva without looking at it.

"Why *of course*?" Sullivan paused to admire the painting.

Kia didn't answer. When Sullivan looked at her, she was fidgeting with the edge of her Kia Gourmazing T-shirt.

"I can't believe you're *not* blushing."

"Look at the brushwork here." Sullivan pointed to a curl of pubic hair at the juncture of the woman's legs. "Do you think that's oil or acrylic?"

Kia laughed. "Read the plaque, Sullivan. I don't look at the bushwork and think, *Is it acrylic?*"

"*Bush*work." Sullivan caught Kia's slip.

"Brushwork. I said *brushwork*."

They proceeded around the perimeter of the hall admiring the paintings and giggling a little at how very, very large they were. The last one featured a woman sitting naked, legs spread.

"Now she's just showing off." Kia rolled her eyes. "Let's eat a sandwich. These are inspired by Ms. Domingo herself."

Kia spread a waxed tablecloth over one of the benches set in the center of the gallery. She set the picnic basket at one end and opened the parchment wrappers to reveal juicy grilled chicken with pickled red onions and creamy avocado, all nestled between slices of crusty ciabatta bread. The meat was topped with a vibrant slaw of shredded cabbage, oregano, pepper, vinegar, carrots, and cilantro.

They sat, side by side, at the other end of the bench, their shoulders almost touching, sandwiches—on reusable Corelle dishes—balanced on their laps.

"I don't need to tell you this is the best sandwich," Sullivan said, covering her mouth as she spoke. "You already know."

"I still like to hear it."

"This is the best sandwich ever."

"Thank you." Kia bumped Sullivan's shoulder.

After they had chewed in silence for a few minutes, Kia took a deep breath. "Can I ask you something personal?"

"How I clean my sous vide machine?"

"No, and not what you paid for your stand mixer."

"What could be more personal than that?"

"You absolutely do not have to answer this—" Kia sucked in her lower lip. "But was Aubrey a good lover?"

"Wow. You're not interested in my stand mixer."

"I'm sorry. I shouldn't have—"

"It's okay. It's just us. The Domingos aren't listening."

The gallery full of nudes felt like a place out of time. If they stayed here, there was no lawsuit. Kia wasn't leaving. They weren't even online. Kia hadn't taken out her phone once. It felt safe. It felt like they'd been here forever.

"At first. I love being in my body. Cooking. Eating. Hiking. Sex." Sullivan realized she'd leaned into Kia ask she spoke. The length of their thighs touched. Kia had not pulled away, so neither did Sullivan. "I'd try most things twice with the right person. I *have* tried most things with the right people. Aubrey was on that page at first, but the more she did her social media, the more she acted like I wanted sex too much. I never pressured her, obviously, but she spent so much time on her phone. I did suggest that having sex was more fun than watching climbing goat videos."

"I would much rather have sex with you than watch goat videos." Kia covered her face with her hand and shook her head as if to say, *I just said that, didn't I?* But when she looked up, she was smiling.

"High praise. I'll take it," Sullivan said.

They both laughed.

"Nothing kills an orgasm like thinking maybe she'd rather be watching climbing goat videos," Sullivan said. "I think she lost interest in sex because she couldn't put it online. So what was the point of spending all that time in bed when it didn't produce any content."

"How could anyone want to film content more than have sex with you?"

"I know, right?" Sullivan pulled her shoulders back in a cocky pose, then let them drop. "I started to feel like she wasn't attracted to me at all even though she swore she was."

"Well, you're hot as fuck. If you needed someone to tell you, I'm telling you."

Kia was still blushing, but she looked Sullivan directly in the eye, and her gaze felt like a punctuation mark that meant *what I just said is unequivocally true.* It made Sullivan glow with pride. Kia's statement felt like a soothing balm to the one-sided love of her past. A wave of attraction and desire washed over Sullivan as she held Kia's eyes.

"You don't have to answer," Sullivan said, "but why do you want to know if Aubrey was a good lover?"

"This is the dumb part," Kia said. "I'm pretty sure I'm not. I kind of missed the part—in your teens and early twenties—when you get good at sex. I was living on a yacht with my dad and a thousand spaniels, and then I was with Gretchen. I should have learned something. We dated for four years. But we never lived in the same city. When we saw each other every two or three months, I wanted to have sex. She wanted to talk marketing strategy. When we broke up and she became *just* my manager, I could barely tell the difference."

"And you're a romantic."

"Exactly. Sometimes I think I could ditch the romantic thing and hook up with someone, but I'm afraid she'd be disappointed. I've built my career on too-much-of-a-good-thing-is-fabulous, but my sex life is stale saltine crackers."

"You couldn't be a disappointment, and nothing about you is like stale saltine crackers."

"You've never slept with me."

The intensity of the moment was palpable, and the silence hung between them for so long Sullivan could have counted the motes of dust shimmering in the air if she could have torn her gaze away from Kia's beautiful, serious face. Sullivan considered just how much more complicated her life could get.

"Kia?"

Sullivan thought she saw a shy smile at the corner of Kia's lips. God, she'd love to feel Kia's thigh between her legs, grinding against her. And it would feel even better to make Kia feel good, feel confident, feel like the goddess she was.

"Yes?" Kia's smile spread into eagerness. She reached for Sullivan's hand and lightly stroked each one of Sullivan's fingers.

It wouldn't matter if Kia had no experience. Sullivan would love to guide her. Would love to explore Kia's body, touching all the places Gretchen had neglected. Sullivan looked into Kia's eyes.

"I showed you how to cuddle on a sofa, and you were a natural. Would it be wrong to make this all more complicated?" Sullivan hadn't noticed when they both set down their sandwiches and wiped their hands, but they had. Against her best judgment, Sullivan traced her fingertips down Kia's thigh, watching Kia's face for any expression that said Kia didn't want to be touched. "We're consenting adults and we're married."

Kia's grin was sunlight on a brand-new convertible cruising down Highway 101. She rested her head on Sullivan's shoulder, then turned and planted an awkward kiss on Sullivan's neck. And Sullivan knew how much fun they would have learning each other's bodies. Sullivan began to speak, but her phone went off with Miriam Makeba's "Pata Pata" playing at full volume.

"Miss Brenda." She shook her head and silenced the phone. "She gets a special ringtone."

Of course the outside world would interrupt just as she was waiting for Kia's official answer to her barely spoken question.

"Do I get a special ringtone?" Kia asked, grinning.

"What's your special song?"

Sullivan's phone buzzed again. Sullivan pulled it out again to silence the vibrations. Why were there so many ways for your phone to take you away from the moment?

She caught the first lines of a text from Brenda.

Brenda: *HELP Roof is flooding*

chapter 24

Kia watched Sullivan take the call, hating Miss Brenda for the interruption. Sullivan tapped her lips nervously as she spoke.

"That's not a *little* problem. No, it's—yes, that's—" Finally she interrupted the speaker. "If it keeps raining, you're going to have leaks in every corner of the restaurant. I'm coming over." She hung up the phone. "I'm so sorry. I have to go."

"What's wrong?"

"Miss Brenda, you remember my grandfather's friend, owns the Biscuit Box, and her green roof is flooding again."

"What are you going to do?" Kia tried not to sound sullen.

Sullivan was already getting up. "Bail her out. Literally."

For the first time in Kia's life, she was not in favor of supporting a small, Black-owned business.

"I'm so sorry, Kia. This"—Sullivan gestured to the gallery—"was the best date anyone's taken me on."

Sullivan had referred to their afternoon like a real *date*. There were no implied quotation marks around the word. And Sullivan had just asked her to have sex. *Had* Sullivan asked her if she wanted to have sex? God, Kia wished she were better at this stuff.

"Miss Brenda had her nephew install it," Sullivan said,

gathering her coat from the floor. "Jersey is a sweet kid who watched a lot of YouTube videos. But you need horticulture, engineering, ecology. You can't get that just by watching YouTube. Fuck. Miss Brenda should have hired a professional."

Yes. Miss Brenda should have. Kia had wanted Alice Sullivan since she was twenty. *Twenty*. She couldn't even drink the first time she'd fantasized about Sullivan. And they'd had a moment, and now Sullivan was fumbling with her phone.

"I'm *so* sorry. I have to go. These roofs. If it gets to the point it's at now, it can collapse. Shit. Miss Brenda could lose everything. I've got to get up on the roof and pull oak tree sprouts out of a clogged drain."

What if pulling oak trees out of drains cooled Sullivan's ardor? What if she decided sleeping with Kia would be too complicated? What if she came back from Miss Brenda's roof and pretended that they hadn't had a moment?

"I'm coming with you." Kia began packing up the picnic stuff.

"It's going to be a mess up there. You are too pretty and too glittery for drain cleanup."

"I am offended, Chef Sullivan." Kia put her hands on her hips. "Do you know how many times I emptied Old Girl's septic tank before I could afford an incinerating toilet? I bailed water out of the Diva in Florida because everyone said, *The hurricane isn't going to hit inland*. If I'm going to bail that much crap, I want to get credit for bailing crap."

Sullivan stopped her light-speed departure, her face hovering on the edge of impressed.

"You're on, Jackson."

"And by the way," Kia said as they headed out, "I *am* too pretty for bailing crap."

*   *   *

Back at the house, Sullivan changed and grabbed tools. Kia donned green striped overalls and colorful rain gear. Bad weather was no reason to wear industrial navy. Outside, Sullivan headed for her sedan.

"Sully," Kia called out. "This is not a sedan situation. It's time for an all-American"—Kia dropped her voice to a masculine drawl—"truck."

"You're cute, Jackson," Sullivan said, and she headed to the truck.

"Tell me more about Miss Brenda," Kia asked as Sullivan pointed directions.

"You remember the elegant Black woman with my family at graduation? That was Miss Brenda. She was my grandfather's *younger friend*. They always helped each other with their restaurants."

"So there's a history of seducing younger women?" Kia quipped. She glanced at Sullivan to see how the comment landed. Hopefully Kia hadn't misread their conversation in the museum.

Sullivan looked like she was going to say something. It came out, "Turn left at the light," but she was fighting a smile.

Kia turned back to the rain splashing off the windshield. A few minutes later, they arrived at a bustling storefront on an oak-lined street. Colorful flower boxes adorned the windows. The words BISCUIT BOX were painted in a whimsical font on the door. A crowd of people stood on the sidewalk watching water pour off the roof of the two-story building and inappropriately, Kia thought, eating biscuits.

"This place looks popular," Kia observed.

"Miss Brenda is an amazing baker. You should try her signature sugar-stuffed sweet potato biscuit; it's to die for. And don't worry. She'll feed you more than you can possibly eat."

"You eat Miss Brenda's sugar-stuffed biscuit, and you mock the tursnicken?"

Kia parked in front. An older woman in a flowered apron burst out of the front door, hugging Sullivan.

"I'm sure it's nothing," she said in a Virginia accent. She kissed Sullivan on both cheeks. "And this must be your bride. You must tell me all about yourself, darling. I am so happy that Little Sully finally found a decent woman. I like her already. Look at you all ready to work in those pretty overalls."

"Little Sully," Kia whispered as Miss Brenda led them to a fire escape that went to the roof.

"Call me Little Sully, and I will never speak to you again," Sullivan said.

"Little Sully." Kia put her arm around Sullivan's waist.

Sullivan shot her a murderous glance, which softened immediately. She paused just long enough to kiss Kia on the forehead.

"I'm calling your father and getting embarrassing baby pictures."

The marriage was fake, but teasing each other in the rain and the smell of biscuits…that was real. You learned that when you moved every week. Special moments didn't last, but that didn't mean they weren't real.

The next real moment included climbing a fire escape under a waterfall of slime.

Ahead of her, Sullivan leaned back to avoid the water, but there was only one way to make the turn on the fire escape, and that was through water pouring off the roof. Sullivan pulled up her hood. She glanced back at Kia.

"You still in?"

This was the universe teaching Kia a lesson about showing off to impress hot women.

"Absolutely," Kia called over the sound of rain and slime falling.

Sullivan closed her eyes, then stepped through the sheet of water.

"Fuck me!"

Kia couldn't help but laugh.

"That water is like thirty-two point one degrees," Sullivan screeched, her voice going high into the treble range.

Kia stepped through. If you were going to show off, you had to go all the way.

"It's not that bad." A string of urban seaweed slipped down her neck toward her collar, and she screamed and flailed every muscle in her body to get it off.

Now it was Sullivan laughing.

"You got another one." She picked a bit of greenery out of Kia's hair.

The building created a pocket space out of view of the crowd of onlookers eating biscuits below.

Sullivan put her hand on the back of Kia's neck. Kia jumped.

"Do I have more slime on me?"

"No. I was just thinking you looked good in rain gear."

No amount of rain gear could have kept them dry. By the time they reached the roof, they were soaked. They climbed over the retaining wall that surrounded the roof, keeping them from slipping off and also holding four or five inches of water.

Sullivan took a tentative step. "Erosion and uplift. It's bad." She reached into the water and pulled out a handful of juicy-looking weeds in one hand and dark green leaves in the other. "See?"

"Yes and also no. What is it?"

"Sedum that you want. And oak tree saplings, which you don't." Sullivan nudged something with her foot.

Under the slime, a canvas hose lay like a bloated boa constrictor after swallowing an alligator...or a small woman with a big Afro.

"So are green roofs ever a good idea?" Kia asked.

Sullivan tipped her face skyward, eyes closed to the pelting rain. Kia couldn't tell if Sullivan was enjoying the rain or repenting ever having praised the green roof concept. But when Sullivan looked at Kia again, she was smiling.

"Right now, they are a terrible, terrible idea." She shook her head slowly, looking bemused despite the rain. "In general, they can be great. They save energy, reduce temperatures in the city, manage water runoff. If every building that could have a green roof did, we wouldn't get urban heat islands." Sullivan rattled off more facts, then stopped herself. "Sorry, you didn't want to know all that."

True, Kia had not planned on a lecture about green roofs in the pouring rain, but now that she knew, one question burned in her mind.

"If they're so good, why are there so few of them?"

Kia guessed the answer before Sullivan spoke.

"They cost more." Sullivan shrugged. "And if you fuck them up, you get this." She gestured to the lake of sludge. "Shall we get to work?"

Troweling and scraping and throwing baby oak trees over the side of the building with nothing to shield them from the rain and the wind should have made her hate Sullivan, her own pride, roofs, plants, and life, but a half hour in, they were laughing so hard they were crying.

"You know that painting of George Washington crossing the Potomac...Delaware? That's me." Sullivan struck a pose, her chin held high and her hands on her hips.

"You look very—" *Sexy. Adorable. Wonderful. Silly.* "Washingtonian."

Sullivan pulled up some stringy vegetation. "Why can you not live in a garden?" she asked the plant. "In the river? But nooo, you have to get up on the roof, because you're sooo special."

Sullivan talked to most of the greenery, the conversation getting more and more irate and more and more for Kia's entertainment. Every time Sullivan pushed her hair out of her eyes, she smeared mud on her face. When Kia tried to wipe it off, she made it infinitely worse. And everything was funny. A heavier gust of wind. A particularly slimy root ball. The crowd eating biscuits below.

Finally, Sullivan stood up, shivering and triumphant.

"The water's going down!"

They'd loosened the vital root ball. Suddenly the water was draining like a bathtub. They heard someone below yelp.

"Serves them right for eating biscuits down there," Kia said. She slogged through the diminishing water and threw her arms around Sullivan.

Sullivan hugged her back and tried to kiss her, but all she did was get mud in their mouths, and it was almost as good as a mud-free kiss because they were in it together.

"Is there one part of you that's not covered in mud?" Sullivan said, laughing.

"There is," Kia said.

Sullivan opened her mouth and then shut it.

"Look who's blushing now," Kia said, although to be fair, it was hard to tell if Sullivan was blushing or just flushed from the cold.

Even with the rain pounding and urban seaweed splashing around them, Kia felt warm all the way through.

"Let's get you home, Ms. Jackson. I owe you a hot shower." Sullivan trailed her fingers down the front of Kia's raincoat. "And a whole lot more."

chapter 25

Sullivan let them into the house dripping mud.

"We wrecked your cab," Sullivan said apologetically.

"Trucks are meant to get muddy." Kia dropped her jacket in a pile in the foyer. "Haven't you seen the commercials?"

"No one drives a truck that nice through mud, do they?"

Kia wasn't thinking about the truck. Sullivan could have exploded paintballs in the cab, and she wouldn't have cared. What she cared about was what came next. In the museum, when Sullivan said, *We're consenting adults and we're married*, Kia was ready to say yes. A hundred times yes. Kia didn't know how to make a move now. Luckily she didn't have to.

"Do you want to shower upstairs or downstairs?" Sullivan asked.

"Which one do you want?"

"I want the one you're in."

"Yes," Kia said.

Sullivan held out her hand.

"Downstairs?"

Kia nodded.

"Watch out for the Turkish rugs," Kia said as Sullivan led her down the hallway.

"I don't know if they're Turkish. I got them from Wayfair."

"You said they were Turkish." Kia tiptoed around the edge of the runner.

"Because I didn't want you stepping on them."

That night felt like a long time ago.

"You can step on my Turkish rugs now. I don't mind."

They were going to take their clothes off. Kia was going to shower with Alice Sullivan. She wished she could catapult herself back in time for a minute, grab the hands of her twenty-year-old self, and jump up and down with her. *We're going to do it!*

"We don't have to do anything you don't want to," Sullivan said.

"Chef Sullivan, I've wanted to see you naked since the day I met you."

"At the grange?"

"At school."

"In Introductory Pureeing Techniques?"

"Yes. In Introductory Pureeing Techniques."

"I must be quite something. That class was fascinating." Sullivan turned on the shower.

"Only because you were in it. Now take off your clothes already, Chef Sullivan."

Slowly, Sullivan stripped off the layers of her clothing. Kia watched her. Sullivan's body was everything. Muscular legs. Full breasts. Her abs defined enough to say, *I hike up and down mountains on purpose*, her belly soft enough to say, *Just because I cook organic doesn't mean I live on microgreens.*

"Help me out of this bra?" Sullivan asked.

Kia laughed as the bra stuck around Sullivan's ribs.

"I'm not good at this."

"No one is good at wet sports bra."

Kia pulled her shirt over her own head and turned her back so Sullivan could unclasp her lace bra.

"Some of us are not that complicated." Kia tossed a smile over her shoulder.

Sullivan unclasped Kia's bra. The shiver that ran through Kia's body had nothing to do with the cold. She felt Sullivan's eyes caress her as she undressed down to her underwear, then whisked it off before she lost her nerve, even though Sullivan had seen her naked in the living room posing with the Janice Domingos.

She stepped toward Sullivan and let her fingertips glide down Sullivan's side. The way Sullivan shivered made Kia feel more confident. Sullivan had said she loved sex. She loved being in her body. Kia might not be experienced, but Sullivan still wanted to be touched. Kia drew Sullivan under the water. Mud streamed off them both.

"Turn around," she said.

Sullivan turned around, and Kia ran a bar of soap over Sullivan's neck and shoulders, down her back. Sullivan let out a soft moan of appreciation. It was exhilarating. Kia was touching Sullivan. Sullivan liked it. After all these years, a fantasy Kia had never shared with anyone—why would she when it was so impossible it was embarrassing?—was coming true.

She ran her hands over Sullivan's tattoos.

"What do they mean?"

Sullivan glanced at her arms as though she'd forgotten she had tattoos.

"This one…um…"

Sullivan's eyelids were heavy. She was blissed out by Kia's touch. Alice Sullivan had lost her words because Kia was touching her, holding her hand in one of her own and running the fingertips of her other hand up and down Sullivan's arm.

"That one is a pagoda near where I worked in Japan. Stylized. You can see the rooftops in the triangular lines."

Tattoos wrapped all the way around her arms, almost to her armpit. On the right, the designs covered her shoulder too. Sullivan turned her arm so Kia could see the delicate skin on her inner upper arm.

"Showoff," Kia murmured.

"Why?"

"This must have hurt like hell."

Sullivan chuckled. "I had to show up the guys I cooked with. Look here." Interlaced with the geometric patterns on Sullivan's inner arm was a date. Kia recognized the year. She wasn't sure about the day.

"This is…?"

"The date we graduated."

"Did you get it because that's the date we graduated or because that's the day we first kissed?" Kia liked the confidence in her own voice, and she'd be okay with Sullivan saying, *The date we graduated.* That was the correct answer.

"I thought it was the day we graduated." Sullivan cupped Kia's face. "Now I think it might be the day we first kissed."

Sullivan leaned in and kissed Kia softly. When Kia responded, Sullivan pressed against Kia, their thighs touching. Now it was Kia who gasped in pleasure. They kissed for a long time. (Sullivan had to be entranced, since she was definitely wasting water.) Kia's body relaxed. Her legs melted. She was one with Sullivan and the water and the world. This must be what Sullivan meant when she talked about being in her body. It was wonderful.

"Is there anything you do or don't want to do?" Sullivan

asked, pressing a kiss to Kia's temple. "We don't have to go any further than you want."

"All I want—" Kia took Sullivan's face in her hands and kissed her fast but deep. "Is to learn how to be point six percent better than you at sex."

"I think I'll enjoy teaching you, and I don't mind coming in second again."

Upstairs in Sullivan's room, Sullivan turned on the baseboard heater. They both shivered.

"Usually, I'd go a little slower, but do you want to get under the covers now?" Sullivan asked.

Kia was already diving under the covers. "Why are sheets always cold?"

Sullivan climbed in next to her, and they wrapped their arms around each other, luxuriating in the heat of their bodies. They kissed, their bodies pressed together. When the room warmed up, Sullivan pushed the covers down.

Sullivan kissed with her whole body. She swirled around Kia until it felt like every part of Sullivan's body touched every part of Kia's. Kia could feel Sullivan's desire mounting. Sullivan's breath grew faster, her touch was gentle, but Kia could feel her straining to move slowly. And she was so wonderful. Kia wanted to pull away and say, *Do you know how perfect you are?* She wanted to give Sullivan everything Sullivan wanted, everything she needed.

It was perfect until Kia realized that every time she thought about kissing Sullivan's neck or stroking her thigh, Sullivan was kissing *Kia's* neck or stroking *Kia's* thigh. She felt like a commis chef right out of culinary school working alongside a master. Then the lawsuit flashed into her mind like a spam call. She was getting sued. Sullivan was saving her ass. Now Sullivan was doing everything in bed. If Kia didn't do something sexy, Sullivan would lose interest.

Sullivan stopped kissing her and lay beside her.

"Are you okay?"

"I'm sorry," Kia said.

"What for?"

"I really want this."

"But…?" Sullivan asked, cupping Kia's face so Kia had to look at her.

"I'm…" Kia couldn't tell Sullivan that her heart, soul, and body wanted to be in the moment, but her mind had decided that, right now, it needed to remember the difference between *material issue* and *issue of purported fact*.

"Is it hard to relax?" Sullivan asked.

"It's not that I don't want this. I totally want this."

"But you're human, and it's hard to stay in the moment when you've got the whole world banging on your door?"

How did Sullivan sum up Kia's chaotic emotions in one sentence?

"I got you," Sullivan said. "Can I rub your back?"

The offer was too delicious to resist. Kia promised herself that next time—please, let there be a next time—she would do everything for Sullivan. But right now Sullivan straddled Kia and began massaging her back, slowly, as though she was trying to tell Kia she could rest under Sullivan's touch for as long as she needed. After a few minutes, Kia's mind relaxed. Desire surged through her. Suddenly Sullivan's weight on her ass was a sensual tease. She pressed up against her. Sullivan groaned. Kia thought she could feel Sullivan's wetness.

"Do you want to know what I do when you're not in the house?" Sullivan whispered.

"Besides planting microgreens in every window?" The teasing comment came out as a sensuous sigh.

"Yes. I want to tell you about my microgreens." Sullivan rocked her hips, pressing into Kia's ass. "I want—" Sullivan moaned.

Kia lifted her hips to press against Sullivan.

"That feels good," Sullivan groaned. She rocked back and forth, her movements growing more frantic. "Yes. God, yes!" Then Sullivan stopped, slid off Kia, and lay panting next to her. Kia could feel Sullivan's need in the way Sullivan's hips still undulated as she lay next to Kia. It turned Kia on more than she'd ever been turned on.

"You don't have to stop," Kia said.

"Right now is about you. Ready for my secret?" Sullivan whispered into Kia's lips.

"I want all your secrets."

Sullivan crawled over Kia.

"Excuse me, miss," she said amiably.

It was an awkward, intimate gesture, like reaching around someone to get in a high cupboard when it would have been easier just to ask them to move over. From that position, Sullivan pulled a wand vibrator out of her bedside table. She plugged it into the base of her lamp, then turned on the device. Kia had vibrators, but she'd never used one with another person.

"It's called the Labianator," Sullivan said.

"That's an action hero name."

"What movies are you watching?"

"Not a porn name!"

"No shame. I watch porn."

The vibrator roared as Sullivan turned it up.

"It sounds like a leaf blower," Kia said.

"It's very frustrating because I can't use it when you're in your bedroom."

Kia touched the vibrating head, which was apparently designed to imitate an earthquake.

"Oh my god, that's fierce. How do you use it at all?"

Sullivan pulled her pillow from where it had slid off the bed and placed the vibrator under it.

"You can straddle it."

Kia felt herself blush. Modesty and desire fought for control of her body. Then Kia took a deep breath and straddled the pillow. She felt absolutely ridiculous. And she was pressing her pussy into the pillow Sullivan slept on! Even if Sullivan washed the pillowcase, she'd think about Kia when she laid down her head. Some of Kia's self-consciousness melted. Sullivan wanted her. It made Kia feel powerful and gorgeous.

"It's okay to laugh," Sullivan said, her voice warm. "It is funny. I mean it's called the Labianator. The classic wand is called the Hitachi, but nooo, I had to buy the Labianator because it's from a carbon-neutral sex toy company."

In that moment, Kia loved Sullivan for buying green sex toys, and she loved Sullivan's confidence and her playful cockiness. That combination had drawn her to Sullivan (after Sullivan's lips and cheekbones and dope grandpa fashion) their first day at school. Sullivan took her work, her craft, her values seriously, but not herself. That thought breezed through Kia's mind, but it didn't take her out of the moment.

"Can I get on top of you again?" Sullivan asked.

At Kia's enthusiastic yes, Sullivan mounted her again, sitting on Kia's ass, pressing Kia into the pillow and the vibrations.

"You can let me do everything." Sullivan rolled her hips against Kia's ass.

The mix of sensations made Kia moan with pleasure.

"Or you can take over."

Kia felt Sullivan take a deep breath, and it felt like Sullivan was relaxing herself and holding herself back at the same time.

"No one's looking," Sullivan said. "There's no audience. You can just be in your body."

If someone had built Kia a perfect roller coaster where every dip and rise was designed exactly for her, it wouldn't have been as much fun as the sensations flooding her body. The hardness of the vibrator cushioned by the pillow. Her own hips thrusting, Sullivan adding just enough pressure and movement to take control away from Kia but not so much that Kia couldn't find the place and pressure she needed.

Kia moaned again.

"Too much?" Sullivan asked.

"Perfect," Kia gasped.

Sullivan rocked back and forth. Kia's hips bucked, her cries grew faster and higher. Kia gripped the sheets. And nothing had ever been more perfect, not the most delicate lavender-honey and lemon panna cotta or the freshest heirloom tomato.

"Oh, Sullivan, yes!" Then Kia was silent as she came.

Sullivan kept up her rhythm, taking Kia higher and higher, until a wave, like sugar carried on champagne, claimed Kia and she went limp. Sullivan lay on top of her, supporting some of her weight on her arms. And when Kia's breath had returned to normal, Sullivan rolled off her, keeping one arm around Kia's waist and holding her close.

"What can I do for you?" Kia asked, turning toward Sullivan. The orgasm had washed away her performance anxiety. If Sullivan liked sex, she'd know how to ask for what she wanted. Sullivan snuggled closer.

Sullivan chuckled. "I took advantage of your gorgeous ass."

"You came?"

"Easily."

"But is there anything else?"

Sullivan pulled Kia against her.

"Don't get up and check your phone."

"I forgot I had one," Kia said. "I know what I should do. Roll over." Kia gently rolled Sullivan onto her side. "I'm the big spoon this time. You have to tell me if I've mastered cuddling."

Sullivan felt so good in her arms. Being the big spoon felt as much like being held as being the little spoon. Sullivan nestled against her. Their breathing fell into rhythm together.

"That was fun," Sullivan said dreamily. "Thank you."

"Anytime, Chef," Kia whispered. "Anytime."

She felt Sullivan twitch as sleep took her. And Kia determined that she would stay up all night long so she didn't miss a second of the time with Sullivan. But like a haze of magic pollen, Sullivan's sleep drifted over her, lulling her into pastel dreams. She'd closed her eyes for only a moment, but when she opened them, it was morning.

chapter 26

Sullivan woke to the lovely chocolate-coconut smell of Kia's hair and Kia's arm around her. Kia blinked her eyes open.

"Hi," Kia said.

"Hi, lover," Sullivan said. "I never say this, but I so wish I didn't have to go to work today. I'd rather stay here with you."

"Take me with you."

"To Mirepoix?"

"Let me share my point six percent with your restaurant."

Sullivan had loved the thirty minutes they'd spent in the kitchen at the Tennis Skort. She couldn't think of anything better than cooking all day and night with Kia. Well…she could think of a few things that'd be better, but spending the day in the restaurant with Kia would be wonderful.

"This morning is mostly prep. You okay with chopping and making sauces?"

"Absolutely."

They arrived at Mirepoix late. Opal was already there. Her eyebrows lifted above her red-framed glasses, but all she said was, "Hey, Kia. Sullivan putting you to work?" Kia fit seamlessly into the kitchen.

She insisted on working in the smallest space possible, dicing pounds of vegetables on a cutting board made for mincing garlic. Her knife flew over the tiny cutting board. Her movements were fast, and yet every cell in Sullivan's body understood innately that the knife wouldn't slip. Kia's arms flexed with the movement. Her hips swayed.

"Like this, Chef?" Kia called out, holding up perfectly obliqued parsnips and zucchini in the shape of diamonds.

"Perfect. Like you are," Sullivan called back.

Opal looked back and forth between them.

Kia was a joy to cook with and not just because she looked stunning with her hair tied in a purple scarf, her borrowed chef whites crisp, her black-and-white-houndstooth joggers clinging in all the right places. When Sullivan surveyed Kia's work, her brunoise of onions, celery, and carrots was also stunning.

"If you ever get sick of the road, I got a place for you," Sullivan said.

Sullivan didn't realize her offer had been half-serious, until she felt the pang of disappointment. The time they had together was temporary, an arrangement. But the impact of that sad fact quickly dissipated when Kia breezed past her, letting her hips graze Sullivan's seductively. Kia's energy was electric. And even if fleeting, Sullivan wanted to savor every moment of the irresistible attraction drawing her closer to this enchanting woman.

"Watch out, Chef." Kia looked over her shoulder. "I might take you up on it, and where would you be when your customers started asking for more tursnicken?"

Their eyes met. Had Sullivan just asked Kia to stay? Had Kia said…something that wasn't no? Kia waltzed past Sullivan. Sullivan felt a thrill of excitement form in her core. One probably shouldn't feel this level of sexual energy at work, but maybe it'd make the food taste better. Maybe all the couples who ate at Mirepoix that night would go home and make love.

When Opal walked by Sullivan (definitely not brushing her ass), she whispered, "I was so right about you two."

The day passed happily. During the afternoon lull, Kia, Sullivan, and Opal drank coffee, and Opal told funny stories about eccentric customers, and Kia described food truck mishaps. Sullivan mostly listened, happy to watch her best friend and her…what was Kia to her?…her *Kia* enjoying each other's company.

By eight, the first seating was complete, and the second seating was bustling. Sullivan managed six burners, searing mountains of mushrooms and grilling the whole sea.

Orders came in.

"Heard!" Sullivan and Kia said in unison.

"Behind you, babe!" Kia said, passing through the tight galley carrying a heavy stockpot. Now that they were cooking, Kia wasn't distracting Sullivan with her touch. She was focused. They were working. A perfect team. The touching would come later.

"We're running low on casoncelli," Kia called out. "Want me to roll some more?"

"We'll let everyone know it's sold out," Sullivan called out. "You can't roll casoncelli in the middle of service." Too bad. The casoncelli were a top seller.

"You've never cooked short order," Kia said. "I can roll casoncelli and cook you a burger."

"Just try it," Sullivan called over her shoulder.

"Don't try," Opal said.

A few minutes later, the lead server breezed into the kitchen.

"We're officially out of casoncelli," Opal told him.

"We're not," Kia said.

"Are we or aren't we?" he asked.

"Chef, does this look good?" Kia held a perfectly formed

casoncelli in her hand. "I can make five dozen more if you give me five minutes."

"Thanks, Chef," Sullivan said. "It looks great."

Kia worked for another few minutes, then slid a tray of the hand-rolled pasta onto the prep table as casually as passing a clean plate. Before Sullivan could say anything, Kia was back at rolling pasta. Sullivan transferred six of the candy-wrapper-shaped ravioli into boiling water, and they floated immediately, delicate but perfectly secure around their filling of ricotta, dates, and shallots.

Damn, Kia was good at this.

Sullivan plated. In what seemed like one movement, Kia stepped to her left, placed the round tian next to the pasta, wiped the splatters from it, and brought the earthenware into the service window.

"We're serving these?" the head server looked at the pasta with the kind of concern he'd leveled against Blake's sloppy plating.

"Kia has made beautiful casoncelli," Sullivan said.

The head server didn't move.

"What?" Sullivan asked.

Sullivan glanced over at Kia, who shrugged as if to say, *I have no idea what the problem is.* Then Sullivan looked at the plate more closely.

Casoncelli always looked a little vulva-like if you were thinking about vulva while you ate stuffed pasta, but these were an unambiguous tribute to the anatomy, with their delicate folds and curled edges. Sullivan's mind flew to the image of Kia's hands gently coaxing the casoncelli into shape. Sullivan felt a pulse of sexual need, as though her body remembered every empty day and night before Kia woke her again with a kiss. And she was looking at pasta. And thinking about her pretend wife. And they were still in the middle of the second seating. And half a dozen people had already ordered the vulva-celli.

"Chef Jackson!"

Kia strolled over. "I showed you one, and you said they were good."

"You included a *clitoris*." Sullivan tried not to laugh as her voice soared. "These look like a straight girls' bachelorette party."

"Straight girls have penis pops," Kia said.

"That is not the point. The point is—"

Kia leaned closer and placed her index finger on Sullivan's mouth. Sullivan gasped, taking in the rich scents emanating from Kia's finger. Dill. Lemon. Sumac. Sullivan wanted to lick those fingers. That was definitely against health code.

"I told you I want to be point six percent better at handling casoncelli."

Sullivan regarded the pasta, then she looked directly at Kia, touching the tip of her tongue to her upper lip in a gesture she hoped was subtle enough only Kia saw it. She held Kia's eyes until Kia squirmed. *I want you.* Maybe Sullivan had always wanted Kia, she just hadn't traced the outline of that desire, hadn't realized how much deeper it went than the desire to make a richer bourguignon.

Sullivan turned back to the head server.

"They look fine to me. Serve them." When Kia handed her another plate of casoncelli, Sullivan held them at eye level and whispered, "You little temptresses." Then she looked right at Kia to let her know she wasn't talking to the food.

"We're going to get murdered," Nina said as they sped—at least lumbered—up I-84 in Opal's rugby van. "And the van smells like wet socks."

"Then why did you come?" Sullivan leaned forward with her elbows on the front seats.

Opal was driving. Nina rode shotgun.

"Because if you get murdered," Nina said, "I want to get murdered with you, and this gives me a couple of hours to practice what you're going to say on the stand. Let's start with first principles. Only answer what they ask. Don't volunteer anything, no matter how useful it seems. They'll set traps that way. And they'll try to rattle you. Let's try some questions."

An hour's worth of questions later, Sullivan had mastered the art of three-syllable answers.

"Are we done with that?" Opal asked.

"We are talking about Sullivan's *life*," Nina said. "We're done when I say we're done."

Sullivan wished Nina didn't sound so fierce. It was good to have friends protect you. It was not good to need Nina Hashim's protection.

But even the impending lawsuit couldn't totally quell the excitement of cars zipping past them and Billie Eilish on the radio. The gas station snacks tasted like high school road trips, not like chemicals that caused cancer in the state of California. Sullivan had found a Wind Searcher Pop-Up Pavilion. She'd spent hours on Craigslist. She'd done a deep dive into local newspaper ads and flea market sites. She'd even reactivated her Facebook page so she could message with potential sellers. And she'd found Kia's dream RV accessory. The exact make and model to fit Old Girl. For a thousand dollars cash, which Nina insisted on calling *unmarked twenties*. And Sullivan had had sex with Kia. Beautiful, funny, unguarded sex. Fuck all the sad things that could happen later. Like Nina had reminded them, the wheels could fall off the rugby van at any moment. (Nina had no faith in lug nuts.) Carpe diem.

"Opal says this old-ass RV accessory is on point," Nina said.

"This present is for Kia, but did Kia talk to you about your birthday?" Opal asked.

"No. We'll have to plan something for her socials."

The idea didn't fill Sullivan with dread anymore. For one thing, posing for socials would mean more time with Kia and touching her on screen would lead to touching off screen.

Nina sipped from her gold-rimmed travel mug.

"What Opal's asking is, are you sleeping with her?"

"How did *did you talk about your birthday* turn into *are you sleeping together*?"

Nina chuckled into her mug. "The witness will answer the question."

"Yes." Sullivan hadn't believed in auras until she felt her whole aura glow with the memory.

"Good job," Nina said. "Don't give them anything more than they ask for. I knew it. Now spill the tea."

"How did you know?" Sullivan asked.

Nina shot Sullivan a look. "I can tell if an estranged husband in another country is sleeping with his assistant. I can certainly tell if my best friend is falling for someone."

"I saw you bumping hips in the kitchen," Opal said. "You seemed to be getting very close. And I heard you ask Kia to come work with us and dump her life on the road. So of course I told Nina all about it. And you halfway said you loved her."

"I didn't."

"She did," Opal said to Nina. "And that was before they even slept together."

Sullivan couldn't stop the smile from spreading across her face. She could see Kia's delight when she saw the Wind Searcher Pop-Up Pavilion strung with lights. She'd throw her arms around Sullivan. Sullivan could feel the way Kia would lift up for a kiss. A second later Kia would pull out her phone and tell Sullivan to reenact the gift, but for a moment it'd just be Kia, childlike in her delight. Sullivan felt her chest contract and expand at the same time. Everything tasted better and smelled better—even the ghost of rugby socks in the van—just because Kia existed. And Sullivan felt fully alive.

"Sooo…" Opal began slowly. "I'm so excited you've met someone you like. We're all on team Kia. Kia is amazing." Opal seemed nervous, like she was about to tell her team they didn't make the playoffs. "For a young Black chef to accomplish what she has…" She continued with some statistics about bias in the culinary arts.

Nina cut her off. "We're just saying, be a little careful. I don't think she'd hurt you on purpose." Nina frowned as though she couldn't believe she'd just said that. "But sweet, loving grandmothers would finesse their favorite grandchild when this much money is at stake. But I don't think she'd *try* to hurt you. But it's a lot of money. And if the shit hits the fan, she could be in a lot of trouble legally."

"You said she'd be okay?"

The sparkle of happy adrenaline in Sullivan's blood turned to pinpricks of anxiety.

"I think so. But if shit goes down, there's a chance—small chance—she'll be able to save herself by throwing you under the bus. If I see that coming, I'll have to destroy her. And then you'll be mad at me for life."

"She wouldn't."

Sullivan was certain in a way she'd never been certain about Aubrey. It wasn't that she'd thought Aubrey would deliberately hurt her, but if someone had asked, *Do you think it's possible Aubrey could hurt you, know she was doing it, and not stop?* the answer would have been *I don't think so.* For a relationship to work, the answer to that question had to be no.

"And she's on the road a lot too," Opal added. "That's hard on relationships. We like her, but be careful. That's all we're saying."

chapter 27

It had been years since Kia let her guest chefs close up the truck without her. But tonight was different.

"You got this?" she asked the local chef she'd invited to cook with her.

They'd featured his recipes and handed out his business cards with every meal. The customers had loved him.

The lights were on in Sullivan's house when Kia got back. She'd timed it right. Sullivan was still up, probably stretched out on the sofa listening to an audiobook. Kia had struggled with a birthday card. How could she capture her feelings and their strange situation in a card? Hallmark didn't have a message for that. Sitting in the cab of her truck, she picked up a pen. *I'm taking you camping. Itinerary and packing list included.* She placed a carabiner on the card and traced it, like the chalk outline that would mark where she fell when the snake got her. *What are these things even for?* She drew an arrow to the carabiner outline and tucked the card and carabiner into the envelope.

When she let herself into Sullivan's house, Sullivan wasn't listening to an audiobook. She was standing at the kitchen sink, staring out the window. She whirled around, like she'd been caught at something. But she looked happy, no trace of gazing-at-my-lost-wilderness in her eyes.

"Happy birthday." Kia held out the envelope.

"You remembered."

"You're my wife, and I have all your vital stats on my phone. And…I like you. In case you haven't noticed. Of course I remembered your birthday."

Sullivan sat down at the kitchen island and slipped her finger into the edge of the envelope, opening it slowly.

Sullivan read the message out loud. *"Dear Sullivan, despite my better judgment, I am taking you camping. We will probably be eaten by snakes. I've planned everything. All you have to do is show up."* Sullivan pressed the card to her chest. "Aww, Kia, that's my dream birthday."

"I know."

Sullivan read on. *"Supplies: RV. Propane. Emergency power supply. Sixty-gallon freshwater tank. Snakebite kit. Bear spray. National Forest Service maps."* Sullivan laughed. "Where are we going?"

"Opal's rugby team's camping trip. She said it's okay."

"Digital compass. Magnetic compass. Book on using a compass? We can live off the grid with this stuff."

Hearing the list out loud it did sound like overkill. "I carry most of this stuff anyway," Kia lied.

"A magnetic compass and bear spray?"

"Okay. Not those. But you never know what's out there in the woods." Kia chuckled. "Fine, you probably know, but I don't. Do you want to go or not? Don't make me buy bear spray for nothing. Those sporting goods stores are terrifying."

Sullivan jumped up and threw her arms around Kia.

"Of course I want to go. Thank you. I can't wait."

And Sullivan held on, her forehead resting on Kia's shoulder. Nothing had ever felt as right or as natural to Kia as wrapping her arms around Sullivan and holding her.

"You're welcome," Kia whispered. The moment felt joyful and solemn, like hello and goodbye and a promise all at the same time.

Sullivan lifted her forehead from Kia's, but she kept her arms around Kia's waist.

"You talked to Opal about camping?" Sullivan asked.

"I asked her how I could take you camping without going too far into the wilderness. She told me the She-Pack was going on their annual camping trip, and they could only get a big campsite Sunday through Tuesday. It's perfect. You're off. Mirepoix is closed. And friends and family were all invited. There'll be kids there so it can't be too dangerous."

"They bring children to distract the cougars while the adults get away."

"Sullivan!" Kia slapped Sullivan's chest gently.

"Don't worry. It'll be safer than crossing a street in New York." Sullivan pulled Kia a little closer. "Now I know why Opal was asking if I'd talked to you about my birthday. It's really special you've done this. I know camping's not your thing."

"That's how much I like you." The word *like* was a sugar cube compared to the fantastic sugar sculptures in Kia's heart.

"I like you too." Sullivan kissed Kia's nose. "And I have a present for you too."

"But it's *your* birthday."

"You'll be gone by your birthday." A shadow crossed Sullivan's face for a second and then passed. "If we're going camping, it really can't wait."

Sullivan led Kia to the back door and turned on the porch light. Sullivan had set up a little canopy, like the kind that might house a small vendor table or a wedding couple prepared for a light rain. In its shelter, she'd placed a bistro table and two chairs. String lights, like the ones in the Mirepoix garden, warmed the space with their golden-white glow. A bottle of wine sat in an ice bucket between two glasses.

Even though it wasn't on top of her RV yet, Kia recognized the 1968 Wind Searcher Pop-Up Pavilion immediately.

"Oh my god, Sullivan, how?"

Sullivan bounced on her toes, her excitement like a champagne tower about to spill over.

Kia approached the structure. She touched one of the supports. Embossed on the metal with a care no one would take with a modern RV were the words WIND SEARCHER POP-UP PAVILION.

"You found one! I have a Google Alert on them. If there's one west of the Rockies I should know about it." Kia jumped up and down with excitement like a little kid on Christmas morning. "Oh my god. Thank you, Sullivan! I've been looking for one for years. I showed you one picture and you found one IRL!"

"I saw it a minute or two after it went on Facebook marketplace. Then the guy selling it took it down."

Kia threw her arms around Sullivan and squeezed her.

"Thank you. Thank you! Do I owe you any money? Whatever it cost—"

"It's a present."

Sullivan had found a 1968 Wind Searcher Pop-Up Pavilion. It was a miracle.

"How long did it take you to find it?"

"Long enough that I could have come up with the menus for all of next year. You're welcome."

Kia hugged Sullivan with her whole body, burying her soft Afro into Sullivan's chest, feeling its rise and fall. Kia pressed her cheek to Sullivan's chest, catching the sound of her heartbeat as they embraced.

"This is so sweet. I don't know what to say."

Kia took Sullivan's hand and pulled her under the Pop-Up Pavilion.

"It's the original canopy, isn't it? Did Opal tell you I was taking you camping?"

"She kept your secret."

"She must like me. You don't keep a secret for someone unless you like them."

"Nina could come up with some exceptions," Sullivan said, putting her arm around Kia. "But yes. Opal and Nina both like you. Do you want to take some pictures?" Sullivan asked. "We can reenact the moment."

"No." A thousand times no. Everything might come crashing down around her, but this happy memory belonged to her.

"Think about all the people who've sat under this." Still holding Sullivan's hand, Kia gazed at the string lights. "All their stories. Old couples and families with kids, teenagers who bitched the whole time and then later they realized it was one of their happiest memories. And us."

She pulled Sullivan into a hug and swayed to imaginary music. And she kissed Sullivan, languid and slow and full of affection, and their kiss became part of the story. Like Sullivan had pointed out at the fair, things didn't have to be perfect to be wonderful.

chapter 28

Not being eaten by bears was the number one reason to camp in an RV instead of a tent. The number two reason, Kia saw as soon as they pulled into the campground, was that tents hate people. And if you weren't getting eaten alive by your own tent, camping consisted of making millions and millions of trips to your SUV while your children jumped off every dangerous thing they could find in hopes of breaking a leg, so you'd have to drive all the way back to civilization.

"Watch this," Kia said as she eased her truck and the RV down the narrow paved road.

Campsite number twelve waited for them. An eight-point turn positioned Old Girl over the gray water drain, and the truck pointed toward the exit for whatever reason might necessitate a fast departure.

"Now we pop up the pavilion and drink a beer."

Kia and Sullivan stepped out and stretched their legs. At the neighboring campsite, two women in rugby jerseys explained to a boy why he couldn't use the camping mat as a raft while a girl of about the same age stole a second mat from their pile of camping supplies and raced toward the creek.

"August Chrysanthemum Lowell!" one of the women yelled when she saw the girl splash into the water.

Another pack of kids was playing a game that seemed to involve shaking cans of soda and spraying each other with Coke. Several teenagers sat on a log, earbuds in, heads down, typing frantically on their phones.

"I should probably help," Sullivan said. "Can you get the pavilion up by yourself?"

"Sullivan." Kia folded her arms and pretended to glare. "Out there"—she tipped her head toward the campground—"I fear everything." She nodded at Old Girl. "Back there, I can flush the radiator, change a tire, and filter gray water. In. My. Pajamas."

Sullivan rolled her eyes, but she was smiling.

"Okay, Miss Point Six Percent."

"Is it sexy?" Kia asked, climbing halfway up the ladder on Old Girl's side and hanging off casually.

"That you can filter gray water?"

"And change a tire and flush the radiator." Kia swung herself onto the roof of the RV.

"Yes." Sullivan looked up at Kia. "Yes. It is." Then in a voice loud enough to reach the children, Sullivan called, "Anyone want to see a slug the size of your arm?"

One of the teenagers put down their phone. "No such thing."

Sullivan shrugged. "Probably not, but the poisonous newts are cool."

Two children who'd been trying to remove each other's eyes with medieval swordplay put down their sticks.

"I heard one newt could kill seven men," one of them said.

"I guess if seven men shared one on a sandwich," Sullivan said.

Kia watched from the top of Old Girl, amused.

"Ewww," one of the tweens groaned from beneath chin-length purple bangs.

"But we're not going to eat them, because they're so cute," Sullivan said.

Another pack of children had gathered in Sullivan's orbit. She explained something Kia couldn't hear. The children's eyes went wide.

Kia heard Sullivan say, "You want to see? Go ask whichever adult is responsible for making sure you're not eaten by bears if you can go on a nature walk."

"So there are bears!" Kia called out from the top of the RV.

"It's a figure of speech." Sullivan didn't turn around, but Kia could hear a teasing look in her voice.

"*Making sure you're not eaten by bears* is *not* a figure of speech," Kia called.

"It takes a village to keep us safe from bears," the smallest child proclaimed in a high voice.

"That it does." Sullivan patted the child's blond head. "Everyone back here in ten minutes. Can you little monsters tell time?"

All the children flashed cell phones.

"I despair for you." Sullivan threw her arm dramatically over her eyes, but a moment later the kids were back, including the sullen tweens, and Sullivan was showing them how to use the food setting on their cameras to photograph close-ups.

"Every single thing in the forest is magical. You just have to look closely enough. But remember, look with your real eyes first. There's no filter that's ever going to be as beautiful as this moment."

The kids started listing filters that might contradict Sullivan's declaration.

"Indio Glow?"

"Lo Fi?"

"Sedona?"

"Nope. Nope. Nope," Sullivan said. They were still standing in the middle of the campground surrounded by people unpacking tents, but Sullivan held the children's attention. She knelt down and pulled a piece of moss so small Kia only knew it was moss because she heard Sullivan tell the children that it was.

Sullivan's camping clothes matched everyone else's: hiking boots in earth tones and Patagonia microfiber. But somehow Sullivan looked cooler than the other campers. She looked like she had in school: confident, cocky, profoundly in her element.

"Now look closely," she said to the children. "Really look. See the little stalks? Those are like moss flowers. And here, the green part, imagine you were a tiny, tiny fairy and this was your whole world. And did you know that all the trees around us talk to each other? I'm serious. Guess how they do it?"

The children guessed, and she said no to all of them but not like a stern teacher telling them they were wrong. She was a magician delighting them with the mystery.

Finally, she said, "The trees are connected by a giant, underground mushroom, it's not like the kind you eat. It's like the internet. Except it's real! Let's go see the forest."

Kia was on the ground before Sullivan took ten steps.

"Wait, Sullivan."

Sullivan's smile was sunlight coming over a mountain.

"I want to hear about the giant slug."

Apparently, there was no slug big enough to impress Oregon children. The hand-sized yellow and black banana slugs impressed Kia, but the children all declared that they'd seen bigger. They were still riveted as Sullivan rattled off facts about the moist, slow-moving creature covered in a slimy mucus. Kia was too. Sullivan found one of the poisonous newts ambling across the path, the same color as the dirt, with a bright orange belly. She scooped it up.

"See how chill he is?" The newt ambled over her thumb and onto her other hand. "He knows I'm not going to eat him. And look at his little smile." She knelt down and held the newt up for the smallest child to admire. "Who wants to touch him? We don't want to scare him, so just let him walk off your hand and onto the next person's."

"But it's poisonous," one of the tweens pointed out, echoing Kia's reservations.

"If you lick your hands. Who's going to lick their hand after handling a newt?"

The children laughed. Sullivan shook a finger at each of them.

"Are you going to lick a newt? How about you?"

A hush fell around them as the children reverently let the creature walk from hand to hand. When it reached Kia, the boy with the newt held it out.

"You don't have to," Sullivan said.

But this might be the only chance she ever got to touch a poisonous newt in a forest with a pack of strange children and a woman who was her wife, and whom she'd been kind of in love with since she was twenty and was…really, really falling for now.

She held out her hand, waiting for the burn of poison. The newt felt cool, light but solid. It didn't burn. It wasn't slimy. It looked up at her with tiny gold eyes.

Sullivan went on to describe the network of fungus biologists believed passed messages between trees. She encouraged the kids to press their thumbprints into sap oozing from a pine tree. Everything smelled like freshness and pine. When they returned to the campsite, the tents were up. Grills were lit. Camp chairs were out. Phones were put away. A few people sat around a firepit stacked and ready to go when it got dark.

"Wash your hands!" Sullivan said by way of farewell.

"I didn't tell them half of it," she said to Kia as they walked toward the bathroom and the soap that would save them from the fate of the legendary newt sandwich. "When the banana slugs mate—they're hermaphrodites—they both have a penis that comes out of the side of their heads, and sometimes if the penis gets stuck on the other one, one of them will chew it off."

"Ewww." Kia sounded a lot like the tweens.

"And the newts, when they mate, they create these flotillas, like newt sex rafts. All twirled up together, so you can't even pull them apart. Or you shouldn't."

"I have no desire to pull apart newt sex rafts."

They washed their hands and wandered toward the creek. Sunlight dappled the mossy ground, and the water glittered. Kia could almost imagine splashing into it without giving a thought to what might brush past her legs or the disturbing fact that snakes could, indeed, swim.

"You're good with them," Kia said when they were sitting, side by side on a large boulder overlooking the creek.

Sullivan had retrieved the binoculars Kia had picked up for their trip in case they got lost at the top of a mountain and had to look for help. Sullivan said there was a blue heron on the other side of the creek, and she wanted to get a better look.

"I'm good at talking about stuff I'm interested in," Sullivan said, raising the binoculars to her eyes.

"They were totally hooked," Kia said. "You could have told them about dirt."

"I think I did tell them about dirt."

"And they loved it. You'd be a good mom."

Sullivan handed the binoculars to Kia. She put the strap over her head.

"It's over there." She pointed. "I wouldn't be a *bad* mom. But what kind of legacy can I leave them?"

Kia looked for the bird but saw only wet children with their dripping child-hipster mullets.

"You mean what if they didn't keep the house?"

"I mean what if there's no planet to leave them. No fresh air. No…snow?" Sullivan stared at the stone beneath them.

Kia let the binoculars hang heavy around her neck. She thought Sullivan might have teared up, but her expression was calm and still.

"Hey, look at me." Kia tipped Sullivan's chin up and looked her in the eye. "You're fighting all that with Mirepoix."

"Sometimes I think I'm just trying to make myself feel less guilty." Sullivan's shoulders slumped as she exhaled a long sigh. "Mirepoix costs forty dollars a plate. Yeah, we're carbon neutral, but we only serve fifty people a night, if that." Sullivan's eyebrows furrowed. "It's not enough. Sorry. That was heavy."

Kia gently rubbed Sullivan's back.

"You get to be heavy if you want."

Sullivan covered Kia's hand with hers in an absent-minded way.

"Do you want kids, wife of mine? The banana slugs make it work. I don't see why we couldn't impregnate each other with the penises that we'll grow out of our heads. Right side only. It's always the right side."

Kia tried to laugh. "I don't want you to chew off my head penis." She still felt heavy. "I don't want kids."

"Why not?" Sullivan threaded her fingers through Kia's.

"I live in an RV. At least my dad had drag queens to tutor me.

I'd have to teach them everything. And there's the environment, like you said."

Sullivan looked surprised.

"I've always tried to put it out of my mind. When I lived on my dad's yacht, we sailed to places that weren't touched by pollution. I mean, of course, they *were*, but they were places where you didn't see it, places that had been cleaned up, like Boston Harbor, or places where people kept things clean for the tourists, like Cabo. And since my dad sailed more than he ran the engines, it felt like we weren't hurting anything. But I know my food truck is part of the problem. You're right about the forks. We go through thousands."

"You're trying to help people."

"What good is it if there's no planet to live on?"

"There's hope," Sullivan said emphatically.

"You just said you felt like you weren't doing anything, and you're more environmentally conscious than anyone I know."

Kia nestled closer to Sullivan. The sunshine on Kia's face was warm, but the air was cooling. She felt Sullivan release a long breath.

"I'm just one person. If I were the only one trying to make a difference, it wouldn't matter at all, but there are people protecting the Amazon rainforest. There's a Kenyan woman turning plastic into bricks for building. Mushroom farmers making cloth out of fungus in petri dishes. There's a fair outside of Eugene where the vendors, restaurants, and a lot of performance spaces are built into a forest. There, people and nature and business are symbiotic. Once a year. For a few days a year, like magic, this model of how we could live if we really tried. If you're in Oregon in July, I'll take you. It's kind of like a food truck pod. Lots of small vendors. No big, established buildings."

"Maybe it should be more than once a year." Kia scooched forward on the boulder so she could look at Sullivan. "We could…" Kia began. "With what you know about sustainable cooking and my food pod…"

Sullivan's eyes lit up. Her body filled with energy. She was waiting, breathless, for Kia to say what Sullivan herself was obviously thinking.

"We could expand the Country Fair model," Sullivan jumped in. "We could prove that you can run food trucks sustainably and help the people you want to help."

"Minority communities get left out of environmental activism. A lot of the chefs I've invited are coming from places with industrial pollution, like cancer alley in St. James Parish in Louisiana. They want a better environment for their kids. They know their towns have higher rates of everything bad."

"We could have community gardens, teach about small-scale food production. Camps for kids," Sullivan said.

"Some sort of shared plate and fork dishwashing so no one has to use disposables."

"It'd be beautiful too. There are lots of food trucks in Portland, but this would be better than eating in a parking lot. This would be a place to be more…alive, more in nature, to feed your soul too."

"I could teach the food trucks I visit around the country how to use our practices."

"Maybe there's money out there to help people install solar panels," Sullivan said. "I opposed the sale of the Bois because I wanted my nonprofit to buy it, but, realistically, there's a good chance we wouldn't have raised the money in time, and the association would have sold it to a developer anyway. And who knows… maybe, long shot of all long shots, maybe some of it will rub off on

Mega Eats or another company like that. Maybe we'll do something that makes them see they can make money and waste less of our planet. Wait, look! It just caught a fish." Sullivan motioned to the creek. Kia turned. A tall bird stood in the water gulping something down its long neck.

"I see it."

When she looked through the binoculars, it felt like the bird was watching her back.

"If we did do something together, you could put it all on your socials," Sullivan said. "It'll be like a home renovation show meets a nature show meets a cooking show."

Kia laughed. "Do I have to? Can't I get off social media?"

"It's your job."

Kia handed the binoculars back to Sullivan, sitting close to her again, as though they could share the binoculars like sharing earbuds. Sullivan admired the bird.

"Hello, you fine fellow," she said. "Would you like to get gourmazed?"

"You make it sound like I'm going to eat him. Wait, do we have to go vegan?"

"It's a responsible choice, but we could do what I do now and buy sustainably and humanely raised meat. I know it's a big pivot. And you don't have to make my thing be your thing. That wasn't the deal."

Kia leaned toward Sullivan and whispered in her ear, "Neither was living with you or having sex with you." It felt so easy to be with Sullivan. She'd stopped worrying about whether her flirting was perfect. She could be totally herself. Maybe she'd take a picture of herself and Sullivan on her digital camera. Those pictures were always taken alone, and it was wonderful to be herself around another person. Being authentically yourself made it easier to dream. Challenges that would have seemed insurmountable or worries—like the lawsuit—that would have devastated her before felt manageable. Maybe it was because being with Sullivan reminded Kia that Kia was herself, no matter what happened. No one could take that away from her.

"Maybe I'll be an environmentalist influencer," Sullivan said. "Did you know that the blue heron's eyes turn red during mating season?"

Did you know I love you? Kia looked at Sullivan and tried to press the words into Sullivan's mind. *Love me back.*

chapter 29

Sullivan was prepared to let the She-Pack handle the cooking. Just because she owned a restaurant didn't mean she should rob people of the pleasure of cooking beans in the cans they came in. But as soon as they returned to the campsite, one of Opal's friends hurried over, pointing to a picnic table loaded with ingredients.

"You don't have to take your work on vacation, but if you'd like to give us a hand…"

This time, it wasn't a competition at opposite ends of the bar. Kia and Sullivan surveyed the supplies and planned the menu. Apple-stuffed vegan sausages. Marshmallow-glazed beef burgers. Flame-grilled summer squash and green beans.

Kia seemed to have every spice imaginable in the RV. When Sullivan commented that her seared iceberg salad needed a hint of za'atar, Kia rolled her eyes. "Did you forget your za'atar, Chef? I can help you. Do you want a Middle Eastern blend or a North African blend? But I'm only sharing if you put some crushed Corn Nuts on your salad. They're America's crouton."

"Isn't the crouton America's crouton?" Sullivan joked.

"Oh, Chef, have you forgotten everything we learned about the croûton?"

With that she skipped off, blowing a kiss to Sullivan, and returning a moment later with two spice jars.

"Hello, my friends," Sullivan said, taking the jars from Kia. "You don't want to season Corn Nuts, do you?"

"I love the way you talk to your food." Kia made a heart with her hands and held it over her chest. "You can always talk to my za'atar blends."

They cooked for an hour, maybe more. Sullivan lost herself in the satisfaction of snapping green beans and the smell of charcoal grills heating up. Everyone agreed it was the best campsite food ever, with the campers getting up for seconds and thirds until the improvised buffet tables were almost empty.

"That's what I like." Sullivan kissed her fingertips and let out a smack. "No waste."

"But everyone got enough," Kia added.

"Perfect." Sullivan put her arm around Kia.

Kia snuggled closer, and Sullivan felt full of anticipation for what the night would bring but also completely at peace. She could sit here forever watching the sparks dance and then go out.

"There's stuff for s'mores, but someone else has to get it ready," Sullivan said.

Opal and three other people jumped up with a chorus of "you've done enough" and "can I get you another drink?" Someone brought Kia and Sullivan two marshmallow skewers and plates of chocolate and graham crackers. Kia and Sullivan teased each other for the entertainment of the crowd, riffing on Sullivan's plan to char the Hershey's chocolate bars to make a mole drizzle and Sullivan groaning in horror as Kia melted Cheetos into s'mores. The children decided Cheetos s'mores was the best food ever eaten by human beings.

"To our chefs." Opal raised a beer. "To one of the sweetest couples I know."

The team and their families echoed her toast.

From across the campfire, Opal caught Sullivan's eyes. Because they'd been friends since they were making mud pies, Opal conveyed and Sullivan understood everything without words. Love and warning. Worry and hope. A dash of *this would be so much simpler if you'd just gone out with my cousin from Savannah.*

Kia didn't ask Opal to repeat her toast so she could get it on camera. Kia just wrapped her arm around Sullivan's and snuggled closer.

"I adore you, baby, but you're still wrong about the Cheetos," Kia said.

Slowly, the fire died down. Children fell asleep in their parents' laps. Couples disappeared into their tents. Eventually, Kia and Sullivan were the only ones left by the embers. Sullivan hadn't invited Kia back to her bedroom after they'd slept together the day of the green roof. She would have liked to. She would have liked to invite Kia into her bed every night, every afternoon she wasn't working. But Kia had been out late working at the NoPo Spring Street Festival and up even later working at her laptop, her eyes getting redder and her eyelids heavier as she typed reply after reply. Once Sullivan had stood behind Kia, massaging Kia's neck. She'd read a few sentences over Kia's shoulders. Kia was writing a long reply to a teenager who had just come out to his friends. Kia told him he was brave, and even if his friends weren't supportive right now, they might come around. And when they did, he got to choose whether to let them back into his life or not. *That's really good*, Sullivan had whispered. Kia had leaned back against Sullivan. *Only ten thousand more to answer.* Sullivan wanted to say, *Just leave it, and come to bed*, but that would be like Kia asking her to leave Mirepoix in the middle of service, so Sullivan just kissed the top of Kia's hair, careful not to deflate Georgie. Kia probably hadn't even felt it.

Now Kia said, "I guess we should…" at the same time Sullivan said, "Do you want…"

Sullivan wanted to bury her face in Kia's pussy, but first she put out the fire using the four-step water-stir-water-cover method.

"You take care of the world," Kia said quietly as they walked toward the RV.

She threaded her fingers through Sullivan's and leaned close as they walked hand in hand.

Inside the RV, Kia turned on a soft light over the sofa. She looped her arms around Sullivan's waist.

"I want to sleep with you again but no pressure. The sofa folds into a bed if you don't want to," Kia said shyly.

"How could I possibly not want to sleep with you? And also I don't want to pressure you if you don't—"

"I do." Kia gave Sullivan a delightfully awkward kiss, their lips colliding as Kia pulled Sullivan closer.

"Good."

They climbed a narrow staircase into the loft. Kia had a small footprint, a whole life in this tiny camper. The mattress filled the whole loft. A wall kept them from rolling off while giving them a view into the living area. You couldn't stand up, but Kia could rise up on her knees without her Afro brushing the ceiling. Kia rolled back a panel to reveal a skylight and pushed up on it to let in a cool breeze. Her RV was like a good kitchen, spacious enough to do anything you needed with no space wasted. For all Kia's glitter and tursnickens and adorable live stream mishaps, she was meticulous. The space was colorful and comfortable. Strings of felt beads adorned the windows. The bed was covered by a velvet quilt, obviously handmade by an artist.

Kia wrapped her arms around Sullivan and playfully pulled her to the bed like a gentle wrestler. But when Sullivan tried to pull Kia to her, Kia sat up, lifting her shirt over her head to reveal an iridescent pink bra that hid as much of her breasts as a summer breeze. Kia straddled Sullivan and caught Sullivan's hands behind her head. The way she looked at Sullivan made Sullivan smile, not just with her lips but with her body. She loved to look at bodies. She loved to be looked at. She loved to be touched. Her body glowed, not just with the promise of release, but with the feeling of being alive in the world, every muscle awake. It was like standing in a mountain meadow, breathing in the perfectly clear air, feeling the sunshine.

"How am I going to get point six percent better if I don't practice?" Kia said.

Kia explored Sullivan's body with guileless simplicity. She kissed Sullivan's lips, then moved to her ears, her neck, her shoulders. She cupped Sullivan's breasts in her hands and sucked on her nipples until Sullivan thought she might come like that.

Sullivan had had more adventurous sex (anything twice with the right person) and sure, sometimes you wanted the tursnicken of sex: every toy and strap and dirty word. But people said vanilla sex like *vanilla* was bad. Vanilla focused your mind and body. Vanilla called you to appreciate this moment, this caress. Some of the best food used only two or three ingredients in a dish. Simplicity made you appreciate. Simplicity made the chef search for the perfect tomato, organic sage, the freshest butter, a single vanilla bean oily and dark. If the dish was simple, you had to love it more.

Sullivan luxuriated in Kia's touch. While her clit and vulva swelled in anticipation, her thoughts were unhurried. She let her mind slip away until she was all body. She felt Kia's lips and hands on her, but she also felt the soft sheets, a corner of the velvet quilt, the pleasant memory of sun on her face. But mostly she felt Kia.

Kia kissed down her belly.

"May I?" Kia asked.

"Of course." Sullivan might be mindfully enjoying every moment, but her clit was also throbbing for release.

"What do you want me to know about your body?" Kia asked, massaging Sullivan's belly just above the curls of her hair.

"I come really fast, but after that…don't stop." It had been a long time since Sullivan had described what she wanted, and she felt unexpectedly shy. "The first time is just a warm up. If you keep going, that's when it gets really good."

"I'll keep going." Kia grinned. "As long as you like."

Kia spent what felt like forever caressing Sullivan's inner thighs and admiring her spread legs.

"You're so beautiful," she said, looking at Sullivan's vulva and kissing lightly around the edges of her labia.

"If I'm beautiful…" Sullivan let the need in her voice finish the sentence.

"What?" Kia asked, kissing Sullivan's pubic hair just above where Sullivan wanted her to kiss.

"You would—"

Kia drew her tongue all the way from Sullivan's opening, across her clit and back down.

"I would do that?"

"Yes!"

Sullivan forgot that the skylight was open and the entire She-Pack rugby team (fifteen players plus alternates) was nearby, and cried out in pleasure. Then she laughed and gasped and stifled another cry as Kia drew Sullivan's clit into her mouth so gently Sullivan felt like the pleasure and the tenderness might break her. Kia continued, asking Sullivan what she liked and where it felt best. How hard? How fast?

A few times, Sullivan lifted herself onto her elbows to look at Kia because she couldn't believe this was real. Kia was making love to her. Kia, the brilliant kid from school, who Sullivan had tried so hard to beat, whose company she'd enjoyed so much Kia defined her culinary education. Kia Gourmazing with hundreds of thousands of followers. Kia, who showed up on her lawn to ask the most outrageous favor. Kia, whose presence made Sullivan's house feel like home. Kia was kissing her and massaging the tight cords of muscle in her legs and sucking and—

The first orgasm washed over Sullivan like a shallow wave. Kia hesitated, then resumed, pressing her thumb against Sullivan's hip flexor while she slid two fingers inside her. Sullivan didn't know if she luxuriated for seconds or minutes or hours. Time vanished. Then pleasure claimed her, and exploded like a piñata cake full of Pop Rocks.

chapter 30

Sullivan wished they could stay at the campsite forever, but too quickly it was time to head home. Kia took an exit off Highway 26 and wound her way through the busier northwest streets into the hills that cradled the Oakwood Heights neighborhood. The rhododendrons were in bloom. Daffodils popped out of mossy rock gardens. But something wasn't right.

Construction equipment, two semitrucks, and three shipping containers—all in Mega Eats–brand orange—lined the street that ran alongside the Bois. On the other side of the street, a man stood in front of his house watering his lawn with a handheld sprinkler, looking shell-shocked.

Kia parked, lining Old Girl and her truck up against the curb behind the semi.

"What's going on," she called to the man with the sprinkler.

"They just appeared," he said. "I didn't realize the sale went through."

"It hasn't," Sullivan said.

Mega Eats slogans covered every piece of equipment. MEGA EATS: CHOOSE FLAVOR and on the back of the semis Mega Eats franchises were listed in bubbly red font: MEGA MEXICAN, MEGA BURGER, MEGAPOLITZ, MEGA PIZZA, MEGA SOUTHRN COOK'N.

"This is unbelievable," Kia muttered, scanning the street. "It's like they've moved in overnight."

A woman with a brown ponytail and an orange Mega Eats windbreaker hurried up to them, a flyer and a handful of coupons extended. When she saw Sullivan, she stopped.

"Sorry about the other day."

Sullivan's jaw tightened.

"You served me."

"It's not personal. I work for Mega Eats. We're excited to work together to build a happier, healthier Oakwood Heights."

"*Healthier?*" Sullivan's voice soared an octave.

"The off-ramp will cut an average of four to seven minutes off commute times. If you factor that over years..."

"That's health? An arm of freeway chopping through our neighborhood so we can eat pink slime?"

The woman shrugged as if to say, *If that's what you want to call it, I don't care.* She turned to Kia, who cut her off before she could speak.

"There is a court case to decide who buys this land. You do not get to build on the Bois just because you want to."

"Standard operating procedure. We want to be ready to go as soon as the verdict comes in."

"You better go!" Kia shoved her hands in her pockets.

"I mean ready to get building. You must be Kiana Jackson." The woman held out her hand.

Sullivan was glad she'd never pissed Kia off, because an angry Kia looked like an avenging goddess.

"I don't want to know you," Kia hissed.

"Well, my company is suing you, Ms. Jackson, so we're

acquainted, but this isn't personal. Mega Eats is a multibillion-dollar company. You're not going to win. I've overseen a dozen projects like this. Mega Eats moves their equipment in so they can break ground the minute the judge signs the papers, and he will rule in favor of Mega Eats. You can pour a bunch of resources into fighting them and then lose, or you can get your lawyers to strike a deal. Mega Eats is actually pretty reasonable." She looked at Sullivan with fake sympathy. "They'll buy your house and your restaurant at more than fair market value." To Kia she added, "They'll probably pay to relocate your food pod. I could negotiate something. Would twenty thousand make it right?"

"You falling off a cliff would make it right," Kia shot back, then stopped herself. "Not you personally. I'm sure you're a decent person when you're not hawking pink slime for the devil."

"That's the nicest thing anyone's said to me this week," the woman said dryly. "Mega Eats just wants to provide delicious, economical food options to make hungry Americans, happy Americans." The woman winced as she quoted the slogan. "They're not out to fuck with you, but they will if you don't back down. It costs a lot of money to bring in this kind of equipment, to have blueprints drawn up, workers hired. They wouldn't invest that money if they didn't know they'd win. Go to them with an offer, but if you don't do that, when they come to you, whatever they offer you, say yes. You seem like nice people, and I don't want to see you ruined."

They walked back to the truck in silence.

"It's going to be okay," Sullivan said, her faith in that sentiment shaken. "That's the woman who served me. She's a flunky. She's just flexing because she doesn't have any real power. She doesn't know what the judge is going to decide."

"She doesn't!" Kia's conviction sounded brittle.

"Whatever happens, I've got you." It felt good to speak those words to Kia. She might not believe they were going to be okay—whatever okay was—but it felt good to be in it together.

The next day, Sullivan woke to find Kia gone out of bed. She expected to see Kia in the kitchen at her laptop. Instead, Kia was outside, dressed, and sweeping leaves off Old Girl. She waved.

"Come on up, babe. The view is great. I can see your weird squash vines and into the bedroom of the most beautiful woman I know."

Sullivan could tell Kia was trying to brush off yesterday's encounter with Mega Eats. Mega Eats wanted to intimidate them. Better to pretend they hadn't.

"Why are you sweeping leaves at eight in the morning?" Sullivan shielded her eyes from the morning sunlight cutting through the trees and silhouetting Kia like an angel.

Kia clambered down the ladder, jumping off the last two rungs. She put her arms around Sullivan's neck and gave her a kiss.

"Can we go camping again?" Kia asked. "Just get in Old Girl and drive away and never do anything except cook hot dogs and watch the birds?"

"So you like camping now?"

"In Old Girl with my pavilion." Kia leaned her forehead on Sullivan's shoulder. "I have to go out of town tomorrow." She sighed. "I don't want to, but these great chefs—I call them the Chets—they're supposed to take their truck to the Grants Pass Spring Festival, on their way up here to...Taste the Love Land. But Chet Jr. got the flu, and his dad and granddad, who work with him, are worried they're getting sick too. If they don't find someone to replace them, the festival will charge the Chets the lot fee and a penalty for being a no-show. The festival organizers are kind of strict. I get it. It's a new festival. They've only got five food trucks. If even one of them cancels, the lines will be insane. People will get frustrated." Kia sank into Sullivan's arms. "I told him I'd fill in. But what I'd rather do is just run away with you."

"I'll run away to Grants Pass with you," Sullivan blurted. She shouldn't leave Mirepoix, but Opal would chide her if she acted like the restaurant couldn't survive a day without her.

A road trip would give them a few more days before reality set it. The court case was approaching. It was quite possible they'd lose everything in a few days. The judge would rule against them. Kia would leave. Sullivan would start looking for a new place for Mirepoix. If she was smart, she'd sell her house before Mega Eats broke ground on the Mega Plex. But they could steal a few more days of joy.

"Ah, babe. I wish you could come with me, but I shouldn't bring company. I am so far behind in everything I need to be on top of. And I can work the whole time I'm gone. We hire a driver for the Diva. Deja drives Old Girl, and I sit in the back and work."

Kia was turning her down. Sullivan was ready to throw responsibility to the wind, and Kia wanted to travel alone and work. Sullivan's brain understood work. In her heart, she felt like a kid who'd expected a hug only to be told to go away and play in her room.

"I'd love to have you there, but you'd be a wonderful, terrible distraction." Kia kissed Sullivan again. "I mean it. I can't believe I'm so nice I volunteered to be away from you for forty-eight hours. I will die of missing you. Deja will just bring back a little box of ashes that says, *Kia was an idiot and went to Grants Pass when she could have been with Sullivan.*"

That made it a little better.

"But I've done fairs in Grants Pass. You know those guys

who drive decommissioned police cars because they wanted to be cops but the police didn't want them and now they think they're protecting America by buying guns? It's that vibe. It's not really the interracial lesbian couple vibe down there." Kia pulled back, a disappointed frown on her face. "I go to places like that all the time…I used to before I got so many sponsors. I can charm Grants Pass, but I don't need to put you through that."

chapter 31

Kia felt bad for throwing shade on Grants Pass. Kia and Deja had installed the Diva at the festival, unhitched Kia's truck, and gone looking for food they didn't have to cook themselves. By twilight, they were walking into Shayla's Diner. Behind the diner, the sky was turning purple. In front of the diner, a man in an eagle T-shirt and leather vest stood by his motorcycle and glared at them. But when Kia waved, his glare disappeared like a wisp of smoke, replaced by a cheerful "ma'am" as he tipped an imaginary hat.

Like so many other places she'd visited, Grants Pass was mostly good. Good people trying to get along, staying out of each other's business, and hoping tomorrow would be better than today. A beautiful landscape that Kia wouldn't have appreciated before hearing Sullivan talk about the ecology of the forest. Gritty, vacant lots that Kia appreciated for their stark beauty and a feeling of sonder. Everyone who crossed those lots had a story that was as important to them as Kia's was to her. Thinking about that was like looking at the night sky without light pollution. So vast.

More than feeling vaguely guilty for dissing Grants Pass (after all, Grants Pass didn't know; it wasn't like she'd broadcast it on social media), she regretted telling Sullivan to stay home. Sullivan had looked so wounded and so worried. Kia wanted to hug Sullivan until Sullivan believed her when she'd said she would so much rather be at home with Sullivan than working a fair in southern Oregon.

"This way, dears." A waitress in a white apron and red slacks guided Kia and Deja toward a booth.

Outside the window, dust stirred in the breeze, catching the last daylight slanting between the buildings across the street.

"Now our specials are the pies," the waitress began. "Pecan pie, filbert pie—that's hazelnuts, if you aren't from Oregon—banana pie, coconut pie, boysenberry pie."

"What *are* boysenberries exactly?" Deja asked.

The woman's face lit up as though she'd been waiting her whole life for someone to ask. And perhaps she was an ageless vampire, because as far as Kia could tell, nothing in the diner had been updated since 1949. She guessed 1949 because a calendar turned to May 1949 hung behind the register, the paper fraying. Despite that, everything had been kept up. As much as it could be.

Once they'd made their selection and the waitress left, Deja said, "Did you see the bowling ball on the road when we were coming down I-5 near Creswell?"

"No."

"I wonder about the stuff on the side of the road. How does it get there?"

A second before remembering the plague of plastic waste poisoning the earth, Kia opened the straw that had come with her water. No point in not using it now. She accordioned the wrapper until it was a tiny knot, then dripped water on it to watch it expand like a snake, then plunked the straw into her glass.

"Cool," Deja said, then continued with things she'd seen on the roadside.

Kia stared at the table. It was spotless. Not a speck of ketchup on the outside of the ketchup bottle. And from across the room, she saw a young busboy wiping out the inside of the ketchup lids. Maybe he was like Blake. Kia's heart throbbed with affection at the thought of talented, disciplined Chef Sullivan mentoring this struggling kid. Sullivan hadn't fired him yet, Kia had noticed, and she loved Sullivan for it. Not that she would be disappointed if Sullivan did fire him. If Sullivan did, she'd admire Sullivan's decisiveness and the way she'd surely be calm and kind about it. Kia would love her for that too.

Love, love, love. The word kept scrolling across her mind.

The waitress returned a few minutes later with a burger for Deja and an unappetizing-looking chicken-fried steak for Kia. If the cook put the gravy on the side of the steak and added a few green beans, it would improve the plate a hundred percent. Right now it was a white biscuit, white mashed potatoes, and a steak entirely covered in whitish gravy. She texted Sullivan.

Kia: *It's very white down here*

Sullivan didn't write back within half a second, which did not mean Sullivan was mad at her. Kia knew that logically. She had not fucked up by not dragging Sullivan five hours down I-5 to spend two days waiting for Kia to get off her twelve-hour shifts. That's what she told herself. She still felt like maybe she'd fucked up. Sullivan would have enjoyed the trip. She wouldn't have hunkered down. She'd have gone hiking, and probably met a bunch of cool, outdoorsy people.

"Are you texting Sullivan?" Deja asked.

Kia nodded.

"How are things going?" Deja propped her elbows on the table, folding her hands above her hamburger in a gesture that said, *After I say my grace, I'm going to sit like this until you tell me everything.*

"Good."

"I can see she's living rent-free in your head. Are you at the part where you're trippin' over everything she says?"

"No. What do you mean *part*?"

"Of the relationship. First you see them and, you're like, *They're so fly*. Then you get that they-like-me vibe. All that walking on clouds stuff. Then you freak out about everything because you're convinced they don't like you. Then you calm down and live happily ever after." Deja stabbed her knife through the top of her burger. "Or break up." She neatly cut the burger in half. "But you two won't. You're totally into each other."

Sullivan wasn't going to break up with her because Kia didn't let her fry tursnickens in Grants Pass.

"Should we do a live stream?" Deja asked after Kia was silent for a while. "I think it'd be fun to get Marley in on it."

"Marley?"

"Our server. She could talk about boysenberries."

There was probably a lot to say about boysenberries: growth patterns, pest resistance, conditions for agricultural workers. Sullivan could probably talk about the boysenberry industry for an hour. But Kia and Marley wouldn't have a real conversation. Kia would croon, *We're getting gourmazing at Shayla's Diner in beautiful Grants Pass, Oregon. Marley, tell us what you're serving today.* Marley would recite the pies. Kia would pretend to faint. Maybe they'd film a clip of Kia with a dozen pies in front of her, frantically sticking her fork in each one. They'd throw away the rest, but it wouldn't matter. She'd pay for them. Plus two minutes on Kia Gourmazing would bring in so many road trippers, Shayla's would wish they'd never heard of Kia Gourmazing.

Kia took out her phone with a sigh and opened U-Spin.

This account has been closed.

She read the screen again.

"Deja?" It felt like that moment in a horror movie when one friend turns to the other with a look that says, *Is that what I think it is?* She held out her phone. For once, Deja was speechless.

"It must be a mistake," Kia said.

It felt like food poisoning. Her stomach cramped. Her heart raced. Sweat dampened her skin, leaving a sick chill as it evaporated. She'd been shut down. She'd heard of this happening. People got shut down for copyright infringement, inappropriate content, false advertising (although U-Spin needed to police that one more carefully), but she had Deja constantly monitoring for any potential issues. She paid $199 a month for a program that scanned for and blocked hacks, trolls, threats, people engaging in hate speech in the comments, and copyright issues. Unless she was sponsored, you'd never find an errant Pepsi bottle in the background or a snippet of a song that wasn't included in U-Spin's approved music options.

But there were the words on a blank profile page.

This account has been closed.

Her account was everything. This was her income, her job, her life. Fuck. Some U-Spin employee or, more likely, algorithm could end her life. Yeah, she was getting tired of life on the road and pumping American Spirit breakfast sausage, but she didn't have a living without her account.

"Let me check my email."

There'd be a message with a link. They'd stopped a hack. Click here to verify your password.

There was a message, but there was no link to restore her account. The message read, *Your U-Spin account has been closed for the following issues: 7.4 and 13.2-7. Please see user agreement for details.*

Kia's hands began to shake. She couldn't breathe.

"Is everything all right?" It was Marley.

No, no, no. Go away. Kia didn't have the energy to find something polite to say.

"We're fine," Deja cut in.

She took the phone from Kia's trembling hands.

"Article seven is about violating community standards."

Ordinarily, Kia would stop to praise Deja for knowing even part of the user agreement off the top of her head. Most people had never read it. Now Kia felt like she was drowning and all Deja had to toss her was a tiny float, not nearly big enough to hold Kia up. Deja handed Kia's phone back. Without her social media accounts, Kia's career was dust. It was broken concrete in a vacant lot. Her other accounts! She opened them one by one. Closed. Closed. Closed.

"The Oak Tree Snacker's account got closed once. They got it back," Deja said. "And Mission Spider Plant. It was basically just a glitch."

"I know." Kia's voice got fainter. "This is different. Mega Eats did this. I don't know how, but those companies can do anything."

"Clause 13.2-7 says U-Spin can decide what meets community guidelines and if they say it doesn't, it doesn't," Deja said. "There's no way to challenge them."

"This is it. I'm fucked."

It was like the moment when you learned someone had died. Everything was normal, and in a second everything changed. Except Kia Gourmazing was the deceased. Deja reached over and put her hand on Kia's forearm.

"We need to reject all the direct payments coming in from

your subscribers, or we'll be taking their money for nothing. And we need to let your sponsors know, stop all direct deposits. We're in breach of a lot of contracts right now. I'm going to get started. Are you okay? Can you call Lillian or Sullivan?"

Kia nodded. She watched Deja pay at the hosts' station and head out the door. When Deja was gone, Kia slid out of the booth and stepped outside into the crisp, dusty air. Across the street an antique store, a veterans' support office, and a store selling glass pipes all looked well maintained and unloved at the same time. Everything was tidy, but nothing was loved. Nothing distinguished this block. Nothing said, *I want to be here.* That was probably just her mood blanketing the scene.

Kia's phone buzzed in her hand. She jumped. A text from an unknown number flashed onto her screen. A GIF showed a skeleton dancing on top of a grave, in a loop of jerky movements. On the tombstone read the words R.I.P. KIA GOURMAZING.

The last finger of light had lost its hold on the street, leaving charred shadows at the feet of the buildings. A bunch of motorcyclists emerged from the bar, dressed in leather and affiliation patches that might belong to middle-aged fathers grasping at adventure or might have been a gang. They revved the bikes to life, pumping handles and pedals to increase the roar. One by one they peeled out. They must have loved that moment when they all tore down the road. If only she and Sullivan could ride into the sunset like that. But she couldn't ask Sullivan to help her solve this problem, because she was the problem and, like Sullivan had said that first night they saw each other, Sullivan's life was collateral damage.

chapter 32

The Mirepoix kitchen was humming, clanging, and sizzling as it should. The latest shipment of shiitakes from Rainland Mushrooms was delicious. For the herculean task of not using his phone in the kitchen for a whole week, Sullivan had let Blake name the dish Let That Shiitake Go. The name mortified her a bit, but the customers thought it was cute, and it had sold more orders than vegetarian dishes usually did. Maybe Kia was right; maybe cute names did sell product.

Sullivan wasn't happy though, not since Kia drove south. Camping with Kia had been magical. It was the birthday date she'd always wanted. Fun and sexy. Surrounded by nature and friends but held closest by a partner who cared about her, who knew her. Kia hadn't taken any videos for Kia Gourmazing, but she had taken a picture of Sullivan on her digital camera. In the picture, Sullivan was standing by the creek, her back to the camera. Early morning light streaking through the trees blended the edges of her curls with dawn. *This is exactly how I want to be*, she'd said when Kia showed her the picture, and Kia had kissed her. They'd been a couple, and Sullivan had forgotten about everything else until they got back home to Mega Eats' trucks and Kia left for Grants Pass and wouldn't take Sullivan.

Through the service window, the head server called out, "Chef Sullivan, there's a customer with a question about the grass-fed bison. Nothing bad, they said they loved it, but they seriously want to meet you."

"We gotcha covered," Opal said. "Don't we, Blake? We got Chef's back because we're not on our phones."

Blake gave Opal a surly look, but he agreed, "Yes, Chef."

A man in khakis and a blue button-down shirt sat alone in the corner, his face pleasantly illuminated by the recycled wax tea light that graced every table.

"Please, Chef, sit down," he asked imploringly.

Hopefully he didn't have a crush on her. Occasionally customers flirted with her. In school, when her hair had been longer, her walk swishier, and herself flirtier, she'd had no shortage of interested men. Interesting men. She wasn't interested in anyone now that she'd fallen asleep in Kia's arms. Sullivan pulled out a chair and sat down on the edge of it, ready to hop up again. "Just for a minute."

"Of course. Of course. You've got work to do. You don't need me to tell you how amazing your food is."

"Thank you."

"Or how special Mirepoix is."

"Thank you."

Something in the man's pleasant demeanor hardened. The man reached into the breast pocket of his shirt and slid a business card across the table, face down. She reached for it, but he placed his hand over the card before she could pick it up.

"Before you do," he said, "hear me out. Have you heard of the *Saville* case?"

The name sounded vaguely familiar, like an actor from a movie everyone else thought was good but she hadn't seen.

Was he going to tell her about a male chef he thought she should study because obviously a female chef—she hated when people referred to women as females—could improve with some male guidance? Maybe he'd even ask for a job.

"I'd love to chat more, but I need to get back to the kitchen," Sullivan said.

"It's a marriage fraud case that the fraudsters lost. Our attorneys will use it to nail you to the wall."

Sullivan's breath died at the bottom of her lungs. The man was from Mega Eats.

"Good night." Sullivan rose.

"Your grandfather started the process of getting his land surveyed and his lot lines redrawn but died before he could register the paperwork."

"Excuse me." Sullivan turned away.

Customers at nearby tables were watching.

"A third of your house is in the Bois. The lot line goes right through what I'm guessing is your kitchen. Mega Eats is going to win this case, and if you don't help us, we're going to build anything we want, and we're going to build right up to the lot line. Do you understand what that means? We're going to shear off a third of your house."

He was bluffing.

"That's not true, and even if it was, you can't do that. Lot lines get adjusted all the time."

"Not when Mega Eats wants them to stay the way they are." He reached in his pocket again and passed her a flash drive. "All the documentation is here."

Her home was her sanctuary. The Bois was her cathedral and

her meditation room and the place where she talked to her grandfather when she was worried or sad or excited. Mirepoix was her pride and joy. She looked around the restaurant at the servers moving gracefully between tables. She'd have to lay everyone off.

"I am not putting your virus-laden drive anywhere near my computer," she spat.

The man shrugged. Sullivan sat back down so as to draw less attention from her customers.

"If you came here to intimidate me…fine, I'm intimidated. Job done. And I'm comping your meal, but you're leaving right now."

"I don't want to intimidate you. I want to help you."

Fuck off, Sullivan mouthed.

"You see, Mega Eats wants the Bois, but more than that, we don't like to lose. We don't want to give the impression that a couple of lesbians—"

"I'm not—"

The man rolled his eyes as if to say, *Whatever, close enough.*

"Nothing can stop Mega Eats. Not everyone appreciates a Mega Plex until it moves into their neighborhood."

Sullivan clasped her hands tightly, feeling the strength of her chef's scars.

"If we let citizens," the man went on, "neighborhood associations, etcetera prevent us from building, people will never know how much they really do want to try our new Mega Southrn Cook'n."

"That name is offensive. The south can spell perfectly well."

"But you aren't the issue. You're not trying to buy the Bois. You're just one local who doesn't like change. Our problem"—he enunciated each word—"is Kia Jackson. So here's the offer. You file for divorce and you testify in court that Kia Jackson tricked you into marriage. Spin that however you want. You were lonely.

She promised you a payout. Whatever. For that, Mega Eats will amend the lots. We'll leave fifty feet of green space around your house and around Mirepoix."

"I am not going to divorce Kia or tell some lies about how we did this for money. I love her."

The truth came out so fast, Sullivan almost kept going, but she froze. It felt like someone else had told her, but it was someone with absolute knowledge, someone who said something and made it true in the saying. It almost felt like her grandfather reaching down from whatever mysterious existence followed this one, and said, *You're in love with Kia.* He'd have followed that with, *I'm happy for you.*

The man must have taken her pained expression for guilt.

"You can't even keep up the lie in your own restaurant. How are you going to do when our lawyers cross-examine you in court?" The man sneered.

"I love her," Sullivan said again.

"Fine. You love her. But I want you to take my card and think this through. You can stay married to a woman you've known for a few weeks—"

"I've known her since—"

He waved Sullivan off.

"Whenever and think you love." He said *love* with more scorn than Nina had on her most jaded day. "And if you do that, we destroy your house, and we build a Mega Plex as close to your eco-friendly restaurant as we possibly can."

A vision flashed in Sullivan's mind: Mirepoix empty. The last fixtures sold at deep discount. Sullivan locking the door for the last time.

Sullivan would never drive through the Oakwood Heights neighborhood again. It would break her heart. She'd literally crash her car, not on purpose, but because grief would blind her like burning steam from a baozi cooked with too much liquid.

"Lots of cars. Lots of exhaust. Maybe some halogen lamps. How do you think that's going to play with your outdoor seating?" He turned over his business card like a dealer revealing the card that lost everyone at the table a round of blackjack. "You can basically keep everything the way it is. Your customers will barely notice. You'll see trees out your windows. You can have Kia Jackson and we basically raze your house and destroy your business. Or no Kia and you keep everything you have almost exactly the way it is now. Is she worth it?"

Sullivan rose again, slamming her chair into the table, not caring who noticed.

"Yes, she's worth it."

"Who was that?" Opal asked when Sullivan burst back into the kitchen.

"It was Mega Eats. I can't think about it right now. Let's just finish the night."

"Tell me. This is my life too, Sullivan." Opal brandished a spatula in a decidedly unprofessional manner, drops of ragout spattering the floor.

How could Sullivan forget that Opal was in it with her, for good and bad? If Mirepoix closed, Opal would be out of a job. Sullivan might open in a new location, but that meant weeks without work for Opal. Could Sullivan afford to keep paying her? Before Mega Eats, the answer would have been of course. What if she ended up with fifty thousand in attorney fees? She'd looked it up. That wasn't an unreasonable sum. Fighting with a giant corporation wasn't cheap.

"I'm sorry."

"Hey, you two," Blake called out. "I mean *Chefs*. We need three trout, one with sauce on the side."

"The guy said if I don't throw Kia under the bus, they'll destroy my house. He said half my house is technically in the Bois. If they buy the Bois, they buy...everything."

"He's just trying to freak you out."

Sullivan shook her head. A vague memory of her grandfather told her no.

"I think he's right," she gasped. "I remember my grandfather saying something about redrawing property lines. He said it was just a formality to make things easier for me when he passed. And then he passed before he could do it." She choked back a sob. "I can't think about this right now. Let's just get through dinner."

"Let's *you* get out of here and call Nina."

"I—"

"Blake and I've got this, right, Blake? We'll just tell people we're sold out of the specials. Keep everything simple and we're good."

Sullivan stumbled out the back door and headed through the Bois toward her fragile, impermanent home. It wasn't until she reached the empty spot where Old Girl had hunkered since Kia moved in that the really bad thought hit her. Kia had left in a rush and refused to let Sullivan go with her. Why wouldn't Kia want company besides Deja? Wouldn't someone newly infatuated with their fake-wife-possibly-starting-to-be-real-girlfriend want to spend all the time they could together? Sullivan wanted to spend every minute with Kia. It killed her to go to work, to be away from Kia's laugher. She wanted to bury her face in the chocolate-coconut smell of Kia's hair and then bury her face other places.

Had Kia left because Mega Eats had gotten to her too?

Sullivan called Nina the moment she walked in her house. She hadn't even taken off her chef's coat, and she never wore it out of the restaurant. She sat on the edge of the couch and stared at the Janice Domingos.

Nina answered the phone, "What's wrong?"

Sullivan repeated the story. She could feel Nina's attention vibrating through the phone.

"So they're threatening to take half your house, if you don't denounce Kia," Nina summed up when Sullivan was done.

Done except for one part.

"I think they did something to Kia. She left to do some fair in Grants Pass." Sullivan sprang off the sofa, then began pacing. She couldn't sit still. She had to do something, but there was nothing to do. "And I said I'd go with her, and she turned me down."

"Because?"

"She said it was because she'd be working the whole time, and she didn't think Grants Pass was interracial lesbian couple friendly."

When she said it like that, it didn't sound like Kia had cast her out of the book of love. Sullivan looked out at the trees, trying to calm herself. She waited for Nina to point out that new couples always agonized over little things like this, and it would probably take months before they actually broke each other's hearts.

"Mega Eats definitely got to her," Nina said. "We're close to trial, and that's time to offer last-minute deals. If they offered her a deal, it probably involves destroying you and Kia coming out of it without as much grief as they'd give her otherwise. At least that's what they'll tell her. The deal will be ugly, and it'll be irresistible. Brace yourself. They'll make it an offer she can't refuse."

"I was hoping you'd say I was overreacting." Sullivan wanted to cry, but she needed to focus on what Nina was saying.

"Kia is crazy about you, and Grants Pass isn't *that* bad. You can rent a whole ranch for two thousand a night. She's either racked with guilt at what she's going to do to you, or Mega Eats told her to leave you alone."

"You don't think she was just...telling the truth?"

Nina sighed as though Sullivan had said everything on the internet was true.

"Everyone lies when they're desperate."

Did they? How could Kia throw away everything they had? But how could Kia throw away her dreams for a woman she'd only reconnected with a few weeks ago?

"What should I do?"

"Take the deal," Nina said matter-of-factly.

"What?! No! I'm not going to say our marriage is a fraud we cooked up to stop Mega Eats from getting the Bois."

"But that's exactly what it is. I mean, even if you do say Kia tricked you into this, Kia's attorney can still argue that you loved each other. You just couldn't handle the stress of the lawsuit, and you broke her heart—and yours—by leaving. He could argue that Mega Eats coerced you to lie and say it was a fake marriage on the stand. That's not a strong argument, but it's an argument."

"What do you mean *her attorney*?"

"I'm withdrawing representation."

"Kia and I are in it together."

It hadn't felt that way when Kia left for Grants Pass. Disaster scenarios crashed in Sullivan's mind.

"I'll call her," Nina said. "And tell her I'm dropping her."

"Before you even know if she'll take the deal?"

"Your interests have diverged. I like her. Opal's right. She's fab. But you're *you*. And saving your ass is the hill I'll die on."

Sullivan had good friends. She was lucky.

"But I might have to bury Kia under that hill."

Sullivan lowered her voice. "I can't betray her."

"You can. You don't have to perjure yourself. If you simply tell the court exactly what happened."

"I can't hurt her like that."

"She started it."

"She didn't mean for this to happen. I care about her."

I love her.

"As your lawyer and your friend, I'm going to walk you through this. Are you ready to lose your business, all its professional and personal assets, and your house for a woman you've known for less than half a year?"

"I have an LLC."

"They'll pierce your LLC. Then Mega Eats will cut your house like a cake. They'll take everything and Judge Harper will make you pay attorney fees, which Mega Eats will have inflated like a fucking hot-air balloon."

"They keep saying less than half a year, but that's not right." Why didn't anyone get how important their time at the Jean Paul Molineux School had been? "I've known Kia since she was twenty. I wouldn't be who I am without her. Mirepoix wouldn't be Mirepoix without her pushing me to be the best chef I could be."

"That's very noble. But I want you to *really* think about this. Yes, you slept with her. Yes, you think you love her."

"I didn't say—"

"I'm a divorce attorney, Sullivan. If I can't spot someone about to throw themselves under the bus for love, I shouldn't be in the business. But are you ready to be that noble? If you find out she doesn't feel the same way? When she leaves? And here's the thing: You can't ask her. You can't say, *Do you love me, because if you do, I won't denounce you in court.* You won't know if she wants you or if she's desperate. When you're starting over, and she's gone, will you still be happy with your choice? And Mega Eats might offer her the same deal. She's the one they want to nail. They want to show people what happens if you fuck with Mega Eats. They want you both, and if they can only nail one of you, they'd rather it's Kia but..." Nina didn't need to finish the sentence.

Sullivan paced across the room. Her life felt like an escape room she couldn't win. "I won't do it."

Part of her had never been so confident of anything in her life. Another part desperately scanned the future trying to figure out if she herself was lying. Would she really give up everything for Kia? She wanted to be that strong.

"I won't hurt her," she said again. "Call Mega Eats and tell them I won't take their deal." There. She'd said it. She didn't have time to change her mind.

"I won't call Mega Eats."

"This is my decision!"

"Shh, girl, calm down. I won't call them tonight or tomorrow. Go to one of those hideous campsites you like and sleep on it. Spend a night in a tent crawling with bugs. Then if you're sure, I'll tell them whatever you want."

chapter 33

Kia was getting ready for a day of frying tursnicken and angsting over the fact that Sullivan had only responded to her texts with emojis. She hadn't told Sullivan about her profiles. The emojis were a wall, and she didn't know if Sullivan wanted her to scale it. Kia had texted *good night*, and Sullivan had texted back 😊🌑. She'd texted a picture of a minimart sign advertising GUNS, AMMO, WINE, WORMS. Then she'd texted *one stop shopping, move over Walmart*. Kia waited for some text banter to let her know that Sullivan wasn't mad that she'd left, but all she got was a laughing emoji a few hours later. With that cold response, she couldn't write, *They closed down my accounts. I can't make money. I know they want me to back down.* What if Sullivan texted back with, *Now you know how it feels to lose your business.* That didn't seem like Sullivan, but Kia didn't know anything anymore.

Kia was checking the propane connection when her phone rang. She jumped to answer, but it wasn't Sullivan. It was Nina. Nothing Nina had to say could be good, could it? Nearby, Deja was talking with one of the fair organizers. Kia excused herself, trying not to look panicked. Deja's sympathetic expression said

Kia had failed. She walked quickly through the maze of hoses and supply crates. A few people waved at her. She heard someone say, "That's Kia Gourmazing," and someone else say, "She's hard to miss. Did you see her truck?"

"Hello, Kia." Nina was all business, not a trace of familiarity in her voice. "I'm very sorry, but I need to withdraw from your case."

"What?"

"I've got Mark Bretton on the line."

Nina said it like Kia should know who Mark Bretton was.

"He's ready to take your case, if you want. He's one of the best family law and contract attorneys in Portland."

"Thank you, Nina," a man's voice said.

"He's even beat me in a few cases, which does not happen often. Naturally, you're welcome to find your own attorney, but given the time-sensitive matter, I think it'd be wise to transfer your case to Mark."

Kia sat down on a crumbling Jersey barrier, snagging her pants on a bit of metal sticking out of the concrete.

"And do not try to do this pro se. You will lose," Nina added.

What was pro se? And more importantly...

"Why are you dropping the case? We need you."

"I will not be representing *you*. Mega Eats has made Sullivan an offer. She's taking a day to think about it. It is likely that, as we proceed, your interests and Sullivan's will be at odds. It may be to Sullivan's advantage to disadvantage you and vice versa."

Kia interrupted. "Mega Eats shut down my accounts. I'm off U-Spin."

"These are things you can talk to Mark about. You can also ask me to withdraw from Sullivan's representation because I know details about the case that another attorney wouldn't. Mark can explain that to you."

"I don't care if our interests are different. I would never ask you to do something that hurt her."

"But if it comes to it"—Nina seemed to be choosing her words carefully—"I will apprise her of the benefits of hurting you. I will tell Sullivan of her options, including the significant advantages of taking the Mega Eats deal. She and Opal are my best friends. They're my family. And law is my other love. My clients aren't always noble like you and Sullivan. I'm not saving the rainforests or inspiring minority business owners, but I don't risk my clients' interests. Goodbye, Kia."

With that, Nina hung up.

"This is a lot to take in." Mark spoke up quickly as if to reassure Kia he was still on the line. "I can give you a moment. Then we can talk about your social media accounts and anything else you want to share. Do you want to call me back after you've had a chance to collect yourself?"

"No." Kia's voice trembled. She needed a moment. She needed a year. "Talk to me."

"First, tell me about your accounts getting closed."

Kia explained, then finished, "Could it be a coincidence?"

"Sorry, no," Mark said. "When Mega Eats thought Nina was still your attorney, they contacted her with a deal. If you stop any attempt to buy the Bois and relinquish your legacy owner status and admit to everything they say about the fraudulent marriage, they'll *make sure your business isn't affected.* Those are the words they used, and they're keeping it vague so we can't prove that they got your accounts shut. But they did. They know you'll put two and two together."

"Can they do that?"

"Legally? They shouldn't. But it would take us a while to prove that Mega Eats has anything to do with your accounts being closed. We might never be able to prove it."

"If I relinquish legacy owner status, does that mean Sullivan does too?"

A whiff of natural gas and charred burger drifted through the air as another food truck owner got their truck up and running, oblivious to Kia's imminent breakdown.

"Not per the charter."

"So she could buy the Bois if I could talk my investors into investing in her?"

It was a long shot. Gretchen said one of her investors was already getting nervous, but maybe there was a way. Maybe she could ask her father, aunt, and uncle. She could do a GoFundMe, except that she didn't have any followers to ask.

"Per their deal, you're required to relinquish your right to buy and not to help anyone else get the land."

"What if the investors came to her on their own?"

"That'd look like too much of a coincidence. Even if your investors jumped over to Sullivan without your involvement, Mega Eats would punish you and Sullivan for it. Basically, you can back down, lose the Bois, and get out from under a mountain of attorney fees, or we can go to court and risk losing the Bois and getting hit with upwards of seventy-five thousand in fees."

"How is that even possible?" Kia slid off the Jersey barrier and sat on the ground, her back to the concrete. She put her head in her hand.

"They claim to have hired the top partners at a very expensive firm. We're talking people who bill eight hundred an hour. It's an intimidation technique."

"And Sullivan has to pay those fees too?"

"If you take the deal, you get your accounts back, and she'll have to pay attorney fees. You'll have to admit to all the accusations, so effectively, you're saying you're both guilty. They promise to only go after her."

"What are our chances of winning the case if I don't take their deal?"

"Slim, but the law is on our side. Judge Harper might do the right thing. Here's the catch though. Because Mega Eats hasn't acknowledged that they've got your accounts hostage, they don't have to release them. If you win in court, they still won't give them back. You'll have to rebuild, and there's nothing to say they couldn't get your accounts shut down again."

"The only way to keep my accounts is to say we did it," Kia said slowly. "And sacrifice Sullivan?"

"Yes. Do you want to take their deal?"

Stating the answer was as easy as stating the boiling temperature for water, as easy as separating an egg into its white and yellow elements, as easy as breathing clean forest air.

"No."

That night, after an exhausting day of serving tursnicken and trying to convince people fried beets were not unapproachable, Kia retired to Old Girl. Deja had been planning on sleeping on the foldout couch, but Kia got Deja a hotel room. Kia needed to be alone.

Now she set her phone on the table of Old Girl and called up the international routing number that would connect her with her father's emergency radio. She put in her personal code. A moment later, her father's voice answered.

"My little angelfish!" he exclaimed. "Is everything all right?"

"I ruined everything." Kia burst into tears the way she hadn't since she was a kid. Even then, she had had some of her aunt's reserve in her. She'd been seven or eight the last time she'd cried to her father.

"Angel, what's wrong?" Her father's voice dropped an octave in concern. "Talk to me."

"No one died." Kia tried to swallow her sobs. "Or got cancer or abducted or killed anyone."

"Okay. We've established no death or illness. What happened?"

"So much has happened." Why hadn't she called him on his emergency radio the day she won the American Fare Award? Why hadn't she filled him in on every development? The emergency radio cost by the minute, but not hundreds of dollars. Now she had too much to explain. "I won the American Fare Award, and then Gretchen said I should buy this land, which I wanted, and there were all these nice, liberal middle-aged white people with water bottles—"

"Slow down. What kind of water bottles?"

"Water bottles with liberal stickers on them. Wait." A bubble of laughter broke the surface of her tears. "That's what you care about? The water bottles?"

"I live at sea, Angelfish. Water is very important. But go on. I talked to Eleanor yesterday, and she told me a little bit about this land deal. Start from the beginning and tell me everything."

"How do I know where the beginning is?"

"There's always a golden glow around the beginning because no matter what happens later, everything begins with love. You just have to go far back enough to find it."

"Love," Kia sobbed.

"That's right, my dear. And love does make us cry sometimes, but it's still worth it."

"I'm *in* love."

"That's wonderful."

"It's not wonderful."

"Love is always wonderful, even when it hurts."

"But I hurt *her*."

"Start at the beginning."

"It was the first day I walked into school and saw Alice Sullivan."

"The one you kissed," her father said. "We always wondered what you hadn't told us about her."

Kia poured out the story, from her first crush on Sullivan to the careless way they lost touch to the American Fare Award, the Bois, her canceled accounts, Mega Eats' offer.

"Dad, Sullivan could lose everything, and it's all my fault."

"You took a risk on the land and on love, and it is as serendipitous as your cousin finding true love. You know we didn't expect Lillian to fall in love like she did. Your aunt and uncle and I always thought it'd be you who ran off with a burlesque performer. But Lillian and Izzy found each other, and now you've found Sullivan."

"But Lillian and Izzy worked out. Lillian didn't bankrupt Izzy."

"You and Sullivan will work everything out. Love always works out if you believe."

That was absolutely not true. If her father was going to lie to cheer her up, he really should find some more realistic lies. Maybe he should spend some time with Nina. Sullivan wasn't going to tease her again. Sullivan wasn't going to give her shit about her tursnicken and then add that Kia was the best chef she'd ever met. And asking Sullivan to go back to their sweet new way of being… that wasn't fair, not after the hell Kia had rained down on her. Somewhere in the back of Kia's mind, a reasonable voice said that all was not lost. Couples went through hard times. People forgave each other. But that voice was drowned out by the rest of her heart and soul weeping over the real possibility that she and Sullivan were over.

chapter 34

Sullivan sat in front of her one-person tent unwillingly listening to Journey played from a nearby SUV parked on the sand. If you wanted a good campsite in the spring or summer, you reserved it in February or you backpacked a long day into the forest, which is why Sullivan ended up on the side of a lake watching motorboats trying to whip around fast enough to make the water-skiers they were towing fall over in a chaos of waves from the wake. It was apparently a consensual act as were the ATV races taking place on the sand. And these people were probably half the reason this lake wasn't built up with vacation homes. They made it a *recreational area*. Why did people have to use something to see its value? Why couldn't people just save the lake to save it?

She closed her eyes. She remembered standing in her grandfather's living room, eight years old, stomping her feet, tears streaking her face. *I hate loggers. Why do they have to cut down trees?* Her grandfather had sat her down on his lap and pointed up to the ceiling. *What do you think this house is made out of?* Trees. *How do you think our family owns this beautiful old house?* At eight, she hadn't understood what her grandfather had meant by *timber money*, but she'd gotten the message. *Plus Oregon can grow trees fast. If we don't grow them, people will cut down forests that take hundreds of years to regrow. We're all part of the problem. We can all be part of the solution.*

A gang of boys raced in front of her waving sticks at each other. They'd been going all morning. Up and down the beach until one of them got hit and went weeping back to his mother, who lifted her head from her lawn chair long enough to say, *What did you think would happen if you played with sticks*, which the kids seemed to take as instructions to go back to hitting each other with sticks. The cycle of life.

She should call Kia. This wasn't Kia's fault. Opal was right; Kia was a talented, ambitious Black woman entrepreneur who'd taken advice from a knowledgeable consultant and live streamed a deal she had every reason to believe was a sure thing. How could Sullivan just blow off Kia's texts and go camping? Wasn't closing someone out one of the worst things you could do in a relationship? But what would she say if Kia said she was going to take a deal from Mega Eats? Or what if Kia didn't answer her call? Didn't even do her the favor of telling her they were breaking up and Kia was taking a deal from Mega Eats? Sullivan couldn't bear it. At least if she didn't talk to Kia, part of her could pretend, for a few more hours, that Kia cared for her, and that they would be all right as a couple even if they lost the lawsuit.

She swatted at a mosquito, although it was only trying to live its best life on her elbow.

If she called Opal right now, Opal would tell her they were not going to end up broke and alone. Kia still had her followers. Sullivan was still one of the most respected chefs on the West Coast. Any restaurant would hire her. Kia could hit the road again. And her thoughts ended up back where they started: watching the taillights of the RV as Kia pulled away for the last time.

Nina's name appeared on her phone.

"Sorry to interrupt your forest contemplation," Nina said.

"I'm at a lake. It's not forested."

"Are there bears? It's all the same if there are bears."

"No, ATVs and Jet Skis."

"Worse. Look, I wanted to give you more time, but Mega Eats called with an ultimatum. You take the deal by five today or it's off the table."

The kids with sticks stopped hitting each other for a moment.

"How much more time do you need to think?"

"None. I can't testify against her."

The kids returned to their stick wars. An ATV threw sand on a woman's beach blanket, and she yelled, "You're dead to me, Brad!" In the water, a jet boat was doing doughnuts in its own wake.

"Can you please think this through, Sullivan. Really, really think about how you're going to feel in a year if you say no."

"I want to get married for real someday." Sullivan drew her hands over her face, getting a grain of sand in her eye. A tear chased it away.

Nina waited.

"I want something that lasts, and there's no way I can believe that kind of love is possible if I hurt Kia just to save myself. How can I believe in love if I can't be the kind of person I want to be with?"

"You'll end up like me: jaded and alone?"

"I didn't say that."

"I call it savvy and independent," Nina said. "You don't have a lot of time, but take a minute and think this through."

"I don't need to."

"You're really going to stay in? Risk everything?"

A man and woman walked by. She caught a snippet of their conversation.

"I love you, but your brother is a loser, and you act like an ass when you hang out with him."

"Don't say *I love you* if you aren't going to…"

Their voices faded away. It didn't sound like they loved each other, but if they did, they should stop fighting. They should realize what a blessing it was to have a partner and be with someone you cared about.

"One more time, Sullivan. Are you sure?" Nina asked.

It felt like a fairy tale where you had to say no to the poison apple three times before the curse broke. No one ever got it right in fairy tales. And baby-queer Kia had preferred the frog over the prince (despite her feelings about nature). That was so sweet and innocent. How could Sullivan betray Kia?

"Yeah." Sullivan felt calm and sick to her stomach at the same time. "I'm sure."

"Okay." It sounded like Nina had something else to say.

"What is it?"

"You know love is just propaganda to hide the fact that romantic"—Nina spoke the word in quotation marks—"relationships are economic agreements based on survival and self-interest."

"You've said." The tiniest smile tugged at Sullivan's lips. Nina was nothing if not consistent.

"As an attorney, I think you're making the wrong choice. If Mega Eats makes Kia the same offer, she'd be smart to take it. And as your friend, I wish you had *some* sense of self-preservation. And I will perjure myself before I admit this." Nina's voice softened, and she became someone Sullivan only glimpsed in split-second moments separated by years. "But as a person…just a person who wants to think there's something worth saving in this world, I'm glad you said no."

With that Nina hung up. Sullivan didn't call back. If she had, she knew Nina's voicemail would have picked up before the first ring.

Kia arrived home the next day, desperately hoping to see Sullivan, but Sullivan's sedan was gone. A note on the table read, *I hope you had a good trip. I've gone camping. Miss you.* The *miss you* was a good sign. The silent house wasn't. Finally, Kia worked up the courage to call Sullivan instead of sending intentionally casual texts. Sullivan didn't pick up. She was probably out of cell range. Maybe she'd climbed some mountain and fallen in a ravine and broken her leg. No one would find her, and she'd have to crawl down the mountain, and her leg wouldn't heal right, and she'd never stand in a kitchen again, and it'd all be Kia's fault. Everything bad in Sullivan's life was Kia's fault, and she hadn't even invited Sullivan to go to Grants Pass with her. At least if Sullivan had been there when Kia realized her accounts had been canceled, she wouldn't have to agonize over whether to tell Sullivan.

If Sullivan was communing with nature, maybe Kia should try that too. She put on a light sweatshirt, one of Sullivan's that hung by the door for quick jaunts to the mailbox or to check on whatever Sullivan checked in her vegetable garden. Kia walked into the Bois, which was looking ridiculously lovely. Where was the rain when it would've fit Kia's mood? Today, she wanted to beg Sullivan's forgiveness, then burst into tears and pour out all her fears and disappointments while Sullivan held her.

She felt something touch her neck. Something had fallen from the forest canopy. It was touching the collar of her shirt. It was—

"Fuck!"

Something had gone down her shirt. It was slithering down her back. She knew communing with nature was a bad idea. She flung off her shirt. What if it went down her pants? She almost stripped those off too. But the thing was off her. She looked around. A movement caught her eye. A green ribbon had come to life, graceful as a coil of light. The miniature Oregon tree snake! She shuddered, the memory of its body still slithering down her back. The snake that only lived in the Bois and was seen once a year had fallen on her. More accurately, the hand of karma had plucked it off a branch and dropped it on her. The snake was probably pissed. Kia had ruined its day too. *Why do I have to fall out of a tree because* she *messes up everything she touches?* What were the chances?

Slim. As slender as the now-disappeared snake. The board should put it on their liberal water bottles. Save the whales. Save the Redwoods. Save the miniature Oregon tree snake from Kia Gourmazing's bad karma tossing it out of a tree.

"That's it! I've got it!"

And with that, Kia was flying over the roots and rocks and jumping over blackberry vines like a hurdler.

chapter 35

Sullivan felt exhausted after talking to Nina. She crawled back inside her tent and lay down. She didn't know how long she slept for. It was still light when she woke up. The ATVs were still blaring classic rock as they roared up and down the beach. She'd slept the dead-deep sleep of a woman trying to escape her life. Her throat was dry. She felt slightly oxygen deprived. And someone was shaking her tent.

"Sullivan! Sullivan?"

"Kia?"

A shadow crossed her tent, then Kia was unzipping the flap. She looked flushed, and her hair was a collection of nests and springs and wisps. It was a one-person tent, barely tall enough to sit up in, but Kia crawled in, nonetheless. She wrapped her arms around her knees, rocking back and forth.

"I figured something out." She looked like she was going to bubble over with excitement and cry at the same time.

If Sullivan had been angry at Kia, her anger would have drained away. But she didn't feel angry. Sullivan drew her into a hug.

"How did you know where I was?" Sullivan murmured.

"Opal has an app," Kia said tearfully.

Right. Sullivan and Opal always shared pins on their hiking app.

"Then I asked around if anyone had seen a hot woman with curly hair who looked like she wanted to murder someone."

"I don't want to—"

"I got your note about camping, and I went out in the Bois because people think it's so calming in nature." Kia pulled away. Her eyes shone. Her hair vibrated against the roof of the tent. "And I don't know how it can be calming because a snake—a fucking snake—fell down *my* shirt. You would have been excited. I wasn't. But I had to come tell you because the miniature Oregon tree snake is the answer."

It took Sullivan a moment to take in Kia's words. Sullivan didn't realize until now how much she'd wanted Kia to run after her. And now Kia was here, and she wasn't telling Sullivan she'd taken a deal from Mega Eats. She was complaining about slithery nature. And this was exactly what Sullivan had wanted when she added *miss you* to her kitchen note. Behind those words was *please come find me. Don't leave me.*

Then Sullivan took in Kia's last words.

"The tree snake?! You've been here a few weeks and you've already seen a tree snake. Jealous!"

"I will not say it was lovely, although it did kind of look like a magic ribbon. If you can overlook that they're little Satans." Kia gave a watery laugh. "I can't save us, but I think I can save the Bois. If the snakes are only in the Bois and you almost never see them, it's got to be endangered. And people in Oregon love endangered species. We have to get the judge to give us a…what was it called? An injunction. Like Mega Eats got to stop the sale until our court case resolved. And we say they can't build on the land because they'll ruin the snakes' habitat. We'll save it. It's brilliant, right?"

It was…absolutely brilliant.

With one catch.

"If we did that," Sullivan said slowly, trying to contain her excitement until she heard what Kia said next, "you won't be able to build on it either."

"I don't care."

"What about Me'shell and everyone you've promised to help? We still have a chance in court."

Kia's face fell for a moment, but she said, "I can find other locations for them. We'll pivot. It won't be exactly what they planned, but I'll stay in Portland until everyone who needs me gets what they want."

That'll be forever if Kia counted Sullivan among *everyone who needs me.*

"Sullivan, there's one other thing." Kia's expression was as serious as her LED likeness on the Diva was cheerful. "Mega Eats got my accounts canceled."

"Fuck."

Everything Kia had built depended on her social media accounts, everything she'd dreamed of on graduation night was tied to those accounts.

"They threatened that if I don't give up my attempts to buy the Bois and say that what they're accusing us of is true, they'll cut them off permanently. They shouldn't be able to do that, but they can, and we can't prove it's them. It's a problem with influencing. You're at the mercy of these huge corporations."

"If we save the snake, do you get your accounts back?"

"Nothing except taking the deal does that. I should take it."

"I understand." Sullivan's heart cracked. She'd stood on this precipice herself, and Nina was right, a sensible person would have taken the deal. Kia knew that. "Why did you bring up the snake if you have to take the deal?"

"Chef, I'm offended." Kia looked shocked, although not angry. "Of course I didn't take the deal."

"Mega Eats offered me the same deal," Sullivan blurted, "except it's my house they want. It's on Bois property. I lose it entirely if they buy the Bois. I didn't take the deal either."

They stared at each other. Sun coming through the tent's red nylon cast a soft pink glow on Kia's face.

"We didn't take the deals." Kia looked incredulous but also happy. "We. Didn't. Take. The. Deals."

"We didn't take the deals." Sullivan felt a bubble of giddy pride. Excitement. Glee. Strength. The feeling that they'd won just by saying no to the devil's bargain. "Fuck Mega Eats."

"Fuck them!" Kia flung her arms around Sullivan. "We are so much better than anything that company has ever done."

Sullivan held Kia tight. *I love you.* The words almost slipped out. Instead she said, "Okay, how are we going to get everyone to care about the miniature Oregon tree snake?"

Kia wished she could ride home with Sullivan, but at least she could call Deja from her truck and not subject Sullivan to Deja's exuberance. She waited until she was on a quiet stretch of highway, then asked her truck's computer to call Deja. Deja picked up on the first ring.

"Deja—" Kia braced herself for the torrent of fangirl love. "I need your help."

"Is this about the lawsuit?" Deja asked, uncharacteristically serious.

"How did you know?"

"My friend Trey. They're not a hacker, but they helped me set up an alert."

There was so much wrong with that Kia didn't know where to begin. What kind of alert? Why did Deja need an alert? Why did Deja always introduce Trey as *not a hacker*?

"Don't worry. It was just a Google Alert to see how the food pod was going, so I could help if you needed me, and I was checking to see if your accounts came back. Then I saw some stuff about Mega Eats. It's so wrong. I mean, anyone who sees you two can see that this is what love looks like! Hashtag 'relationship goals.' And hello, Mega Eats is serving a side of homophobia. A gay marriage isn't real because blah, blah, blah. You couldn't possibly want to marry a hot woman you've been in love with since you were twenty and—" Deja stopped. "Sorry. I talk too much. I am ready to help. What do you need?"

"Do you have any friends who are into the environment or hate capitalism?"

"Oh my god, do I have any friends who *don't* love the environment and hate capitalism? No, no I do not."

"I need some publicity around an issue."

Deja didn't say a word as Kia described the lawsuit and the snake.

"Sullivan says it shouldn't matter whether people like an animal. If it's endangered it's endangered, even if it's hideous."

"The miniature tree snake is *gorge*. But I get it. You need people to rally for the snake."

"Yeah."

"Like a *rally*!" Talkative Deja was back. "We'll get local food trucks to serve food. And I can get your friend's burlesque troupe to make snake costumes. And I know some anarchists that—"

"Maybe no anarchists."

"Okay, no anarchists, but we'll get—" Deja hesitated, probably googling. "People from the Mount Hood Environmental Front, and the Urban Green group." Deja listed a dozen other groups, ranging from the obviously environmental to the bud-tenders union. "Do you think Saturday or Sunday? Maybe we can have a drag show. All snake themed. Barb, Mike, Benny, Greg, and Mira will totally be on board."

"Barb, Mike…?"

"The board. You know. The white people with woke water bottles."

That basically described all of Portland. Maybe all of Portland would come.

There was one more thing. Kia took a deep breath.

"Deja, I need to tell you something. I don't want you to feel like I didn't tell you because I didn't trust you."

"Okay," Deja said.

"What Mega Eats said about us just getting married to get the land deal…that was partly true. And I'm sorry I let you believe that and call us hashtag 'relationship goals.' I should have trusted you with the truth."

"But you've been in love with her since school, and she has been too, but she didn't realize that she was in love with you too until she saw you again." Deja recited the words like an article of faith.

"That's just what we told people."

"No, that's what *I* told *you*."

"What?"

"I saw the video of your kiss at graduation. Total fire. You don't kiss someone like that and just forget them. I saw the way you and Sullivan looked at each other. Legit from day one.

Whatever you *thought* you were doing getting married, I know you did it for Sullivan. You didn't have to buy the Bois to save Sullivan from Mega Eats. You could have gone anywhere. Your investors didn't say it had to be the Bois."

"The Bois was a good deal."

"Since when has getting sued by Mega Eats been a good deal? You did it because you want Sullivan in your life."

"Are you hurt that I didn't tell you?"

"A little." Deja's voice dipped toward sadness, then perked up again. "But you don't share your business. I get it. Half your life is online, you don't want to spill the tea after that."

"How did you know I was in love with Sullivan?"

"You don't have to spill to me, 'cause I see you, girl. I know everything you know before you know it. GOAT assistant."

Kia smiled. "Yeah you are."

chapter 36

Sullivan sat in the living room that evening, happy to be showered and away from the ATVs. Kia, Deja, and about a dozen other people were clustered around the kitchen island, eating Kia's Pop Rocks–crusted bacon caramel corn and talking like revolutionaries. Sullivan picked up her phone and dialed Aubrey's number. She still had it memorized. A few weeks ago, that might have felt significant. Now Aubrey was just an acquaintance whose number she happened to have, and Sullivan needed a favor.

"Do you have contacts at any environmental protection group?" Sullivan asked after a quick hello. "Someplace who could help stop a development that's going to destroy an important habitat? Maybe the only habitat for this species?"

"The tree snake," Aubrey said with so much love and sadness. "Remember when we went looking for one? It was in the fall. It was getting cold. We thought we'd figured out where they might be and we got binoculars?"

"I'm sorry. I don't remember." She almost wished she did so they could have a moment of nostalgia and then get off the phone, but she really didn't.

"I'm sorry, Sullivan." Aubrey's voice broke. "Love Sullivan n Aubs was the worst mistake of my life. I got addicted. People say that now. Social media addiction is like gambling addiction. You get hooked on the endorphins every time a post goes viral." Aubrey paused. "I know it's not fair to ask you to forgive me, but I need you to know, I wouldn't have done it if I wasn't hooked. It was like getting a hit of a drug or taking a drag off a cigarette. And when I didn't get likes or when another influencer got more, I felt this…" She seemed to struggle for words. "It was like, *What good am I? I should quit everything. I suck, and there's nothing I can do about it except make another video. A better one. Funnier. Sexier.* And you are so fucking photogenic. How could I not put you online? But I hurt you with my addiction. I used you to make myself feel good. It was wrong." Aubrey choked back a sob.

Aubrey's tears elicited only a vague human sympathy. Sullivan didn't want anyone to be sad…well, maybe everyone who ran Mega Eats. She didn't want Aubrey to suffer, but she wanted the conversation to jump over this part.

"It's okay," Sullivan said. "Um…thanks. Don't worry about it." They had more important things to talk about. "Mega Eats wants to cut down the Bois. If we can get someone's attention, we can get an injunction, get the judge to stop them until we find out if we can protect the land for the tree snake. Do you know anyone who can help?"

"Yes. Yes! Of course." Aubrey cleared her throat, jumping at the chance to help. Nina would say it was useful to have an ex who was racked with guilt. "I got a job with Portland Metro Conservation." She hesitated, probably remembering that she'd quit her day job when she started making money online.

"That's great," Sullivan said before Aubrey started apologizing again. "So you said you know some people?"

Aubrey started listing off names and organizations.

"I can call all these people today," Aubrey promised. "And I'll text you their numbers so you can call them too."

"Thank you."

Sullivan was already taking the phone from her ear when Aubrey said, "I went to therapy. I know that doesn't take away what I did to you. But I worked on myself a lot."

Sullivan's attention wandered to the kitchen full of activists. They let out a cheer that Aubrey almost certainly heard on her end.

"I know we can't…couldn't just pick up where we were, but would you…would you like to—"

Sullivan could feel Aubrey working up her courage to finish the sentence.

"Go on a date with me? Maybe we could give it another try."

A really good person wouldn't have felt a rush of satisfaction as she spoke the next words, but Sullivan wasn't quite that good.

"Oh, Aubrey, you didn't hear? I'm married."

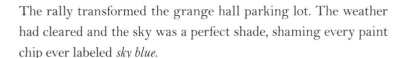

The rally transformed the grange hall parking lot. The weather had cleared and the sky was a perfect shade, shaming every paint chip ever labeled *sky blue*.

Kia heard one of Deja's friends explaining, "If Mega Eats shows up, we're going to do a call-and-response. He cupped his hands around his mouth. I say, *Savor local flavor.*"

The people around him answered, "Reject Mega Eats!"

Someone walked by with a sign reading MEGA EATS: GREASE IS THE WORD.

Kia had already opened the Diva. Her own face beamed from the LED screen on the side of the truck. The four other food trucks that Kia had invited lined the parking lot: Me'shell's Soul

Food, a Mexican-Thai fusion, a truck called K-Pop Corn Dog, and a classic American burger truck with the name MAN BUN BURGERS emblazoned on the side. The food truck staff were running around, passing cords and sparking pilot lights. Miss Brenda was helping at Me'shell's truck. Opal was chopping cilantro at the Mexican-Thai fusion truck, trying to talk the owners into joining the She-Pack. Several people in green tights were fitting themselves into a green snake puppet reminiscent of a Lunar New Year dragon. The White People with Woke Water Bottles were walking around shaking hands. It seemed like every environmental organization in Portland had a booth or spokesperson handing out flyers.

Nina had apologized; she could only stop by for a moment. She had a meeting with a client about tracking down the wealthy absentee mother of his two children and relieving her of several million in past due child support. But Nina had made Sullivan an authorized user on a platinum credit card and told her to buy whatever she needed for the rally. When she'd asked Nina how much she could spend, Nina had looked miffed and said, *You don't have to ask, because I can afford it.* With all the support from the community, they didn't need much, but Sullivan had a screen printing company print SAVE THE SNAKE on a hundred thrift store T-shirts, in the same glittery script as Kia's LET'S GET GOURMAZING! tees. Kia sported one proudly.

Everyone was taking selfies and live streaming, even Sullivan.

"I have to cook," Kia said. "But I'll sneak away when I can for our speech."

Sullivan put an arm around Kia's waist, holding her back for a moment.

"It's beautiful," Sullivan said. "I see what you want. I see how good it is."

"And I see why we have to protect that." Kia turned toward the woods that lined the parking lot and spread her arms. She wanted to say something about how it felt like the forest held them, but she couldn't find the words, and the tursnickens wouldn't deep-fry themselves. But if they survived the lawsuit and she got to run a food truck again, she'd be buying only free-range turkeys.

"Before you get to work," Sullivan said. "I want to show you something." Sullivan took out her phone and held it out shyly. "I still think social media is problematic, but you showed me you can reach a lot of people."

The screen showed an Instagram profile with three posts and one reel. The profile picture featured a selfie of Sullivan. The handle was @servetheworldPDX. She clicked on the reel. Sullivan stood in her vegetable garden looking awkward like she'd never seen a cell phone camera before. She waited a beat before speaking. *A lot of people feel like they can't grow their own food because they don't have space or time or they don't know how, but there are a few simple vegetables you can start with.*

The video went on longer than any social media post should, but it didn't matter because Kia could have watched another hour of Sullivan outlining how to fertilize tomatoes with old banana peels. Sullivan looked dapper and outdoorsy. A couple of times she said, *My wife is going to tease me about this*, then held up a slug or some other hideous garden pest.

"This is beautiful," Kia said.

"I'll never be good at it like you are."

"You're passionate about this. Part of having a good channel is finding something you can talk about all day, every day. You know a ton. And you're smokin' hot, which never hurts on social media."

Sullivan rolled her eyes.

"I want to teach people about organic slug control, not be smokin' hot."

Kia clicked on the last picture and stopped. Kia at her food truck. It must have been at the fair when they kissed in the Love Tunnel. The lights of her truck set off the dark sky. Kia was in the window, leaning out as she handed a plate of food to a customer. Her hair glowed. In the caption, Sullivan had written *my beautiful wife*. The colors were cheerful and the picture captured nostalgia, like the photo was saying, *This is going to be a long time ago someday, so appreciate it now*. Kia raised up and placed a kiss on Sullivan's lips. "This is brilliant. You have to do this."

Later in the evening, Kia and Sullivan took the stage for their speech.

"Thank you all for coming today." Sullivan held the mic close to her lips, and her voice resonated across the parking lot, soft despite the amplification, as though she had pitched it so as not to disturb the wildlife tucking itself in for the night. "I know that not everyone loves snakes."

Kia gave a dramatic shiver to illustrate, and the crowd laughed.

"But I think everyone here appreciates how important it is to protect our environment. Behind me is the Bois. Mega Eats wants to build here."

The man who'd explained call-and-response called out, "Savor local flavor."

His compatriots answered, "Reject Mega Eats."

"So often the default is *build*," Sullivan went on. "Cut it down unless a bunch of obnoxious environmentalists tie themselves to the trees."

Someone called out, "I'm an obnoxious environmentalist!"

"But what if we change it around? Let us be conservationists in the truest sense of the word. Let us *conserve*. Let the default be to save it for the next generation and the next and the next. There is a Mega Eats complex thirteen and a half miles from here. We can live without one here. Let us ask, *Must we develop?* rather than, *Where can we develop?*"

She was everything Kia had adored in school and more. Not just confident but dignified. Not just strong but strong despite her insecurities and vulnerabilities. Real strength wasn't being fearless; it was walking forward into fear because you believed in your cause.

"Doesn't this snake thing help you?" The Mega Eats woman had appeared out of nowhere. Beside her sat a golden retriever, blameless in the whole snake–Mega Eats conflict, its tongue lolling to the side. "You own a restaurant next to the Bois."

"It does help me. And it hurts my wife. And that's not fair," Sullivan said.

"But we both believe that this is the right thing for Portland," Kia added.

"Your wife." The woman strolled closer to the stage. "Didn't you get married a few weeks ago?" She turned to face the crowd, commanding their attention although not quite bold enough to walk onstage. "Kia Jackson and Alice Sullivan got married so she could take advantage of a legacy clause prioritizing existing legacy owners with the first right of purchase for the Bois."

The crowd quieted.

"When that didn't work, they invented the miniature Oregon tree snake. Has anyone even seen a miniature Oregon tree snake?"

"We haven't because it's *endangered*," someone answered.

Near the front of the crowd, a little girl in a gunnysack dress let go of her mother's hand.

"I caught one. And I wanted to put it in my dollhouse, but my mom said wild things stay in the wild."

Kia could see the Mega Eats woman hesitate. You couldn't shut down an adorable girl in pigtails.

"I'm sure you're very good at catching snakes," she said with the syrupy sweetness people used on children when they didn't understand children were actually people.

"No. I need you to use your ears and listen right now." The girl's cadence was perfect. Some adult in her life said that frequently. "I said I caught one. It's little, and it has a little smile on its face. Its tongue goes like this." The girl flicked her tongue.

"I think that's all snakes," the woman said.

The girl's face hardened. "They're not all little. The green anaconda is five hundred fifty pounds and—"

The girl's mother pulled her back into the crowd.

"The point is," the woman went on, "this marriage is a fraud. You barely know each other, and, from what I've heard, you don't even like each other."

"I absolutely do know Sullivan," Kia said. "I know she grew up in these woods and that her grandfather taught her about the forest. I know she can catch a newt, and she knows way too much about the mating habits of slugs. I know she talks to her food while she's cooking and grows squash. I've tasted her coq au vin, her stuffed salmon, her handmade pasta. I know she can make an anchovy-cornichon vinaigrette that will change your life and a crème brûlée that will make you cry it's so good. She drinks her wine too young, and her hair looks like a tornado in a wheat field in the morning. And I was jealous of every guy she dated when we were in school."

Sullivan took the microphone from Kia.

"And I know Kia grew up on a yacht and read Sappho off the

coast of Greece. I know she had a spaniel named Julia Child. I know she makes every place she visits better, and when she serves people at her food truck—which she calls the Diva—she cares about every one of them. I know she spent years looking for a 1968 Wind Searcher Pop-Up Pavilion to go with her RV. I know she's afraid of snakes, and she's still here today. She's that kind of person. She's brave, and she's confident, but she doesn't put herself in front of everyone or everything else. And I know she can cook things with Pop Rocks that should never touch candy, and that whatever she makes tastes like love itself."

The crowd cheered. The giant snake puppet undulated. Someone yelled, "Boooo Mega Eats." The woman checked her watch, and in the most anticlimactic response to an impassioned speech, she said, "I don't get paid enough for this. We're not union," and walked off, her dog snagging a stray french fry on its way out.

chapter 37

Kia spotted Mark and Nina in the courthouse hallway as soon as she and Sullivan arrived.

"Let's huddle in a conference room for pregame," Nina said as they crossed the glistening floor to the escalators.

"I thought we were going up against each other," Kia said to Sullivan.

"Not since you two decided to throw yourselves on your proverbial swords." Nina rolled her eyes. "God, you're perfect for each other."

In an elegant, windowless conference room near the courtroom, Nina took the lead.

"How are we feeling?" Nina went on without waiting for an answer. "Let's get the nerves under control." Nina took in a deep breath and beckoned them close with a hand wave. "Come on, just a few deep breaths."

It was a helpful exercise since Kia had forgotten how to breathe.

"The time is going to fly by," Nina went on. "I need your full focus. We've been over this before. Mulroney is going to try to trip you up. Take you off your game. Don't take the bait. We want you to tell your love story, but we don't want you getting all emotional. Emotional means there's lots of words spilling out. Emotional means mistakes. We don't want that." Kia and Sullivan nodded their understanding.

"Just answer the question asked and no more," Nina said.

"We got it," Kia and Sullivan said in unison.

"This is Mega Eats' shit show, so Mulroney will present his case in chief, and then we'll present ours. Mark and I agree when it's our turn, Kia will testify first and then Sullivan." Nina looked at her watch. "We'd better head in."

The bailiff unlocked the courtroom and they took their seats at counsels' tables.

"All rise. The Honorable Judge Edward Harper presiding," the bailiff boomed.

"Please be seated." The judge shuffled some papers on the bench and adjusted his glasses. "Are there any prehearing motions this morning?"

The attorneys all said no.

"Is everyone ready to proceed?"

Nods all around.

"Thank you, Judge." Mulroney stepped forward, looking determined. As Mulroney presented his case, Nina and Mark, ever vigilant, raised appropriate objections, strategically disrupting Mulroney's flow. Finally, Mulroney rested his case. He had a satisfied look on his face as he fake smiled in Nina's direction.

"Respondents, call your first witness," the judge said.

"The defense calls Kiana Jackson to the stand," Mark announced.

Kia had taken to heart the lectures about courtroom decorum: nothing distracting.

She wore professional attire: a fitted blazer in a rich shade of emerald green paired with a flowered pencil skirt. Beneath the blazer, a crisp white blouse provided a clean and classic contrast. She'd even bought a pair of sleek, black stiletto heels that added a touch of elegance and height to her usual glittery appearance. Simple yet elegant gold jewelry adorned her ears and wrists, adding a subtle sparkle without being too flashy. And, of course, she wore her wedding ring.

Mark started with a basic question.

"How long have you known Alice Sullivan?"

Kia took a breath before answering.

"Since I was twenty."

"How long ago was that?"

"Almost ten years."

In the conference room, Kia had felt so nervous the room had gone fuzzy. Now that she was on the stand, looking out at the courtroom, she felt completely calm. She was here to tell the judge how she felt, how she'd always felt. Despite Nina's warnings, her emotions bubbled to the surface, her words laced with protectiveness for her culinary arts school rival and ride-or-die.

"How long have you been in love with Ms. Sullivan?"

"I fell in love the day she walked into the practice kitchen at school."

She looked at Sullivan. Sullivan crossed her hands over her chest, as if sending Kia a hug. That part could have been for show, but the look in her eyes had to be sincere. Kia saw the same joy and desire she felt. *I love you.*

"Where did you meet?"

"We met at the Jean Paul Molineux School of Culinary Arts in New York City."

"What were your first impressions of Ms. Sullivan?"

"The first day when she walked into class, I wanted to be her friend." Kia spoke slowly. "She walked in serving all this nineteen twenties lesbian swagger, then all the guys fell for her because she was so effing cool. Every time she'd go out with one of them, I'd be jealous, and I'd go back to the practice kitchen and try to make a better beef Wellington than Sullivan. Whatever she was good at, I tried to be better. People at school didn't get that that didn't mean I didn't like her. It meant I *adored* her. She inspired me to be my best, just like she helped me see how important it is to preserve this land. I think love means trying to be your best for the person you adore. Love inspires us to be our best. At first love makes you look at each other. Then it makes you look out together."

"Objection: these musings are irrelevant," Mulroney said.

"Sustained. Please stick to the question, Ms. Jackson."

"Your Honor, Ms. Jackson's comments are relevant. They speak to the heart of Mega Eats' accusation that she isn't in love with Ms. Sullivan," Mark Bretton said.

"Objection is sustained," the judge said with an unnecessary rap of his gavel.

Harper was definitely in Mega Eats' pocket. Somehow that didn't frighten Kia anymore. If Sullivan heard what Kia said next and celebrated it, that was all that mattered. In fact, the love Kia felt was so deep, so much a part of her, there was a way in which it didn't matter whether Sullivan shared her feelings. Of course, later, if Sullivan didn't share them, she'd be devastated, but for now, there was nothing truer than what she was about to say. Unfiltered, unvarnished fact. And she felt the wild, glittering exuberance of asserting her truth. *I am me. I am real.*

"During the time you and Ms. Sullivan were out of touch, how did you feel about her?"

"I thought about Sullivan all the time. I had this dream that we'd meet again. She'd see me and she'd say, *I always loved you, Kia.* I didn't date people because it'd fu—mess with the fantasy. If I was with someone, I wouldn't be available if I met Sullivan on a busy street in New York…or at a meeting at a grange hall in Oregon."

Mulroney stood up. "This is all very romantic, Your Honor, but—"

"Yes, it is very romantic," Kia cut in. "And Sullivan is even better than I realized. Back then I thought she was cool. Now I know she's so much more than a hot, rizz chef with amazing knife skills. She's everything. And if you're going to sue me, don't pile on with *you're not in love with her.* I will not be unrequitedly in love for my whole life and then get sued for not being in love. Do you know how many girls I could have hooked up with if I wasn't dreaming about Sullivan all this time?"

"Objection!"

"Sustained."

"State the basis of your objection, Mulroney," Mark Bretton snapped.

"Indecent—"

"That's not an objection."

"I will hold you in contempt, Mr. Bretton, if you continue like this," Judge Harper said.

Bretton sent Kia a *better tone it down* look. She'd already said her part, and her words had landed the way she needed them to. Sullivan was beaming, still clasping her hands over her chest. Nina must be rolling her eyes on the inside.

Sullivan took the stand next.

"Ms. Sullivan, please tell the court about the inappropriate communications Mega Eats initiated with you without the knowledge or consent of your attorney," Nina began.

She shot Mulroney a look that could have frozen the CO_2 right out of the atmosphere and then set it on fire.

"Mega Eats sent someone to my restaurant. He contacted me outside of the official settlement negotiations."

"And what did this representative from Mega Eats say?" Nina asked.

"He suggested that I say my marriage to Kia Jackson was fake, that Kia was using me, and I was duped. He said they would release me from all blame if I did this. And if I didn't, I'd end up here, at risk of losing everything."

"For the record, Your Honor, I've filed a bar complaint against Mr. Mulroney for permitting this likely violation of the professional rules of conduct," Nina said. "I find it very unlikely Mr. Mulroney was unaware of this contact. So, Your Honor, you can see what we've been dealing with."

Harper glanced at Mulroney with a disapproving glare.

"Now, Ms. Sullivan, during your courtship with Ms. Jackson, did she make any false representations about herself?" Nina asked.

"No."

"How about any other material fact to induce you to marry her?"

"None."

"So you weren't scammed?"

"Objection. Leading," Mulroney said.

"I'll rephrase, Your Honor. Tell us about your awareness of the circumstances surrounding Ms. Jackson's marriage proposal."

"She wanted to marry me."

Sullivan was sticking to Nina's no-extra-information rule.

"Were you always in love?"

"Interesting question. Complicated answer. Back in school I wasn't interested in love, so I didn't see it sneaking up on me. I liked going out. I liked flirting with the guys in our program. But you know what I loved more? Cooking with Kia. The more time I spent with Kia, the more I'd rather stay up all night cooking with her than go out to a bar with someone else. I had fun with Kia. Kia inspired me to be my best. She had my back when I forgot an ingredient or was about to miss a step in a demonstration.

"But when I think about it now, I know when I started to fall for her. It was winter in New York. Really, really cold. She was out in the school parking lot trying to deep-fry a turkey, stuffed with god knows what, probably caramel corn, which was going to be delicious even though I'd never admit that in public. I can see her. She was wearing some ridiculous nylon jacket with graffiti hearts all over it. She had her hair up in two puffs. Before she saw me coming, I watched her. Everything was gray. You know that low gray snow sky. Gray snow piles on the side of the parking lot, but that day it was too cold to snow. She looked so serious. Then when she saw me, she smiled so big I felt warm all over. And I loved her. And I didn't realize it.

"I realize it now, and I realized it at the grange the night she showed up. Through all the noise. All the bull—I mean *stuff* from Mega Eats, I saw her and I thought, *I've missed you. So. Damn. Much.* Kia is kind, honest, and committed to what she believes in. She wants to make the world a better place. She makes me happy, and she's beautiful inside and out, and when I wake up in the middle of the night when I'm eighty, I want her next to me. And that started in school. How could I not say yes to her when I'd missed out on all these years we could have been together."

Mulroney asked Sullivan several questions after Nina finished. When Mulroney finally gave up trying to trap her, Judge Harper struck his gavel. Sullivan stepped down from the witness stand.

"Ms. Hashim, Mr. Bretton, Mr. Mulroney, I'll take this under advisement and get my decision to you by the end of next week."

"That's it?" Sullivan asked when she, Nina, Mark, and Kia were standing outside the courthouse, Portland city life bustling around them. "Does he just email you the verdict?"

"Yeah. Not nearly as exciting as on TV," Nina said. "It's a bench trial. No jury so it's just Harper and his conscience."

That wasn't comforting.

"Come on. Even I need a martini today," Nina said.

Nina's driver delivered them to the Makers Bar. Opal and Deja joined them a few minutes later. Nina gave the group a rundown on the legal fine points of Mulroney's case, most of which they understood. Sullivan and Kia held hands under the table. Sullivan glanced at Kia as often as she could without being ridiculously obvious. Every time she looked at Kia, Kia was smiling back at her.

"To Nina," Sullivan said when Nina finished her recap and explanation. "I can't thank you enough. No matter what happens. I am so lucky to have a friend like you." Sullivan nodded to Opal. "And you. And new friends." She nodded to Mark and Deja.

"What?" Deja had been on her phone since she arrived.

"I was saying, I'm glad I got to meet you and Mark."

"Thanks." Deja's face lit up. She held up her phone. "Sorry about this. My friend, they're not a hacker, but they're trying to get Kia's accounts back up."

Deja really was delightful.

"I'm lucky to have such good people in my life." She turned to Kia and kissed her lightly on the lips. "You too. Whatever happens, I'm lucky because this brought you back into my life."

Kia laid her head on Sullivan's shoulder. Opal and Deja said, "Aww." Nina said, "Jesus save me." Mark looked embarrassed.

Sullivan didn't care how she sounded. She didn't want to be anything other than madly in love with Kia Jackson.

"See?" Opal said to Nina. "We said they were perfect for each other."

"We said we liked Kia better than Aubrey," Nina said. "Sorry, Kia. That's a low bar."

"Nina!" Opal and Sullivan said together.

Nina put her hand up in a *hold on a minute* gesture.

"But now, I'm going to say, I like you very much, Kia. You stood by Sullivan when it mattered. You didn't crack on the stand. And you're strategic. I said *ruthless* before, but now I'm just going to say *strategic*."

"See what I have to deal with?" Sullivan said. "They want me to date someone ruthless and strategic. I just thought you were cute and kind of a good chef."

Sullivan tickled Kia's side. Kia giggled.

"I'm ruthless and strategic for the greater good," Kia said.

"Check this out." Deja looked up from the phone that had once again trapped her attention.

"Did Not A Hacker But get my accounts back?" Kia didn't sound as thrilled as she should have been by the prospect.

"Sorry no, but look at this. Sullivan took some videos at the rally and they're going viral."

Kia reached for her own phone, remembered she didn't have accounts, and said, "Sullivan, look it up."

"The whole world is talking about that hideous little snake," Nina said. "Sullivan, you went from no social media presence to nine thousand overnight!"

Now everyone was scrolling through their feeds, except Kia, who was leaning over Sullivan's arm, touching her as much as one possibly could under the pretense of sharing a phone.

"Nine thousand isn't a lot." Sullivan knew enough about influencing to know that.

"It's a lot to get overnight for someone with just a few posts whose videos are superlong," Kia said. "I love that you didn't edit them, by the way. You're talking about things that are too important to cover in six seconds."

In addition to likes and comments on Sullivan's posts, people had shared GIFs showing snakes swallowing Mega Eats complexes with captions like *Who's mini now?* Channel 8 had interviewed the leaders of several environmentalist groups. One of them called the miniature Oregon tree snake the *rallying cry of our time.* The hashtag #WhatsInTheMeat accompanied Mega Eats employees slamming Mega Eats food. Foodie influencers were urging a boycott: #MegaNo. Kia gave Sullivan an exuberant hug, nearly knocking over everyone's drinks. Maybe the cooking bloopers on her feed weren't *all* manufactured.

"We're going to do it. We're really going to save the tree snake!" Kia rattled off details about the snake and its unique tree-dwelling habits.

If Sullivan hadn't already been in love, she would be now.

They discussed the rally for a while, filling Nina in on what she'd missed, savoring the details, applauding Deja's organization. Finally, Nina downed her drink and said, "I wish I could stay, but I've got a husband giving some serious piece-on-the-side vibes, and me and his wife need a convo on how we're going to take his money. This one's too good to sit on." Nina looked at Sullivan and Kia. "I'm happy for you. This looks good for the snake. Now Mega Eats knows there's a movement to stop the development. What a clapback."

* * *

Nina was gone for less than an hour before bursting back through the door. She pulled up her seat again and planted her elbows on the table.

"Listen to this." She read from her phone. *"Mega Eats will be dismissing their complaint against Alice Sullivan and Kiana Jackson. It has come to our company's attention that the* Portland supply chain *wasn't strong enough to support the* volume of customer demand."

She couldn't have looked more excited if lightning bolts were sparking off her shoulders.

"Does that mean...?" Kia began.

"We're...?" Sullivan didn't finish the question.

"Free. Clear. Done with that bullshit. Yes!" Nina said.

"They don't think they'll be able to sell enough slime burgers in Portland?" Kia asked. "Or was it the snake?"

"It was the snake lovers," Nina said.

"They don't want to look like they're destroying the earth," Kia surmised.

"Nope. And based on what we're seeing online, the publicity would be *bad*. Period. The snake is adorable if you like that sort of thing." Nina gave Sullivan a pointed look. "And with so many people rallying around something that looks like the best Ralph Lauren belt this season...it's too much bad press." Sullivan was pretty sure no one had rallied around the snake because it looked like a Ralph Lauren belt, but you never knew. And it didn't matter.

"We won." She wanted to kiss Kia with lips and tongue and her whole body, but that seemed inappropriate in front of her friends. She clasped Kia's hands instead. "We beat Mega Eats."

Kia squeezed her hands, bouncing in her seat. "By way more than point six percent!"

chapter 38

Their celebration lasted into the evening and seemed to involve most of Portland. They started with a bottle of champagne at the Makers Bar.

"So glad you've moved on to champagne," the waiter said. "Congratulations."

Then they went to a lavish dinner at the ridiculously overpriced but truly fantastic restaurant Apollo and Diana. Nina's treat. Kia ordered fern fronds with house-distilled balsamic glaze. Sullivan ordered a drink with cotton candy floating like a cloud around the biodegradable paper straw. By six, they were at the Tennis Skort, and by seven the She-Pack was there, sweaty from practice. Deja brought her friend Not A Hacker But. Me'shell and her daughter arrived with a half a dozen other food truck owners, followed by the waitstaff from Mirepoix. Blake showed up.

"I deleted Mickey's account," he said over the clamor of voices.

"I think Mickey will be okay with that," Sullivan said and gave him a hug.

Maybe she wouldn't have to fire him.

Just when Sullivan thought it couldn't get more festive, the burlesque troupe paraded by the window in their dancing snake puppet costume.

Kia stood beside Sullivan, her hand tucked in Sullivan's back pocket, Sullivan's arm around her shoulder.

"You could live stream this on Serve the World PDX," Kia said. "It'd play really well. Activism is fun. By saving the snakes, you're part of this beautiful diverse community. I know we're supposed to save the snake for the snake, but people are motivated by a lot of things."

"There's nothing wrong with being motivated by community." Sullivan looked at the crowd. She couldn't stop smiling. One of the She-Pack women was explaining how to drink beer out of a cleat to an activist who—despite their shaved head and militant outfit—looked horrified. Deja was flashing a QR code on her phone that took people to the Save the Snake website Not a Hacker But had set up.

Kia texted everything to her cousin, who texted back at lightning speed even though she was in Paris.

"She wants a picture of you and me," Kia said, leaning over to sip on Sullivan's straw.

Then they took half a dozen bad selfies, their smiles wide and the angles all wrong. Kia sent them all to Lillian.

Sullivan heard Opal whisper, "They're so cute."

Nina said, "They're frickin' adorable, but don't tell them I said it."

And Sullivan even live streamed a bit of the celebration.

"Let's go outside and see the massive Oregon snake," Sullivan said to the hearts that were popping up on the screen as she live streamed.

Outside, she showed her viewers the burlesque troupe's snake.

The snake costume engineer talked about using recycled plastic to make the snake's frame, and he invited Sullivan and her camera into the head of the snake. Holding the snake's head and live streaming at the same time was not easy, and eventually Kia popped into the tiny space in the snake's papier-mâché head and took over filming.

Sullivan felt good when she finally turned off the live stream and pocketed her phone. There'd be trolls, and there'd be haters, but everyone who liked her live stream was one tiny bit closer to understanding one tiny, precious part of the natural world. And they got to see diverse communities coming together for a common cause and, yes, to drink beer and watch burlesque performers in a giant snake costume…but in the world with all its strife and divisions, that was a win too.

The party was still going on when Kia and Sullivan snuck out of the bar.

Back at the house, Kia and Sullivan mounted the stairs without discussion. Once in Sullivan's bedroom, Sullivan kissed Kia tenderly, running her fingers through Kia's hair for the first time. Georgie had felt off-limits. The way Kia sighed and leaned into her touch said Georgie wasn't anymore.

"I can't believe it worked out," Sullivan said, unbuttoning the top button of Kia's shirt.

"We always win," Kia said.

She fumbled with the button on Sullivan's pants until Sullivan had to help her.

"I'm still worried that I'm not good at this," Kia said, toying with the waistband of Sullivan's pants. "You said you've done everything twice. What if I'm boring?"

"You could never be boring." Sullivan tipped Kia's chin up and cupped her face. "And yeah, I've tried a lot of things twice. Like raw abalone. It's okay but twice is enough."

Kia laughed. Sullivan kissed her forehead.

"What I want is to be with you. I want to do all the fun things way more than twice. I want to learn what you like and what we like as a couple. I don't need or want anything more than that."

"So you're not going to lick abalone off me?"

"If you want me to lick abalone off you, I will lick abalone all up and down your beautiful body."

"You could just kiss me instead." Kia beamed.

Soon they were naked, their movements both urgent and tender as they burned off the adrenaline of the day and found a place to put all their joy.

Sullivan was just waking up when Kia brought coffee and scones to bed, strutting in naked with two mugs in one hand and a plate in the other. A marshmallow floated on top of both cups.

"I won't even complain about this high-fructose pillow floating on my coffee, Jackson."

"You better not. You know it's good." Kia set her mug on the bedside table, handed Sullivan the plate, and snuggled back under the covers.

"Are the scones the best you've ever had?" Kia asked, nudging Sullivan's bare calf with her own.

"They're the best. I admit it. And you are the best wife."

"I thought I was kind of a wrecking ball," Kia said, her eyebrows furrowing ruefully.

"I think life is a wrecking ball sometimes. I want to be with someone who's by my side throughout it and someone who tries to make things better when, maybe, they had something to do with the wrecking ball."

"Are you saying you like me?" Kia nudged Sullivan's foot with hers. "After everything."

"Of course I like you, Jackson. I've always liked you."

"Not enough."

"Enough for what?"

"Enough to throw yourself at my feet and say, *Kia, I want you more than anyone else in the world.*"

She was so cute, and Sullivan did want her more than she'd ever wanted anyone, more than she could imagine ever wanting someone else.

"Do I have to get out of bed to throw myself at your feet, or can I just do it here sitting up?"

"Where is the romance, Chef?" Kia said with mock indignation and behind that a brittleness that said she was afraid this conversation wasn't going to go the way she obviously wanted it to.

Sullivan couldn't leave Kia hanging even for a moment.

"I do want you more than anyone else."

She felt Kia's body relax.

"Were you really in love with me in school?" Sullivan would have to revisit all her school memories. Kia had loved her!

Kia paused for a moment. "I think so. It's probably good we didn't date back then, but it wasn't just a crush. You impressed me more than anyone else I'd ever met, and I come from a family of professional ballerinas, so that says a lot. I guess one of the things I loved about you was that you weren't just one thing, like my cousin and my aunt were for a long time. You took your work seriously, but you were playful. You have this sexy masc lesbian vibe, and you dated all the men in the program."

"Not *all* of them."

"A significant number of the men in the program, significant if you're in love with the woman dating those men. You know, after we lost touch, I didn't look you up because I didn't want to find out you'd turned out to be an ass."

"Did you think I'd be an ass?"

"Of course not, but you were so amazing, after we lost touch, I didn't want anything to ruin that memory."

"I wish we hadn't lost touch. I got so busy; I lost touch with everything."

"Did you ever think about me?"

"Honestly, if you'd asked me back then, I would have said, *Not a lot*. But that wouldn't have been true. When I look back, you've been everywhere in my life. You were so much a part of me, I didn't see it. There's only one dish I serve every single night. It's the Golden Crisp Experience dessert. It's puffed rice cooked in brown-butter mixed with homemade marshmallows. Then I finish it with a pear-infused glaze."

"It's a Rice Krispies treat!"

"We are not talking Jet-Puffed and Rice Krispies, but it's all about you. It always has been. When I saw you in *American Fare*...I was happy for you. Really happy, even though I was distraught over all those forks."

"I know. I know. I've reformed."

"I didn't realize how much it mattered to me that you achieve your dreams until I saw you there. And in case you haven't noticed, I am in love with you, Kia Point Six Percent Jackson."

"I am *still* in love with you, Chef Alice Sullivan."

Kia turned toward her, and they kissed.

When they finally parted, Sullivan said what had been on her mind since they lay down the night before.

"We didn't take a chance back in school." Sullivan felt a flash of déjà vu. They were back in the practice kitchen staring down an unspoken possibility. *We could stay together.* It had been a ridiculous idea then, and it was a ridiculous idea now. "We didn't complicate things with a relationship anyone would have told us was crazy to start. I know you'll want to get back on the road, but I'm willing to give long distance a try."

"I don't want to travel like I used to. I want to find an empty used car lot and build Taste the Love Land somewhere where I'm not hurting the environment. I think I could find a place like that in Portland. But mostly, the times in my life when I've been the happiest were when I was with you, staying put in one place. I'd rather be here with you. Is that too much too soon?"

That was exactly what Sullivan wanted to hear and knew she shouldn't wish for since she shouldn't stand in the way of Kia's dreams. But if Kia's dreams didn't include serving tursnickens in all forty-eight contiguous states, that was just fine with Sullivan.

"That's not too much at all."

"I'm not saying we have to live together if you want your space."

Sullivan took a sip of her deliciously sweet coffee. She felt her brow furrow.

"What is it?" Kia asked.

"We're still married."

"We are." Kia looked everywhere but at Sullivan. "Nina would tell us we should get divorced," Kia said. It sounded like a question. "Mark emailed me the paperwork."

"Nina sent it to me too."

They looked at each other.

"I haven't even asked you if you wanted to be my girlfriend," Sullivan said. "It's too early to be married."

"It makes sense to get divorced."

Kia was right, but her words hurt…but only until Sullivan noticed the tremulous look in her eyes.

"If we weren't married, and I asked you to marry me right now, you'd be like, *Whoa. Too much too soon.*" Sullivan was asking, not saying.

Kia answered, "I wouldn't." She held Sullivan's gaze with her golden eyes.

"I don't want the first thing we do in our real relationship to be you moving out and us getting divorced," Sullivan said.

Kia curled up against Sullivan, their warm, naked bodies melting into one. Sullivan couldn't bear the thought of getting out of bed, let alone ending the morning with divorce papers.

"I always thought when I got married it'd be forever," Sullivan said, "and deep in my heart, I wondered if I made a mistake when I left after graduation without at least seeing what we might have been together. What if I didn't make that mistake this time?"

"Are you asking me to stay married to you, Chef Sullivan?"

"And live with me. Cook together. Camp in your RV. Have abalone sex if that's your thing. Build Taste the Love and build a life together. Yes to all of that."

Kia cuddled even closer, wrapping her arms around Sullivan and pressing her cheek to Sullivan's chest. She was a very successful cuddler.

"I do," Kia said. "I do. I do."

epilogue

Kia stood in front of the gates to the new Taste the Love Land. Behind her, trees grew from holes cut in the concrete of what was once an RV lot, then an abandoned RV lot. It'd be years until the fast-growing hybrid poplar trees created the canopy she dreamed of, but that was years, not decades. A willow tree grew in the center of the space, fed by gray water from the plate-washing station where teenagers were washing dishes with organic detergents at their first summer jobs. Birdhouse boxes set around the perimeter of the space had already attracted the black-capped chickadee and the Northern flicker. Sullivan stood beside her dressed in her chef's white coat. Kia wore the new edition of the Kia Gourmazing T-shirts made from recycled materials and screen printed by an artists' co-op in Guadalajara.

A crowd gathered in front of her and Sullivan, including two of the local news stations and several environmental influencers. A reporter from *American Fare* was also there to document *American Fare's most dynamic winner.*

Deja stood on the sidelines ready to live stream for Kia's and Sullivan's feeds.

And most exciting, Kia's father, her aunt Eleanor and uncle Erik, Lillian, and Izzy stood front and center. Erik had immediately hit it off with Sullivan's parents, all of them academics, and Izzy regaled Sullivan's brother with the history of burlesque. It had been nice meeting Sullivan's family. She didn't talk about them much, but their relationship, while not as close as Kia's family, seemed supportive and uncomplicated.

"Thank you all for coming to the opening of Taste the Love Land Portland."

She handed the microphone to Sullivan.

"When it comes to the environment, I used to feel like I was doing my part, but it didn't matter. The problems were too big. I could serve sustainable food, but it was too expensive for most people. Together Kia and I have created a model of affordable, sustainable dining for communities across the country." She went on to describe the solar power and to-go-container return program. "And yeah, we've had a few setbacks."

The cardboard forks drooped and melted. Attracting starlings had been a mistake.

"But I think we can say the soft opening of Taste the Love Land has been a success, and we're very excited to welcome you to the official opening."

They'd invited the girl who'd stood up for the snake at the first rally. She was dressed in a one-piece printed with snakes. Kia gave her two thumbs-up for fashion. And Kia handed her a pair of scissors to cut the hemp ribbon that fluttered across the opening.

"Welcome to Taste the Love Land," Kia said.

The food trucks were ready to serve. Live music played beneath a shaded canopy made of vines grown on a large trellis.

"We did it," Kia said as the crowd ambled past them into the food truck paradise, the little piece of Eden.

"We did." Her wife, Alice Sullivan, put her arms around her.

"I have been in love with you since I was twenty. No one can say we didn't know each other long enough. You just had to see the fabulousness I am."

Sullivan kissed her head.

"I always knew you were fabulous. I just didn't know how fabulous we were together. Now are you ready to defend your point six percent?"

"Chef Sullivan, you are on!"

"Don't get too proud, Jackson. I might just stuff a tofurkey with a free-range duck with a whole fern. Where would you be then?"

"Taking your bouillabaisse recipe to the next level with cola and a splash of PBR."

"And it'll be amazing." Sullivan made a show of rolling her eyes, but her whole aura was smiling. "You don't lose."

"Well…" Kia scrunched up her nose as she thought through all the disasters of their early marriage. "As long as I have you, I feel like a winner."

"Same." Sullivan lifted Kia's hand to her lips and kissed it. "I guess it's a tie."

acknowledgments

First, we'd like to thank the farmers and agricultural workers who bring us fresh local food. Western Oregon is a land of bounty. We feel blessed every time we drive through the fields of corn or squash or blueberries. Vineyards stretch across rolling hills. The dense foliage of filbert orchards creates corridors of shade. It always seems like something magical could happen under those branches, and it does. Filberts grow. And wherever there are fields and orchards, there are people bent over or reaching up, lugging crates, working in hot sun and pouring rain. Thank you.

We'd also like to thank Chef Matt Bennett, Janel Bennett, and Sybaris Bistro for giving us a glimpse into the world of high-end cooking and restaurateuring. If you're ever in Albany, Oregon, be sure to visit Matt and Janel's restaurant.

Thank you to our agent, Jane Dystel. Thank you to the whole team at Forever. Thank you to Venessa Vida Kelley for another gorgeous cover.

Thank you to Rachel Spangler and Anna Burke for letting us join the Bywater Books contingent at Women's Week in Provincetown, Massachusetts.

Thank you to the organizers of the Steamy Lit Con and the Golden Crown Literary Society for giving diverse writers a place to connect with each other and with our amazing readers. Karelia thanks her Golden Crown Literary Society Writing Academy students for keeping her motivated and inspired.

Thank you to the influencers who spread the word about the books they love. A special shout-out to Tasty Cherry @sterling_ sapphic_reads for supporting us and the community and for designing the fabulous IYNYK T-shirt.

Thank you to Albert Stetz, Elin Stetz (1940–2022), and Cheryl Paules for your love and support. Thank you to our friends. We are blessed to have too many to mention, but a special thank-you to Mitzi, John, Maria, Shannon, the Lizzes, Scott, Terrance, Measy, Keith, Jerred, Jessica, Johanna, and Eric.

Many people ask us about our writing process, and quite a few ask us if we ever fight over our books. The answer is no. Co-authoring a book requires excellent communication. We pride ourselves on being good at that. Writing together is a joyful, playful exercise and a wonderful escape from the stress of real life. And we craft characters who model healthy communication. We hope *Taste the Love* holds you like a warm hug from a good friend. We hope everyone can take something from Kia and Sullivan's relationship and the kindness and respect they show each other even when the proverbial sh*t hits the fan.

Finally, and so importantly, we want to thank our readers. Thank you for loving our characters and celebrating their happily-ever-afters. We want happily-ever-afters for all of you.

Thank you for writing to us and sharing your lives with us. (If you haven't already...subscribe to our newsletter at kareliastetzwaters.com so we can stay in touch!) It is an honor to think of our characters accompanying you through the ups and downs of life. We hope there are more ups! But we'll be with you through all of it.

Karelia and Fay

PS: Lillian and Izzy say *hi*. If you haven't read their against-all-odds love story, be sure to check out *Second Night Stand*. Kia is there too, and she's looking forward to seeing you again.

recipes

Kia and Sullivan's Miso-Marshmallow Burgers

A perfect opposites-attract burger. Miso lends an umami flavor, while the sweetness of marshmallow nods to barbecue sauce. The recipe can be scaled up or down to feed your sweetheart or your whole rugby team (fifteen plus alternates). The recipe below makes four sliders.

INGREDIENTS

1 pound ground meat of your choice (recommended free-range beef)
2 teaspoons red miso (soybean paste)
½ cup hot water
100 mini marshmallows
Arugula
Hawaiian sweet burger buns, warmed
Other burger toppings as desired (caramelized onions, pickled jalapeños, etc.)

INSTRUCTIONS

1. Form meat into patties and set aside.
2. Mix the miso in hot water until dissolved in the pan over medium heat.
3. Reduce heat and gradually add marshmallows over low heat

until they melt into miso mixture, stirring constantly until it reaches a caramellike consistency.
4. Grill burgers to an internal temperature of 150–155°F for medium-well.
5. Transfer burgers to warm Hawaiian sweet burger buns. Top with miso-marshmallow sauce and arugula.

Rice Krispies Treats with Pear Reduction

Brown butter is the secret to Rice Krispies treats. With brown butter, even the most sophisticated foodie will fall in love with this gooey dessert (or main course…we're not judging).

INGREDIENTS
1 cup butter (2 sticks)
12–15 ounces Rice Krispies cereal
22 ounces marshmallows
3 cups pear juice

INSTRUCTIONS
1. Cook pear juice on medium-low heat until the juice is reduced by two-thirds.
2. Meanwhile, line a lasagna pan with parchment paper and set aside.
3. Place butter in a pot on medium heat. A light-colored nonstick pot is ideal.
4. The butter will bubble first. Watch closely until the milk solids turn golden brown. Reduce to low heat immediately. Butter goes from golden brown to burnt quickly, so don't walk away from the stove.

5. Add marshmallows to the pot with the brown butter and stir until marshmallows melt.
6. Gradually add ⅓ cup of pear reduction.
7. Add Rice Krispies and stir until incorporated.
8. Press Rice Krispies treats into lined pan and cool in refrigerator.
9. Cut Rice Krispies treats when they are solid, and drizzle with remaining pear reduction sauce for added stickiness.

Sullivan's Butternut Squash Risotto with Fried Sage

Fried sage is essential to this dish. Do not substitute marjoram. You have standards.

INGREDIENTS

1 cup arborio rice
1 large butternut squash (local, organic)
6 tablespoons butter (freshly churned)
1 shallot (chopped)
7 whole sage leaves (homegrown in windowsill)
Zest of 1 lemon (organic)
½ cup pinot grigio
7 fresh thyme sprigs (homegrown in garden)
2 sprigs of rosemary (homegrown in garden)
2 tablespoons extra-virgin olive oil
½ teaspoon each salt and pepper
6 cups heritage broth (homemade broth made from kitchen reserves and vegetable scraps)

INSTRUCTIONS FOR HERITAGE BROTH

1. To make heritage broth, save vegetable scraps and bones until you have enough to fill approximately half a stock pot.
2. Add water to cover vegetables and bones by at least 3 inches.
3. Simmer for four hours, skimming fats and oils. Add additional water if needed. Add salt and pepper to taste.
4. Cool and strain.

INSTRUCTIONS FOR RISOTTO

1. Plant sage, rosemary, and thyme. Wait until plants are large enough to harvest (at least 10 inches tall). Alternatively, purchase fresh herbs at a local market.
2. Preheat oven to 350°F.
3. Cut butternut squash lengthwise. Scoop out and save seeds on a damp cloth napkin for planting later.
4. Drizzle generously with extra-virgin olive oil and season with salt and pepper.
5. Roast squash for 45 minutes at 350°F.
6. Cool and scoop out flesh.
7. In a dry pot, add the butter and chopped shallots, and cook on medium heat for 3 minutes.
8. Add the arborio rice and toast in the skillet for 4 minutes.
9. Add rosemary, thyme, and ½ cup of wine.
10. Using half of the squash, scoop one tablespoon of squash at a time into the mixture until incorporated. Reserve the other half.
11. Add heritage broth ½ cup at a time until the rice absorbs the broth. Stir gently and constantly. Cook until a creamy consistency.

12. Add the remaining half of the squash, keeping large pieces.
13. Fry the sage leaves in extra-virgin olive oil until crispy, and remove before the leaf color deepens. Crumble some leaves and leave others whole.
14. Top risotto with crumbled sage leaves and serve.

Vulva-Style Sausage & Ricotta Casoncelli

While pasta making can feel intimidating, it is easier than one might think. Remember there is a great diversity in vulva shape and size, so your casoncelli do not have to be uniform.

TOOLS

Stand mixer with pasta-making attachment or hand-crank pasta maker

Rolling pin

INGREDIENTS

For the pasta:

2 cups all-purpose flour, spooned and leveled

3 large eggs

½ teaspoon sea salt

½ tablespoon extra-virgin olive oil

For the filling:

1 pound pork sausage (local and humanely raised)

4 cups whole milk

2 tablespoons lemon juice

¼ teaspoon salt

Or 2 cups commercial ricotta (to replace the whole milk, lemon juice, and salt above)

For the toppings:
½ cup shaved Parmesan cheese
1 tablespoon chopped parsley or your favorite herb
2 tablespoons melted butter

INSTRUCTIONS
1. Mix flour, water, eggs, olive oil, and salt.
2. Knead until a smooth ball forms, about 10 minutes. The dough will feel dry initially but should become pliable. Add a small amount of water if necessary.
3. Roll the dough into a thin sheet using a rolling pin, then pass it through a hand-crank pasta maker or stand mixer attachment until it is paper-thin.
4. Cut the dough into 2-inch squares. Cover with a damp cloth.
5. For the sausage: Fry in 1 tablespoon of olive oil, crumbling the sausage as you go. Remove and drain the fat.
6. To make the cheese, heat the milk in a saucepan on medium heat until the milk temperature reaches 195°F (takes 5–6 minutes) and remove from heat.
7. Slowly add the salt and lemon juice. Curds will form. Gently stir the mixture for 1 minute.
8. Line a mesh strainer with cheesecloth and set over a glass bowl.
9. With a slotted spoon, remove the curds and place them on the strainer. Let the curds sit in the strainer and drain for 20–30 minutes until they have a firm texture.
10. Place 1 teaspoon of sausage and 1 teaspoon of ricotta in the center of each dough square.
11. Fold squares to approximate the shape of the vulva.
12. Bring water to a gentle boil. Place casoncelli in the water, and boil for 2 minutes or until they reach desired texture.
13. Top with Parmesan, fresh herbs, butter, or sauce.

Easy Tursnicken

Sweet, salty, and aromatic, the tursnicken surprises everyone with its delicious flavors. You can top it with any sauce or gravy you like, but Kia and Sullivan recommend mole, which pairs beautifully with the Snickers bar.

While the classic tursnicken uses a whole turkey and a whole chicken, this simplified recipe makes a smaller portion, reducing prep time and avoiding food waste. Baking instead of deep-frying reduces the risk of kitchen injury. If you would like to make a classic tursnicken, follow recipes for the fried turducken, substituting four Snickers bars for the duck.

INGREDIENTS

1 large turkey breast (humanely raised; butterflied and pounded thin)
1 chicken breast (humanely raised; butterflied and pounded thin)
1 12-ounce box commercial stuffing (or four cups homemade stuffing)
1 cup pecans, chopped
1 cup dried cranberries
2 cups chicken broth
1–2 full-size Snickers bars
½ teaspoon kosher salt
½ teaspoon black pepper and dry herbs of your choice

INSTRUCTIONS

1. Brine the meat by mixing 2 tablespoons kosher salt in 2½ cups water until salt is dissolved. Soak meat in brine for 1½ hours.
2. Moisten stuffing according to box recipe (but do not add onions or vegetables). Add pecans and cranberries. Set aside.

3. Cover a cutting board with plastic wrap. Place the turkey on the cutting board and butterfly.
4. Place another layer of plastic wrap over the turkey breast, and pound with mallet until approximately ½ to ¾ inch thickness.
5. Repeat with chicken.
6. Preheat oven to 350°F.
7. Lay turkey on cutting board. Cover the turkey in 1 to 2 inches of stuffing. (Save remaining stuffing to serve at table.)
8. Place the chicken breast on the turkey.
9. Place one to two Snickers bars in the middle of the chicken.
10. Carefully roll the tursnicken lengthwise (around the Snickers bar).
11. Wrap tursnicken with kitchen twine and secure.
12. Place several slices of butter in a roasting pan and lay the tursnicken on top.
13. Roast the poultry breasts at 350°F for 45–75 minutes until the thickest part of the tursnicken reaches 160°F.
14. Remove tursnicken from oven. Let rest for 10 minutes.
15. While the tursnicken rests, warm mole sauce (or another sauce of your choice). Drizzle mole sauce over tursnicken.
16. Slice and serve with extra mole sauce (or sauce of your choice) for dipping.

Kia's Mole

When you're cooking in a food truck, you don't always have time for elaborate recipes. Simplify your tursnicken with this two-ingredient mole.

INSTRUCTIONS
1. Simply take commercially made mole paste and prepare it according to the directions on the jar, substituting Coca-Cola for water. Try to find Coca-Cola manufactured in Mexico, where it is made with sugar instead of corn syrup.

Sullivan's Mole

Sullivan says that mole must be made from scratch. She includes the following recipe for an elevated mole experience.

INGREDIENTS
2 each fresh, organic whole dried guajillo, New Mexico, mulato, and pasilla peppers
4 organic tomatoes
6 cups heritage broth
1 tablespoon thyme
5 bay leaves
2 tablespoons black peppercorns
½ cup butter or EVOO (extra-virgin olive oil)
⅓ cup slivered almonds
⅓ cup yellow raisins
2 slices of bread
2 tortillas (corn or flour)
2 Mexican hot chocolate tablets

INSTRUCTIONS

1. Add 5 cups of heritage broth to a large pot and heat on medium heat.
2. Roast 4 large tomatoes for 20 minutes at 350°F.
3. Cut and deseed peppers. Measure 4 tablespoons of the seeds and set aside.
4. Tear the whole dried peppers into pieces and toast the skins in a hot skillet for 2 minutes.
5. Then soak the toasted peppers in a bowl of hot water for 30 minutes.
6. After 30 minutes, remove the peppers and ½ cup of the soaking liquid and blend them in a food processor. Set this **paste** aside.
7. Grind the dried ingredients, meaning the pepper seeds, thyme, bay leaves, and black peppercorns mixture. Set this **dry mixture** aside.
8. Heat butter over medium heat to coat almonds and raisins. Remove this **moist mixture** and set aside.
9. To the skillet, add the bread and tortillas until crispy. Remove **crispy** toasts.
10. To the heritage broth, add the roasted tomatoes, the **paste**, the **dry mixture**, the **moist mixture**, and the **crispy** toasts. Heat for 10 minutes, then remove from heat.
11. Allow the mixture to cool. Using a sieve, strain the mixture. This will take some time. You want a super smooth mole.
12. Pour the strained liquid into the pot. Add the remaining cup of heritage broth to the pot, and turn up to medium heat.
13. Simmer mole sauce, and add the Mexican hot chocolate tablets. Stir occasionally and simmer for an hour.

about the authors

Ambassadors of real-life happily ever after, **Fay** and **Karelia Stetz-Waters** have been together for twenty-five years. They live in Albany, Oregon, with their pug mix, Willa Cather, and a garden full of dragonflies and hummingbirds. Their writing process involves many afternoons spent at local coffee shops and brewpubs outlining scenes, going over drafts, and high-fiving each other. The process works beautifully. *Taste the Love* is their second novel together but definitely not their last.